An Embarrassment of Riches

An
EMBARRASSMENT
of RICHES

A Novel of the Count Saint-Germain

Chelsea Quinn Yarbro

TOR®

A TOM DOHERTY ASSOCIATES BOOK

NEW YORK

AN EMBARRASSMENT OF RICHES: A NOVEL OF THE COUNT SAINT-GERMAIN

Copyright © 2011 by Chelsea Quinn Yarbro

A Tor Book
Published by Tom Doherty Associates, LLC
175 Fifth Avenue
New York, NY 10010

www.tor-forge.com

Tor® is a registered trademark of Tom Doherty Associates, LLC.

Library of Congress Cataloging-in-Publication Data

Yarbro, Chelsea Quinn, 1942–
    An embarrassment of riches : a novel of the Count Saint-Germain / Chelsea Quinn
Yarbro.—1st ed.
        p. cm.
    "A Tom Doherty Associates book."
    ISBN 978-0-7653-3103-8
    1. Saint-Germain, comte de, d. 1784—Fiction. 2. Vampires—Fiction. 3. Bohemia
(Czech Republic)—History—To 1526—Fiction. I. Title.
    PS3575.A7E63 2011
    813'.54—dc22

                                                                                    2010036539

First Edition: March 2011

Printed in the United States of America

0 9 8 7 6 5 4 3 2 1

This one is for
STEVE RAWLINS.

You know why.

Author's Note

The map of Europe is constantly changing; countries arise, expand, contract, relocate; many eventually disappear. Most of these changes have happened to the Kingdom of Bohemia, which, at its height in the thirteenth century, included not only what is now the Czech Republic, and Slovenia, but also most of Austria, Styria, Carinthia, part of modern Poland, and Moravia. A significant factor in this enlargement was due to the energies of the Przemysl dynasty, in particular, Vaclav (Wenceslaus) I and his son Otakar (Ottocar) II, known variously as the Iron, the Golden, and the Great. At a time when Bohemia was a mining center of eastern Europe, the Przemysls made the most of their mineral resources, and turned Bohemia into one of the wealthiest kingdoms of that age, which enabled Vaclav I and Otakar II to finance major military campaigns. For more than a quarter century, Przemysl Otakar II did his utmost to make an empire out of Bohemia, and very nearly succeeded. He also did his best, upon the death of Richard of Cornwall, to be elected Holy Roman Emperor, but lost that contest to Rudolph von Hapsburg, who became his implacable foe.

Otakar married twice; both were political unions, the first to Marghete of Austria, who was almost thirty years his senior, who retired, handsomely recompensed, to a nunnery in 1260; the second in 1261 to Kunigunde of Halicz, granddaughter of King Bela of Hungary, whose kingdom included most of modern Romania, the northern third of Bulgaria, eastern Croatia, Slovakia, and the eastern end of Austria. Kunigunde, younger than Otakar by about fifteen years, was the mother of Otakar II's three children, including his only legitimate son, who became Vaclav II; her father was Rosztiszlo, Grand Duke of Kiev and King of Bulgaria, and her mother was Anna of Hungary, all very desirable political connections for Otakar.

At this time in history, most of the people of Europe—and the rest of the world, for that matter—were illiterate. Nearly all the centers of education were run by the Church, and as such, perpetuated the Church's role of record-keeper, historian, diplomatic liaison, and document-maker. Even the upper classes were largely dependent on Church-schooled scribes—usually monks—for the preparation of their official papers. As a result, almost all contemporary records of this period are in Church Latin, often with an admixture of local usage and dialect. Most of eastern Europe was a linguistic hodge-podge of Slavic, German, Baltic, and Balkan tongues with some Latin influences; spelling was not standardized, and names of persons and places appeared in many forms. By far the most disconcerting country for such confusion was Hungary; it had five distinct languages being used at the time of this book; Magyar was the most common of the lot, but it was not unusual for Hungarians living only a few miles apart to be completely unintelligible to one another.

For the sake of clarity rather than authenticity, I have chosen one version of all city, country, and personal names and used that consistently throughout the book. Whenever possible I have chosen the ones that are most commonly found in the records of the time; when that has been impossible to determine, I have chosen the word or name closest to modern usage. Titles of nobility were generally recorded in their Latin versions, and I have maintained that in this novel to avoid confusion and to make it easier to equate the old titles with current ones: hence, *dux,* meaning leader, which becomes duke in English and doge in Venetian, or *comes*—pronounced CO-mays—which becomes comte in French, count in English, and conte in Italian; other titles such as *pan* are uniquely Bohemian: pan is roughly the equivalent of baron, meaning something along the lines of land-holding-martial-aristocrat-not-directly-related-to-the-ruler. Otakar II, in most of his official documents, preferred the German derivative *rytir* (rider) for knights, meaning titled men who were permitted to ride horseback in royal processions and were expected to provide fighting men for the King's use in war; it was also the title conferred upon mounted fighters who distinguished themselves in battle. Customs of conferring knighthood were not as strictly defined in Bohemia as they were in England and France. Traditionally, knighthood usually bound the knight directly to the King rather than to a chain of aristocratic command, and the honors knighthood conferred did not pass to the heirs of the knight, but lasted only for the life of the knight. In terms of religious titles, Latin is also used, with a few regional variations of the period—*Pader* (Bohemian) and *Pater* (Hungarian), father, for priests; *Episcopus* for bishops; *Frater*, brother, for monks; and *Sorer*, sister, for nuns. As regards Otakar himself, he used both *Rex* and *Konig* for his titles, so I have opted for *Konig* for him and *Konige* for Kunigunde. The honorific used for the rulers in Bohemia at the time translates roughly as *dear Royal*, so that is how the honorific appears in these pages.

Being a younger son and therefore intended for the Church, Otakar himself seems to have had a rudimentary level of literacy, enough to be able to leave a small amount of personal letters and lyrics that are not in the handwriting of his clerks and scribes, and are consistent with his signatures on various official documents. As was the custom of the time, he left most of the writing chores to his scribes and clerks, such activities being considered inappropriate for reigning royalty. Like most aristocratic men of his time, Otakar could read music and play stringed instruments. Also in keeping with his position Otakar had a Court Scholar for most of his reign, lavishly rewarding the men who fulfilled this post, as was his habit, for providing him with reliable information; the Court Scholars, whose names have not come down to us in any verifiable form, were charged with interviewing travelers as well as pursuing more academic studies, and with sponsoring the making of books.

Like many Medieval rulers, Otakar's amusements were hawking, hunting, carousing, and gambling. Legend says he was given to bouts of self-indulgence and occasional debauchery, but there is little solid evidence of these lubricities; then again, there is no sure indication that he did not indulge, either. That he was reported to have been involved in orgies is hardly surprising, since similar tales were circulating about most of the aristocrats and royalty at that time. While Otakar II often had the opportunity for such behavior, and may very well have enjoyed himself in ways that officially scandalized the Church, his private activities remain more rumors than facts. What we do know about him is that after his rebellion against his father, until he was forgiven and reinstated as Vaclav's heir, he spent most of his time hunting and in riotous living; once he became King of Bohemia, his ambitions burgeoned and he appears to have devoted most of his time to territorial expansion and political maneuvering.

For most of the two-plus years covered in this novel, Otakar was on campaign, a significant part of his personal Court accompanying him into battle. Konige Kunigunde divided her time between Praha and Pressburg, apparently staying in Praha during her pregnancies because the city was far from the dangers of disputed territories and the threat of kidnaping, where her lavish and opulent Court could take care of her. Contemporary records imply that she was not well after the birth of her first child, Kunigunde of Bohemia, in 1265; her two later pregnancies evoked great concern for her health, emotional as well as physical. It is likely that she suffered from some form of postpartum depression, given that one of the more reliable observations of the time says that Kunigunde was prone to melancholy following the birth of her three children. Other accounts of the time often describe her as meek and submissive—both considered desirable virtues at the time—but subject to occasional outbursts of passion, which were attributed to her Hungarian nature.

In matters of nomenclature, the aristocracy and royalty of most eastern European states put their family names before their personal names if they were male—Przemysl Otakar II—or occasionally, when dealing with Germans or Italians, he styled himself Otakar II of Bohemia, in the manner of most western European royalty of the time. Aristocratic females put the personal name first, with their estate name following *of* or *from*—Rozsa of Borsod—and did not take their husbands' names. Royal children were usually identified by the names of their estates, in the same manner as noblewomen were. Merchants were usually identified by the goods they sold—Josko the mercer—or by the city from which they traded—Vlach of Bruno. Working men also often had a personal name, followed by an *of* or *from*, indicating where they lived—Gazsi of Raab. However, when a family had been established in a profession for three generations or more, then the family name appeared before the personal name, many times derived from occupations, the founding ancestor's name, or nicknames, and usually followed by the name of the city, town, or village of residence—Tirz Agoston of Mures. Peasants and common people had no family names as such, but often had either a patronymic— Donat-son-of-Mozes—or an occupation name—Antal-the-smith.

Like all European Medieval societies, Bohemian and Hungarian merchants and aristocrats kept slaves to do the most unpleasant, most basic labor of household and personal maintenance. They also controlled most of the land and the serfs who worked them in conditions almost identical to slavery. The vast majority of these slaves came from the territories to the east of their countries, especially the Principalities of Russia, although some came from the Middle East, where the slave-trade flourished. Slaves were expensive, not only to purchase but to keep, and as such were something of a status symbol for those who owned them.

Standards of measurement were a bit haphazard, but in terms of measuring distance, the Bohemian league seems to have been a bit shorter than the Roman one, being about two and a third miles as compared to the Roman three-mile leagues. Various other regions of Europe had slightly different versions of leagues, so calculating distance was never an easy task. Nautical measurement of distance was also different from region to region: the ships of the Hanseatic League used a different standard than the Venetian Empire did, and Spain used still another standard. Italy, although fragmented, kept to the Roman league. To limit the confusion, I have used the Bohemian league throughout, applying it to both land and sea. For acreage, the plowing standard seems to have been maintained, and will be used here. Tuns, bushels, crocks, and bales had a great deal of leeway in terms of sizes. Animals and people were measured in terms of hands—horses still are—which has been standardized to four inches—fifteen hands equals sixty inches, or five feet. Although the hand was not so fixed at the time, for clarity it is reckoned by the modern four inches in this story.

The middle of the thirteenth century was a busy time elsewhere: in France the cathedral of Notre Dame in Amiens was completed (1268) and King Louis IX went on Crusade, but died of plague, along with most of his army (1270) before reaching the Middle East; the Crusades were finally winding down. Albertus Magnus and Thomas Aquinas were writing. In what is now Turkey, a severe earthquake in 1268 caused three years of social and economic chaos and ended up helping the Turks take over Anatolia, beginning the first steps toward the Ottoman Empire. The Hanseatic League was expanding, and the increased trade from their member-cities spurred international trade, which strengthened Bohemia's economy, for the overland routes—not as active or as visible as the sea routes but important nonetheless—between the Venetian Empire and the Hansa cities went through Bohemia, making it a trading power to be reckoned with. The great German minnesinger Tannhauser died in 1271 at the considerably advanced age of sixty-five. Another significant death, that of Pope Clement IV in 1268, brought upheaval in the Church when he was succeeded by the Anti-Pope Gregory X, who reigned unofficially from 1271 until 1276. Also in 1271 Kublai Khan founded the Yuan Dynasty in China, the same year that Niccolo, Maffeo, and Niccolo's seventeen-year-old son Marco Polo set out from Acre, bound for Asia. In England the following year, Henry III died while his heir was on Crusade; upon notification of his father's demise some two months after the event, he returned to England the following year to reign as Edward I. Europe at that time was crowded, the population at levels that would not be seen again until the latter part of the eighteenth century. 1275 to 1345 would see Bohemia lose ground to an expanding Lithuania, the increasing belligerence of the Ottoman Turks, the end of what is sometimes called the Medieval Warm Period, the start of the Little Ice Age, and the arrival of Bubonic Plague in Europe, which from 1346 to 1379 reduced the population of Europe by between 35 and 40 percent, creating a social and economic vacuum that would open the door for the Renaissance, sixty years later.

Incidentally, Otakar's monetary activities left one lasting impression on the world: the standard silver coin struck during his reign was named for the Bohemian town in which it was mined— the town of Tolar, which the Germans called Thaller, and resulted in the name *dollar.*

As with all the books in this series, I have some people to thank in the preparation of this one: to Lucas Bortin, for access to his material on Medieval manuscripts and diplomatic documents of the period, including some of the remaining records of Otakar's Court Scholars; to Juana Cardones, for information on Bohemian Medieval architecture, furnishings, and household management; to Betty Fuller, for access to her research on the end of the Medieval Warm Period; to Klaus Lowenstein, for information on Court life in Medieval Bohemia; to Jamie Mattissen, for access to her library on eastern European textiles and clothing in the thirteenth and fourteenth centuries; to Inge Porrenheim, for information on Konige Kunigunde's Court; to Janet Tworek, for information on the economy of Bohemia and the transition from a barter-and-labor standard of exchange to a money-based one; to Peter Quarterod, for information on mining and smelting in Medieval Bohemia, and Bohemian coinage policies; and to William Wilson, Jr., for information on the Bohemian/Hungarian military campaigns of the thirteenth century, including disputed accounts of certain events associated with them. If I have strayed from their excellent information, I plead exigencies of storyline, and take full blame for my errors, with apologies to these good people who have been so generous with their help and expertise.

At the publishing end of the process, my thanks, as always, go out to my agent, Irene Kraas; to my online publicist, the incomparable Wiley Saichek; to my editor at Tor, Melissa Singer; and to all the good people at Tor. Also I wish to thank my attorney, Robin A. Dubner, who continues to protect Saint-Germain; to Lindig Harris for her e-newsletter, *Yclept Yarbro;* to the Yahoo C. Q. Yarbro chat group; to Paula Guran, who womans my Web site, www .ChelseaQuinnYarbro.net; to Libba Campbell, who proofreads my chapters as I complete them. Thanks also to Tony Harrison, Eleanor Prinus, and Chris Webster, my recreational readers; to Sharon Russell, Stephanie Moss, Elizabeth Miller, Maureen Kelly, and Alice Horst for their interest and support; to Gaye, Megan, Marc, Brian, Charlie, Peggy, Lori, Christine, and Jim, with nods to David, Peter, and Eggert, just because; and to Crumpet, Butterscotch, and Ekaterina the Great for their splendid feline companionship. Most especially, thanks to my readers and the bookstore owners who supply them with these tales. I wouldn't have made it to this, book #24, without you.

CHELSEA QUINN YARBRO
Berkeley, California

PART I

ROZSA OF BORSOD

*T*ext of a letter of introduction from Frater Sandor, scribe to Konig Bela of Hungary, to Konig Otakar II of Bohemia and the Counselors of Praha, written in Church Latin on vellum, carried by a royal herald, and delivered thirteen days after it was dispatched.

On the order of Bela, Konig of Hungary, presently established at Buda, I send his greetings to Przemysl Otakar II, Konig of Bohemia, and the Counselors of Praha: at Konig Bela's pleasure, I present to your notice the following men and women:

Gazsi of Raab and his three sons, Miksa, Adorjan, and Nandor, all silversmiths and Masters within their Guild, who have made jewelry and other prized objects for Konig Bela; they will supply Konig Bela's granddaughter, your Konig's Konige, Kunigunde, such items she requests for herself or members of the Konige's Court, as they have done for our Konig Bela. They will require housing and the support given to members of the Konige's household.

Tirz Agoston of Mures and his wife, Jolan, and their two youngest children, their son, Imri, and their daughter, Alida. The family has made musical instruments for three generations, and their older sons are presently apprenticed in Mures to their cousin Tirz Lajos; at the completion of their training, they will once again join their parents for their living, thus continuing the honor of the craft. Tirz Agoston will make such instruments as mandolas, gitterns, rebecs, fiddles, and psalteries as may please Konige

Kunigunde; Jolan can teach the Konige, and any of her ladies she may select, in the art of playing these instruments. The family will require a house and a workshop near to the Vaclav Castle but will require no support beyond their house and workshop, so long as Tirz Agoston is given permission to make instruments for those outside the Konige's Court.

Vili of Gran, who is a superb furrier, skilled in every aspect of his art, from skinning to preserving hides and furs, and will, at the pleasure of Konige Kunigunde, fashion such garments and other items as it will delight her to have or to present to members of her Court. He, too, is to have housing and the support of the Konige's household. His wife and children will remain in Hungary for at least a year, his wife being newly pregnant and unable to travel; she will require at least a year after giving birth before she may safely take to the road with her children, and so will not arrive in Praha for at least two years.

Klotild of Jilish, the widow of Szilard, and her daughter Emese, who is seven years of age. Klotild is widely recognized as an herb-woman and midwife. She has delivered many noble children and has only had four die among more than thirty births. Konig Bela believes that Klotild of Jilish will be able to use her skills to ease his granddaughter's labor and ensure her a safe delivery. She will also attend the infant through its first year, as a member of the Konige's household. Her daughter will assist her in her work, and serve as a companion for the Konige's daughter.

Rakoczy Ferancsi, alchemist, who has the knowledge to make jewels, which he will be honored to concoct for Konige Kunigunde. This man comes from an ancient line of Comesi, as the Latins have it, and is due the rights of his title, that of Santu-Germaniu, a fiefdom at the far eastern edge of Bela's Kingdom, an ancient holding of his family, the safety of which fief is in his hands. Aside from his abilities to produce jewels, Rakoczy is also familiar with many languages. Being a man of some wealth, he will provide residence and maintenance for himself and his man-servant, and employ such household as he may require, without cost to the Konige. He has made arrangements with the Counselors of Praha to purchase a mansion in Praha which he will keep from his own purse. He has also provided his own escort and wagons for the journey to Praha, and provided all funds for such stops as this company of travelers may make along the way. Konig Bela asks that the Comes be restricted to his own mansion, the Konige's Court, and the public places and buildings of the city, and that he not be allowed to pass beyond the city's walls; further, Konig Bela relies upon the Konige's Court to make regular reports on his activities, for he is a figure of great interest to the Konig.

Elek of Buda, master of horse, who will bring ten horses with him to augment the Konige's stables, all from Royal blood-stock. In addition, he will bring his wife and five children with him, all of whom are to be enrolled in the Konige's household, as servants of whatever capacities as will please Konige Kunigunde to assign. This man is skilled in all manner of equestrianship, and will not only train the Konige's horses, but will also train such members of the Konige's household that she may require, to ride.

Hovarth Pisti of Buda, master tapestry-weaver, and his six apprentices: Fabo, Geza, Andras, Bartal, Jeno, and Tivadar. These artisans are the most accomplished tapestry-weavers in Hungary; they will prepare such tapestries as the Konige shall desire them to weave. Hovarth is the highest member of his Guild, and has been enrolled among the Counselors of Buda to represent all members of his Guild of Tapestry-Weavers. His absence has required him to appoint a deputy, who will fulfill his duties in Buda while Hovarth Pisti remains in Praha in the service of Konige Kunigunde, and a member of her household.

Rozsa of Borsod, Teca of Veszbrem, Gyongyi of Tolna, and Csenge of Somogy to help the Konige's four other women tend to her in her pregnancy. All four women are from noble families; Rozsa of Borsod is the wife of Notay Tibor of Kaposvar, already in the Court of Otakar II; Csenge of Somogy is the cousin of the Konige's waiting-woman, Imbolya of Heves. Teca of Veszbrem and Gyongyi of Tolna are high-born widows of distinguished soldiers of noble birth. These four women will remain to wait upon Konige Kunigunde until her second child is three years old, and longer if the Konige gives birth again during that time, for they are charged with assisting in the care of her children as well as of her. They will be kept by the Konige as members of her Court.

In addition, Konig Bela has purchased twenty slaves for Konige Kunigunde's household, to be employed as she sees fit. Most of the slaves are from the East, and have only a rudimentary knowledge of the Magyar tongue and none at all of the Bohemian one, and so will have to rely upon those knowing Magyar to be in charge of them, or to be assigned tasks that requires little or no instruction and supervision. They have the appropriate brands on them, and they range in age from about ten to about twenty. There are twelve men and eight women. Three of the women are needlewomen capable of simple sewing. One of the men is quite strong and may be used for heavy labor. Konig Bela has clothed them and provided them with round cloaks to spare his granddaughter that expense.

The escort and transportation for this company, led by Padnagy Kalman, Dux of Oradea, consists of ten mounted men-at-arms, five drivers of wagons pulled by mules, ten walking escorts for the wagons, eight walking escorts for four large carts pulled by bullocks, and six small carts pulled by ponies. There are an extra four horses and six mules assigned to this company, in order to ensure that there will be fresh mounts at all times. The slaves will walk to augment the escort, but the others will ride in the wagons except when ordered to leave the wagons by the Dux. In addition, there are two cooks, five grooms, three monks, a priest, a scribe, two couriers, and a physician. All these will return to Hungary with the Dux unless it should please Konige Kunigunde to keep one or more of them to serve her. Since they will be traveling in the two weeks before Easter, it is to be hoped that they will be far safer than they would be during times that battle is permitted and the Peace of God is not in effect. They depart two days *following the courier carrying this, and for ten days they will be in God's Hands. After the 24th of March, the escort will have to be more diligent, even on Bohemian roads.*

Given Konig Otakar's encouragement to German settlers in Bohemia, Konig Bela has no doubt that Konig Otakar will extend the same welcome to these Hungarians, for the sake of his Konige and the deep affection that is shared between these two Konigs. It is Konig Bela's hope that the presence of these excellent Hungarians will bring about an end to the hostilities often expressed to their fellow-countrymen, which would please both Konig Bela and his granddaughter, Konige Kunigunde, both of whom seek an end to border skirmishes.

May God bless and save Konig Otakar, and send him a son this time, and may his line never be extinguished in Bohemia from this day until the Last Judgment.

In Buda on the 12th day of March in the 1269th Year of Our Lord, at the behest of Konig Bela of Hungary, by the hand of

Frater Sandor, Hieronymite and Scribe
(the seal and sigil of Konig Bela)

1

Rakoczy Ferancsi looked around the entry hall of his manse, his only expression a flicker of disappointment in his dark eyes. "Well, we have seen worse; at least they disposed of the rushes; we will have to do something about the rats," he remarked in Imperial Latin to Hruther, who was three steps behind him, carrying a red-lacquer chest strapped to his shoulders, its legs removed and bound to the body of the chest. The two went through the arched door and into the main hall; at the far end of it was a large fireplace badly in need of sweeping; two benches lay upside down in front of it. "We will need a staff of fifteen at least to manage this place, inside and out." He swung his black-and-white badger-pelt mantel off his shoulders and draped it over the nearest plank bench, revealing a black bleihaut with Hungarian-style sleeves and long, black-embroidered riding panels in the front of the garment. His Roman braccae were heavy black cotton; his high boots were thick-soled and made of tooled red leather from Aleppo. He wore no jewelry or indication of rank so as not to tempt robbers to stalk him during his travels; his head was bare, revealing dark wavy hair, cut shorter than the current fashion, with a touch of gray at the temples, and just now, his attractive, irregular features were severe. His simplicity of clothing would change when he went to the Konige's Court to present himself along with the rest of those subjects Konig Bela had sent to his granddaughter, when grandeur would be expected of him on account of his title; richness and variety in dress were required for members of the Konige's Court, and failure to present a splendid appearance would be regarded as a slight to the Konige.

"More like twenty, and more for the bake-house, the bath-house, and the stable," said Hruther, setting the chest down and sniffing the chilly air. "It's musty."

"True enough."

"The air is stale."

"It has been empty for more than a year," Rakoczy said, a suggestion of doubt about this in his observation. "According to Counselor Smiricti."

The building was less than fifty years old, made of wood and stone, two stories high, with ten rooms and a kitchen in this central manse. It stood on a shoulder of a hill not far from the Vaclav Castle, surrounded by a tall stone wall; this manse was on the highest part of the mansion-grounds. The main hall reached up to the roof, heavily beamed and shadowy above the rows of shuttered windows that ran along the gallery on three sides of the hall providing what little light filtered into the room. Large as it was, the main hall was sparsely furnished with rough-hewn benches and two standing chests, both of which were open, showing all contents were gone; there was an overturned table in the far corner of the hall. To the left of the fireplace, a narrow, steep stairway led to the gallery above.

"The private rooms—six of them—are upstairs, but for the withdrawing rooms, on the other side of the main hall," said Hruther as he carefully put down the bundled legs of the chest. "According to the information we were given."

"There are two of those, are there not? withdrawing rooms?" Rakoczy asked.

Hruther pointed to the right. "You can see the doors; one is supposed to have three tall windows."

"I'll decide which one of them will serve as my study; we can turn one of the upstairs rooms into my workroom, with space for my books; we will have to determine how accurate the description we were provided actually is," Rakoczy decided aloud. "The work already paid for is still not done."

"It isn't quite what we expected," Hruther said. "This will need a lot of work."

Rakoczy nodded his agreement. "Fortunately we have four men from our escort with us for another ten days before they return to Santu-Germaniu. We can get some work done here until we have hired the servants we need."

"Escorts and a groom," said Hruther of the four men who had accompanied them to Praha. He crossed the room to the maw of the fireplace. "The chimney will need cleaning before a fire can be safely lit. At least the Bohemians have chimneys—not like the English. By the smell of it, there are rats in the flue." He glanced at the floor. "By the droppings, there are rats everywhere."

Although it was April, the day was overcast, threatening rain, so the house was chilly and damp. Hruther stretched to ease his shoulders. "The eight wagons with your furnishings should be here in a few days. It was wise to dispatch them separately; I think now you were right about that. Konig Bela would have been suspicious of you taking so many of our own goods with the Dux of Oradea's escort. Bela would like your exile to be as limited as possible, but since he needs Santu-Germaniu to help keep his heir in check in Transylvania, he cannot deny you at least a few of your things. Bela has good reason to contain Istvan, and without Santu-Germaniu he won't be able to." He looked at the nearest of the open chests, shaking his head. "We can manage for four days on our own. You have enough gold to hire help before the rest of your goods arrive."

"And you dare to speak the heir's name aloud?" Rakoczy asked, his tone gently mocking.

"Who but you can hear me, my master?" Hruther countered. "I will say nothing that could create more suspicions than have already accumulated around us."

"We may yet need my gold for bribes, though Bohemia is rich in gold."

Hruther gave a wintery smile. "Jewels will be most welcome, in any event. The Konige will want them."

"I wish I had been allowed more of my servants to come with me," Rakoczy said, taking a turn about the main hall, feeling increasingly desolate as he took stock of all the work to be done. "There is so much to be restored."

"True enough," Hruther agreed.

"As you say, we can probably manage well enough until the household goods arrive. This is hardly the Silk Road, nor is it Leosan Fortress, or Cyprus, thank all the forgotten gods." Memories of those three places rose in his thoughts; he looked toward the maw of the fireplace as the images faded.

Hruther pinched the bridge of his nose, then rubbed his eyes, doing his best to banish the fatigue that was taking hold of him now that they had reached the end of their journey. "The Dux set a hard pace for us," he said as if offering an explanation for his weariness. "Doubtless Konig Bela required it of him."

"So he did," Rakoczy said.

"Still, we should make some effort to settle in as soon as your goods arrive," Hruther declared, making himself stand straight. "It's expected. The Konige's Court will expect it of you." He stretched his arms, laced his fingers, and pushed his hands out ahead of him.

"We should probably fetch food from the market before that; as you say, it is expected and the men are hungry," Rakoczy said, and then added, "Or I could give them money for a meal and entertainment. What do you think, old friend?"

"They'd probably prefer the latter, and it will postpone our first visit to the market until tomorrow; I can wait until then to purchase a lamb or a brace of ducks for my own needs," said Hruther. "It's been a long trek from your native earth. The men have earned their respite—no doubt they'll be glad of a night of revelry and soft beds."

"Then they shall have such a night, and as many of them as we may need to provide," Rakoczy nodded, and continued his stroll around the room. "We should purchase a proper table from the local wood-workers, with chairs, not benches, to go with it. The servants' quarters are behind the kitchen opposite the stable, as I recall from the Counselor's description."

"I'll go and look, if you like," Hruther offered.

Rakoczy laughed once. "You have the right of it; neither of us has been here before, and we are both seeing it for the first time. That plan the Counselors sent has its limits in—" He paused, pondering for a moment. "I suppose I should send a gift to the Counselors of Praha for selecting this place for us."

"They probably expect something for their help," Hruther agreed. "There'll be time enough tomorrow to present yourself to them, when you can report your plans for this place." He pointed to the empty sconces on the wall. "We'll need some torches by nightfall. We don't want to fumble about in the dark."

Rakoczy nodded. "And not fumbling about would lead to awkward questions," he said; he saw nearly as well in the dark as he did in daylight. "I'll put incense in the sap on the torches, to take the disused odor out of the air."

Hruther moved to the center of the main hall, taking stock of the place. "It's a bit drafty."

"We will have to find where the drafts are worst and hang tapestries there until proper caulking can be done." Rakoczy sighed. "Do you suppose we should send a messenger to the Konige's Court to announce our arrival? Or is that the Counselors' duty?" He stopped. "You have no more notion than I do. I am speaking to the walls as much as to you, for which I ask your pardon."

"You needn't," said Hruther; his faded-blue eyes showed a trace of amusement. "There are busy days ahead of us."

"Truly," said Rakoczy. He strode to the staircase next to the fireplace. "I trust the Counselors will advise us on where we might find dependable servants. In any case, we'll need their permission to engage the staff."

"I'll find out tomorrow," said Hruther.

"I will consult the Guildmaster to engage masons to build an athanor for me," Rakoczy said, his eyes fixed in the middle distance, his lips pressed together as he weighed his decision. "Better to have it done by a Bohemian than by me, and by a Guild member."

"There may still be raised eyebrows," Hruther warned. "Athanors are not the usual work of masons."

"So long as I am considered to be in the service of Konige Kunigunde, however marginally, having local masons build the athanor will provide a measure of protection against rumors." Rakoczy lapsed into thought again. "We will need more furnishings than what is coming. I'll find the Carpenters' Guild as well as the Masons'."

"Except for those rumors the masons start, you can contain the worst of them, so long as the Konige is willing to support you," said Hruther.

Rakoczy sighed. "You have the right of it: there will be rumors—since I am twice-exiled from my native earth." He nodded once. "Still, it was prudent to leave Santu-Germaniu before Konig Bela decided to attack once more and claim it as his own, not only to keep his son in check, but as an excuse to seize my wealth." He shook his head slowly. "I am well-aware of what Konig Bela wants, and my fief is the least of it. By accepting his terms of exile and coming here, we avoid any more difficulties with him, and his son, for that matter—Istvan is still eager to rule beyond Transylvania—and spare the peasants on my land further raids and losses." He paused. "But now we are here, we must take care not to be overheard when we speak of this."

"Of course." Hruther pressed his lips together. "For the sake of Santu-Germaniu and your vassals."

"Among other things," Rakoczy said. "It is a relief to talk about it while we are private. It is a relief not to have spies all around us."

"But you disliked leaving," Hruther pointed out.

There was an ironic note in Rakoczy's response. "It *is* my native earth, and I am bound to it. Though I have left it many times, leaving of my own will and leaving in exile are not the same thing.

Konig Bela wants me out of Hungary, but not so far that I might make mischief for him. Praha serves his purpose admirably."

"I don't think you could have negotiated with him, not to any advantage for you," Hruther remarked.

"Nor do I. What assurance could we have that our terms would be honored?" He went quiet. "It was best to leave, but—"

"You would rather not be required to go," said Hruther; he had been aware of Rakoczy's sorrow since they had gone from Santu-Germaniu.

"It was how I went to my death, the first time—as an exile and captive. I am less a captive now than I was thirty-three centuries ago, but just as much an exile." He felt the impact of that time, so long ago, when he had been captured by the enemies of his father and his country, made a slave destined with men from his father's army to take the brunt for his new masters' army in battle, and was disemboweled for his victory when his captors had expected his defeat; they had feared that he and all the captive slaves he led might rebel . . . To keep from dwelling on his breathing life, he slapped his hands together, saying, "What did you make of the bodies?"

Hruther showed no emotion. "You mean the four hanging in chains outside the main gate?" He saw Rakoczy nod. "Otakar doesn't suffer treachery, or flouting of the Konig's Law."

"So I thought," Rakoczy concurred.

"And the Counselors of Praha will not deny him his justice, such as it is, unless they want to join the bodies hanging outside the gate," Hruther added in a carefully neutral voice, rubbing his clean-shaven cheek.

"As they are certainly aware. Those corpses—" He had felt the odor of the bodies like a blow, and it struck him again in recollection. "I wonder how long he leaves them hanging?" It was more a question to himself, so he was a bit startled when Hruther answered.

"Until they come apart," Hruther said. "That's the way of most rulers in this region of the world, or so I heard one of our escort explain to the scribe."

"It would appear to be true," said Rakoczy, making a fastidious gesture as if to banish the vision of the men hanging by the gate.

"There is a bath-house—yes?" Hruther asked into the silence that had fallen between them.

"So I was told; behind the bake-house," Rakoczy answered, his manner mildly distracted, as if the recollections of his breathing days were lingering. "And you have the right of it: bathing is needed."

"If the furnace is clean enough to use safely, then I believe I should start it warming." Hruther folded his arms. "You will not want to call upon the Counselors still grimy from the road, and in clothing less than worthy of your rank. You know what sticklers these municipal Councils can be."

"None better," Rakoczy agreed as he fingered his neat, close-trimmed beard, relieved to have such a mundane matter to consider. "I will want the Hungarian bleihaut in dark-red silk, and the black-silk gambeson trimmed in ermine. The Hungarian braccae and the Persian boots, I think. I will present myself to the Counselors tomorrow after Mass, and to the Konige in the afternoon."

"With jewels," said Hruther, glancing over at the overturned table as a mouse ran out from its protection and skittered toward the corridor leading to the kitchen.

"Certainly," said Rakoczy. "Konig Bela would demand it, if only to prove my deserts of position to his granddaughter. The black-sapphire-in-silver eclipse pectoral on the ruby-studded chain, and rings for every finger." He began to pull off his Spanish gloves. "And my coronet, too, I suppose. They will expect the full display."

"What gift will you offer the Counselors?" Hruther inquired.

"I have to think about it; perhaps silver buckles?"

"There is plenty of silver in Bohemia," Hruther pointed out. "Some of the Counselors might consider such a gift insulting."

"Then a selection of ivory boxes should be welcome; there are no elephants in Bohemia," said Rakoczy, his expression remote.

"There should be a dozen of them in the banded trunk. You'll have no difficulty in locating them."

"We can search for them later," Hruther said, aware of Rakoczy's discomfort. "But for now, the bath-house, don't you think?"

"I do," said Rakoczy, and dropped his gloves on top of his mantel, preparing to follow Hruther.

The kitchen, tacked onto the east wall of the manse, proved cavernous, with two huge fireplaces, one equipped with spits for turning meat, the other with an assortment of hooks for hanging cauldrons. The room smelled of stale oil and burnt flesh. An oven with an iron door was set in the wall between the two fireplaces, and another small fireplace in the center of the room was topped with a thick iron sheet that was in need of cleaning and oiling. The windows were high in the wall, the thick, greenish glass filling them in diamond patterns of heavy leading, giving the kitchen a quality of fretted light that made the room seem as if it were under water.

"The utensils are gone; we will have to get new ones, and whatever pots and pans are required," Hruther remarked as he continued on toward the larder and the door to the outside, where the information the Counselors had provided said there was a kitchen garden; there was, but it had been allowed to run riot.

"We have time enough to restore many of the herbs; the rest may have to wait a year to be replanted," Rakoczy said as the two of them made for the small gate that led out into the courtyard.

To the right of the garden wall stood the bake-house and the bath-house, both of stone with wooden roofs topped by slates, many of which were chipped or broken; they shared a brick chimney. A large wooden bin backed onto the bath-house; a lift of its lid disclosed a fair supply of very dry cut wood and the distinct odor of rats, accompanied by a scuttling under the sawn branches. Hruther dropped the lid back into place.

"We will need a cat or two," said Rakoczy. "At the least."

"Male and female, so there will be kittens." Hruther nodded.

"For now, we'd best see to the furnace. I'll wager it needs cleaning, with so many rats about." He chuckled. "Konig Bela would be pleased to see you so deprived."

"So he would; it would give him profound satisfaction to see me destitute, but he would not be endorsed by the Church if he ordered it himself, my title being older than his for more years than he realizes. He wants to keep track of me, so that he need not fear my making alliances with Galich or Polovtsky. Do not say those words aloud if anyone other than I can hear them: Bela might learn of it and change his mind about exile in favor of something more absolute. We must guard our tongues in this place," Rakoczy said sardonically, looking for the loading chute for the bath-house furnace. "We need to have all the chimneys cleaned, and repaired if repairs are needed, which I suspect they will be."

Hruther shrugged to cover his relief at Rakoczy finally talking about the reasons for his departure from his native earth. "Along with everything else; we'll need an army of cleaners." He went around the corner to the bath-house entrance. "The hinges are rusty."

"They will be oiled and cleaned, or replaced," said Rakoczy, coming up behind him. "Will the door open?"

"It should," said Hruther, taking hold of the latch-handle, shoving it down, and pulling outward. With a groan the door swung wide reluctantly, exuding an odor of mold and revealing a heap of damp rags.

"More cleaning, and more repairs," said Rakoczy. "I suppose it would be as well to wash in one of the kitchen tubs tonight. Tomorrow I will put my native earth under the bath and I will inspect the old bathtub to see how much can be salvaged. Most of the boards will have to be replaced, in any case, by the look of them."

Hruther stepped inside the bath-house, taking stock of the small undressing room and the ajar door that led into the main bath-room. "Not very big."

"It will suffice," said Rakoczy, his expression darkening as he studied the ceiling for signs of leaks. "We will need to have the roof repaired."

"For all the buildings," said Hruther. As he left the bath-house behind Rakoczy, he inquired, "What became of the previous owner? do we know?"

A frown flickered between Rakoczy's fine brows. "I will inquire of the Counselors tomorrow. Knowing what became of its previous owner would be useful."

"Do you think they'll tell you?" Not waiting for an answer, Hruther closed the door. "I'll check the furnace, and if it's in good form, I'll do what I can to have it ready in a day or two."

"The same will be needed for the bake-house," said Rakoczy.

"And every hearth inside the walls. The attics and cellars will need attention as well; you were told the mansion was ready for occupancy." Hruther started toward the door to the furnace, noting with misgiving that the iron door was scabbed with rust. "This door will need to be replaced; it's rotted at the hinges."

"It is not the only one," said Rakoczy, turning as he heard a thud from the stable. "I think I should see what the men are doing with the horses and mules."

"The stalls may be falling apart," said Hruther, his face showing no emotion. "Or they are trying to move fallen stall slats out of the way. Or there could be vagabonds hiding there, and your escort is trying to evict them."

"I should go," said Rakoczy, signaling his appreciation to Hruther as he made his way across the uneven flagging of the courtyard, being careful to watch where he stepped, for the paving stones were broken and uneven, providing poor footing. He tripped only once, on the handle of a fallen rake. Reaching the stable door, he tugged it open and stepped into the dark interior.

Illes of Kotan, the groom, was the first to look toward Rakoczy, and to duck his head in respect. "Comes," he said loudly enough to alert the three men-at-arms; they turned and offered a simple salute.

The men-at-arms took a few steps toward Rakoczy but made

no effort to help contain the furious mule that demanded Illes' attention.

Rakoczy had taken in the general confusion, and realized that the noise had come from one of the mules, the on-side wheeler attempting to kick the wagon he pulled; he was half-rearing in his harness, ears laid back, and eyes rolling, while the other three mules did their best to lean away from their unruly comrade. Rakoczy went up to the aggravated animal, speaking softly as he reached for the reins to steady him. "There, there. No bad conduct now, when you've done so well for so many leagues." The mule gave an angry squeal; Rakoczy laid his hand on his noseband. He spoke to Illes. "Unbuckle him from the wagon—slowly. Do it as calmly as you can. Then lead him around for a short while until he's used to this place."

"Yes, Comes," said the groom, hastening to his work as he had been ordered.

"Brush off his legs as soon as the mud dries," Rakoczy went on, still patting the mule's neck. "No need to fuss," he added to the mule.

Illes worked as quickly as he could, trying to stay away from the mule's feet, for he was stamping in annoyance. "Comes, he's almost free."

"Thank you, Illes," said Rakoczy, preparing to lead the mule away from the wagon. "As soon as I get him at the end of the aisle, come and take charge of him."

"And the rest of the hitch?" Illes asked, aware that the other three mules were very nervous. "They're restive."

"I will attend to them, with some help from your comrades," he said with a significant glance at the three men-at-arms. They might consider caring for mules beneath them, but refusing their assistance when the Comes himself was willing to handle them was demeaning.

"I'll deal with the lead pair," said Zabolcs of Hrasty, the senior of the three, a man of medium height with powerful arms and shoulders and a swagger in his walk.

"I'll take the other wheeler," said Domonkos of Pest, falling in beside Zabolcs as they approached the mules. Endre son-of-Odon hung back, then went to help out.

Rakoczy held the mule's head low so that he would not be inclined to rear again and led him at a slow trot toward the far end of the stable. He saw that none of the box-stalls were bedded; he added straw to the many things he would have to purchase the next day. "Where is my horse, and my manservant's horse?"

"In the paddock behind the stable. The fence is sound enough, and I didn't want to stall them just yet. I'll bed stalls for them while they're turned out in the paddock, assuming I can find enough straw to do it." Illes reached up and took the lead from Rakoczy. "Where do we put the wagon? We can't leave it here in the aisle." He made a gesture of confusion.

"There should be a place for it near the tackroom," said Rakoczy with more hope than certainty. "If there is no place for it, put it in the mare's stall at the end of the row. Give them all oatmash for their suppers, and vinegar," he added, tossing him a scoop that had been hanging on a nail. "Put oil in the mash, and on their hooves."

"Yes, Comes." This time all the men answered in a ragged sort of unison as they took reluctant steps forward.

"And when the horses and mules are groomed and fed, come to the main house and I will have silver for you all, so you may go down into Praha and enjoy yourselves." He was not surprised to see the men's eyes brighten at the prospect. "I will provide you money to put up at one of the inns until there are rooms ready for you. I see no point in asking you to sleep on the floor."

"Why not?" Domonkos asked. "The Konig demands it often enough."

"Ah, but I am not Konig Bela," Rakoczy said.

Zabolcs laughed. "Would you want to be?"

"No," Rakoczy said quietly. "Little as he may believe it." He regarded the four men. "Are you able to manage for yourselves?"

Endre son-of-Odon, lead-rope in hand, swore as the off-side

lead mule lashed out at him with her teeth, barely missing his shoulder; Rakoczy moved swiftly to bring the frightened jenny under control. Endre stepped back into the nearest stall, regarding the mule warily. "Be careful, Comes."

"Do not fret, Endre," Rakoczy said, his Carpathian accent stronger than usual. "He's settling down. You can handle him safely now."

Reluctantly Endre came out of the stall and attached the lead-rope to the bit-ring. "There. I'll have her out of harness in three finger-snaps."

"Steadiness is better than speed," said Rakoczy, and looked toward the door as Hruther came through it, appearing uncharacteristically flustered. "What is it?"

"Counselor Smiricti has just arrived, with two deputies," Hruther said. "I've asked them to wait in the main hall." He was not panting, but he took a deep breath, as if to clear his head. "I have told him we haven't had a chance to make the house ready to receive guests yet, that most of your goods have yet to arrive, but—"

Rakoczy stared at Hruther for a moment, and said, "Then I must go and welcome him as best I can." There was an ironic note in his words; he turned to Illes and the three escorts. "I will leave you to your tasks. When you have finished them, come to the manse and I will give you your money."

"Thank you, Comes," said Zabolcs for all of them.

Hruther held the door for Rakoczy as he left the stable. "The deputies are armed," he said in the tongue of Visigothic Spain.

"That is hardly surprising; I believe any man of means goes about the city with some form of protection." Rakoczy lengthened his stride, taking care not to trip on the flagstones; he avoided the bake-house with the small laundry attached to its back, and made straight for the low-walled and much-neglected kitchen garden. "That is not a matter for concern; the deputies are guards for the Counselors."

"Possibly," said Hruther, keeping pace with Rakoczy.

"They're in the main hall, you said?"

"Yes. I apologized that we wouldn't be able to offer them bread and salt, or wine. Or a chair to sit in." Hruther reached the kitchen garden and its dilapidated gate. "At least the Counselor can see the state of this mansion he has allowed you to purchase."

Five steps brought them to the kitchen door; they passed inside and closed the door, then went past the two pantries, through the kitchen, and down the corridor to the main hall.

"Comes Santu-Germaniu," said the tall, angular, middle-aged man in the elaborately fur-trimmed huch of dark-blue Milanese velvet worn over a long chainse of rose-colored silk; his braccae were dark-brown, as were his low boots. His hair, a steely gray, was cut fashionably short, curling next to his jaw and blending into his trimmed beard in the style of merchants; his soft hat of amber velvet brought out his light-brown eyes and minimized his large ears and hatchet-nose. He offered a mannerly bow, although the deputies with him did not; they remained standing, their hands on their swords and an air of belligerence about them.

Rakoczy returned it. "Counselor Smiricti."

"I was told you had arrived, and I wanted to bid you welcome to Praha." He signaled to the two men standing behind him, indicating that he wanted to be private with Rakoczy. "I will be here some while. The Comes and I have much to discuss. If you will keep watch at the door?"

The two deputies turned and left the room, their spurs ringing on the stone floor.

"I regret that the stable has not yet been prepared for horses. My escort and groom can provide grain and buckets of water for your horses from our traveling supplies, but there is no bedding in the stalls, and no hay in the loft. I trust your men will not be too displeased with that," Rakoczy said with as much geniality as he could summon.

"I feared there would not be anything here for you to use," said Counselor Smiricti. He gestured to the room. "I had hoped that the Counselors would allocate the funds you provided to set this place in order before your arrival, in accordance with your instructions, but no one could agree on the amount to spend, so nothing was done." He clicked his tongue. "Since your gold that bought this mansion was in our hands, we should have made an appropriate disposition here, in accordance with your wishes, but, as you see . . ."

Rakoczy made a small bow. "I understand. Matters of this sort are always difficult, are they not?" He went and righted one of the two overturned benches in front of the fireplace. "At least I can offer you a seat. I am sorry it is only a plank."

Counselor Smiricti went and sat down. "I was examining that chest," he said, pointing to the red-lacquer one that stood at the other end of the room, its detached legs lying in front of it. "A handsome piece."

"I agree," said Rakoczy. "I have had it for many years." That those years were reckoned in centuries he did not mention.

"Excellently made." He rubbed his gloved hands together. "It occurred to me that you would need some help in making this house habitable. I felt I should give you what advice I may."

"Thank you. I would appreciate it." He managed to keep the irony he felt from his voice,

The Counselor cleared his throat. "You see, the previous owner, Pan Belcrady Jaromir, had many mines, mostly silver mines, and he drove a hard bargain for his silver with Przemysl Vaclav, and then was exiled, two years ago. His estates now are the fiefs of Konig Otakar, and the revenues they produce are owned outright by the Crown." He coughed. "The manse was cleared out by order of the Konig, and Belcrady's kin have been ordered not to leave their country estates, or face imprisonment for rebellion. There is some hard blood between the Konig and the Belcradys. I thought you should know this, since this mansion is regarded with misgiving by many, and not without good cause. In order to avoid problems, I will tell you what Guilds to deal with, and whom to approach for servants. That is, if my offer is welcome to you."

"An exile's manse for an exile," Rakoczy mused aloud, a trace of amusement in his midnight eyes. He nodded to Counselor Smiricti. "Thank you for this information. It will help me to make my arrangements to set it in order. In that regard, your advice would be very much appreciated; I am grateful for your offer."

"I feel it is fitting that I do what I can to make up for this unpromising beginning. Let me know what you require and I will tell you where to obtain it, and at what cost," said Counselor Smiricti, and gave Rakoczy his full attention as the Comes began to list all he would need to put the manse and the mansion in order.

Text of an order from the Carters' Guild of Praha confirming the transportation of deliveries to be made to Mansion Belcrady.

To the Comes Santu-Germaniu, Rakoczy Feransci, the following items are to be brought to Mansion Belcrady:

Delivered today, April 29th, 1269th Year of Grace:
   Three wagon-loads of cut stone from the Italian quarry, as presented by the Masons' Guild
   Six wagon-loads of lumber from Styria, as cut by the Woodsmen's Guild
   Two wagon-loads of straw and two of hay from the farm-market of Roztoky

Delivered tomorrow, April 30th
   On a flat-bedded cart, three sheets of iron, from the Blacksmiths' Guild
   On a flat-bedded cart, four completed new doors from the Carpenters' Guild
   Three wagon-loads of household furnishing as ordered from the Furniture-Makers' Guild

Delivered on May 4th
  Fourteen beds and eleven chests, also from the
    Furniture-Makers' Guild
  Two wagon-loads of fencing lumber, as cut by the
    Woodsmens' Guild
  Two large bathing tubs of caulked wood

I have been paid thirty-five gold Vaclavs and ten silver Episco-
puses for these deliveries, which is a full and complete payment
for the services required. Payments to all other Guilds must be
arranged with them, and no claim for undischarged debt to them
may be applied to the monies paid to the Carters' Guild.

  Jaroslav of Praha, Guildmaster (his mark)

by the hand of Josko, clerk and Premonstratensian monk

2

Four youngsters in the Konige's colors stood on the threshold to
Rakoczy's manse, at once pugnacious and shy. They ranged from
about nine to no more than twelve; their stiffly embroidered cotehardies did not fit particularly well, and they all four were uncomfortable in their grandeur, for though it was early, the day was
warm. Two of the younger pages fretted at their posts while the
oldest—a gangly lad with wary eyes and the first hint of a mus-
tache on his upper lip—announced in a high voice that broke
once during his recitation, "To Comes Santu-Germaniu: this day
after High Mass, the Konige's lady-in-waiting and messenger to
the Konige, Rozsa of Borsod, will visit this mansion on behalf of
the Konige."

Hruther, arrayed in a dignified bleihaut of dove-gray linen

over a bleached-cotton chainse and tan-linen trews, studied the four pages, and was startled by the sudden memory of his son, dead twelve centuries ago. "Thank you for your message. The Comes Santu-Germaniu will be honored to receive the Konige's messenger, Rozsa of Borsod."

The tallest of the four bowed for them all; he was slightly younger than his companion who spoke first. "You will make ready to receive her and her escort of four men-at-arms."

"We will welcome her and her escort most gladly," said Hruther. "We thank you for this notice, and for the distinguishment the Konige shows to the Comes."

After an awkward moment, the four youths stepped back and made for the gate in the wall. As they went through to the outside, two armed men fell in with them, making their way toward the narrow street that led up the ridge toward Vaclav Castle.

Closing the main door, Hruther stepped back into the entry hall; three workmen were finishing the repairs to the shutters, and two women were laying down new rushes intermixed with rosemary needles; the manse was nearly ready for invited guests. Hruther nodded to the workers and went into the main hall, now fully restored, with a new table capable of seating twenty dominating the room, wanting only padded benches to be complete. Climbing the stairs next to the fireplace, he continued along the gallery and the central corridor to the door to the nearer of two north-facing rooms. Here he rapped on the door, and being bidden to enter, he lifted the latch and stepped into what had become his master's workroom and library.

"What news, old friend?" Rakoczy asked in the Persian of a thousand years ago as he removed a flask from the athanor that sat at the far end of the room on a footing of bricks, and carefully set it down in a small stone bowl. "Sapphires this time: the Konige likes sapphires. They will be cool enough to touch by mid-day. I'll add them to the rest."

"You may be glad to have them," said Hruther in the same Persian. "One of the Konige's ladies is coming here after Mass."

"I thought I heard the bell," said Rakoczy, his attention still fixed on the flask.

Hruther chuckled. "Four pages, from Vaclav Castle—they came to give us time to prepare for the visit, and to make sure you would be here. Not that you have been granted leave to go about the city unguarded."

"Do we know which of her ladies will arrive?" It was slightly more than a month since he had first presented himself at the Konige's Court, and since then he had had no direct contact with anyone from Vaclav Castle. This, he knew, was a sign of change, and given the elaborate notification, it seemed to imply the Konige's favor and interest.

"Rozsa of Borsod." Hruther kept his demeanor exquisitely neutral.

"The wife of Otakar's favorite, Notay Tibor of Kaposvar? I believe I saw her at Bela's Court, five years ago," Rakoczy remarked, curious as to why Konige Kunigunde would send one of her highest-ranking ladies as her messenger unless the visit was official. "She was a pert bride, as I recall, very young to be married."

"I believe so, from what we have been told by the Counselors," said Hruther. "She may be bringing you a request of some sort, my master. Why else would the Konige's messenger be coming here?" This was not quite a warning. "Do you think that the Konige has an assignment for you?"

Both men knew that a request was likely, and they exchanged knowing nods. "I already have a pouch of diamonds and rubies for the Konige. It may be best to entrust them to Rozsa of Borsod, as a show of respect, both to Kunigunde and to her. Whatever else the Konige may want of me, the jewels should please her, and satisfy Bela."

"Not the rubies," Hruther warned him. "Remember, she's pregnant."

Rakoczy frowned, then said, "Rubies and blood. Some would say they would bring about a miscarriage. So nothing red or otherwise hot."

"The sapphires will be cool enough," said Hruther.

"Yes. And a pair of rubies will be a gift for Rozsa of Borsod." He looked toward the window. "Thank you, old friend. I should have remembered."

"Why? The lore is Bohemian, not of your homeland."

"Still," said Rakoczy, his dark eyes becoming troubled.

"How should Rozsa of Borsod be received?" Hruther asked, intending to redirect Rakoczy's concerns. "Given that the manse is still largely unfinished? We can't yet have the kind of grand display she may expect. You don't want her to offer a disappointed report to Kunigunde."

"We will receive her as formally as we can, and with apologies for the manse not being fully ready. Make sure the servants are in clean clothes; that should help. Have wine and bread and salt set out for a proper welcome, and ask Pacar to make up a plate of pickles and sausages and sweetmeats for our guest. We must not be lacking in attention to one of the Konige's ladies-in-waiting. Have flowers strewn at the door. Also, see that her escort have beer and bread, and cheese if we have any to spare." He stared at the open window, and the serene blue sky beyond. "I suppose I ought to change my clothes," he said, looking down at his stained leather apron that covered an old-fashioned black-cotton dalmatica. "This is hardly fitting for Rozsa of Borsod."

"The Antioch silk huch and the embroidered braccae?" Hruther suggested. "They're fairly grand, but not over-much."

"With the red-silk chainse; yes," Rakoczy agreed. "I will finish up here and go along to my apartments."

"I'll go down to the kitchen and then will meet you in your quarters, unless you have more for me to do?" He started toward the door, glad that they had a strategy for the visit. "High Mass should begin in a short while."

Rakoczy held up his hand to slow his manservant. "Hruther, the second withdrawing room is the most complete; have it prepared for the visit. It can be made quite comfortable. Have the housemaid bring the silk cushions down from my apartments to set on the chairs." The second withdrawing room had been chosen to be his study, and although books were stacked on the reading table and the floor, it was more truly ready for occupants than the first, which was in the process of having its woodwork replaced. "A bowl of cinnamon and rose petals should sweeten the air. Also, be sure the shutters are fully open. It will be hot this afternoon."

"A good thing then that the dung farmer came yesterday," said Hruther with a faint smile.

Rakoczy nodded. "There's only the stable midden to contend with, and it is on the leeward side of the house." He paused, mentally reviewing what more ought to be done. "Tell Pacar to use the brass platter and the Chinese plates, and the glass goblet for wine. A wooden platter will do for her escort."

"Yes, my master," said Hruther, and hurried toward the stairs, climbing up them with unusual haste. By the time he entered Rakoczy's private apartments, he had had the satisfaction of seeing the kitchen in a bustle and two house-servants set to furbishing the withdrawing room according to Rakoczy's instructions in preparation for the official visit; he had dispatched two other house-servants—the seamstress Magda and the herb-woman Jozefa—to the main gate to greet Rozsa of Borsod as soon as she arrived, and to bring her into the manse. He himself had changed from his simple linen bleihaut to one of polished cotton the color of mulberries over a chainse of pale-gray cotton.

Rakoczy stood in the main room of his quarters, wrapped in a drying sheet, rubbing the water out of his hair with the end of it. "I see you have put camphor in the clothes chests," he remarked. "Or rather, I smell that you have."

"In all the chests and garderobes, yes. And added burdock to the latrines, to keep down the smell."

"I will give you some essence of cloves to hang in a vial. That should help." He stared at the garderobe that stood next to the open window. "Do the servants think me peculiar to demand weekly baths?"

"They fear you may be a follower of Mohammed, at the very least," said Hruther, his tone level. "Most of them have Confessed their bathing, and two are doing penance for it."

"I will have to account for my requirements, I suppose, to avoid unwanted attention," said Rakoczy, watching Hruther remove his clothes from the chest and the garderobe, hanging them on pegs set in the garderobe's door.

"I have said it is the custom of your House, and you follow it to honor your ancestors. So far they haven't balked: you are master here. I tell them that if they bathe on Saturday night, while they are fasting, they can go clean in body and soul to Mass on Sunday morning." Hruther handed a breechclout to Rakoczy, and saw him turn away to drop the drying sheet and don the undergarment. "Do you want me to trim your beard?"

"That would probably be advisable," said Rakoczy as he fingered his jaw. "It must look a bit ragged." He had long since become accustomed to lacking a reflection and had learned to rely on Hruther to look after his appearance.

"A bit," said Hruther. "And I'll shave the line for you as well." He handed over the red-silk chainse.

"Let me finish dressing. You can use a cloth around my neck to catch the trimmings." Rakoczy managed a rueful smile. "We must do our best to ensure that Rozsa of Borsod reports us favorably to Konig Bela."

"Do you really think she will do that?" asked Hruther as he offered the braccae to Rakoczy.

"She is a Hungarian noblewoman waiting on the granddaughter of Konig Bela. I think it is required of her to tell not only the Konige but her grandfather of how the meeting goes." He bent over and stepped into the close-fitting braccae, pulling them up and tying them to the braiel of the breechclout. "I think the Byzantine solers, not the estivaux—that would be too foreign."

"The solers," said Hruther, taking them from the box of footwear in the garderobe.

"The soles have been refilled—"

"—last week," said Hruther, sensing Rakoczy's nervousness. "It will go well, my master."

Rakoczy gave a deprecating shrug and finished fastening his solers. "I have done this enough in the past that you would think I would no longer be troubled by these little tests, would you not? I suppose it comes from living in this imposed isolation that magnifies my anxiety." As he rose, Hruther held out the heavy, black-silk huch and tugged the open square sleeves so that they would hang properly while Rakoczy fastened the lacing on the front of the garment.

"I'll get my razor and scissors," said Hruther as he handed Rakoczy his silver-linked eclipse pectoral.

"Very good." He dropped the silver chain around his neck and positioned the black-sapphire heart of the eclipse at the center of his chest. "To your trimming, old friend."

By the time he left his quarters, Rakoczy was superbly turned out, his clothes not truly Bohemian, but not strictly Hungarian, either, as was appropriate for an exile; he wore a signet ring and his pectoral but had decided against other jewelry. He made his way along the corridor to the gallery, then down the narrow stairs to the main hall, where half a dozen of the house-servants had found some excuse to be so that they could view him in his elegance. He went into the second withdrawing room to satisfy himself that it was ready for his guest; then he made his way to the entry hall, opening the door himself in preparation for Rozsa of Borsod's arrival.

Hruther appeared at Rakoczy's side. "This may sweeten your greeting," he said, and put a red, five-petaled rose into his master's hand. "I took the thorns off the stem."

"Deft as always," Rakoczy approved. "Is Pacar ready?"

"Almost. The food will be done very shortly. He said he prays that she does not come too late." He took his place two steps behind Rakoczy, and felt the sun beat down upon him, too hot to be entirely welcome; what Rakoczy was feeling he tried not to think.

In a short while, an elegant little wagon pulled by a pair of spotted ponies and escorted by men-at-arms in the Konige's colors—black and gold—carrying lances as well as swords made its way up the hill toward the mansion, preceded, followed, and flanked by armed men. The device of Borsod—gules, a wolf's head argent, erased to the chief; langed sable and dented or—was painted on the door-panel of the curtained wagon.

From his vantage-point above the gate, the warder, Minek, called out that their noble guest had arrived. The two women with their flowers straightened up and smoothed the fronts of their housses and tweaked their linen caps. The warder opened the gate, and the first armed man stepped through.

"In the name of Konige Kunigunde, her waiting-woman and messenger, Rozsa of Borsod, comes to this mansion."

Magda and Jozefa stepped toward the carriage, garlands in their hands.

Rakoczy came to the front steps. "Where she is most welcome. Pray bring her into our forecourt." He waited while the little company moved forward and the gate closed behind them, then stepped forward as the man-at-arms on her right opened the half-door for her and helped her to get down from the vehicle.

Veiled in elaborate swaths of linen secured in her elaborate coronet with long golden pins, falling in graceful folds that concealed everything about her except for the russet hem of her hammered-silk bleihaut and the embroidered inner sleeve, Rozsa of Borsod turned to face her host, courtisying, and waiting for him to bow while all the servants abased themselves to honor the Konige in whose stead this noblewoman had come.

Holding out the rose, Rakoczy ducked his head while Jozefa and Magda went to hold the door open. "You do this mansion much honor and favor, Rozsa of Borsod," he said in Magyar.

She took the rose, sniffed it. "A pretty conceit, Comes."

"I am pleased you like it," he said, offering his hand on which she could lay her own; the men-at-arms bristled at this familiarity. "It is a pleasure to see you again."

Her laughter rippled like the warm breeze. "He is of ancient title, and from Hungary, as am I," she said to the men in the Bohemian tongue. "It is fitting that I should accept his courtesy. And he is right; I met him the day before my wedding." Very deliberately she put her hand on his. "I leave my men and my wagon to the care of your household."

Hruther signaled to Illes of Kotan to come to take the wagon in charge, and then motioned to Domonkos of Pest. "See to our visitors. Domonkos, there is food and drink for the lady's escort in the kitchen. Make it your purpose to be sure that their needs are provided for."

"Very well done," approved Rozsa to Rakoczy as he brought her to the threshold of his manse. "I particularly liked the women at the gate with their garlands. You have a refined way with you, Comes—not what I would have expected from a Carpathian lord." Behind her veil her eyes were unreadable; her practiced grace the result of her time at the Konige's Court.

Rakoczy offered her a Roman-style bow. "What would you expect, Rozsa of Borsod?"

"Oh, someone more like my husband: a crapulous, quick-tempered, debauched, uncouth—" She broke off. "The match was arranged by my father, with Konig Bela's approval." With a wave of her hand, she banished the topic, looking around the entry hall with interest.

"The work is not yet finished on most of the manse," he said deferentially.

"I heard about that: you sent the funds to put the place in order and they were spent elsewhere. It was to be expected." She released his hand, reaching up to her coronet and loosening the end of her enveloping veil, revealing her pert, feline features and green eyes. Her dark hair was done up in a complex braid and held in a golden snood.

"So Counselor Smiricti explained," Rakoczy said.

"Were you surprised?" The lilt in her voice was belied by a keenness in her glance that revealed she knew more of the incident than her question implied.

Rakoczy gave a half-smile. "Not surprised; more disheartened than anything else."

"Ah," she said, her face softening as she went toward the main hall. "So you have had some experience in these matters. Just as well." She paused to take in the room. "This will be very nice when it is complete."

"That is my hope," Rakoczy said, following her.

She turned toward him. "You will receive the Konige's Court as soon as the manse is ready? Is that your plan?"

"If that would please the Konige, then of course I will consider it a privilege to do so," he said, continuing to watch her.

"It will please her; I'll see to it." She went to the table and ran her fingers along its glossy top. "You could offer a fair banquet here."

"Once the chairs and benches arrive," Rakoczy said.

She laughed, the sound deliberately musical. "Yes. It would be easier with chairs and benches." Her gaze lingered on him, speculative and sensual. "But you already have a few benches, I see, certainly enough for our use. Why not be satisfied with those until you have more guests to receive?"

"A quirk of mine." He bowed her in the direction of the second withdrawing room, following two steps behind her as decorum required; he tried not to notice the servants who had come to the main hall to catch sight of their noble visitor. "If you would? There are refreshments waiting for you, and a small gift that I trust you will convey to the Konige."

She twitched the rose she held. "You will have to show me what it contains," Rozsa said, going toward the second withdrawing room ahead of him.

"Certainly." He moved to open the door for her, saying as he did, "The Anatolian chair is the most comfortable."

She stepped inside and halted, staring at the books. "Mary's Tits!" Her voice was hushed. "Are these all yours, Comes?"

"I collect them," he admitted.

"So many . . ." Her words trailed off. "Do you *read* them?"

"Of course: what would be the point of having them if I did not." He saw suspicion and awe in her eyes; he moved to guide her to the center of the room, saying as he did, "Let me offer you some refreshment." On the low table there stood a brass platter with bread and salt at one end of it and plates of sausages, sweetmeats, pickles, a mound of fresh cheese, and shelled nuts. Next to them stood a bottle of pale wine and a glass goblet. A lean, two-pronged iron pick and an Italian knife lay on the platter, a concession to Rakoczy's foreign manners. "May I pour a glass for you?" Rakoczy asked, picking up the bottle.

"I'd like that." She watched the glass fill as she put her rose down on the tray. "And you? Where is your goblet."

Rakoczy set the bottle down. "Alas," he said, "I do not drink wine."

"Whyever not?" Rozsa asked as she lifted the goblet.

"A condition of my blood will not permit it," he said with the ease of long practice.

"How sad for you," she said, and drank, looking at him through her lashes as she did. "This is excellent."

"I have more laid down; if you think the Konige would like it as well, you may take some bottles with you." He waited while she sank into the Anatolian chair and set her goblet on the table once again; her wide-skirted bleihaut draped her body like a caress.

"This *is* very comfortable," she said.

He pulled up his Spanish chair. "With your permission?"

"Do sit, Comes; this is your manse and I am your guest, not your—"

His interruption was as elegant as he could make it, combining elements of modesty and propriety with practiced courtesy. "You are here in the name of the Konige, and you are entitled to the full respect she deserves," he said, moving the platter a little nearer to her.

"She will be glad to know of it," she said, and pulled a small portion of the bread off the loaf, dipped it in the salt and popped it into her mouth, drank another generous sip of wine and put the glass down once more. "There. Bread and salt. Now my welcome is official."

"May I fill your glass again?" He had already picked up the bottle.

"You may." She continued to watch him, her green eyes alight, as he poured. "I like a generous host."

"You are kind to say so," he said, knowing it was expected of him.

"The Konige will be happy to hear good of you." There was a hint in her words, and he responded to it.

"What would the Konige desire me to do for her?" he asked as he sat down once again.

Rozsa sighed. "You're right, I am here at her behest and it is fitting that I present her request, and then we may become better acquainted." She licked her lips, flashing a provocative glance at him that was gone as soon as he had seen it. "I am charged with telling you that there is to be a tournament in ten days, for celebration of the arrival of May; she has chosen the sixth day so that the Episcopus cannot accuse her of giving credence to pagan rites." She waved her hand as if to reprimand herself. "Be that as it may, Konige Kunigunde would like you to compete in the lists for Hungary."

Of all the things he had been expecting, this had not been among them. Rakoczy did his best to conceal his surprise, saying with only a slight pause, "The Konige does me great honor, but I fear that her grandfather has forbidden me to bring arms with me into Bohemia, but for those reasonable weapons a man of rank might carry for his safety. He would forbid me to fight in armor even for a tourney." He was comforted by the knowledge that he spoke the truth.

Rozsa pouted a little. "The Konige will not be—" She stopped herself, her eyes narrowing. "But if Konig Bela has restricted you, then of course, it is out of the question that you should joust." She ignored the utensils on the platter, picking up one of the pickles and nibbling at it. "What else can you do that might entertain her on her festival day?"

"I have a lyre and a gittern. I can play for her."

"A gittern and a lyre." She ate a little more of the pickle. "If you would be willing to play for her between the contests, I think she may be satisfied."

He snapped his fingers as if a thought had just occurred to him. "In ten days this manse will be ready to receive guests. You were gracious enough to suggest that the Konige would accept an invitation to dine at this manse." He paused to allow her to question him; when she did not, he went on, "If it would not be too forward for an exile, I would be highly favored indeed if Konige Kunigunde and her Court would consider dining here at the conclusion of her tournament. There is room enough for a large company, and there is a room for servants that the Konige's Court might require." That should be enough to mitigate his refusal to joust for her, he told himself, and give Rozsa of Borsod something more to report.

"A banquet at night!" For an instant she collected her thoughts. "We don't see many of those in Praha. A great undertaking." She offered another of her feline smiles. "And all the cost will be borne by you?"

"Of course," he said, more certain now that he had struck the right note. "If you will advise me, I will try to provide entertainment to the Konige's taste."

She finished the pickle and licked her fingers before picking up one of the sweetmeats. "Entertainment which you will pay for?"

"Yes." He resisted the urge to embellish his answer, for he was aware that they were overheard and that her response, whatever it might be, would spread through his household like dust in summer.

"It may be possible. The Konige likes banquets and festivities. She likes mountebanks and jongleurs and troubadours, too." She tasted the sweetmeat. "You have a good cook. I hope you pay him well."

"I do, to both of your concerns." He regarded her with good-mannered interest, alert to the tests she was posing to him. "May

I entrust a gift to Konige Kunigunde to your care, to assure her of my devotion to her House? I will provide you a token of my gratitude for your conveyance."

"It is my duty as her lady-in-waiting to do so," Rozsa said, a speculative angle to her brows. "What do you want to give her?"

Rakoczy rose and went to take a small gilded pouch off the nearest shelf. "These are for Konige Kunigunde, with my duty to her, exile though I am." He handed the pouch to Rozsa. "You may look inside."

"I am required to look inside," she said, her tone sharpening. "I would be responsible if you sent her any unwholesome or ill-omened thing." She pulled open the mouth of the pouch and poured its contents out into her lap, then sat still in amazement as the diamonds and sapphires shone back at her. "So many," she whispered, impressed in spite of herself.

"Nine sapphires and thirteen diamonds," he said.

"And all of them large, and so well-polished," Rozsa marveled, touching them as if she were afraid they might burst.

"One of many such gifts I hope to provide for the Konige." Rakoczy went to the shelf and took down another, smaller pouch of tooled Florentine leather. "This is for you, for your willingness to carry the jewels to the dear Royal." He gave the small pouch to her and watched her try to discern its contents by pressing the leather. "Open it, if you wish."

Rozsa set her pouch aside and carefully gathered up the diamonds and sapphires for the Konige, counting them aloud as they went into the pouch. Once its neck was closed, she reached for her gift and opened the securing laces of twined red silk, turning it over so it emptied onto the palm of her hand. As she caught sight of the two cabochon rubies the size of currants, she let out a little shriek of excitement, the first truly spontaneous sound she had made since arriving at Rakoczy's manse. "Are they real?"

"Most certainly. I would be a fool indeed to offer false jewels to a noble of the Konige's Court." He said it smoothly enough, concealing the stab of dismay that had gone through him at her exclamation: what had Konig Bela said of him that would lead anyone to suspect that he might offer counterfeit goods? He made himself smile and bow. "I hope you will enjoy them, Rozsa of Borsod."

"Will you make fittings for them, so I may wear them as eardrops?" Her eagerness was entirely genuine. She laid the two rubies down next to the rose he had offered her.

As he filled her goblet once again, he met her green eyes with his dark ones. "It will be my delectation to do so."

Text of a dictated message from Hovarth Pisti of Buda, Master Tapestry-Weaver, at Praha in Bohemia, to Donat, monk and clerk to Konig Bela of Hungary, at Buda, carried by the apprentice Jeno of Buda, and delivered twenty-four days after it was dispatched.

To Donat, clerk to my most puissant Konig, Bela of Hungary, the dutiful greetings of the Konig's servant Hovarth Pisti of Buda, on this day, the eighteenth day of May in the 1269th Year of Salvation,

To the Konig, His Grace,

We are now all well-established in the household of your granddaughter, Konige Kunigunde, with the exception of Rakoczy Ferancsi, Comes Santu-Germaniu, who has set up his own household at Mansion Belcrady, which makes it difficult for me to keep the close watch upon him you have charged me to do. The rest of us have been given apartments in Vaclav Castle or provided housing outside the walls but near to the Castle. Slaves have been presented to all of us but the Comes, who refuses to have slaves in his household. The Konige has permitted him to maintain his customs in this regard without insult to her for offering him such a gift, for it is known that his blood have not kept slaves for more than five hundred years.

It is two days since the Konige's tournament, and the Comes Santu-Germaniu's banquet, and the Court is full of talk and ru-

mors. There were twelve jousts, to honor the Apostles, and three interludes of diverse entertainment, to honor the Trinity. In the jousts, German and Bohemian knights prevailed, but there were only two Hungarians entered in the bouts, so it is no disgrace to the Konige or to you. One knight, Bubna, Rytir Oldrich, suffered a broken leg when his horse was fatally lanced and fell with Rytir Oldrich still in the saddle, and Thun, Rytir Dake, took a hard blow to the head and is much affected by it, his memory seeming faulty due to the ferocity of the impact he endured. One Hungarian contestant, Nitra Akos, bested three Bohemians before he was unhorsed and disqualified from competition. Konige Kunigunde presented Nitra with a wreath of silver leaves, and proclaimed him to be her champion for the month of May. Since the Konig is not presently in Praha, no greater honors were awarded, although it is likely that Nitra Akos will be advanced to the official rank of Rytir, and as Rytir Akos will be able to take his place among the officers of the Konig's army.

The evening of the tournament, we were all welcomed to Mansion Belcrady, which Comes Santu-Germaniu has bought, as I have mentioned. This is a very fine mansion, consisting of a manse of ten rooms, a bake-house, a bath-house, a creamery, a small mews (currently vacant), and a stable with stalls for sixteen horses. Rakoczy has put many craftsmen and servants to work to make the manse not only livable, but an example to all the nobles of Praha, so it would appear that his wealth is undiminished in spite of your denying him the right to take his gold with him. Clearly he has other sources of treasure, and not just from the jewels he has presented to the Konige.

The Comes offered a banquet of nine courses, beginning with a pottage of oats and new onions, then a stew of eels, ducks turned on a spit and basted with wine, collops of veal cooked in beer, a subtiltie of pork in the shape of a hunting horn, dried berries cooked in cream, pastry boats filled with forcemeat and garlic, venison with bitter herbs, ending with a cream-bastard and candied flowers. There were four different wines poured and in such quantity that anyone might drink his fill three times over. What this hospitality must have cost the Comes is beyond my reckoning, but I cannot fault him either in the quantity or the quality of the food he provided. Among the twenty-four of us, no one had cause to complain. Rakoczy busied himself serving the courses with his own hands and did not join us to eat. This troubled a few of the Konige's Court, but none of them refused any of what they were offered, and none has had cause to regret their decision.

Along with this magnificent meal, we were treated to songs from the Konige's Court singers, as well as a celebrated minstrel from Venezia; they say Rakoczy paid him ten pieces of gold to come to perform for your granddaughter. There were two men with four dogs who had been taught to do things of such skill that it is almost beyond the nature of dogs for them to behave in such a way. The Episcopus who attended the banquet declared that such displays by simple animals smacked of diabolism, and was only dissuaded from arresting the trainers on the spot by the Konige, who put the two men and their animals under her protection.

I have sought an audience with the Comes in the hope of learning more of his activities here in Praha, but so far he has continued to delay offering me any time for a discussion. His obvious wealth has made him wary of those less fortunate than he, and given the envy his riches inspire, I am sure he has cause to be cautious, but I will persist in my efforts. It is my hope that as the time of the Konige's delivery grows nearer I will be able to take advantage of our shared interest in her well-being and turn that to the acquisition of information that I may relay to you.

This, with every promise of my devotion to you and to the mission you have entrusted to me; I pray daily that God will bring you victory and the esteem of the world as well as a place of honor in Heaven,

Hovarth Pisti of Buda (his mark)

by the hand of Lukash, scribe to Konige Kunigunde's Court

3

Konige Kunigunde lay back on her padded-leather Byzantine couch, frowning with discomfort. Five months into her pregnancy and she was feeling miserable; her back hurt, her feet were swollen, her guts were in turmoil, and the heat had given her a vise-like headache. If only she might be allowed to remove her heavy damask-silk bleihaut and lie about in her linen chainse, as a merchant's wife might do—but that was unthinkable. She was Konige, and that imposed certain duties upon her, no matter how she felt; she was obliged to maintain her appearance for the sake of her position. She would have to endure as best she could. But this afternoon not even her solarium offered her any relief from her distress; the open windows brought only the odors of the middens. She felt her baby shift inside her and she made herself lie still, thinking as she did that she had to carry herself as if her womb were made of thin glass, and everything she did required her to consider first the potential heir she carried. Hating what she saw in her mirror, she made a sound between a groan and a sigh.

The two of her ladies assigned to her company came to her side: Csenge of Somogy and Imbolya of Heves, both of them dressed on account of the heat in light unbleached cotton bleihauts with the thinnest of linen chainses beneath them. Csenge, being the older of the two, spoke first. "What would you like us to get for your relief, dear Royal?"

"I don't know," muttered Kunigunde. "Cover my looking-glass. If you could make the room cooler, or the day less oppressive . . ." She waved her hand to show she knew this was impossible.

"Pray God, we shall have rain soon and the air will clear." Csenge, too, was enervated by the sultry weather, but knew she did not have the right to rest while the Konige was in her care.

"Shall I fetch Klotild? Or ask her to prepare a cordial for you?" asked Imbolya, tentatively, her face flushed from the heat. She was younger than Kunigunde was when she married, not quite fifteen, a slender birch of a girl with a generous mouth, a straight nose, light-brown hair, and hazel eyes; she had a youthful lack of certainty in herself.

"What use is a midwife now?" Csenge challenged as she selected one of three chairs in the room and moved it nearer to the couch. "There is no sign of trouble."

"She is also an herb-woman, cousin," Imbolya reminded Csenge with the kind of helpful eagerness that made her cousin flinch. "She may have some means of making our Konige more at ease. For the good of her baby."

"Pray God it is a son," said Csenge piously, and all three women crossed themselves.

"For the sake of Bohemia and Hungary," said Imbolya.

"Do you think Klotild could help me?" Kunigunde asked, trying not to whine; she reminded herself again what was expected of her as Konige of Bohemia—the production of a viable heir and an example of conduct worthy the wife of a Christian King, as well as securing the terms of the treaty between her grandfather and her husband.

"I'll go and ask," said Imbolya, and left the Konige's side.

Csenge watched her leave. "A bit skittish," she said as if to herself.

"She's still half a child," Kunigunde said quietly, as if she were vastly older than Imbolya. "Your guidance will help her."

Satisfied that she had impressed the Konige, Csenge shrugged. "Yes. She's new; she'll learn. Shall I send for Tirz Agoston to play for you?"

"No." She knew she should explain her refusal, but nothing came to mind.

"Would you like me to rub your feet?"

"I suppose so," said Kunigunde, who realized that her lady-in-waiting needed to do something for her. "Yes, if you would. And turn the mirror away." Her chainse was sticking to her body and it was not a pleasant sensation. "Do you think it would harm my child if I were to bathe?"

Csenge considered the question. "Klotild would know better than I, but if bathing would make you more comfortable, I doubt it could be too harmful." She dropped into her chair.

"I will speak to her myself, later." She took a deep breath. "Who is with my daughter this hour?"

"Rozsa and Betrica are with Kinga," she said, using the four-year-old's nickname. "They will tend to her until Teca and Milica take her into their care at sundown."

"She was fussy this morning," said the Konige.

"It's the heat," said Csenge. "The leaves are wilting on the trees."

"Well, at least it should bring us a rich harvest." She tugged at her bleihaut, exposing her lightest solers.

"Would you like me to use wool-fat while I rub? It should soothe your skin, soften it. There is the jar of it that Comes Santu-Germaniu sent four days since, in your private room. He said it has ginger and arnica mixed in it." She spoke soothingly as she removed the Konige's solers, exposing Kunigunde's bare feet, the upper flesh puffy from pressing against the straps of the solers. "Would you like me to wash them first?"

"That would be nice. If you can find some cool water," said the Konige.

"Cool water it shall be." She rose and went to the door. "Gyongyi, the Konige would like a basin of cool water," she called to the waiting-woman sitting in the open window at the end of the corridor.

Gyongyi of Tolna, a sturdily built woman with pock-marked skin and a lantern jaw, who was a few years older than Csenge, got up quickly and ducked her head before hurrying away toward the stairs and the distant kitchens.

On her couch, Kunigunde turned her head toward the windows. "No clouds," she said in disappointment.

"Not in the east, no: there may be some in the west," said Csenge, coming back to the Konige's side. She wished Imbolya would return so that she could have a little rest. They could not leave the Konige alone, but Csenge was so uncomfortable, she wondered why Kunigunde had not sent her away to rest, as she had done with her body-servant Davni, who was a commoner, and a Bohemian, not Hungarian and noble as she was. Feeling ill-used, she patted her brow with the edge of her sleeve. The heat had made her nauseated and she knew she would soon become dizzy if she had no chance to lie down. It had happened before, but not with such vehemence as she feared might now be the case. There was a sourness in her mouth and a tightness in her throat that did not bode well. If only Erzebet of Arad was not laid low with a fever, she could demand some relief, and not only from her flibbertigibbet cousin—running off to the midwife like that!—but from tried and tested women of maturity and good sense, women who would not abandon the Konige so recklessly.

"Pader Stanislas said it will rain tonight, or tomorrow at the latest," Kunigunde said; the Polish Augustinian served as her scribe and secretary and was the most educated man in her immediate Court, one whose pronouncements were highly regarded. "He has been praying for rain for the last three days."

"A pity God hasn't answered him yet," said Csenge, forcing a smile to her face to avoid a rebuke for such irreligious sentiments; she remembered to turn the mirror arround.

Kunigunde did not return her smile. "He says it must come."

"May God hear his prayers, and say 'Yes'," said Csenge, her smile widening to a grimace, for it seemed as likely to her that God would say "no", and such an idea was truly blasphemous. The heat was working in her, like the flames of Hell.

"And say *we* all 'Amen.'" Kunigunde rubbed her forehead.

Acquiescently Csenge crossed herself. "Amen, dear Royal."

"We often have a few hot days around the Solstice, don't we;

this is more of the same," Kunigunde observed, as if acknowledging it made it more bearable. "It sets the fruit and heartens the fields."

It took an effort for Csenge not to make a sharp retort; it took all her training to remain courteous. The smile remained fixed on her lips, and she drew up a chair to the foot of the couch, saying as she did, "Gyongyi will bring the basin shortly, and my cousin will return from Klotild, and soon you will be more comfortable, dear Royal, and your babe less restless."

"I would rather he be active; it would mean a lusty child, which would please the King." She pressed her lips together, recalling the remonstration she had received for delivering a girl as a first-born.

"A boy born at harvest-time is said to garner plenty to himself," said Csenge.

Kunigunde sighed. "That's all to the good, but—" She stopped. She had no right to complain; she had a duty to Hungary. God had put her in her high position to do His Will, and if that honor brought occasional discomfort, she needed to renew her faith so that she would not become prey for Satan and his thousand Devils who were said to find every weakness in women.

Csenge patted Kunigunde's foot, speaking to her gently to provide solace as well as relief. "Don't fret, my Konige. Summer will end and your boy will be born, and Bohemia will rejoice with Hungary, in spite of the war." She wiped her brow again. "God provides the heat in summer so that we will not starve in winter. To doubt His Wisdom and Mercy is the course of damnation." She had heard this often from Episcopus Fauvinel, as had all the Konige's Court.

"*Deo gratias,*" Kunigunde murmured, crossing herself; she waited a moment for Csenge to do the same. "We must have faith, Csenge."

"Certainly we must," said Csenge, masking her irritation with a prim humility.

"Without faith, we are lost to God," Kunigunde persisted.

If only it were not so hot, thought Csenge. If only it would rain. She realized she had to say something. "And God tests our faith through hardships—yes, I know." This was more skeptical than she intended. "Just as He sends this heat to fortify the land and try His people, to strengthen them."

"So we must endure this trial." Kunigunde sighed again.

"Episcopus Fauvinel will offer Mass for rain tomorrow," Csenge said by way of providing encouragement.

"And it will rain in France," said the Konige, whose misgivings about the French bishop were well-known. She put her hand to her mouth, more for form's sake than any real desire to unsay the words.

Because it was expected of her, Csenge laughed. "So it may."

A tap on the door announced the return of Gyongyi, a basin in hand. "From the cistern in the kitchen cellar," she said as she came into the solarium, ducking her head in recognition of the Konige. "I brought a drying cloth with me."

Before Kunigunde could speak, Csenge was on her feet, reaching for the basin and cloth. "You come in good time. Did you happen to see my wandering cousin?"

"No," said Gyongyi. "Where has she gone?"

"To Klotild, to see if she has anything that might ease the Konige's present distress. So much heat may prove harmful to the child, my cousin believes." She pursed her mouth to show her opinion of the notion. "What herbs can do to change the weather, I cannot think. If she has such power, it would smack of witc—"

"She made a poultice for Erzebet," said Gyongyi, keeping Csenge from finishing the word.

"And Erzebet is still feverish, so perhaps Klotild isn't—"

"Remedies take time," said the Konige sharply, cutting off the exchange between the two waiting-women; she went on in a quieter tone, "Erzebet has been ailing for some days. It will be a while before her fever passes."

"Of course," said Gyongyi.

"Let me tend to your feet, dear Royal," said Csenge, ignoring Gyongyi's efforts to claim the opportunity to tend to the Konige, taking her place in the chair, the basin balanced in her lap against the foot of the couch. To secure her command of their circumstances, she added, "Gyongyi, there's a chalcedony jar on the table in our Konige's private room. Would you be good enough to fetch it for me, so I can rub its ointment into Kunigunde's feet?"

Gyongyi gave Csenge a sharp look, but went to get the chalcedony jar.

With a little maneuvering, Csenge managed to get Kunigunde's right foot into the basin, where she washed it gently, noticing how truly swollen the foot was. "You should lie here for an hour or more, for the sake of your feet, my Konige."

"It is an accumulation of phlegmatic humors in the body," said Kunigunde, repeating what Pader Stanislas had told her the day before.

"All the more reason for you to rest," said Csenge, lifting her foot from the water and patting it dry with the cloth.

"The coolness is very pleasant," said Kunigunde, offering her left foot.

"Then I am more than gratified," said Csenge, gently massaging her foot and ankle. When she had dried the Konige's left foot, she dropped the cloth on the floor next to her chair, then rose and went to dump the water out the open window, and returned to her chair. "As soon as Gyongyi comes back, I'll—"

As if answering a summons, Gyongyi came through the door, the green chalcedony jar in her hands. "I found it, dear Royal," she said, ducking her head before giving the jar to Csenge.

"Thank you, Gyongyi," said Kunigunde; her headache was making her feel slightly dizzy, which she strove to conceal, reminding herself that she could give her suffering to God and the Blessed Virgin.

Csenge opened the jar and dipped three fingers into the yellow ointment. "It smells very nice," she declared as she reached for the Konige's right foot.

"How pleasant," said Gyongyi, starting toward the door. "Is there anything I may do for you, dear Royal?"

"Not for the moment, thank you," said Kunigunde.

Gyongyi ducked her head, then left the solarium to return to her place at the corridor window; she was fanning herself with her open hand as she pulled the door closed.

Carefully Csenge spread the ointment over Kunigunde's foot, making sure to work slowly. "There is much virtue in this," she said as the scent of the ginger filled the room.

"Won't it make my foot swell more?" Kunigunde asked, unable to hide her anxiety.

"I suppose that's what the arnica is for," said Csenge, feeling her hands start to tingle. "Lie still, dear Royal, and let me tend to you."

Kunigunde closed her eyes, and tried not to see the vivid depictions of Hell that Pader Stanislas had impressed upon her during morning devotions. There were special torments in Hell reserved for women who did not present their husbands with sons, and if her next child should also be a daughter, then she would have to answer for her failure before God. At the time she had asked if the birth of daughters was not God's Will, as all things on earth were. But Pader Stanislas had reminded her that only God or the Devil could change the world, and when a woman obstinately refused to deliver sons, as it was her duty to do, it showed that she had come under the influence of the Devil. Had not God sent His Son, to save mankind? Why, after such a sacrifice, would He send daughters to Christians? Daughters, like Eve, were the allies of the Devil. She murmured a protest, and was jarred from her unhappy reverie by Csenge breaking off her massage and beginning an upbraiding of her cousin. The Konige opened her eyes.

Imbolya was back, holding out a cup. "Dear Royal," she said, a bit out of breath. "This is from Klotild; she says it will make you more comfortable and release the waters pent up in your body, but do no harm to your babe."

"Pader Stanislas said it is phlegmatic humors that try me," Kunigunde told her two waiting-women.

"This will help those humors as well," said Imbolya. "Phlegm attracts water, according to Klotild." She gave the cup to the Konige.

Kunigunde sniffed at the dark-green liquid suspiciously. "What's in it; did she say?"

"She told me it had juniper berries, parsley, celery seed, milk thistle, willow bark, and feverfew. I will drink some if you like." She ducked her head. "They were ground with a mortar-and-pestle and mixed with spring water. It will encourage the elimination of moisture and lessen the tendency to accumulate heat in the flesh."

With a slight shrug, Kunigunde made herself drink. "I don't like the taste."

"Klotild said you would not," Imbolya told her. "She also said that if this provided relief she'll make more for you tonight."

Setting the cup down, Kunigunde said to Csenge. "The ointment is quite pleasant. The prickle it gives is . . . agreeable. You may rub my other foot."

"What pleases you, dear Royal, pleases me to do." It was the required response, and she made no effort to attempt to sound sincere. Csenge brushed the wisps of hair that had fallen around her hair, using the back of her wrist so that she would get none of the ointment on her face. "If you will recline again?"

"I thank you." With a sigh, Kunigunde lay back once more and let Csenge rub her foot. She tried to keep her mind on happy things, so that her child would have a good-natured temperament, but her thoughts kept turning to Pader Stanislas' exhortations, and little as she wanted it, she could not keep from recalling the horrendous visions the priest had conjured.

"Be easy, my Konige," Csenge whispered as she finished her task and rubbed her hands on the drying sheet.

Imbolya, who had been sitting on the bench away from the windows, rose and came toward the couch. "Should we let her sleep?" she asked her cousin in a hushed voice.

"For a while," said Csenge, feeling Imbolya's quiet inquiry go through her head like iron spikes. "Is Gyongyi still in the corridor?"

"I suppose so. Would you like me to go and look?" Imbolya asked.

"If you would be so good," said Csenge, trying not to make her request abrupt; Imbolya was too young to think brusque responses anything but chastisement; by the way Imbolya's lips thinned, Csenge realized she had been too short with her. "Thank you, cousin," she added, to soften her request.

"Of course," said Imbolya, and went to the door, her head held a bit too high.

"Do you dislike her?" Kunigunde muttered, her eyes still closed.

"She's very young," said Csenge.

"True enough, but do you dislike her?" The question was slightly louder but much more pointed.

Startled, Csenge stared down at the Konige. "I . . . It's hard to say . . . I don't dislike her . . . exactly. She can read, you know." She disliked Rozsa of Borsod for her prettiness and the high favor her husband enjoyed in the King's Court; she disliked Teca of Veszbrem for her endless praise of her dead husband. Imbolya annoyed her, and that was entirely different.

"Then what is it, exactly? Is it family rivalry, perhaps? Have you been agonistic in any way? Do you dislike having her at my Court? Or is it simply that she is so young? What bothers you about her?" Kunigunde inquired; caught off guard, Csenge could think of nothing more to say. "Csenge of Somogy, I asked you a question."

The ringing in her ears was louder; Csenge saw spangles around the center of her gaze, and as her queasiness grew worse, she put her hand to her mouth. "Pardon, dear Royal. I fear I am about to be sick," she said, and without ceremony, stumbled up from her chair and hurried unsteadily out of the solarium, making for her small room on the floor below. All but tumbling down the steep staircase, she leaned against the wall as she rushed for her apartment. She found the chamber-pot just in time, and when she had vomited into it, she remained on her knees, panting, trying to stop the clamor in her head. She was astonished by what she had done; what would the Konige make of her flight? She might well be offended that Csenge had not answered her. Perhaps she would order her to absent herself from the Konige's Court. If that were to happen, how would she reestablish her position with Kunigunde? What would her husband say when he learned of what she had done?

A soft knock on the door warned of the arrival of Imbolya, with whom she shared the cell-like room. "Cousin Csenge? Are you all right?"

"I will need a house-slave to—"

"—remove the chamber-pot, yes. I've sent for one of them already." Imbolya opened the door a crack; the wedge of light this admitted made Csenge's eyes burn. "Do you want water, or wine, or apple cider?"

Just the mention of these made Csenge's stomach clench. "Not now."

"Then a damp cloth for your forehead? Would you like me to get a potion for you from Klotild?" Imbolya sounded so sympathetic that Csenge ground her teeth.

"Don't bother. I will be better presently. Attend to the Konige." She felt another cramp in her abdomen, and she shivered as her muscles tightened. "God and the Virgin!" she mumbled. "What's happening to me?"

"Are you certain you don't need any help?" Imbolya persisted. "You don't sound—"

"I will be well shortly."

"Shall I send for Frater Lovre to aid you?"

The thought of the half-blind monk patting at her with his flaccid hands sent another surge of nausea through Csenge. She swallowed convulsively. "I do not need anything," she said with great precision. "I will be better if you leave me alone."

It took a long moment for Imbolya to accept this rebuke; she remained at the door, peering into the dark room. "Shall I come back later?"

"It is your room as well as mine; I can hardly keep you out."
She felt very, very tired. "Do as you think you must."

"I'm worried for you, cousin," said Imbolya in a tone that
meant she was worried for herself. "You are not well, and it may
be that because of you, our Konige is not well. We are sworn to
preserve her in health at all costs." She stood very straight at the
edge of the door. "Do let me come in. I can succor you."

"Not just now," said Csenge. "I am still at some loss . . ." Her
bowels twisted once more. "I'd like to think that . . ." She bent
over and retched.

Imbolya pushed the door open enough to see Csenge; the two
stared at each other. "What am I to do, if you are so compromised?

"You fear I have taken a contagion? Is that it?" Csenge
demanded, putting the chamber-pot aside. "You think I should be
moved out of the Konige's Court until I recover, like Erzebet?"
The very notion was intolerable, for once out of the Konige's Court,
she could as easily be replaced as allowed to return.

"I . . . I . . . don't know," said Imbolya unhappily.

"Then keep your thoughts to yourself," snapped Csenge as she
wiped her mouth.

"But if the Konige should become ill—"

"It is the heat," said Csenge. "Everyone is suffering from it."

Imbolya hesitated, unwilling to go against her influential cousin,
yet keenly aware of what she was required to do as a lady-in-waiting.
Finally she put her hands to her eyes and wept with frustration. She
took a step toward Csenge. "You should lie down," she said, trying
to stop her tears. "Truly, cousin, you are not well."

"No, I shouldn't lie down; I should go and help Rozsa with
Kinga. It is time." Csenge got unsteadily to her feet, one arm extended to secure her balance. After an attempt at walking, she gave
up. "But I'm going to send you in my stead. Since you are worried
that I might have a fever, it would be best if I didn't venture near
the child, or the mother." She tottered over to her bed. "There. Are
you satisfied? Do you want anything more of me?"

"Shall I help you to undress?" Imbolya asked.

"I can manage for myself," said Csenge firmly. "Tell dear Royal that I'm overheated and need to lie down. Then go to—"

"Rozsa of Borsod," said Imbolya, accepting her task.

"Tell her you'll remain with Kinga through supper and see her to Teca and Betrica's care for the night." Csenge resisted another urge to throw up, and wondered briefly if her dislike of Rozsa was the cause.

"I will," Imbolya promised her.

Bile rose on the back of Csenge's tongue, and this time she noticed a second taste in its acridity. "Did you eat the fish-stew at dinner?" she asked.

"No," said Imbolya. "I had the lamb-ribs. And the pheasant with chestnuts; it was dry."

"Ask if others who had the fish-stew have felt unwell," said Csenge. "I keep tasting fish." Very carefully she sat on her bed, doing nothing hurriedly; she felt her insides roil.

"Do you think that it was tainted?" Imbolya's shock was tempered with relief.

"Fish taints quickly, and in this heat . . ." She left the rest unsaid.

"It would be a bad thing, of course, and many may have suffered from it, but better tainted fish than fever," Imbolya said, and dared to touch Csenge's arm. "Shall I ask before or after I watch the dear Little Royal?"

It was tempting to lash out at the girl, but Csenge decided she needed Imbolya's help just now too much to berate her. "Before, of course. If the fish was tainted, then there's no need to alarm the Konige with rumors of fevers, is there?" This last was pointed and underscored by a single, hard stare.

"N . . . no," said Imbolya, keenly aware of her cousin's intent. "I wouldn't want to add to dear Royal's upset, considering how wretched the heat has already made her. But if there is another cause for your—"

Csenge nodded. "If it isn't the fish, you may tell the Konige that I am prostrated by the heat, but say nothing about a fever. Nothing."

"If Rozsa asks? What am I to tell her?"

"The same thing," said Csenge. "You have to make it plain that I am not ill, just struck by the weather. I'm not the only one, by the Virgin, I'm not."

"They say the Devil revels in the heat," Imbolya remarked, crossing herself. "He could summon up a plague, couldn't he?"

"If God allows it," Csenge said darkly. "If we have strayed from Him, God will chastise us for our failure." This time, when she crossed herself, she longed for the comfort of Pader Lupu, her old Confessor, who always made her see God's Plan in every misfortune. Here at Court, she knew better than to rely on the priests to support her. "Go on. Find out about the fish and then take up my post with Kinga."

"Of course. Of course, cousin; at once," said Imbolya, and hurried out of the room, closing the door before she went off down the hall that led to the great hall and the kitchens.

Satisfied that she finally would be left alone, Csenge reached out with her foot, snagged the chamber-pot, and pulled it toward her; she could tell she would need it again before long.

Text of a letter from Counselor Smiricti Detrich of Praha to the apothecary Huon of Paris at his shop in Praha, written by Frater Ulric and delivered by messenger.

To the accomplished French apothecary, Huon of Paris, the greetings of Smiricti Detrich, Counselor of Praha, on this, the twenty-third day of May in the 1269th Year of Salvation,

My dear Master Apothecary,

I wish to secure from you such nostrums and potions as you have to treat obstinate flux. I fear that all of my household must succumb to it unless you have a means of treating it unknown to the physicians of the city. One of my slaves, an older man with a habitual cough, has already died of it, and all but two have shown some signs of it. The servants in the household are also afflicted, and that gives me cause for concern, in that it may soon reach my family and me.

The city is afraid the wells may have been poisoned, which would account for the spread of the sickness. If you have some means of determining if this is a justified fear, I and the other Counselors would be most grateful. We would provide you a stipend for any work you might do to improve the quality of the wells, if they are truly the source of the contagion. As the apothecary to Episcopus Fauvinel, we are certain you have the ability to produce a cure for whatever it is that is making so many in Praha sick.

If you would be good enough to call upon me at my house, I will discuss all the aspects of the current outbreak that I have discovered, including the spread of it, and the nature of the miasma that may be spreading from the wells to the people. In the meantime, Episcopus Fauvinel has authorized the priests in all the churches of the city to offer Masses of healing, and encouraged those who are well to show their Christian charity and visit those who are suffering from this affliction. Although there have been few deaths among those contracting the illness, we, the Counselors, have declared that a pit for burial of all those dying of it should be dug and consecrated outside the walls, so that no lingering infection may spread from those interred.

My servant will bring me your answer, and if you require it, will guide you to my door.

May God bless you for your help to those in need.

> *Smiricti Detrich*
> *Counselor of Praha (his mark)*

by the hand of Frater Ulric

4

The contents of the banded coffer glittered in the morning light; more than two hundred jewels lay in the ornate chest, polished and shining with all the glory of a rainbow, colors repeated in the Persian carpets on the floor, making the rest of Rakoczy's workroom appear drab; at the far end of the room, the athanor was heating, making ready for the production of still more jewels.

"You aren't going to give them to the Konige all at once, are you?" Hruther asked as he watched Rakoczy close the lid. He spoke in the Latin of his long-ago youth. "It's one thing to give the Konige's Court a banquet, but so many jewels at the same time? The Episcopus has already remarked on your wealth, and not flatteringly."

"Of course I will not give all these to her at once: she would just expect more and grander the next time she summoned me to wait upon her, and more banquets with more jewels as well," said Rakoczy in the same tongue as he set the padlock in the slots in the two hinged iron bands. "No, I shall give them out judiciously, enough to satisfy Konig Bela that I am upholding the terms of my exile, and to keep the Konige well-inclined toward me but not so much that Otakar decides that he, too, should have his own share of what I provide."

"You're certain it would come to that?" Hruther asked, and knew the answer as soon as the words were out of his mouth.

"Think of Cyprus, old friend." He regarded Hruther levelly, recalling seven hundred years before and his three years there, when he had been faced with the increasing demands for jewels from the island's ruler.

"I take your point," said Hruther, nodding slowly.

"I would not like to have to make caskets and caskets of jewels every month again; that one time was sufficient."

"Even though you could do it," said Hruther with a suggestion of amusement.

"I could," Rakoczy agreed, "but it would put me in a more difficult position than the one I am in presently, for their demands would be likely to increase." He paused, his face unreadable. "I cannot rid myself of the feeling that I may need to have the means of paying for a clandestine departure, and in Bohemia, jewels are more anonymous than gold."

"Then you're planning to escape?" Hruther was not surprised.

"Not at present, but it may come to that, if I can arrange for the protection of Santu-Germaniu before we go. If only Konig Bela had not quarreled with his son after granting him rule of Transylvania, suspicion would not have been turned on Santu-Germaniu." He stifled a yawn. "I sometimes feel I am in a vise, with Otakar on one side and Bela on the other, and that between them they will do their best to ruin me."

"As was tried on Cyprus," said Hruther.

"I trust not." Rakoczy offered nothing more as he glanced toward the window. "There will be more rain this afternoon, by the look of it. There are clouds in the distance, and they are towering already."

"Summer storms," said Hruther. "At least that will lessen the heat."

"And the virulence of the current ailment is fading, thank all the forgotten gods," Rakoczy said. He stretched as thoroughly and gracefully as a cat, then twisted his upper body side to side, which for him was a sign of fatigue.

"Do you think you might rest today?" Hruther asked, a flicker of concern in his faded-blue eyes. "You've been out or working all night for the last three days."

Rakoczy's smile was more wry than amused. "I am better for having been out last night," he said. "It restored me somewhat."

"Did the woman enjoy her dream?" Hruther made no attempt to hide his assuagement. "Are you improved?"

"It certainly seemed she did," Rakoczy answered, a note of unease in his answer; he changed the subject. "How are the servants? Has their distress ended?"

"All are recovered but two scullions," said Hruther, adding, "They should both be fine in a few days."

"Very good." He touched his small hands together. "We will continue to treat the well-water for another fifteen days, just in case; the Chinese are right about that precaution."

"Some of the household have complained about the taste of garlic in the water," Hruther said, his attention on the banded coffer.

"If the animacules in the water are to be killed, they will have to bear with the taste a while longer. And they will have to endure it again next year, when the animacules return." Rakoczy stowed the coffer in a niche beneath the largest window; though it was heavy, he gave no sign of effort in carrying it. "I'll want presentation pouches the day after tomorrow; I am asked to make an appearance at the Konige's Court that day."

"And besides jewels, what does the Konige want of you—more songs?"

"Very likely. She is receiving one of the von Hapsburg ladies, and she wishes the occasion to be as awe-inspiring as possible, with every sign of wealth and elegance. Given how much Otakar dislikes the von Hapsburgs, the Konige will want the von Hapsburgs to envy her, and Otakar." He paused, his demeanor thoughtful. "I should probably offer a few jewels to Aurelie von Hapsburg as a matter of courtesy." He gave a short sigh. "Good stones, but not as grand as the ones I present to Konige Kunigunde, I think. Perhaps the moonstones, and a pair of aquamarines."

"The emeralds to Konige Kunigunde," Hruther recommended.

"Of course, and a pair of diamonds along with topazes and amethysts to the Konige as well. I would offend her if I did not give her something remarkable, and failure to do that would dis-

please her grandfather and her husband, which"—he sighed—
"could lead to trouble, not only here but at Santu-Germaniu, as
almost everything I do can. So long as he can dismantle my estates, Bela has me on a short tether, and we both know it; he can
pretend that he is not coercing me, but he knows he can demand
my compliance on anything that suits him to requi—" Rakoczy
gesticulated his aggravation, swinging his arms then slamming his
hands together. "It is always such a dance, such a costly dance,
and grows more so over the years," he exclaimed, then composed
himself. "Even in my breathing days, court-ship was as artificial as
the smiles of those performing it." He broke off again, turning to
Hruther with an intent expression. "Do you recall that clock in the
Santu-Smaragdu monastery we saw?"

"The one that had the tower with the bell-hammers attached
to figures of Santu Smaragdu and the Devil?" Hruther saw Rakoczy
nod. Curious to learn what had captured the Comes' attention, he
said, "I do remember. What has that to do with—"

"Yes; all they need to ring the bell is a mallet on a spring-
hinge and a chain to release the spring when the clock reaches
the right hour, but they decided to give their spring-hinges an
additional purpose and made the hinges allegorical figures; it is
much the same with court-ship, which starts out simply, as a code
of conduct for those in authority, uncomplicated and direct. Then,
like the bell-mallets, conditions are added, competition begins
among those in the Court. Eventually someone will find a way to
make the iron figures more elaborate, so that marking the time is
only an excuse for grand displays. Court-ship here in Bohemia,
like the clocks, will become more complex than it already is. Think
of the Court of Karl-lo-Magne, and compare it to this one. There
is more display, more grandeur, here. And for most of the courtiers, more to lose." He fell silent, and after a short while went on
in a more tranquil tone, "Pardon me, old friend. I am feeling ex-
asperated, but it is hardly fitting to burden you with my discon-
tent."

"I don't mind," said Hruther. "You listen to my harangues."

"Infrequent as they are," said Rakoczy, a rueful cast to his countenance. "I wish I could quell my apprehensions, but I have not yet been able to." He took a turn about his workroom, his restlessness taking hold of him. Finally he stopped, a frown deepening between his brows. "What have we heard from Balint? His report is overdue." The steward at Santu-Germaniu had pledged to send monthly reports, but he had not been heard from for six weeks.

"You fear that bodes ill," said Hruther, aware that concern for his steward and his lands had given rise to Rakoczy's fidgetiness.

"There is fighting not far from the roads the messenger must travel," Rakoczy said. "Otakar will have to use all the summer to press his advantage; campaigning in winter is madness."

"Do you think the Konig might have conscripted your messenger?" Hruther asked.

"It would be like Otakar to do that. Or it could be the messenger is delayed by illness or injury, or taken as a prisoner, or killed, or any number of unpleasant things. I will dispatch a message to Balint, and hope that nothing dreadful has happened." Rakoczy continued pacing, slowing a little on his fourth pass around the room. "You are right; I am tired. No doubt you're hungry. If the kitchen is empty, go have your meat while no one can see that it is uncooked."

"I will—while you lie down for the morning. The household knows you were up well into the night for three nights. No one will think it odd that you choose to sleep in the morning; they might think it odd if you didn't rest." Hruther's implication was clear; he indicated the door. "Two hours on your bed should ease you, my master."

"No doubt," said Rakoczy, capitulating. "Two hours it will be. Then off to the Counselors' Court." He brought the key to the door out of the wallet hung on his belt. "To keep from tempting anyone," he said as he followed Hruther to the door.

"Do you want me to call you in two hours?"

"If I have not risen of my own accord, please; since I am summoned to the Counselors' Court early this afternoon," said Rakoczy, shutting the door to his workroom and turning the heavy iron key in the lock. "Are the old rushes swept out of the main hall?"

"And the new rushes laid with branches of rosemary. The servants complain that you clear the rushes too often, but they say the manse smells nicer than most, and has fewer rats. The other rooms will be finished by sundown, whatever the weather may bring." Hruther opened the door to Rakoczy's private apartments. "And Pacar and I will finish the plans for your banquet. By the time you rise, we will have all the necessary lists made, and we can begin to make the mansion ready. Forty guests and as many more servants—there's a lot to do to prepare." He moved aside for the Comes. "Do you need my assistance?"

"Not here; I need your skill at planning. Mid-Summer Eve is the banquet; three weeks away," said Rakoczy as he went into his outer room. "The shortest night of the year." He laughed once.

"The nights will lengthen again, my master," Hruther assured him, and closed the door.

Left to his own devices, Rakoczy removed his thick-soled solers and bleihaut, but kept on his chainse of black-dyed linen. With the shutters closed, the room was dim, and the sleeping-chamber beyond was darker still, and monkishly austere. One large chest stood in the center of the chamber, a thin wool-stuffed mattress atop it, with linen sheets and a single rough-woven blanket to dress it. Rakoczy pulled back the blanket and upper sheet, and got into the bed, pulling the blanket up to his chin as he lay back and lapsed into the stupor which passed for sleep among those of his blood.

It was nearing mid-day when Rakoczy emerged from his personal quarters, dressed in an eclipse-embroidered black bleihaut over a chainse of white cotton, braccae of dull-red linen, and high, thick-soled estivaux; his eclipse device hung from a thick silver collar around his neck. He walked down to the main hall and looked around, generally pleased with what he saw.

Barnon, the steward, lowered his head and snapped his fingers to alert his two underlings to halt their efforts and acknowledge their master's presence. "Comes Santu-Germaniu."

"Good day to you, Barnon," he replied. "I hope I see you well."

"You do, Comes," Barnon mumbled. He took two steps back and respectfully averted his eyes.

"Have you had your dinner yet?"

"No; household servants dine in an hour. The grooms and outside servants dine first. They will sit down shortly." Barnon was quite uncomfortable; no nobleman he had ever worked for had indulged in actual conversation with him.

"I understand you will have spit-turned lamb with turnips and onions today," said Rakcozy, and saw the astonishment in Barnon's eyes.

"I . . . I think so, Comes."

"Very good," said Rakoczy, and was about to move on, but stopped and turned to Barnon again. "Do you know where I might find my manservant?"

"I believe he and Pacar aren't yet back from the marketplace," said Barnon. "There are only scullions and the under-cook in the kitchen."

"Ah." Rakoczy nodded once. "I trust they will return before the rain starts."

Barnon crossed himself. "All is in the hands of God."

Rakoczy did the same. "As you say." Making a gesture of dismissal, he strolled out of the main hall into the entry hall, where two hired men were laying new stones in the floor in a pattern of interlocking chevrons of black and white stone. "You are making fine progress. How long until you are done; do you know?" he asked the older of the men.

"Three more days should do it, Comes, including the marble border," the man answered, not looking up.

Rakoczy let himself out and went around the side of the house to the stable, calling out for Illes as he did. "I know your dinner is almost ready, but will you be good enough to saddle the dapple-gray for me before you go in to eat?" he requested as soon as Illes appeared.

"Of course, Comes," said Illes, ducking his head as he turned back into the stable; Rakoczy followed after him. "She's newly shod, and she's been given her weekly dose of vinegar-and-oil. Her hooves have been treated with wool-fat and turpentine." He reached the mare's stall and whistled softly to her as she pushed her head toward him. "She's a good girl, she is." He reached for the halter hanging from a hook on the nearest column.

"Yes, she is," Rakoczy agreed.

"It's not my place to ask, but do you plan to breed her?" He buckled the halter and stroked her neck.

"She had two foals already. But she is eight, so I may find a stallion to cover her again." Rakoczy stood aside while Illes led Asza out of her stall. "In that regard, do you have any recommendations?"

"No," said Illes, surprised that Rakoczy would put such a question to him.

"If you see a stallion you think would do, will you tell me?" Rakoczy asked, watching Illes brush down the mare's coat.

After a disconcerting silence, Illes nodded. "If I do, I'll tell you."

"Thank you," said Rakoczy, stepping back as three stable-hands came down the wide central corridor in answer to the summons of the dinner-bell. "Do you miss Domonkos and Zabolcs and Endre?" he inquired when the hands were gone.

Illes, who had reached the mare's rump in his brushing, stopped for a moment. "No. They are men-at-arms, and they became riotous when they had nothing to do beyond gambling and drinking. I was glad when they left to return to Hungary."

"The three who work with you now: are you satisfied with them?"

"They're steady workers, for Bohemians." He went around to the off-side of the mare and began to brush her neck, working down and back with the grain of her coat.

Rakoczy almost smiled. "For Bohemians?"

Illes shrugged. "You know how they are—their country is rich and their Konig is powerful, so they're a little lazy, since you're a foreigner. Still, they know enough about caring for horses that they're worth their keep." He set the brush down and reached for a hoof-pick, bending over to lift up the mare's off-rear hoof. "Which saddle do you want?" he asked when all four hooves had been cleaned.

"The Byzantine one, with the embossed leather," Rakoczy said, stepping away while Illes finished grooming, saddling, and bridling Asza; then he came and took the reins before swinging up onto the mare. "Go and have your dinner, Illes of Kotan, and thank you." With that he rode out of the stable and made for the gate.

By the time he reached the Council Court—a large, three-storied building built of stone for the first story and of wood for the two above—the streets were largely cleared; most of the people within the city walls had gone to their homes and taverns to have their dinners. In an hour the streets would be bustling again, but for now, the Council Court Square was all but deserted but for two scruffy dogs fighting over what appeared to be the front leg of a pig. Rakoczy dismounted and secured Asza to the post near the entrance to the Court provided for that purpose. He patted the mare's neck, then trod up the steps and entered the tall doors, feeling discomfited by the lack of activity. He entered the foyer to the empty Council Chamber, and was wondering if he should call out or look further for someone to assist him, when he saw a hump-backed man in clerical habit coming toward him, motioning to him.

"Comes?" the clerk inquired as he came up to Rakoczy.

"Yes," said Rakoczy.

"Santu-Germaniu?"

"I am he."

"Will you follow me? Counselor Smiricti is waiting for you in his private room." Without waiting for an answer, the clerk sidled away, dragging his left leg a little; more curious than cautious, Rakoczy followed him. As they climbed to the second floor, the clerk said, "Counselor Smiricti asks that you forgive him for this manner of meeting, but he knows his coming to Mansion Belcrady would be noticed and reported."

"Indeed," said Rakoczy.

"If you will step through this doorway?" The clerk ducked his head and opened the door for him, allowing Rakoczy to precede him into Counselor Smiricti's chamber; it was a handsome room, paneled in wood and containing an upholstered bench, a German chair, and a trestle-table.

Smiricti Detrich stood at the open window, staring down at the empty square below him. He wore a dark-brown cotton blei-haut over a chainse of fine yellow linen, and braccae of dark-gray sacking, all designed to keep him cool on this hot day. His face shone with sweat. Without turning or offering any other formal greeting beyond a nod, he said, "Thank you for coming, Comes. I trust my clerk has told you the reason for this?"

"He has," said Rakoczy, aware that the clerk was backing out of the room and closing the door. "You coming to my home would lead to those watching making a note of your visit. And I am allowed to answer your summons in the terms of my exile, at least if you call me here to the Council Court."

"True enough," said Counselor Smiricti. "We take a chance here and now, but not so great as the one we would at Mansion Belcrady."

"Then I applaud your prudence," said Rakoczy.

"As well you might," Smiricti approved. "I ask you to take a seat, so that those who might watch from below will not see you." He pointed to the upholstered bench next to the fireplace. "No one will see you there."

Rakoczy moved nearer to the hearth. "As you wish." He made himself as comfortable as possible on the upholstered bench.

Smiricti remained at the window, avoiding Rakoczy's gaze. "There is something you should know, though it pains me to tell you."

"If it is to my advantage to know, then I thank you for your—"

"You have spies in your household, from Otakar and from Bela of Hungary," Smiricti blurted out.

"Of course I do," said Rakoczy calmly. "It is only to be expected."

"Then you have taken precautions against them?"

"How can I, when I have not yet discovered which of the servants is spying, and for whom?" Rakoczy saw the distress in Smiricti's posture. "What more is there: I gather there is something?"

"There is a rumor that you are . . . that you have seduced one of the Konige's ladies-in-waiting." He swung around to face Rakoczy. "If that is true, Otakar will banish you."

"And Konig Bela will sweep down on Santu-Germaniu and destroy it, enslave my peasants, and kill my household, or his son will, although Bela has the larger army, and it was he who sent me here," Rakoczy added, his voice grim. "With so much at risk, why would I do such a foolish thing? It would endanger the woman as well, and for no cause." He waited for Smiricti to speak, and when he did not, Rakoczy went on, "Who has made this claim?"

"One of the Konige's servants," Smiricti said evasively, his face darkening. "She said she overheard Csenge of Somogy talking to Gyongyi of Tolna, and that Csenge accused you of seducing Rozsa of Borsod."

Rakoczy concealed his dismay, keeping his expression neutral and his manner forthright. "And when am I supposed to have done this? When have I been with her unobserved? Surely if I had imposed upon Rozsa of Borsod one of the spies in my house, or in the Konige's Court, would have been aware of it. It is true that I have received Rozsa of Borsod at Mansion Belcrady on two occasions, both at the behest of Konige Kunigunde, and when I have waited upon the Konige in her Court, I have seen Rozsa of Borsod, but we have been watched by more than servants, for I have been in the Court itself."

Smiricti flapped his arms. "I know. I *know*! If I thought there was any truth to the rumors, I wouldn't be talking to you now. I hold you in high regard, Comes, yet I owe you no protection. So you need to be careful: gossip has a life of its own, and this could become a scandal." Now that he had spoken his worst fear, he dropped into the single chair in the room. "If such a thing happens, it could disrupt the good-will that has been established between Bohemia and Hungary. All of the Konige's Hungarian ladies-in-waiting could be sent back to their homes in disgrace and the Konige all but imprisoned by Bohemian ladies-in-waiting, and the current peace would end."

"Is that not something to the advantage of Bohemia?" Rakoczy asked.

"No. It would give Hungary an excuse to set aside the accords we have with them, and that could give rise to open war again. With the Konig on campaign in the south—in territory of Hungarian influence, to be sure—he needs no enemy to the east." He slapped his thighs. "It cannot be allowed to happen."

"What would you want me to do?" Rakoczy asked when it was clear Smiricti would say nothing more. "Shall I abandon my plans for the banquet at the Summer Solstice?"

"No," said Smiricti emphatically. "That would only fuel the rumors." He wiped his face with his sleeve. "You must have the banquet."

"Then what is it you want me to do?" Rakoczy asked again.

"Be careful, for the Konige's sake as well as your own. Guard yourself from any appearance of impropriety. I have dreamed of the crows flying into Vaclav Castle to pluck the eyes out of the Konige's ladies-in-waiting, a clear warning. The spies in your household have most certainly heard the rumors and will be doubly alert to any misstep you might make." The Counselor gathered himself up. "If you aren't heedful of your danger, tragedy will be the result."

"Tragedy?" Rakoczy was puzzled by his choice of the word.

"Anything that could bring about the downfall of the Konige and the end of the possibility of peace with Hungary could be nothing less," said Smiricti. He glowered at the floor. "If you need a woman—and I must suppose you do—it can be arranged. No slut or drab, but a woman of standing. Not one of the Konige's Court, of course, but someone well-born and not unpleasing to the senses. There are many widows, some of them quite young women, who would be glad to have a rich foreign lover. None of them would want to marry, for that would lose them whatever their husbands had left to them, so that shouldn't worry you." He was talking rapidly now, as if trying to explain as much as he could before his nerve failed.

"You need not bother, Counselor Smiricti," said Rakoczy.

"But if you had a woman, the rumors would cease, or lessen. The Konige would not want her Court to be compromised, and she wouldn't object to you taking a woman as your . . . companion." He leaned forward, his elbows on his knees, his hands extended. "Truly, if such an arrangement can be made, you would have less to compromise you. You have only to tell me what your tastes are and a suitable mistress will be found."

"It is unnecessary, I assure you," said Rakoczy.

Smiricti shook his head woefully. "If you won't take a mistress, then your situation may become . . . difficult, for as a member of the Konige's Court, your actions must reflect upon her, as her countryman." He wrung his hands.

Rakoczy gestured reassurance. "Counselor, calm yourself. I will do nothing to disgrace the Konige; you have my Word on it."

"That may not be for you to decide, not the way calumnies of this sort develop, especially in so closed a world as the Konige's Court is," Smiricti said fretfully. "Remember, rumors can have lives of their own, and once they have started, very little is needed to keep them in motion. A word, a look, a smile, a gesture—nothing more is necessary."

"Then I will be careful." Rakoczy stood. "Counselor, I thank you for your concern, and your discretion. I will consider what you have said to me, and I will weigh your recommendation carefully. After the banquet, I will give you my decision."

"I had hoped you might present your mistress at the banquet. That should put an end to all but the most—"

"Outrageous whispers?" Rakoczy suggested. "Perhaps. But since there are spies in my household, such a ploy may lead to more suspicions rather than fewer." He ducked his head respectfully.

"But we must do something." Smiricti got to his feet. "Comes, I implore you to reflect upon the danger to which you expose yourself, for we are all in jeopardy: the Konige, her ladies, you, and I, as your primary deputy in Praha."

Rakoczy studied the Counselor. "You may tell Konige Kunigunde that I will need a little time to consider what is to be done, and when I have reached a decision, I will inform her of what it is, and if she is in agreement, I will inform you. Will that satisfy you?"

Smiricti could think of nothing to say; he lowered his head, his color still high. "Of course, Comes. Whatever you think best."

As he walked toward the door, Rakoczy had the odd sensation that Smiricti's gaze was boring holes into his back.

Text of a letter from Atta Olivia Clemens at her horse-farm in Flanders, written in Imperial Latin on vellum, carried by private courier and delivered twenty-eight days after it was written.

To my most dear, most exacerbating friend, Ragoczy Sanct' Germain Franciscus, or whatever name you use now, the greetings of Atta Olivia Clemens on this, the 19th day of May in the Christian year 1269,

It is six moths since your last letter reached me, and I am curious to know how you have found the Konige's Court of Bohemia, and since you haven't anticipated my desire to learn how you are faring, I have taken pen in hand to inquire for myself. I know how much you dislike being coerced, and this semi-exile Konig Bela has imposed upon you can only be seen as coercion. But you have it in you to accommodate difficult circumstances, so I trust you have established yourself in the Konige's good graces and that you have had no more disagreements with her grandfather.

Did Mansion Belcrady turn out to be all you had been promised, glazed windows and all? You certainly paid well enough to have it precisely as you instructed it should be. If not, how far from your expectations was it, and how much have you had to do to make it suitable for you? My manse here in Flanders needs much done to it, and Niklos has hired a dozen workers from Ghent to come and make it as it should be. They are supposed to arrive in July and work through September. I have agreed to pay them quite handsomely, of course, to ensure their best efforts. And I would not like the local authorities to decide I had cheated honest men, for my claim to this property is shaky at best, and it would take very little to have the magistrate cancel my claim entirely, although the title, as the law requires, is held by my so-called half-brother, Niklos Aulirios.

As awkward as your circumstances are, you have behaved honorably toward your dependents, and have preserved your fief. The Konig and his son are still at odds with your fief in the middle of their dispute. But you have faced more daunting situations than this one and emerged from them without too many bruises, which is probably necessary, given your capacity for taking on other people's problems. From all you have said and I have heard, Konig Bela is a hard man to bargain with. It does not surprise me that he would hold your fiefdom hostage to keep his son from being able to wage war; I am only surprised to learn that Konig Otakar hasn't taken it into his head to try something similar. But he is off on campaign, so perhaps it hasn't occurred to him yet; I suspect that in time he will want to make the most of you or be rid of you. Why, of all things, did Konig Bela decide to keep you so close at hand? If I were he, I would have banished you to a very distant place, where you could do no mischief. Trapped between Bela and Otakar, as you are, must test even your expert statesmanship. How long do you plan to endure it? You needn't worry: I won't maunder on about your problems; most certainly you comprehend them more thoroughly than I do.

Niklos has been working with three new foals; there are six more due to drop in the next month. We bred late last year because of the weather, which was unusually stormy, and two of the mares didn't settle. This year the spring was later in coming than in the past ten years. The farmers here say that the weather is growing cooler, more like what it was when the Goths sacked Roma—I will not remind you how many hundreds of years ago that was. There was hard flooding not far from here, and two small villages were partially destroyed by the high waters. My horse-farm sits on raised land, and the two creeks that run through it, although they may fill their banks, have not yet overflowed, but I have ordered the banks be built up and reinforced with stout logs. If we should have another hard winter, I may have to order some heavier barriers erected so that there will be little flooding here.

I've had word from Sanza Pari that there has been trouble there, and in Roma itself. Apparently there have been riots in the countryside and peasants have marched on the city to demand a resolution to the question of the Pope. A number of them were killed, and the Cardinal Archbishops retreated to the Palazzo Laterano, where they tried again to decide who should succeed Clement IV. Tobaldo Visconti has the most desire for the post, which ought to disqualify him, by the Church's peculiar rules. Ever since Conradin came to Roma, and was betrayed and beheaded at Naples, there has been terrible unrest in the country, and, of course, Roma has taken the brunt of it. Much as I love my native earth, I am glad to be away from it just now.

Przemysl Otakar II seems to be making a name of himself— from what news I have heard, he is taking land from the Hungarians and claiming most of Austria. If Flanders were nearer to Bohemia than it is, I might be concerned enough to seek out a new place to live, but as it is, I believe it is unlikely that he will turn his attention to Flanders for some time. But you must feel his ambitions all around you. Perhaps it's just as well that he is on campaign and not in Praha to impose upon you more than Konig Bela has done.

In your letter that you dispatched to me as you left Santu-Germaniu, you said it was your intention to form no close alliances while in the Konige's Court; while I understand the reason for your decision, I think it may be unwise. In your unusual position I believe it would be prudent to have at least one woman in Kunigunde's Court willing to support your interests, and perhaps help to sustain you, as I have at present a most interesting young scribe to sustain me. I realize there may be risks involved, but I also know that you have enough isolation there to have it be hazardous to you. So I am asking you to reconsider. I would rejoice for you if you decided to take a lover; I am sure that Rogerian agrees with me. Why deny yourself having the one thing that most nurtures you?

If you find that you must depart from Bohemia at any time, I ask you to join me here in Flanders. There is relative peace in this region, and I think we might not rouse suspicions about our true natures for a year or two. I have a trunk of your native earth in my cellar, if that is any incentive. Rogerian would be more than welcome, too.

Keep yourself safe, my oldest, dearest friend. I don't think I could bear it if you were to suffer the True Death before I do.

Your eternally devoted
Olivia

5

"I have come to you bringing gifts, Comes," said Rozsa of Borsod as she entered the main hall of Mansion Belcrady; she was arrayed in an elaborately embroidered bleihaut of dull-red samite over a chainse of light Anatolian cotton the color of primroses. Her head-dress was high and broad so that her long veil hung down over her gorget, wrapping around her head in such a way that her face appeared to float in a cloud. She had bathed a week ago and had disguised the odor of her sweat with a perfume of sandalwood and roses. "The Konige was very much pleased with the banquet, so lavish and excellent it was, and so magnanimous your hospitality, and she wishes to reward you for it." She courtisied him, bending her knees to a half-kneel and ducking her head, a degree of recognition usually reserved for Konigs. "Behold in me her envoy."

Rakoczy nodded respectfully to her. "Dear Royal is much too kind to an exile, and I am much obliged to her for her kindness," he said, aware that it was more a plea than politesse; he was keenly alert to four of his servants who were listening, and that everything they said was being noted, and that the news of the Konige's gift would be all through the city by Vespers. He steadied himself and, with superb gentility, swept her a French bow. "Do come into my manse and be welcome, Lady. As the Konige's envoy, receive the hospitality of Mansion Belcrady in her stead." Fortunately he was elegantly dressed in a huch of Damascus silk woven red-and-black; beneath was a very white chainse of Italian linen. Braccae of black Hungarian leather and French solers completed his clothing.

It was a little more clothing than the hot day called for, but since neither heat nor cold tended to discomfit him, he was not flushed or perspiring.

"Dear Royal wants to make sure a fellow-countryman is properly thanked for his estimable entertainment," Rozsa countered. She held out the large pouch she carried within the folds of her veil. "This is for you."

"I should not accept it," he said, hearing the clinking of coins in it and gauging the weight by the size and hang of the pouch. "It is far too much."

"To refuse would insult the Konige: is that what you want?" She looked at him through her eyelashes, a faint smile playing at her mouth.

"No, I do not," he said, accepting the pouch from her; it was quite heavy. "Dear Royal is overly generous, I fear."

"This from a man who has given the Konige more than twenty fine jewels, and a banquet for her Court with twelve courses and jongleurs, acrobats, troubadours, and players," Rozsa chided him playfully. "After such munificence, it would be churlish of you to slight her gold."

"Has she presented such lavish gifts to others of her Court?" Rakoczy asked cautiously, anticipating the jealousy such distinction could inspire.

"No one has ever given her such jewels as you have," said Rozsa, her eyes lighting with naive greed. "Bohemia is rich in gold, and it is the dear Royal's to use as she likes."

Rakoczy bowed in the French fashion once again. "Then convey my deepest appreciation and gratitude to the dear Royal, and assure her of my respectful devotion." He looked around. "Barnon, will you go to the kitchen and ask Pacar to prepare a tray for our guest?"

Barnon ducked his head. "At once, Comes."

"Had I known of your visit, a tray would have been waiting for you," Rakoczy said to Rozsa. "As it is, I hope you will forgive me for the lapse."

"Certainly," said Rozsa, her green eyes bright with mischief. "I would not expect you to keep bread and salt on hand all the time in case a guest might happen along. That would diminish the value of the offering." She laughed. "We needn't hurry your cook. I have been told to stay with you a while, so that all Praha will know of your favor." She made a sign of gratitude to punctuate her formal announcement. Then she made herself more at ease, and said to Rakoczy, "I am told you have an herb-garden. I would like to see it. Would you show it to me while your cook readies the tray, Comes?"

"As soon as I deal with this pouch, it will be my honor," he replied, misgivings working deep within him. He ducked his head and turned toward the stairs. "I will not be long."

"So I hope," she told him. "While I wait, I will ask one of my escort to be with me, so that no ill-willed gossip will result from my presence in your manse." She pointed to Ambroz, the carpenter, who had been repairing the shutters and was now watching Rozsa with open admiration. "Will you fetch Pasc to me? He is the leader of my escort. You may know him by his surcote, that has vert, a lion couchant to the sinister or. The others wear Konig Otakar's device: argent, a lion rampant sable, crowned and charged with a cross on the shoulder or. You should all recognize it, but those of you new to Praha might not."

Astonished at having been singled out for this honor, Ambroz hurried from the main hall.

"There," said Rozsa, "that should stop any unkindly words in regard to my visit." She walked toward the maw of the fireplace. "In winter this will keep you very warm." No one answered her. "You are fortunate to have so accommodating a master. You would do well to keep it in mind that he has done much for you."

Unusually rushed, Hruther hurried into the main hall, his manner flustered. He bowed to Rozsa, then hurried to remove the long apron over his short cotton bleihaut and braccae of braided leather. "I'm sorry you have not been properly greeted yet, Rozsa of Borsod. The cook is working right now to make a welcome-tray for you. I ask you to forgive his tardiness. I would have brought you bread and salt myself, but I was tending to duties elsewhere, or you should—"

"It's not important. You couldn't have known a tray would be needed," she said. "The Konige sent me without pages to inform you of my arrival."

"The Konige is most gracious," said Hruther with the automatic good manners he had learned over the years, which were measured in centuries.

"Oh, she is, she is," said Rozsa, all but grinning as she saw Pasc approaching from the entry hall, his hand resting on the quillons of his sword, his stride as deliberate as his eyes were wary. "There you are, Pasc," she hailed him with a graceful summons of her arm. "There. All our reputations are maintained."

"Lady," said Pasc, disapproving of her blithe lack of concern.

"You needn't admonish me. I am probity itself." She swung back toward Hruther. "I trust the tray will have enough for Pasc and his men as well as for me?"

"Of course, Lady," said Hruther. "Your escort shall have bread and wine. It is being prepared even now." He met her gaze with calm. "The scullions will bring it out to them in the stable."

"They will be most appreciative," said Rozsa.

"And their horses may go into the stable to get out of the sun," Hruther added. "I assume you came in your wagon?"

"I did," she said.

"We will put it in the stable as well, and see that the pony has a pail of water. If you will excuse me, I will attend to the arrangements." He bowed again and withdrew to the kitchen, where he found Barnon and Pacar locked in a battle of wills, their voices raised enough to make the room echo. "What is it?" Hruther asked in a tone that stopped them for a moment. "What is the reason for all this?" The two men began to speak at once, and Hruther silenced them again. "Pacar, what is the trouble?"

"I am trying to prepare a tray for the guest that is worthy of her; Barnon wants the usual bread and salt alone, which is good enough for the men-at-arms, but hardly suitable for a Konige's lady-in-waiting." He folded his arms for emphasis. "I will not be slipshod in my attention to such a guest, and if others must wait on that account, so be it."

"And in the meantime, the men-at-arms and their horses stand in the sun, at a nobleman's establishment. Pray God the Lady Rozsa does not hold us in contempt for this," Barnon complained. "Besides, all this fussing is taking time. A Konige's lady-in-waiting should not have to wait to be properly welcomed. Offer bread and salt now, and the rest later." He sounded both worried and angry.

"Pacar," said Hruther in a manner that gave no room for argument, "if you will, finish preparing the tray for the Konige's lady-in-waiting. Barnon, be good enough to go out and inform the men-at-arms that they and their mounts and the Lady's wagon may take shelter in the stable. Tell Illes that water and hay should be offered, and that as soon as the cook has attended to the Konige's lady-in-waiting, bread, salt, and wine will be provided for them." He saw that the two men were somewhat mollified. "The Comes will thank you for your good service."

"I'll inform the Lady's escort," said Barnon, huffy but willing to accommodate the demands. He turned on his heel and tromped out of the kitchen.

Pacar indicated the tray he had been readying; it held a round loaf of dark bread, a small dish of salt, a silver goblet, a bottle of straw-colored wine, a plate of dried fruit, a tub of butter, and a bowl of pickled onions. "I thought some carrots and the veal sausage?"

"That should suffice." Hruther smiled his reassurance. "Then the tray for the men-at-arms."

"Of course," said Pacar, continuing with his preparation.

Hruther made his way back to the main hall, where he saw half a dozen household servants lingering to watch Rozsa of Borsod while she made her languid way around the room, stopping now and then to examine the new wood carvings installed between the narrow windows along the walls, or to finger the new tapestry that hung opposite the fireplace. "Return to your duties," he said with composed authority.

The servants complied slowly, taking as long as they dared to get out of the main hall. Ambroz was the last to go; only the sound of Rakoczy descending the stairs made him depart.

"Comes," said Hruther. "There will be trays for your guests shortly."

Rakoczy said, "Thank you; Lady Rozsa and I will go out to the herb-garden, which she has a desire to see, and will return directly, to the rear reception room, where I trust she will have a welcome-tray waiting for her." He looked toward her. "Will you forgive the delay in a proper welcome?"

"Since the herb-garden is my idea, I most certainly will. I have broken my fast, and my hunger is minor," she assured him, and motioned Pasc away with a wave of her hand. "Go join your men, Pasc. You will have your refreshments with them."

Pasc inclined his head. "As you wish," he told her before he made for the entry hall and the door beyond.

"There. I am now ready to view your herb-garden. If you will be kind enough to show me the way? Comes?" Again she offered her sideways smile as she held out her hand to lay on his proffered arm.

"There is a door in the corridor to the kitchen that has access to the herb-garden. We need not go into the kitchen itself," Rakoczy said. At the entrance to the corridor, he moved slightly ahead of her, indicating the large cabinet built into the wall. "This is most useful. We have stored many things in it."

"Better than a pantry, I'd wager; you don't have to have a slave sleep in it if you keep it locked." Her laughter trilled again. Then she asked, "You don't keep slaves, do you?"

"No," he said, stopping at a door set in the wall at the end of the cabinet.

"Whyever not?"

"Slaves can be dangerous for exiles," he said ambiguously, his memories stirring.

"Slaves are slaves. How dangerous can they be?" She moved back as he pulled the door open. "You can certainly afford to own many."

"In terms of wealth, yes, I can; but politically, I cannot; a stranger in a place is at the mercy of his household." While this was true, it was not the reason for his decision—made long ago— not to keep slaves. His experiences with Srau, a millennium in the past, had convinced him that it was unwise and unethical to do so. He stood aside so that she could go out into the herb-garden; he went after her, closing the door behind him, ensuring them a degree of privacy they would not have otherwise. There was a stone bench next to a bed of lavender; he led her to it. "I think you can see all the garden from here."

She took her seat, leaving space enough beside her for him; from here she surveyed the ordered beds. "Lavender, rosemary, thyme, marjoram, savory, basil, tarragon, sorrel, anise, parsley, juniper, hawthorn"—she stopped and pointed to a cluster of unfamiliar flowers—"I don't know that one."

"Saffron," he answered. "Oregano, catnip, mint, nettles, angelica, milk thistle, feverfew, ginger. I would like to plant a willow for its bark, but there is insufficient room for it and all the rest of them."

"Too much shadow, you mean?" She saw him nod. "Perhaps." She patted the empty space beside her. "Come sit with me."

"That might be unwise, my Lady. There are those who would make more of our nearness than either of us would like." He took a step closer to her, asking her with a cordiality that was more form than substance, "What is it you want to say to me?"

"Say to you?" she echoed.

"I supposed that you wanted a private word with me."

"You mean you don't believe all I want is to see your herb-garden?" She laughed again, amused at her suggestion. "You're right, of course. I have a second purpose."

"May I know what it is?" He saw her smile broaden. "Rozsa?"

"In time, Comes, in time." She took a deep breath, deliberately turning away from him. "If I lived here, I would probably spend all day in this garden. The smell is as heady as new wine. I want to bask for a little while, and then I'll explain to you." She put her hands behind her and straightened her arms, leaning back a little so that she could look up into the depths of the endless summer sky. After a long moment, she frowned and gazed toward the city walls. "Oh. I wish those kites and crows would go elsewhere."

Rakoczy squinted at the expanse overhead, making note of the assorted carrion birds that flew above the city gates. "They are attracted to the nine highwaymen hanged yesterday." He felt a rush of pity for the men, for, brutal as they were, their execution had been ferocious and cruel: arms and legs pulled from their sockets, teeth wrenched from their jaws, then hanged in chains where they would rot until their corpses fell apart.

"Of course they are," she said. "But there's dead meat out there." She pointed at the woods a little less than a league beyond the walls. "They should go there for their meals. It is distracting to have them making such a fuss. And they stink almost as badly as the corpses do."

"You mean you want the birds to fly to the forest?" he inquired.

"Yes; why not? They have wings," she said with determination.

"Why should they, when the hanged men are so . . . convenient?" Rakoczy pointed down the hill to the city walls. "If the Guards do not kill them, what do you expect them to do? They are not foolish creatures. They roost all around the city, and will do for as long as they find ready food here. They kill the rats and many other vermin inside the walls when they haven't easier pickings at the gates." He made no attempt to hide his disgust.

"How fastidious you are. Yet it appears you've seen this before," Rozsa observed, her green eyes on his dark ones.

"Yes; I have," he said as his memories expanded back over the centuries: Spain, Aachen, Cyprus, Constantinople, the Cyclades, the Silk Road, Roma, Persia, Roma again, Gaul, Egypt . . . the images flickered through his thoughts like shadows in a high wind.

"As an exile, I suppose you might, traveling the world as they say you have done," she said, reaching out and taking his hand. "And in your situation, I also imagine you might be inclined to accept the favors of those who wish you well? Would you not?"

"It would depend upon the favor," he said, his voice utterly neutral.

"Nothing unpleasant, I assure you," she said, and her tongue flicked over her lower lip.

He concealed the sudden wash of anxiety that swept through him, responding coolly, "If I was certain that the good-will was just that, and not a disguise for advancing a cause, or a clever ruse concocted for some form of maleficence."

"So cautious. But I guess that's to be expected. I know I would be, were I in your . . . situation."

"Then I ask you to be forthright with me, Lady." He spoke softly in Magyar. "Tell me your intentions and your reasons and I will give you my answer."

Rozsa sighed. "No one does anything for pure charity but saints, and there are few of them in the Konige's Court." Her laugh this time was cynical.

"Will you tell me your purpose when you explicate your request?"

"Very likely," she said, getting up from the bench and walking a few paces away from him. "Ever since this gossip about you and me began, I have been thinking: what if there were good cause for the rumors?" She glanced back over her shoulder, mocking excitement strong in her face.

"But there is no cause for the talk," he said.

"There might be; there could be," she said. "I have pondered the matter, and I'm sure we have denied all those allegations so often that most of the Court has grown weary of their fruitless speculations and all the Konige's Court is now searching for something else to be titillated by since you and I have provided so little fuel for their fires. Very soon, no one will pay any attention to what you and I may do, and we may do anything we like—anything."

She stopped to pluck the end of a hawthorn twig, then resumed walking among the raised beds, dallying near the wall where roses climbed. "Consider how readily we might turn this to our advantage." Her fine, angled brows lifted, encouraging and taunting him at the same time.

Rakoczy scrutinized her without appearing to do so. "Is this some manner of test? Have you been told to discover whether I will capitulate when offered such bounty as you possess?"

"Do you think that's what this is?" She all but spat the question.

"Is it not?" he countered.

"Of course not," she said with heat. "I'm not so foolish as to propose something I am not prepared to do. Think of my position as a lady-in-waiting: my husband is gone on campaign, and when he is with me, he is no better than a rutting boar. He beats me before he demands my submission, as so many men do to their wives because the priests encourage it." She fixed him with her green stare. "There is something about you that makes me believe that you might be more accomplished than he is. I don't think you would beat me, or not very much. You would give me what I seek." Desire and another, less obvious emotion simmered in her face. "Do you tell me I am wrong?"

"It would depend upon what you feel you lack," he replied, speaking with great precision.

"The satiation of the flesh," she said at once. "A man with your grace and courtesy must know something of the nature of women's bodies—something more than my husband does."

"Your husband could demand my life if—"

"If he learned of it?" she challenged, coming toward him.

"Or if the Konig did," he amended.

Rozsa tossed her head and one end of her veil came loose. "Who is to tell him? You?"

"If there were nothing to tell, neither you nor I would have cause to fear either your husband or the Konig," he said as gently as he could.

"Are you denying me?" She stopped a stride away from him, anger turning hot within her. "You would refuse what I ask? You disdain what I offer?" Her voice was loud; she spoke again in a near-whisper. "Do you dare?"

"For your safety as well as my own, I am certain I must; you may rely on me to hold your offer in confidence so that nothing ill may come of anything you have said," he answered quietly; adulterous wives were often condemned to the stake for apostasy and betrayal. "I would not want your burning on my soul." He met her eyes and held them.

"Or your own? That could be your fate as well as mine." She pointed at him, wicked amusement in her eyes. "I've thought this over, you see, and my Confession would say you seduced me with diabolical powers. I might be immured in a convent, but you would be given to the flames. I implore you not to force me to such a desperate act. Say you will be my lover and we may be happy together."

He calmed his turbulent thoughts, and said with equable determination, "I am flattered beyond all reckoning that you would seek me out in this way, and, as I have assured you, I pledge never to repeat what you have said. But I could not bear to think you might be burned for betraying your husband—"

"You mean you fear what he would demand of *you* for his honor to be restored, don't you?"

"No, Lady, I do not." He waited for her rejoinder; when she remained silent, he added, "You are a beautiful woman, and if you want to take a lover, I am sure there must be many men within the Konige's Court who would be overjoyed to—"

"I don't want any of them: I want you!" She closed the distance between them, trying not to touch him quite yet. "What use have I for the men at Court? They are the same as my husband. You—you are different. You listen to me: you don't swill wine and stagger into bed, making demands no woman would want. You don't . . . You treat me the way the heroes in the troubadours' songs treat their women." She took his hands in hers.

"They may be only tales, but, oh, Comes, I want that sweetness for myself."

"Which you believe I can provide?" Ruthfully he drew his hand from her grasp.

"Which I *know* you can provide." She stared into his face. "When you have sung for the Konige, you have given such pathos to the songs you offered that I know there is mercy in you. You cannot deny it. I have yearned for such affection as you must have, and there are few men in the Konige's Court who can provide me what I want."

"The kind of passion you seek cannot be demanded or contrived, it must answer the longing—"

"All right; I long for you. Everything within me cries out for what you can offer. Is that enough, or must I abase myself still further?" Her voice was still low, but emotion turned it rough. "What do I have to do? Tell me."

"You have to do nothing," he said, compassion making his tone tender.

"You don't want me?" Disbelief and outrage soared through her. "Can you say that to my face?"

"If I cared nothing for your safety, or my own, yes, I would want you," he told her softly, knowing that when he had first met her, before he became aware of the intricate jealousies of the Konige's Court, he had wondered if she might be inclined to accept a discreet arrangement. After two weeks, he had known that it would be foolish and desperate to form such an alliance, and he had contented himself with visiting women in their sleep to satisfy his esurience. "But there is too much danger for us both if we should decide on such a course. I would rather you suffer only pangs of disappointment than spend your days in a cell, isolated from everything and everyone you know." This was not an unlikely possibility, and both of them knew it.

"I am willing to take the chance," she said, reaching for his hand again and pressing it to her breast. "Tell me this doesn't move you. Tell me your flesh isn't stirred."

"Rozsa, I am not a stone," he responded, dropping his hand. "Your welcome-tray should be waiting."

"I waited for it, let it wait for me," she said severely. "We are not done yet."

"I think we must be," Rakoczy said sympathetically.

"You will not love me?" There was more anger than yearning in her question.

"Not as you wish," he said with an apologetic bow; he started toward the door.

Rozsa remained where she was. "What if I were to say you raped me?" she asked in a remote voice. "What if I Confessed that you forced yourself on me? What do you think would happen to you then?"

He stopped but did not turn toward her. "I would be burned at the stake," he said, aware that it would be his True Death.

"Yes, you would," she said, her words like a closing trap. "Your name would be utterly disgraced, Konig Bela would claim your lands, your dishonor would be complete when your ashes were scattered to the winds, never to rest in hallowed ground."

"Would it please you to see me burn?" he asked, showing little emotion.

"If you hadn't given me what I ask, it would. It would delight me to describe the depravity you unleashed upon me, and to renounce the world because of how you had used me." She approached him, fury in her smile.

"Tell me then," he said levelly, "what you want of me."

"You know already—the rapture sung in the heroic tales. I want to be Blanchefleur, Ysolte, and Messeuline. I want to have what they had for myself." She reached for him, pulling herself to him, rubbing her body against his. "You know the way to ignite my flesh, don't you, Comes?" With a sudden effort, she put her hands around his neck and kissed him full on the mouth, and when she was done, she laughed breathlessly. "Tell me, Comes, am I not sweeter than flames?"

The heat of her body seemed to brand him through his clothes.

"How can you ask?" he told her, all the while puzzling out how he would deal with her if he acquiesced to her demands.

"Then show me," she said before she kissed him again.

Text of a letter from Balint of Santu-Germaniu, steward at Santu-Germaniu in the Carpathian Mountains, to Rakoczy Ferancsi, Comes Santu-Germaniu, at Mansion Belcrady in Praha, dictated to Frater Lorand, written on vellum and carried by personal courier; never delivered.

To the most puissant Comes Santu-Germaniu, Rakoczy Ferancsi, currently living at Mansion Belcrady in the city of Praha in Bohemia, the greetings of his faithful steward Balint of Santu-Germaniu at Santu-Germaniu on this, the first Sunday in July, the 1269th Year of Salvation,

Good Comes:

In fulfillment of the charge you gave me upon your departure, I send you this report to inform you of the current state of your fief, and all that pertains to it, in the hope that you will find what I have done satisfactory and appropriate.

The orchards within the walls of your principal seat bloomed lavishly this year despite the late snow at the end of March, of which I have already informed you, and I am confident that the harvest of apples and plums will be the best in the last eight years, barring summer misfortunes. I have ordered more grapevines planted on the south slope below the orchards, and in time they will yield good red wine. The oats and rye are ripening in the fields and again, the wheat is flourishing but not as abundantly as the other grains. Yet even with that consideration, the assumption is that the harvest will be bountiful unless there are more heavy rainstorms.

The drainage ditches you ordered be dug are finished, and they have done much to keep the fields from being inundated with water during the rainstorms of May. The weather has re-

mained hot, which has been beneficial to the crops, including those of the kitchen gardens, for we have a great crop of beans and onions already flourishing. The berries on the vines behind the kitchen garden are so plentiful that we have had to post men to drive off the deer and bear that come down from the peaks and out of the forest to raid them.

Konig Bela's men have come here twice since the middle of May, and they are warning of high taxes that will be levied on the crops we harvest and the livestock we may breed. To that end, they have already requisitioned three grown hogs, ten lambs, and a yearling calf, with promises that more will be required. After their selection, we have now thirty-four hogs, sixteen shoats, eighty-four sheep, twenty-three lambs, fifteen goats, six kids, twenty-nine head of cattle, thirteen calves, seventeen horses, eight foals, and fifty-eight various fowl. I have, in accordance with your instructions, refrained from disputing with them on any of these demands, and when they return in August, I will do what I can to supply their wants without cavil.

However, I have made a protest to Konig Bela on behalf of Erno the Blacksmith, whose daughter Ildiko was carried off by the Konig's men to be their maid and whore; they paid no price for her, and they boasted that they would share her among them. Ildiko is almost fifteen, and she was pledged to Vida the game-keeper, who is now demanding payment for her loss. If the Konig is unwilling to pay the price Vida is asking, then there will be bad blood between him and Erno for a long time, I fear, and more anger at Konig Bela for allowing the debt to remain unpaid. I ask your permission to send an official petition of redress to Konig Bela.

The Konig has also not stopped the robbers who prey on those traveling into Santu-Germaniu; his men said that because of his war, the Konig cannot spare any fighting men to patrol the roads to rid them of the outlaws. I know you cannot hire men to do it, for then Konig Bela would seize all of Santu-Germaniu and conscript or enslave all those living as your vassals, but surely there must be some way to stop the attacks, which grow bolder *every month that passes. If you have some means of dealing with the robbers, tell me and I will attend to it at once. Something must be done, or no one will be safe on our roads.*

We have heard that there has been some trouble for the river merchants on the Moltava, and for that reason, I have not yet dispatched to you the two boats you have requested, unless you would like me to load them on a lumber-wagon and hitch ten mules to pull it. It may be wiser for you to go to the Boatwrights' Guild and have the craft built there, little as Konig Bela might approve. He would not like you to have boats brought to you as loads of wood, either.

This in all devotion, by the hand of Frater Lorand, who continues to serve as scribe to Santu-Germaniu, and clerk to

Balint, steward of Santu-Germaniu (his mark)

6

An hour after the sliver of moon had gone down in the west and all the world seemed sunken in darkness, Rakoczy slipped a black-wool French cotehardie over his dark-red silk chainse, and added a cowled liripipe of dark-gray wool, with the hood raised; he eased open the shutters in his own rooms, climbed out onto the broad sill, and carefully lowered himself as far as he could from the sill, then dropped to the flagstones beneath, all without making a sound any louder than the fall of a cushion. The stable courtyard was deserted but for a pair of cats on their first hunting sallies of the night, and no one raised an alarm. Quickly he made his way to the stable, going through it to the rear paddocks, then climbed the wooden wall at the back of Mansion Belcrady, into the narrow alley that ran behind the mansion's walls and up the shoulder of the hill to Vaclav Castle. Rakoczy went along to the first back-street that led down toward the heart of Praha, out of sight of the Guards on the castle's battlements and the city's walls.

The heat of the day had dissipated, and a slow, cool breeze slid through streets that were mostly dark and empty in this quarter of the city. Rakoczy made a point of avoiding the few taverns, which were filled with roistering soldiers, tired merchants, gamblers, cutpurses, and loose women; he went along the minor routes where beggars slept in doorways and scrawny boys moved in the shadows, hatchets and hammers clutched in their hands, alert for solitary travelers or strangers to Praha gone in drink. At one point three of the youths began to follow Rakoczy, but fell back when he swung toward them, one hand on the hilt of his Luccan short-sword, the other on the empty wallet that depended from his belt.

Reaching the old Church of the Apostles, Rakoczy paused at the front of the round, squat, thick-walled stone building with its pointed hat of a roof, to listen for the chants of monks; when he was certain that the nightly Hours were being strictly kept, he moved toward the rear of the church to the walled graveyard where the Redemptionist priests and monks buried beggars, madmen, lepers, and pox victims to show their humility and faith. As if the church were a jewel set in a high stone ring, the walls of the compound rose on either side of the church, enclosing a dormitory, a refectory, the new hospice, and, at the farthest end of the compound, the half-finished leprosarium waiting for the patients it would soon house. The enclosing wall beyond was as old as the church—more than four hundred years old—and enclosed the original graveyard and the abandoned charnel house. A single gate gave access to the graveyard; it was not locked, for few people entered the cemetery willingly. He made his way through the wooden headstones toward the charnel house at the rear of the graves; it was an ancient, dilapidated, six-sided building of stone with a sagging wooden roof and windows that were no more than slits. No light came from within it; the only door was buckled so that the crucifix nailed to it hung at a precarious angle. Taking great care to pull the door clear of weeds, Rakoczy stepped into the charnel house, his night-seeing eyes observing the abandoned structure with a mixture of sadness and consternation. Of all the places Rozsa had ordered him to meet her, this was by far the worst and most reckless. He picked his way through the disintegrating pallets where the monks had once treated their patients; his footsteps disturbed mice and other scuttling things. At last he came to an examination table made from sturdy slabs of oak. He leaned against it and felt it hold firm. "That's something," he murmured to the emptiness in his native tongue. Rozsa would like it, for it would let her expose her body to him without the disadvantage of having him lie beside her; she had told him from their first meeting that she disliked closeness, and had insisted upon minimal contact once her clothes were off.

An unmelodious bell struck the end of Vigil; at this signal Rakoczy moved into the deepest shadows in the dark building, for the monks would be leaving their church to return to their dormitory, and he had no wish to give them any reason to suspect that he was in their old charnel house. He chided himself on this extreme precaution, but kept in mind the consequences of being discovered, and remained in place.

Chanting the 88th *Psalm*, the monks moved in a double line away from the graveyard and toward their dormitory on the far side of the compound, the echoes of their voices following them like disconsolate spirits. From where Rakoczy waited, the echoes became a faint, fading harmony as they met and mixed, the dire words of the chant lost. Gradually the sounds died, and only the faint whisper of the night breeze remained.

It was some time later that there was a rustle in the graveyard, with the hushed tread of solered feet. Rakoczy, who had tossed aside his liripipe, and had been spending his time casting back over his last few centuries of travel and debating when and where he might go next—if he could go anywhere without endangering his fief—now gave his full attention to the approaching footsteps, marking their progress with great care; his left hand curled around the hilt of his short-sword.

"Comes?" The word was so soft it might have been his imagination that he heard it. The door moaned as Rozsa leaned on it. "Are you here, Comes?" she called, adding in an undervoice, "You had better be."

"I am," he responded, starting toward her to help ease the door open, giving no sign that he had overheard her last remark.

She came up to him as he swung the door back. "Ah, Comes. I'm so glad to see you. You will make me very happy, I believe." She flung herself into his arms, reaching to press herself against him. Her elegant bleihaut of muted-purple silk scrooped against him; her rose-and-sandalwood perfume wreathed around him. "Here before me, and in such a place. You are eager. Are you overjoyed I've come?"

"Keep your voice down," he warned sharply.

"Why? Do you think the monks would notice? Everyone knows the place is haunted. No one will come searching, not at this hour, for fear of ghosts."

"You are not afraid of ghosts?" Rakoczy asked.

"Why should I be? God gave me audacity of spirit and a taste for things of the flesh. How can ghosts be proof against that?" She caught her lower lip in her teeth and offered him a languid smile. "We could light torches and no one would disturb us. We may disport ourselves without worry." She locked her hands behind his head, looking at him with undisguised satisfaction. "You hate this, don't you?"

"Hate is the wrong word," he said, trying not to resist her as she tugged at his head so she could kiss him. He could feel her teeth through her closed lips, and was aware she intended that he should.

"What is the word, then? if not hate?" she asked as she released him.

He shrugged. "Despair, perhaps?"

Her laughter was an excited ripple in the air. "Truly? I cause you to despair?"

"Yes."

"Despair." She grinned and tossed her veil at him, her grin widening as the filmy fabric wrapped around him before slithering to the floor. "How delightful, to have such a hold on you. I have never achieved that before." Seeing the shock in his face, she licked her lips provocatively. "Yes. It's delightful. To have a man of your position, your wealth, your power, at my beck and call without obtaining even so little a thing as expiation from our dalliance is delicious." She twirled away from him, going between the old pallets toward the examination table. "I may have to accommodate my husband according to his pleasure, but you, Comes, you will enjoy me according to mine." There was mockery in her voice as well as seduction, and as she held out her hands to him, she said, "You will pleasure me, Comes."

"As you wish, Rozsa," he responded with a duck of his head.

"See that you do."

"Have I failed to gratify you the three times we have met?" He knew he had given her what she sought, even as her particular fulfillment deprived him of the intimacy he craved, and left him feeling deprived.

"No," she admitted. "But you give me cause to hope for more— much more. Something along the lines of the passions of the great lovers of the past." She hummed a fragment of a song about betrayed devotion.

"I cannot give you the love of the troubadours' ballads," he said, thinking that the fables they told were beyond any human capacity to achieve.

"You provide more than I would have otherwise, as I intended you should, and that will have to suffice," she countered, a note of spite in her words. "I've told you that you are far preferable to my husband. You have agreed to pleasure me instead of risk accusation. And, true to your Word, you will give me no awkward children to shame me and bring dishonor upon my husband; not that you would escape damnation if you did." She maneuvered herself onto the table. "The monks have gone in to sleep by now. I think you and I should begin our dalliance for tonight. We haven't much time before there will be activity in the streets again, and we must be gone before that begins; as the night leans toward dawn, half of Praha wakens, and the servants and slaves make ready for the day. I wouldn't want anyone to see either of us."

He wanted to ask her how she had managed to get out of Vaclav Castle without being noticed, or how she would get back in without being observed, but he doubted she would tell him, so he said only, "I am here to do your bidding. You must tell me what you want."

"Then come here and embrace me," she said, gloating as he approached her. "I've loosened my lacings, so you should be able to undress me with ease."

He did as she bade him, removing her gorget before he reached to lift her bleihaut over her head, raising it with care so that it did not catch on her gold-fretwork chaplet, and setting it on the end of the examination table where it could serve Rozsa as a pillow. "Byzantine silk," he said as he turned back to her. "Very elegant. Very expensive."

"Isn't it? My husband at least clothes me well." She fingered the ties on her knee-length linen chainse. "Shall I raise this or remove it?"

"Whichever will please you the most," he said without inflection of any kind.

"Then I will take my chainse off and move it away from me. It's too much like a married-woman's nightrail, and in any case, it irritates me. I will have to tell my 'tire-maid to wash it for me, though she will note any stains upon it." Her face revealed her distaste for the garment all married noblewomen were required by Church law to wear when having congress with their husbands: a simple ankle-length rail with a hole cut to allow for intercourse, thus preserving the spouses from the evils of lust. "Since you will not penetrate me to preserve my honor, I suppose it's just as well that neither you nor I wear one, for there would be little either of us could do to rouse my carnalistic urges. One hole in a sack, that's what it is. Only a priest could think of such a thing."

Rakoczy said nothing while he watched her pull the chainse over her head and fling it away from her, then kick off her solers, paying no heed as they clattered on the rough stones. Now there was only the clout around her loins to clothe her. He began to untie the bands that held the clout in place.

"Kiss me," she said, capturing his hands with her own.

Obediently he lowered his head and pressed her mouth with his own; he could sense the fury in her ardor as she clasped her arms around him. He took his time with their kiss, his tongue opening her lips to his exploration, all the while wondering if she might decide to bite him, for he could feel her caprice welling along with her desire, and angry mischief. He ended the kiss and took a step back. "Shall I untie your—"

"Not yet. All in good time," she said, her hand caressing his jaw. "So carefully trimmed. You must spend hours working in the mirror to achieve this."

"My manservant grooms me," he said; he had had no reflection for more than thirty-two hundred years.

She managed an artistic shiver. "Embrace me again. I am cold."

He almost laughed. "I doubt I can warm you."

"Oh, yes you can. You have done so the previous times we have met, and you shall do so again." The edge in her voice reminded him of how perilous their connection was.

"Then tell me what you want me to do," he said, trying not to recall the many, many times he had asked that question, and what the answers had been. He banished the memories and gave his whole attention to Rozsa. "What will make you warm."

"I want you to embrace me and caress me—slowly." She smiled up at him. "If you hurry, I will not be pleased."

"Then you must tell me if I go too fast," he said, closing the gap between them and putting his arms around her; she snuggled against his cotehardie. "Where would you like me to begin?"

She thought for a moment, then said, "I think you ought to kiss my face, many, many kisses. Of all sorts. Everywhere on my face." She tilted her head to make this easier. "Begin at my eyebrows. Now. Do not be too hasty."

Rakoczy did as she ordered, making his kisses light, playful, and sensual; he smoothed back her hair and turned her face with his hands. He made his way from her eyebrows to her eyelids, then across her cheeks, never increasing the speed of his kisses, until finally he reached her lips, where he spent his time outlining her mouth with his own, growing more intense as he lingered, his tongue probing deeply. He was aware of her arousal, and her satisfaction, but he knew beyond all question that she did not want to include him in her fulfillment.

"Use your hands," she said, pushing against him so he would have access to her body. "Start at my shoulders."

Obediently, he began to stroke her shoulders as gently as if he held a kitten. Shoulders and upper arms gave way to her breasts. He fingered her nipples, fondled her breasts, watching her face suffuse with a concupiscence so inward that he felt himself an intruder in her arousal. He bent to take her nipple in his mouth and was rewarded with her quick gasp of pleasure. Carefully he leaned her back, guiding her so that she reclined on the examination table, her head resting on her folded garments, his hands continuing to venture over her body, probing enticingly, finding new ways to evoke her excitement, gauging his success by her shivers and encouraging sighs and moans. Gradually he felt her move into his hands.

"Do more, and do it sweetly," she said, opening her legs. "You know what I like. Run your hands up my thighs."

He faltered, wondering if she were trying to trap him in some way. "There is more I can do before I—"

"I *want* you to move lower. Now. My ardor is rising. I want you to use your mouth and your hands to delectate me. I want to be wrung with ecstasy." She met his eyes with more determination than passion. "You promised me that you would not deprive me of my fulfillment: I hold you to that promise."

Slowly, expertly, Rakoczy kissed and nuzzled his way from her breasts, along the flare of her ribs, the curve of her abdomen, to the dark curls at the base of her hips; Rozsa quivered as he gently tugged at the dense hairs, then bent to tongue the small bud that lay at the top of what she called *my most lovely rose.*

"Not yet," she said, her breath quickening. "Hands first. I want to prolong my exhilaration as long as I can."

"As you wish," said Rakoczy, and separated her sea-shell-scented flesh with his fingers and softly rubbed the little nubbin until it stiffened and grew red as a plum; Rozsa moaned her exaltation. Then he slid two fingers into her, taking his time so that she would gain the most arousal from it; when he tantalizingly withdrew his fingers and entered her again with three, all the while stroking the reddened kernel, Rozsa jolted in response.

"Use your mouth. *Now!*"

His lips closed on the swollen mote; he felt it jump and tremble; he heard Rozsa give an ecstatic whimper as she dug her hands into his hair. He increased the pressure of his mouth and her first spasm seized her, rocking through her like a miniature tide; she shuddered, her hips lifting rhythmically with her culmination, her throes casting her into a private paradise; Rakoczy wondered briefly what she envisioned behind her closed eyes. Her cries were soft, high, like the call of a distant hawk, and they, like her transports, faded fairly quickly. She shivered a last time, sighed a little, then let go of him. "I am most satisfied," she declared, shifting away from him. "You have done what I require of you. I ought to thank you."

"And you will keep your bargain—I have to be grateful to you," he said with a tinge of sardonic amusement.

"You should be." She contemplated him with the attitude of her superior rank. "Yes, I will abide by the terms I have laid out, I will spare you my—"

"Accusations of rape? That is good of you." Rakoczy stepped back from her, feeling her disdain as if it were a cold wind between them. "I fear I may have broken the skin . . ." He gestured toward her loins.

"Did you?" She laughed quietly. "You must have been more determined than last time. You certainly increased my consummation." She sat up and swung around. "You say you broke the skin: did you taste the blood?"

"Yes."

She laughed again. "How perverse. Will you Confess it?" Saying that, she reached for her chainse, her mordant amusement fading rapidly. "Help me dress. I will have to leave shortly."

Her abrupt shift from rapture to practicality, although he had seen it before, still had the capacity to shock him. "What do you want me to do?" he asked, feeling, as he had at the end of their previous trysts, a bit mystified. The very small amount of blood he had taken from her tasted flat, and he knew it would provide little nourishment, for there had been no real intimacy between them, no connection beyond the most superficial; the sustenance it provided was minimal.

"When I have my bleihaut on, you may tighten my lacings," she said as she tugged her chainse over her head. "It is a good thing that you don't undress, for all that it displeases me." Without warning, she reached out, grabbing for his genitals through his clothing and shaking her head in disapproval. "Soft, too soft."

"Does that trouble you?" he asked. More than a thousand years before he had lost all embarrassment from his impotence and offered no apology for it now. "Were you not fulfilled?"

She fastened the neck-bands of her chainse, chuckling. "I'm not troubled; it suits me that you are . . . as you are. In fact, there is something very pleasing in your . . . condition. I feel that I achieve more because you achieve less." This last revelation was accompanied by a wink. She got off the examination table and tugged the hem of her chainse to make it smooth, then reached for her bleihaut, shimmying into it with practiced ease. "The lacings," she said to him bluntly.

"Of course." He stepped behind her and began to secure the silken cords. "How tight?"

"I'll tell you when you've—"

The sound of a door opening in the rear of the church made both of them start, then hold in place.

"The night-warder," whispered Rozsa. "He is going to wake the slaves."

"Then we have to hurry," said Rakoczy, securing her lacings without her approval, and tucking the slip-knot into the neck of her dress. He gave her her gorget and veil. "You will need these."

She grabbed them without ceremony, and bent to guide her solers onto her feet. "The warm nights will soon be over," she murmured.

"Yes?" Rakoczy waited to hear what more she would say.

"When the rains come, the army will return from fighting." Her voice was flat.

"Yes."

She straightened up, still speaking softly. "We won't be able to meet while my husband is here."

"I suppose not," he said, keeping his voice quiet and level.

"We won't be able to speak except when meeting at Court functions, and then only of minor things: gossip, clothes, entertainments."

"I am not completely ignorant of Court life, Rozsa," he reminded her with a quick smile.

"No, no, of course you're not," she said with a dismissing wave of her hand. "But you are an exile, as you often remind me, and customs do vary from Court to Court." She pulled her gorget over her head and reached for her veil. "I'll leave first. Wait until the side-gate is closed before you—"

"I will see you safely away," he told her firmly but without raising his voice.

She stared at him, as if shocked by his assertion. "I will leave first," she reiterated in a tone that did not encourage argument.

"If you will permit me to create a diversion, you should be able to get away without being noticed."

As if to underscore his instruction, a sleepy voice was heard ordering the slaves to collect their bread and then to set to work.

Rozsa nodded. "All right. But be quick. I must be in the castle garden shortly, and delay will do me no good."

"Delay is what I seek to avoid," he said, and went to the door of the charnel house, pulling on his liripipe as he went, making sure the hood was up and his features obscured. "You will know when to take your chance, Rozsa."

She frowned. "If you must, I suppose you must."

Carefully he eased the door open and stepped out among the graves. He stayed in the cover of the wooden markers, keeping away from the path the slaves would soon use, and putting distance between himself and the gate in the wall. Finally he found two grave-markers leaning together and he dropped down behind them, unbuckling his belt and sprawling in their shadow. Once laid out, he began to sing in the language of Brabant, the melody an off-key rumble; the song was plaintive, but his rendition only made it sound disjointed:

> *The wind in the mountains*
> *The wind on the sea*
> *The wind in my lover's heart:*
> *Why has she gone from me?*

He was well into the second verse when he heard hastening footsteps and subdued voices, and saw out of the corner of his eye a monk and two slaves hurrying in his direction, the monk carrying a stout wooden staff. He lolled onto his back, spread out his arms, and sang more loudly:

> *The vines in the valleys*
> *The trees on the hill*
> *The holly in my lover's heart*
> *With thorns that softly kill.*

"Over there!" the monk cried, pointing toward the pair of grave-markers; the slaves followed him through the graves, not quite running, but more than walking. Guided by his song, they hastened up to him, and stopped as they discovered him, lying supine, his face hidden, his clothes in disarray.

The monk stood over him uncertainly, then nudged Rakoczy with his toe. "Good man," he said more loudly than was proper in this place, "wake up, good man."

Rakoczy interrupted his song and blinked at the monk. "What?" he asked in Bohemian with a pronounced French accent. "What's the matter?"

"Foreign *and* drunk," the monk grumbled.

"What's the trouble?" Rakoczy slurred his question.

"You cannot lie here," the monk said, patience and annoyance in his manner.

"Why not?" Rakoczy flailed about in an effort to sit up; he almost struck one of the two slaves huddling next to the monk.

"You are lying on a grave," said the monk, and was satisfied to see the stranger jump and make a serious effort to clamber to his feet. "These are church grounds, and you have been lying on—"

"Yes. Yes. Graves." Rakoczy crossed himself clumsily, then looked around, peering into the darkness. "God have mercy on me."

The monk made the sign of the cross for them all. "Amen." He stepped back as the stranger lurched one step, steadying himself on the nearest grave-marker, then moving away from it, his steps uncertain. The monk made no effort to assist him. "How much did you drink last night?"

"Not much," Rakoczy answered, inwardly reminding himself that this was the truth. "My comrades and I were in a tavern, and then we went and bought a skin of wine." He stared about, befuddled. "I don't remember what . . ." He slapped the front of his bleihaut. "My belt!" He stared down at the ground. "My wallet." He crouched awkwardly and began to feel around the place he had been lying. "My belt," he exclaimed, snatching it up and holding it aloft like a trophy taken in battle. "And my sword. But where's my wallet?" He hoped that when they finally came across it, they would assume it was empty because of theft.

"Help him look," the monk said in a resigned tone, bending over himself. "The sooner we recover it, the sooner we all may return to our duties."

All four of them set about scrabbling among the graves for the missing wallet, the sounds of their labors sufficiently loud to cover Rozsa's careful retreat. Only when Rakoczy heard the side-gate sigh open did he stop searching and sink down on his haunches. "It's no use. It's gone." He slapped the ground with his hand.

"The dead have claimed recompense for you disturbing them," said the monk, relieved to straighten up. "I will order another search after sunrise, if you are minded to wait." He took a deep breath. "You could attend Mass."

Rakoczy shook his head and crossed himself. "Not this morning. I haven't Confessed for a long time."

The monk's expression made it plain that he was not surprised. He motioned to the slaves. "Come then. Be about your work. This man can find his way to the gate that he came in." He shoved the slaves ahead of him. "May God guide you to His—"

"Thank you. You've been good to me, Frater—better than I deserved." He staggered away a few steps.

"The gate is that way," the monk said, pointing. "Leave now, and choose your companions more carefully in future." With that, he swung around and herded the slaves toward the path to the bake-house.

Rakoczy made a show of fumbling his way through the grave-markers until he was sure he was out of sight; then he walked to the gate and slipped through it, mildly surprised that Rozsa had left it open for him; he closed it behind him, then started up the hill toward Mansion Belcrady.

Text of a letter from Frater Castimir, battle-scribe to Konig Otakar II, near Graz in Styria, to Pader Stanislas, clerk and scribe to Konige Kunigunde at Praha in Bohemia, written on vellum in Latin and carried by royal courier; delivered nine days after it was written.

To the most worthy Augustinian scribe and secretary to the exalted Konige Kunigunde, I, Frater Castimir, battle-scribe to Konig Przemysl Otakar II of Bohemia, send the most sincere greetings of the dear Royal to his Royal wife, and entrust the honest reading of this letter to you on this, the nineteenth day of August in the 1269th Year of Man's Salvation.

To the most serene Konige Kunigunde, the greetings of her husband and Konig, Otakar II, bearing with them the hope that this finds her well, her pregnancy advancing without difficulty, and her Court abiding in her Good Will,

My Konige, it is my wish that you be ready to receive me and my Court in Praha by the middle of October; I have had many successes in the field, and the borders of Bohemia are greatly expanded, much to the distress of Rudolph von Hapsburg, and it is my intention to bring my soldiers out of harm's way before the weather turns; I have been told that the signs are for a hard winter and an early one, and I do not want my army to be bogged down in mud and cold that can only serve to weaken them at a time when they will be wanted in strength next spring.

My Court and I will remain with you until the first signs of spring, and then we must go to Pressburg, where we will make ready for another summer on campaign. It is my wish that you and our children be kept away from the turmoil of battle, and I believe that your grandfather, Konig Bela, shares that wish. For that reason, you may choose what festivities we will observe during my stay in Praha, and you will set the tone of the Courts, yours and mine, for the time they are combined.

May God grant you a safe delivery of an heir, and may he be a sound, healthy boy who will be ready to take the reins of power when God takes them from my hands. Know that I pray daily for our coming child, and that I have offered Masses and tribute for our son. As I know you pray for my victories, so your delivery of my heir shall complete my conquests and secure an Empire for our descendants. In this we are united in purpose and in faith.

Przemysl Otakar II
Konig of Bohemia and Moravia
Lord of Styria and Carinthia
Dux of Austria

by the hand of Frater Castimir, battle-scribe to the Konig Otakar
and Premonstratensian monk

PART II

Rakoczy Ferancsi, Comes Santu-Germaniu

*T*ext of a letter from Smiricti Detrich, Counselor of Praha, to Rakoczy Ferancsi, Comes Santu-Germaniu, at Mansion Belcrady in Praha, carried by Council messenger.

To the highly esteemed Comes Santu-Germaniu at Mansion Belcrady, the greetings of Smiricti Detrich, Counselor of Praha, by the hand of the Counselor's scribe and clerk, Frater Ulric, on this, the second day of September, in the 1269th year of Salvation,

Most worthy Comes,

It is my duty to inform you that the Counselors of Praha have met to determine the taxes for the city; those laid upon the Mansion Belcrady have increased, due to the high cost of Konig Otakar's campaign in the south, which is a decision that I have been given the privilege of informing you. I regret to tell you that you will be asked to pay another six standard ingots of gold beyond what you have already provided us to support his campaign. All foreigners are being assessed additional monies, so this is not intended to inconvenience you and no other. However, as you have the grandest establishment, the actual amount required of you is larger than for other foreign residents in the city. I am of the opinion that your rate is too high, even for an exile. The rest of the Counselors disagree, and I must capitulate to their wishes or resign my post; the latter course would benefit neither of us, and so I have acquiesced, in the hope that I might, in future, be in a position to advocate for you. I ask you to comply with these demands now, and trust me to do what is in my power to intercede for you next May.

You will have until the beginning of Advent to pay the amount due or to find other housing. I know this is abrupt, and for that, I ask your understanding; you have been a most upright and responsible resident, for all you are an exile, and it troubles me to see the hand of the Konig's necessity fall so heavily on you, but this must be God's Will, for He has brought you here in Konig Otakar's time of need. Your gold will help the Konig to make the most of the winter without reducing his own treasury. Production of gold has already been increased at the mines, and Konig Otakar has money from those efforts coming to him in quantity, but the bulk of the sums will not be ready until the spring, and the costs he is encountering are immediate. The Konig is determined to see his army enter the field next spring fully armed and ready for whatever Comes Rudolph von Hapsburg of Austria may have in store for him, which requires a large outlay before the Nativity so that the smiths and armorers may spend the winter preparing all that the Konig requires. I am disinclined to deny Otakar what he seeks, for he has succeeded so well that the Hand of God is certainly in his successes, and those of us who aid him now will gain Royal favor in this life and the approval of God in the next. That the brunt of these costs will be borne by you is unfortunate, but as the loyal vassal of Konig Otakar, I must continue to ensure that everything is done to bring about his vision of a Bohemian Empire.

With the Konig preparing to return to Praha and the Konige about to give him his long-sought heir, there will be grand occasions for celebration in the city, and therefore we must prepare to show our loyalty and corroboration of the greatness of this reign: to that end I implore you, if you are able to spare more money, to contribute toward the occasions that will herald the arrival of the Nativity Season. We will put forth the embodiments of our rejoicing. A civic procession and Royal Contest is planned already, and will require stands for those attending, as well as display wagons for the Guilds and great Houses of all Praha. Episcopus Fauvinel has already promised that he will have his troupe of dwarves and hunchbacks perform their antics in the procession. And that he will bless the occasion. Any donation you make to any aspect of the festivities will stand you in good stead with the Council as well as the Konige's Court, and therefore I implore you to do what you may to add to our coffers and our splendid occasions. I also ask that you impart to me any ideas you may have for improving the welcome we will give the Konig when he once again enters our gates. Perhaps you will agree to meet with me in ten days' time?

This week, unless the Konige gives birth, of course, I will be spending most of my days with my fellow-Counselors deciding the suit brought by the Beggars' Guild against the rats that are so plentiful in Praha. Episcopus Fauvinel has given his permission for the suit to proceed as promptly as possible, and the Council is happy to accommodate him in this matter. If the suit is decided in favor of the Beggars' Guild, then we will have to hire an experienced rat-catcher and pay to have the rats killed, as well as offer rewards for those who are willing to help rid the city of the rats, but if the rats prevail, then any member of the Beggars' Guild caught killing a rat will have his hand struck off, and any resident of the city found to be killing rats will be fined three ingots of silver. Since this is an issue of significance, and given that there are so many other demands at this time, until we have reached a decision in regard to the Beggars' Guild suit, I fear I will not be available to you before the ten days have passed.

With deep gratitude to you for your many helpful acts and for your gracious acquiescence in delivering your assessed portion toward our glorifying Bohemia and Przemysl Otakar II in his time of victory,

Smiricti Detrich
Counselor of Praha

by the hand of Frater Ulric, Hieronymite monk

1

"She did not come," Rakoczy said to Hruther as he climbed into his personal quarters through the half-open window; the night was almost ended, and there was a stillness that marked the approach of dawn as much as the beginning activity in the city below them. Rakoczy stepped down from the window-ledge; there was dust on his huch, and his jaw-length wavy hair was in disarray; he held his liripipe in his hand.

"How long did you wait?" Hruther asked in Imperial Latin, putting the last of the books he had been stacking in place on the trestle-table next to the largest upright chest where two oil-lanthorns gave illumination to the room.

"From midnight until a short while ago. I wanted to get off the streets before the slaves and laborers were abroad," said Rakoczy, a faint vertical line forming between his fine brows. "She chose the cellar of an old weavery this time, near the North Gate, where the butchers are. Not a very . . . prepossessing location."

"Still it's probably safer than the charnel house was," Hruther remarked. "No monks or slaves about."

"It stank of old wool-fat and mice. I wonder if she chose it to test me in some way." His eyes were remote. "But to what end?"

Hruther studied Rakoczy. "Do you think she's tiring of you?"

Rakoczy gave an abrupt sigh. "I hope so." He went and pulled the shutters closed, setting the bolt in place before going on, "To-night would have been our sixth meeting. That has been upper-most in my thoughts for the last eight days, and I am no wiser now than I was when she first sent me word of her most recent intentions. So our next contact—limited though it may be—is the sixth contact."

"And that troubles you."

"Of course it does: how could it not. I have no wish to bring a woman like Rozsa of Borsod into my life, but if she insists . . ." He looked up at the ceiling. "If I tell her what is coming when she dies, I believe she will think I am lying."

"Are you sure?" Hruther thought he had not seen Rakoczy in such turmoil for more than three centuries.

"If she does not think me a liar, she will know I am something much worse—and then what? My life is in her hands, and she knows it. Anything that increases her power will please her." He slapped his hands on the tops of his thighs. "The good people of Praha would have me bound at the stake if they knew my true nature."

An unmelodious bell sounded from the floor below, the signal to waken the household.

"I'll let Barnon attend to the household for now," Hruther said to Rakoczy.

"You may want to put some distance between us, to be safe. I may become dangerous to know. Speak against me among the servants, to show you dislike your position." He flung his liripipe across the room.

"You've been dangerous to know for the twelve hundred years I have served you," Hruther said calmly. "I won't malign you to the household unless it benefits both of us."

Rakoczy suddenly shook his head. "I am churlish; pardon me, old friend."

"You aren't churlish, you are vexed, and not without cause," Hruther said, thinking he had not seen Rakoczy so nettled by a woman since Csimenac had abused his gift five hundred years ago.

Rakoczy considered this. "You may be right," he conceded.

"The lady's circumstances may change shortly, my master, and there will be no occasions for her to make more demands of you," Hruther said.

"So I hope," Rakoczy admitted.

"Her husband will be here next month." Hruther looked down at his folded, lean hands.

"I can only hope that she will not insist on more meetings before he comes." Rakoczy clicked his tongue. "It is craven of me, but I do not want to have to explain to Rozsa about the hazards of undead life. At best she will view my warnings with mockery."

"As to that—the word is that Konige Kunigunde has begun her labor; that may account for Rozsa's absence."

Rakoczy looked startled. "Tell me how—"

"A message came from Vaclav Castle three hours ago. Not from Rozsa of Borsod, from Pader Stanislas, that the Konige's labor has begun. The news has been sent to all the great Houses in the city, and all the churches, so that all may pray for her safe delivery." He rubbed his thumb along the edge of the table. "It is her time, isn't it?"

"Very nearly," said Rakoczy, a note of relief in his voice. "You are right: if the Konige is about to deliver, it is not surprising that Rozsa would not dare to leave Vaclav Castle. All her ladies-in-waiting must attend on her childbed."

"It would be a reckless thing to do, leaving the Konige's Court, even for her, at this time," said Hruther. "And she will have to stay near Konige Kunigunde for the first month after the child comes, as all the Konige's Court will." He pressed his lips together, then said, "You will probably be summoned to sing for the Konige and her new child."

Rakoczy nodded. "I and Tirz Agoston of Mures: he has made a new gittern for the Konige, to celebrate her safe delivery."

"Assuming that she has a safe delivery," Hruther cautioned.

"Indeed."

"Of a son," Hruther added, his lean face hinting at an ironic smile.

"They will celebrate a girl, for the sake of Konig Bela, but not as grandly. A girl can seal a treaty with a marriage, as Kunigunde herself has done." He shook his head. "Hungary will expect some rejoicing."

There was silence between them, an uneasy one. Finally Hruther returned to an issue that he realized was causing Rakoczy much consternation. "So you haven't explained matters to her yet? to Rozsa? She doesn't know what's to come?"

"No." Rakoczy paced the length of the room, then rounded on Hruther. "It is not that I do not want to tell her, I do not know *how* to tell her. She has turned aside every sally I have made so far, and short of tying her to a chair and demanding that she listen, I have no notion how to inform her. Not that I think tying her to a chair would work: she would very likely be furious and would upbraid me instead of hearing me out. And she might well denounce me to her Confessor." This admission left him feeling discomfited; he frowned and made a gesture of hopeless frustration. "I *know* it is imperative she be prepared for what will happen before our next meeting, whenever that may be, and that she—" He stopped.

"What is it?" Hruther asked, reading dismay in Rakoczy's countenance.

Rakoczy did not answer at once. "I wish I knew what she has told her Confessor."

"You may be certain that she doesn't tell him everything. Few people do."

"Do you think she would not?" Rakoczy sighed again, this time sadly. "She might enjoy Confessing what we do, since it is not true adultery. She might have to do penance for lust, but she would not be in danger of being dishonored." He tented his fingers under his lip. "If she tires of me, she will want to be rid of me, I suppose." He looked around his room. "I would be sorry to have to leave here."

Hruther was surprised at this. "I thought you aren't—"

"I would be sorry to leave here because of the price Konig Bela would exact from my fief and my vassals if I did leave, and because, having done so much to make this mansion livable; I would prefer to enjoy it a while longer, at least until I can improve my understanding with Konig Bela, and can negotiate a kind of truce with him on behalf of my vassals. To have so much resting on Rozsa's caprice . . ." He shook his head slowly. "Not that there is anything that worry can accomplish." His single, self-deprecating laugh made Hruther wince. "You might as well leave me; I need to get some rest."

"You should consider visiting one of the women you've—"

"Not just now," said Rakoczy, starting to yawn.

"Tonight, perhaps," Hruther suggested.

"Yes; yes. You are right. I need nourishment. I can provide a sweet dream and gain sustenance from the satisfaction I provide: I've done it often enough." Rakoczy loosened the front lacings of his huch. "That will be for later, when I have rested."

"And if a summons comes from the Konige's Court, what then?" Hurther asked in an off-handed way, knowing that Rakoczy was still deeply troubled.

"Wake me, of course," Rakoczy answered. "I will need to make an appearance at the castle."

"I will, if that's what you want," said Hruther. He picked up the liripipe. "Do you need anything more from me just now?"

"No, not just now," said Rakoczy, feeling slightly distracted. He hung his huch on a peg on the side of the garderobe.

"Rest well, my master," said Hruther as he closed the door. He went down the corridor to the stairs and descended to the main hall, taking note of the three servants raking the rushes. "Where is Barnon?" he asked the nearest of the three.

"In the bake-house, collecting the loaves for breakfast."

"I'll find him," said Hruther, and went toward the kitchen and the door to the herb-garden. He stepped out into the early morning and the sounds of birds wakening as the sky lightened; a ragged chorus of cock-crows sounded from many parts of the city, well in advance of the bells that would greet the actual sunrise. As he stepped out through the garden gate, he saw one of the mansion's cats hurrying along, something limp dangling from its mouth. "You do good work," he murmured to the cat.

Barnon was standing in the bake-house door, his arms akimbo, his face turning red in the light from the oil-lamps that lit the stone room where the baker made the household bread; there was an odor of charred and decaying flesh in the room, and an air of conflict that was palpable. He pointed at the baker and raised his voice to a bellow. "If you knew this was a problem, why didn't you inform me?"

The baker shrugged and gestured to the open oven. "We thought the bake-fire would burn the rats out," he said as if this were an obvious conclusion. He was a large man, as soft and swelling as a mound of dough; his face was so rounded that it had only one wrinkle, and that was between his bushy brows.

"And now you have half-baked rats caught in the chimney." Barnon reached out and struck the baker with his open hand. "You say you're a master of your trade? You're worse than a scullion. At least scullions don't—" He fell silent as he saw Hruther standing beside him.

"Yes," Hruther agreed. "Most scullions know to keep the chimneys clean; they fear fire as much as you do." He gave his attention to the baker. "Tell me why you decided to risk a fire in the flue rather than ask for a day to have the chimney cleaned?"

Again the baker shrugged; he was unwilling to look at Hruther.

Hruther said nothing while Barnon and the baker waited uneasily for him to speak. Finally he took a deep breath. "All right," he told them. "Barnon, send one of the servants to buy bread in the market today. Then bring the housemen here to clean the flue. Have the rushes swept from all the rooms that have them, and get rid of any mice and rats found nesting in them. Bring in the cats to help you kill them. Then have the floors washed; I'll give you something to add to the water to rid the rooms of the smell. When the floors are dry, then wait a day before more rushes are put down, and use the time to brush the floors with camphor-water, let the cats have a night to hunt those rats we do not find today." He looked at the baker. "Tymek, I will inform my master about what you've allowed to happen. He will decide what is to be done about you."

"I'm ready to be beaten," said the baker.

"But the Comes might prefer to impose some other punishment," said Hruther, who had rarely seen Rakoczy do deliberate harm to anyone who had not attacked him. "Do you have a wife or children?"

"My wife is dead, and one of my sons. I have one boy remaining." Tymek looked puzzled but ventured no question.

"And where is that boy?" Hruther watched the baker steadily.

"He is apprenticed to Nikula, the butcher in Sante-Hildegard's Square." He stared at the far wall.

"A butcher, not a baker?" Hruther inquired.

"My wife's father is a butcher. He arranged it." Tymek shifted from one foot to the other, his face clouded.

Hruther nodded. "Well, Tymek, I will report this to the Comes, and he will summon you to hear his decision in your regard." He turned to Barnon. "Go and rouse the housemen and the scrub-women and tell them there is work to be done."

A fanfare of crowing greeted the first rosy rays of the sun as they struck the highest points in Praha; Barnon crossed himself and whispered a prayer. "I go now," he informed Hruther as he departed, his footsteps slapping on the courtyard flagstones.

"What shall *I* do?" Tymek asked, his hands flapping at his sides. "I can't bake, and there is nothing for me to do in the kitchen."

"Go to the servants' hall and break your fast. Then return here to aid in cleaning the flue. The bread will be purchased in the market for today."

Tymek blustered at this. "I am a baker, not a chimney-sweep."

"The rats don't know that, nor do they care." Hruther regarded the baker calmly. "You neglected the oven, and it is for you to see it put right. Until the oven is safe, we will not use it. Be thankful that there was no fire."

Tymek wadded his hands into fists but gave no other indication of having heard Hruther. He went toward the door as if dragged by a rope, then halted. "If you disgrace me, then you will be sorry for it." He thrust out his jaw as if daring Hruther to do anything to oppose him.

"I may be a foreigner and the bondsman of a foreigner, but in this place, you will respect my position," said Hruther, so coldly that Tymek took a step back. "Remember who you are, and what you have done, Tymek-the-Baker, and show proper regard."

The baker tapped his foot, then left without another word.

Hruther took a little time to make a cursory inspection of the oven, wrinkling his nose at the odor of spoiled meat; then he set himself in the doorway, giving himself a short time to compose himself before going into the manse to be sure that the necessary chores were being done. He was on his way to the garden gate when he heard the first bells sounding, not a full, resplendent peal, but the repeated ringing of a single bell, soon echoed by other single bells. Hruther stopped to listen, and said to himself, "Konige Kunigunde has another daughter," then went through to the plantations of sweet-smelling herbs.

"What will the Konig say?" Pacar demanded as he saw Hruther in the corridor. "Why has God given Otakar so much, but withheld the one thing that would protect all he has done?" He pointed to one of the scullions, who was filling the largest cauldron with water from the well beyond the garden. "You should find your comrades and go to church to offer prayers for the child."

The scullion went pale. "If you tell me, I must. But I'm supposed to clean—"

The noise from single-note bells was now sounding all over Praha, and their clamor was deafening.

"You can clean after prayers," Pacar said, raising his voice; he reached out to swat the side of the youngster's head. "Be about it. Now! You will eat when you return."

"How do you plan to serve the rest of the household?" Hruther asked Pacar as he watched the scullion run from the kitchen.

"Barnon will send the others to pray." He gave a sidelong glance to Hruther. "Your master will want to go to the All Saints' chapel in Vaclav Castle, won't he? to be with the Konige's Court."

"I'm going to rouse him now," said Hruther, favoring the cook with a slight nod. "And when are you going to pray?"

"When I've fed the household, of course," said Pacar. "You mayn't be so careful in Santu-Germaniu, but here in Bohemia, we know the way such things are done."

Hruther made no reply; he went to the main hall and the stairs beside the fireplace. He climbed quickly and went directly to Rakoczy's private quarters, rapping twice before letting himself in, prepared to wake the Comes from the profound torpor that in those of his blood served as sleep. "My master," he said in Imperial Latin.

"I am awake, old friend," he heard Rakoczy say in that language as he came through the door.

"Then you know," said Hruther in that language.

"The Konige has a girl again," said Rakoczy, emerging from his sleeping-chamber with his hair tousled and a slightly distracted air that told Hruther that he had only just wakened.

"Yes," said Hruther.

"I should dress and go to Vaclav Castle." Rakoczy approached the garderobe. "I suppose the dark-red velvet huch and the black silk chainse, with the tall Hungarian boots," he said, peering into its depths. "The day will be warm, but the occasion demands—"

"You will want the silver-link collar with the eclipse pectoral," Hruther added. "As you say, the occasion demands it."

"Yes, I will." He rubbed the edge of his beard.

"I'll set them out for you, my master," said Hruther, and began on that task while Rakoczy ran his hand over his cheek and along his neatly trimmed beard again. "A good thing you were shaved two days ago."

"Yes," Rakoczy agreed. "There's hardly any stubble yet." He passed his fingers through his hair. "I wish there were time to bathe properly, but I will have to do with a basin and a towel."

"I'll have one sent up," said Hruther, putting the black chainse on a peg before going to the door. "This shouldn't take long."

"Thank you," said Rakoczy, aware that he was going to have a long day at the Konige's Court. When Hruther was gone, he took his ivory comb from his small chest of personal items and pulled it through his hair until he could feel that the waves were neatened. He had long since learned to manage without a reflection, and no longer fretted about his appearance, knowing that what he did not notice, Hruther would. The constant chiming of bells was becoming annoying, and he spent a short while regaining his composure, for the sound would not end until sunset.

Hruther tapped on the door, then came in bearing a basin of steaming water. "Pacar has a large pot on the boil. It's hot."

"I will bear that in mind." Rakoczy used a thick square of boiled wool to shield his hands.

Hruther retrieved the huch and calf-length braccae of embroidered black leather. Next he got out the boots from the chest of footwear and set them on the bench that fronted the hearth. "If you don't need me for anything more, there are problems in the bake-house . . ." He clicked his tongue.

"Problems?" Rakoczy repeated as he tugged his nightrail over his head, turning away from Hruther as he did.

"The flue has a rats' nest in it." He paused. "Tymek decided to bake them out rather than have the flue cleaned."

"Ah." Rakoczy took a cotton cloth and dropped it in the basin of hot water.

"The mess will have to be removed. And all the chimneys scrubbed, as well."

Rakoczy nodded. "I will not keep you." He gestured to his clothes. "I can manage this."

"Then I'll await your return this evening."

Rakoczy heard the door close; he wrung out the cloth and ran it over his naked body. It was a cursory wash, but, he reminded himself, it was more than most of the Konige's Court would do. First he pulled on his simple breechclout, and after it, his braccae; then drew the chainse over his head, smoothing it as the heavy silk settled on his shoulders. Taking the huch from its peg, he opened the lacings at the neck and wriggled into it, adjusting the hang of the wide, rectangular, open sleeves before tightening the lacings and reaching for his belt. When he had finished buckling it in place, he took his silver-link collar and eclipse pectoral from his jewel-case. After he had set it in place on his shoulders and chest, he donned his high, thick-soled, black-leather Hungarian boots; his native earth in the soles was almost as restoring as sleep. Opening his jewel-case again, he took out a tear-drop-shaped pink zircon and a large, straw-colored topaz. These he slipped into his wallet, then flicked his comb through his hair one last time before he chose a soft, red-velvet Florentine hat to complete his ensemble. He took care to lock the door as he left.

At the gate to Vaclav Castle, Rakoczy joined a line of nobles, churchmen, Guild Masters, and foreigners of rank, all of whom had answered the summons of the bells. They were all dressed with the grandeur the occasion required, and some of them were bearing packages and little chests with gifts for the Konige and her new daughter. Rakoczy passed through into the wide forecourt of the castle, then turned toward the south wing of the sprawling stone building and the entrance reserved for Konige Kunigunde's courtiers. He was admitted promptly, along with Sorer Zuza, who was charged with caring for the Konige's linen; the elderly nun was beaming.

"God has given Bohemia another Royal daughter," said Sorer Zuza as she and Rakoczy climbed the stairs to the main floor; Rakoczy said nothing. "God must have a great plan for the two daughters: with wise marriages—and these girls will make great marriages—Bohemia could be tied to all the Royal Houses from Roma to Poland, as it deserves." She crossed herself. "God will give the Konige a son in His good time."

At the top of the stairs there was an antechamber, where they were met by Csenge of Somogy and Teca of Veszbrem, who directed them to the Konige's Chapel. "There will be a blessing of the birth by Episcopus Fauvinel, and then you will be allowed to see the Konige briefly, to present your gifts and to see the child." Csenge stared at Rakoczy, a stern purpose in her dark-hazel eyes. "You will inform the Konige's grandfather that you have seen Konige Kunigunde well, and that her daughter is whole. He will have the letter from Pader Stanislas, of course, and Episcopus Fauvi-nel, but he will want confirmation from you and other Hungarians here at Court."

"If that is the Konige's pleasure, it will be my honor to inform Konig Bela," said Rakoczy, ducking his head before following Sorer Zuza to the Konige's Chapel, where more than forty people were already gathered.

"I am glad to see you, Comes," said Rozsa of Borsod as she came up to him, resplendent in a sweeping bleihaut of rust-colored silk, a chainse of ivory linen, and a veil of dark-red Mosul-cotton; her green eyes were unusually bright. "You will give the Konige comfort, I think. She is very low-spirited."

"For the sake of Hungary, I hope I may comfort her," said Ra-koczy, trying to read her inscrutable expression.

"It must be so. All Hungarians will comfort her."

"For the birth of a second daughter?" Rakoczy asked.

"That, and last night, her lady-in-waiting Erzebet of Arad col-lapsed and now lies in a stupor that—" She stopped, glanced over her shoulder. "Say nothing of this to anyone, not now. It would be an ill thing to speak of death with a birth not yet sanctified." She indi-cated the benches where they would soon sit. "You, and all the Hun-garians sent to be in the Konige's Court, will be allowed to sit toward the front. And you will be permitted to visit the Konige before the Bohemians." There was a glint of satisfaction in her green eyes. Then, mischievously, she added, "Did you get any sleep, Comes?"

"Very little," he told her.

"You were awake, then?"

"Most of the night," he said. "The bells roused me not long after dawn."

"As they did all Praha." She looked directly into his face, her feline expression both satisfied and anticipatory. "It is hardly sur-prising. Every church in the city is sounding the news," said Rozsa as she ducked her head before going to greet Gazsi of Raab and his apprentices.

Hovarth Pisti of Buda and four of his apprentices were already seated in the second row of benches. He raised his hand. "Comes. Well met. A happy occasion."

"Certainly," said Rakoczy, noticing that the tapestry-weaver was wearing three impressive rings, gifts from Konige Kunigunde, as well as a gold chain-and-pendant given him by Episcopus Fauvinel.

"So restrained," Hovarth Pisti murmured to Geza, who sat immediately beside him. "Exile, as you recall. But he is richer than most of the nobles of Praha put together."

"He paid for our hostelries on the road," Geza said, just a little louder.

"Without complaint," added Bartal.

"For the pleasure of Konig Bela," said Rakoczy, not raising his voice, but making certain that Hovarth could hear him. "It is my honor to serve Konig Bela and his granddaughter."

"And now you serve two Konigs; which of them benefits the most—Bela or Otakar?" Hovarth said. "An expensive business, even for you."

"Why be troubled with such concerns on this happy day?" Rakoczy could sense the rancor in Hovarth and was determined to difuse it.

"Yes, why, when you have a rich gift to give, and the thanks of the Konige for your trouble." He motioned to his apprentices. "Our tapestry will take until spring to complete, and we will have to labor well into the night until it is done. It is a large project, and a complex one: an allegory of faith triumphant."

Rakoczy was glad that the jewels he would present to the Konige were safely in his wallet; he nodded to the tapestry-weavers. "Your gift will be the more treasured for the effort you expend to make it. Your skills are well-known and your work is highly regarded everywhere. Your tapestries will adorn Vaclav Castle for all ages to come."

"Unless they are ruined. Jewels don't become ruined." He scowled. "How long do you think the Episcopus will be with the Konige?"

"I have no idea," Rakoczy said with utter candor. "Our thanks-giving Mass will begin soon enough." He turned away from Hovarth Pisti, and was surprised to see Kravar Jurg, Pan of Kravar, motioning to him; he had met the young nobleman no more than three times, and this sudden show of bonhomie struck Rakoczy as strange, but he moved toward the Pan in the blue-and-red cotehardie. "A happy day for Bohemia."

"It could be happier," said Kravar Jurg, moving aside to give Rakoczy some room among the benches. "The Konig was expecting a son."

"A shame that he must be disappointed," said Rakoczy.

"Do you think so? that he must be disappointed?" The young man chuckled, then stopped. "I forgot, you're one of the Hungarians, aren't you?"

"Not precisely; I am from the eastern end of the Carpathians, where my fief is located," said Rakoczy. "Mine is a very old House."

"I thought your accent isn't quite like the rest of them." He looked toward the door. "Monks are coming. We'd best be seated." He took the end of the bench where he had been standing. "Join me, Comes?"

Becoming more curious at Pan of Kravar's geniality, Rakoczy sat down next to him and prepared for the coming Mass.

Text of a letter from Rakoczy Ferancsi, Comes Santu-Germaniu, at Praha, Bohemia, to Frater Sandor, private scribe to Konig Bela, at Kalocsa, Hungary, written in Latin code on vellum and carried by private courier; delivered sixteen days after it was written.

To the loyal and upright Hieronymite monk, Frater Sandor, the greetings of Rakoczy Ferancsi, Comes Santu-Germaniu, on the ninth day of September in the Lord's Year 1269, with the trust that all information in these pages will be imparted to Konig Bela as promptly as circumstances will allow.

To the most excellent Konig Bela of Hungary,

It is my duty to tell you that Konige Kunigunde has, on the 5th day of September, been delivered of a daughter to be named Agnethe of Bohemia, who will be presented to the people of Praha tomorrow, and her name entered in the role of Bohemia's royal lineage. I have seen your granddaughter twice and I can assure you that she is properly formed and active in her movements. She has been given to the Konige's wetnurse, and all of the Konige's ladies have been given their orders for watching over the infant.

The Konige's older daughter, Kunigunde of Bohemia, because she is little more than four, is unhappy to have to share the attention of the Konige's Court with her new sister, and has taken to behaving objectionably toward the Court ladies. She struck her body-servant yesterday and was given stale bread for her supper. Children are often jealous in this way, and in time the rancor will pass, but for now, you may expect reports that single out the Little Royal's bad behavior. If a companion could be found for her—her own age or a little older—most of her antics would likely cease. Perhaps one of her cousins could be spared for the task? If not a cousin, then the child of one of your vassal-lords?

All this is favorable, but there are two matters that are not: first, your granddaughter has been struck with melancholy, which sometimes comes upon women after giving birth, but this shows no signs of lifting, and may be deepening. Her labor was long, but she has rested from that. She has yet to show any sign of concern for her new daughter. As much as she wanted a son, her distress is known, and I am troubled that she is not willing to hold her newborn namesake. I have spoken with Klotild of Jilish to see if there are any herbs that might lessen the Konige's misery, but she has nothing to recommend. If it pleases you, Konig Bela, I will ask Episcopus Fauvinel to say Masses for her restoration, or seek any other service that you would want performed on your behalf.

The other information I have to impart is cause for grief and distraint: your kinswoman Erzebet of Arad died yesterday evening after falling into a profound lethargy that could not be ended, although there were several attempts made to bestir her. She had been declining for some time, wracked by pain in her guts and joints, by failing appetite, and, in the last month, rashes on the skin. She had become so pale that she seemed translucent, and her eyes were sunken in her head, but were luminous. Frater Lovre, who attended on Erzebet in her illness, declared it was heated guts due to bilious humors that killed her, but I must tell you that I fear she has been poisoned. For that reason, I urge you to provide more protection for the Hungarians at the Konige's Court, for if one of the Konige's Court can be murdered, so others might be. May my fears be groundless, but since I have them, I am duty-bound to tell you of them. If you would like me to send a report to Frater Morcs so that he may assess the factors of Erzebet's death and submit his conclusions in its regard, I will do so. As an apothecary, Frater Morcs is familiar with the nature of poisons and can therefore lend his knowledge to Erzebet's case, and his advice must be given full regard. If he finds that I have no cause for alarm, I will bow to his wisdom.

I have acquitted my charged obligation to you, Konig Bela, and will continue to do so for as long as it pleases you that I should. All I ask is that you not forget that all you have required of me in Praha thus far I have done to the limits you have placed upon me. For the sake of the pledge you have made to Santu-Germaniu, I implore that you recall your good-will and your probity on behalf of my land and my vassals.

> *Rakoczy Ferancsi, Comes Santu-Germaniu*
> *(his sigil, the eclipse)*

2

Where there was sunlight there was warmth, but in the shade the first whispers of winter lurked, their chill brushing shivers onto skin and snapping color into the faces of the members of the Konige's Court; in the waning afternoon the shadows lengthened, deepening their touch, and the Konige's courtiers began to struggle to stay warm. Four elaborate pavilions stood in the broadest swath of light, with dozens of men and women wandering between them; in the space at the center of the four a large fire was being laid, and cooks were preparing to spit-broil the game that had been killed that day, while a group of musicians played just outside the closed silken door of Konige Kunigunde's pavilion. Three Trinitarian monks hovered near the entrance to the pavilion, seeking alms for the poor and the Church.

"She has been weeping most of the day," Csenge of Somogy said to Rakoczy Ferancsi in Magyar as he tuned his new Frankish lyre; they were in the alley between the Konige's pavilion and the one of Pan Kravar Jurg. "I hope you can provide her some relief. Something must be done before the Konig arrives."

"And I, as well, hope that my efforts can help her," said Rakoczy, testing the bass string for a third time, then twisting the tuning peg to bring it up to pitch.

"Sing her Hungarian songs, ones she'll know. I think she's been homesick. You could help her to—" She gnawed at her lower lip before flinging out her hands in a show of helplessness. "If only she had had a son, she wouldn't be so downcast. Who can blame her, though? Married almost eight years and only two daughters to show for it!"

"The Episcopus says her daughter is God's Will." Rakoczy plucked at the other eleven strings, taking care to tune them sweetly.

"Then God has been cruel to her, and the Episcopus knows it. The Konig must feel betrayed, to have a second daughter." She shuddered. "Not even the Konige is proof against his ire. She has failed him in the most dreadful way a woman can fail a man." She took the hem of her sleeve and wiped her eyes.

"Surely adultery is a greater failure," Rakoczy said. "Konige Kunigunde has faithfully given him this child. That she is a daughter may disappoint Konig Otakar, but it is hardly a failure: Agnethe is alive and properly formed. She feeds well, and her cry is hearty."

"But the Konig needs a son."

Rakoczy bit back a question that buzzed in his mind, for expressing more approval of the Konige above that of the Konig in these circumstances would be dangerous sentiments, especially for an exile. He looked at the large, red pavilion and said, "How many are with her?" It was a question often asked these days, and Csenge thought nothing of his inquiry.

"Three ladies-in-waiting, two dwarves, and six slaves, and those she has invited into her presence; how many of them are with her now, I have no idea," she replied. "There would be four ladies, but Rozsa of Borsod has been sent for by her husband, and the Konige has released her to go to him. If she doesn't return, she will have to be replaced, as will Erzebet of Arad. Two new ladies in the spring—it will be difficult until then, without Erzebet and Rozsa. The Konige misses them both." A faint flicker of supposition shone in her eyes, fading rapidly when her announcement got no more reaction from Rakoczy than a shake of his head. "As do we all."

"It is sad that Erzebet of Arad is dead and will never return here," he said carefully. "For Rozsa, it is probably better to travel now than later in the autumn. The rains will start shortly, and then it will be too hard to be abroad. Muddy roads make for trouble." He touched his lyre and this time was pleased with what he heard.

"As the Konig knows; the army will leave the front shortly."

Imbolya of Heves walked by, resplendent in a bleihaut of pale-green Damascus silk worked in a pattern of acanthus leaves, a large pitcher of honied wine in her hands; she nodded to her cousin but said nothing.

"And Rozsa's husband will be at Kaposvar before the Konig comes to Praha." Rakoczy waited for Csenge to speak.

"Rozsa won't be able to return until spring, when her husband once more follows the Konig into battle." This time her scrutiny was pronounced. "She will not be here before the Equinox. Unless she becomes pregnant, which will probably result that she remain in Hungary at Kaposvar."

"Among her own people, who will care for her," he said, more because it was the prudent response than because he believed it.

"Would it bother you if she became pregnant?" Csenge asked, her eyes fixed on his.

"Why should it?"

"The rumor is that you might care," Csenge said as pointedly as she dared.

"For Rozsa's sake, certainly," he agreed. "But you imply more, do you not?" His tone was light and sardonic.

"And if a child should come in the spring, what then?" Csenge lifted her chin in triumph. "She boasted that she had the sweetest lover in all the world."

"Then she is a fortunate woman," said Rakoczy and struck a chord, listening to its harmony with satisfaction.

"Proud of yourself, are you?" Csenge challenged.

Realizing his risk, Rakoczy took a chance, asking calmly, "Did she say I was that lover—by name?"

"Of course not. But we know. 'A man from my own country who is not brute, who gives me the pleasure I seek,' whomelse could it be?"

"There are a good number of Hungarians in the Konige's Court," he reminded her. "Have you considered them?"

"Most are artisans and Guildsmen: the rest are monks and priests—not to say that all of the clergy are chaste. You are the only Court noble who is not on campaign with the Konig. You are the one who is an oddity." She sounded slightly less sure of herself.

"Mightn't one of the others be the person she praised? And might she have misled you about her lover—if she truly had a lover." His demeanor was so calm that Csenge began to doubt her own convictions.

"The Konige would not tolerate having a lady-in-waiting who disgraced her husband," she said thoughtfully.

"Did she say that she disgraced her husband with her lover?" he countered, wondering what Rozsa had told the other ladies-in-waiting; how much had been boasting and how much had been simple truth? He thought back to Sophronia in Byzantium, who boasted of her multitude of lovers, often in great detail, and never had any. "Sometimes lovers are more dreams than flesh."

"No; she said that he—"

He held up his hand. "It is not appropriate for you to tell me her confidences. You are her confidante."

"Even priests gossip," Csenge said, her eyes narrowed. "But if you aren't interested—" She shrugged. "We will see what we may, in the fullness of time."

"If she becomes pregnant—if she delivers in the autumn next year there will be no question of her fidelity, which will still all the salacious rumors, and will restore her good name," he said calmly. "If she is delivered about this time, or in early October, there will be no doubt." He nodded as if to end their confrontation. "When we will all wish her a healthy, sound child."

"She said she wants to come back to the Konige's Court, which she won't do if she has an infant," Csenge said, looking away as a shower of sparks rose from the central fires.

"If her husband wants a child, and it arrives next autumn . . ."

He let the rest of his thoughts go unspoken, wondering as he did what was uppermost in Rozsa's mind: her dislike of Notay Tibor of Kaposvar or the power having a child would give her? A son would enhance her prestige and importance to her husband that she presently lacked, and that might be sufficient to keep her at Kaposvar, or would her enjoyment of Kunigunde's Court outweigh her yearning for position within the Notay House?

Csenge sniffed. "As you say, if her husband wants a *legitimate* child . . ."

In the ensuing silence he ducked his head to Csenge. "I should go to the Konige."

"So you should," Csenge said, stepping aside to allow him to pass.

The flap of Kunigunde's pavilion held a large embroidered golden sun upon it, a reminder of Bohemia's wealth as well as a token of hope for the Konige's improved happiness. Inside there were three braziers providing light and perfumed smoke for the nine people attending on Konige Kunigunde, who lay on a Byzantine couch, a soft goat-hair blanket thrown over her legs. She was dressed in a dark-blue silken bleihaut over a peach-colored linen chainse; a collar of gold studded with jewels lay slightly askew on her chest. Her gorget was white and her veil was a muted shade of red. Wisps of dark auburn hair escaped from beneath her veil, slightly damp and clinging to her forehead and cheeks, accentuating the look of fatigue that had taken hold of her. She gave a negligent wave to Rakoczy as he went down on one knee to her.

"Dear Royal," he said, and held out a small white-leather pouch. "Something to brighten your spirits, I hope."

"You're too good to me, Comes; you have adorned me with riches beyond any other but the Konig himself, and always with grace and courtesy," she said in Bohemian with a strong Magyar accent. "What have you hidden in here?" She pulled on the silk cords that held it closed, releasing their knot and holding up the pouch so that she could look down into it. "Ah. What stones are these?"

"Amethysts and rubies: three of each, and a single peridot," he said.

"You're too generous to me. I don't deserve such tribute, though I am thankful to you for your generosity." She handed the pouch and its contents to Milica of Olmutz without a second glance. Again she gazed at Rakoczy, lacing and unlacing her fingers. "They tell me that beyond your pretty gems, you're to sing to me. Are you going to do that?"

"If it would please you, dear Royal, I will," said Rakoczy, rising and touching the strings of his lyre so lightly that only the ghost of a sound issued from them. "Tell me what you would like to hear and I will try to summon just such a song for you."

"That's most acceptable," the Konige said without enthusiasm. "You really are most kind to me, kinder than many who would have more cause to want my good opinion and my . . . I have never been so . . . I shall not forget you in years to come." She spoke by rote, her eyes on the middle distance.

"What do you want me to sing, dear Roy—" he began after she had remained silent for some little time.

"Something new!" she said in a burst of brittle petulance that seemed almost on the brink of weeping. "Everyone sings the songs I've known all my life. For the love of Hungary, Comes! sing me something *different*. I *know* the Hungarian songs."

"Would another language than Magyar suffice?" he asked, for he knew songs in all five languages spoken in Hungary.

She laughed once, deeply sad. "Do you know anything from far away?"

Melodies from Pharaonic Egypt, from China, from the Asian Steppes, from Hispania, from the north of Gaul, from Tunis, from Cyprus, from Roma, rang in his memory; he considered them all, trying to decide which would serve the Konige best. Finally he lifted the lyre. "Here is something Greek, from long ago. It was sung in Corinth when I heard it, by a market-slave who said he had it from a country youth." That had been more than fourteen and a half centuries ago, but the plaintive song remained alive in his recollections. He touched the lyre and began in the ancient dialect of the region:

> *Morning is coming, the stars vanish from the sky,*
> *The lambs are calling on the hillside and birds waken,*
> *Their songs blending with the bleating sheep.*
> *I will follow the flock through the mountains*
> *To the place where my heart longs to be:*
> *Woe to those who do not know the call of love,*
> *Alas to those who deny the rites of Aphrodite.*
> *Tonight I shall lay with my beloved in sweet grass*
> *And drink the wine of our joy; nothing will keep us*
> *From each other, and nothing will break our happiness*
> *But the lure of sleep and the charms of Morpheus,*
> *My only rival and my greatest friend.*

As the last few notes plucked from the lyre's strings faded, Konige Kunigunde nodded her approval. "That was very pretty, Comes. What did it mean?"

"It was the lament of a shepherd who longs to be with the one he loves. He expects to see his love soon." He noticed the Konige wince, and he went on as smoothly as he could. "Is there something else you would like to hear?" Rakoczy saw that Imbolya of Heves was bringing him a goblet. "This is most gracious, but it is not my custom, as you know—I do not drink wine. I am sorry to refuse so mannerly a gift, but for those of my blood . . ."

"So you have told me," Konige Kunigunde said from her couch. "I was hoping you might change . . ." She sighed. "Very well, Imbolya, present the wine to Hovarth Pisti, with my thanks for the progress he and his apprentices are making on their tapestry."

"Dear Royal," said Imbolya with a courtisy. She carried the goblet to the four men in the far corner of the pavilion.

Konige Kunigunde looked up suddenly, her face brightening for the first time. "Can you sing me a children's song, one I have never heard?" She pointed to Rakoczy. "You say you have traveled a long way and learned many things. Surely you must know a children's song?"

He knew several, but he took a little time to answer. "I know one from the Eastern Realms that might please you."

"Then play it for me, Comes." She stretched and did her best to smile at him. "If I like it, you may teach it to me."

"As you wish, dear Royal." He ducked his head, positioned his lyre, then began in the Chinese of the Old Capital, of seven centuries past:

> *One rat, two cups of rice*
> *One hen, two eggs to brood*
> *One dog, two lambs to guard*
> *One fish, two flies to catch*
> *One pig, two wallows to lie in*
> *One horse, two apples to eat*
> *One man, two sons to follow him*
> *Happiness is everywhere.*

"What does it say?" the Konige asked when he moved his lyre aside. "It sounds like nonsense to me."

"It is a counting song," said Rakoczy, aware that several of the courtiers inside the pavilion had disliked the unfamiliar Chinese melody.

"What manner of tongue was that?" asked Pader Stanislas, approaching Rakoczy. "Why did you sing such a dreadful thing to the Konige?"

"It is a song for children in the city of Lo-Yang, in distant China." He thought back to the Year of Yellow Snow and all that had happened during his return to the West in that desperate time, and how few children had wanted to sing during those hard years.

"It isn't Christian," Pader Stanislas pronounced, and turned toward Kunigunde. "You should not ask for such entertainment, dear Royal. You do not know what is being said. Foreign songs could open your soul to the devils that every day seek for ways to ruin Christians."

The Konige crossed herself. "I hadn't thought a children's song, no matter where it came from, would be so dangerous."

"You have only his word that it is a children's song. It might be anything from a curse to a spell, since only he can tell you what it says." The priest glowered at Rakoczy. "Konig Bela exiled you to the Konige's Court for some serious reason. I believe it would be fitting to learn what it might be." He lifted his head, his ragged beard standing out from his chin like an accusing finger. He sighed explosively. "I may have to make inquiry."

"You may do as you like," said Rakoczy, "but I swear to you on my . . . on my soul, that the song was nothing more than a children's song."

"A potent oath," said the priest, measuring Rakoczy with his eyes, seeking for flaws. "If you have endangered your soul in this oath, then it will be the worse for you when the Last Trumpet sounds."

One of the dwarves, a squat man of possibly twenty years with short black hair and a hooked nose, came up to Pader Stanislas. "Your pardon, Pader," he said with a deep bow; his speech was flavored with the accent of Antioch. "I have traveled with jugglers from China, and their children sang just such a song."

Pader Stanislas regarded the dwarf suspiciously. "Do you swear by the Holy Trinity that you speak the truth?"

"By the Holy Trinity, by the Cross, by my hope of Heaven, I swear," he said, his face angled up so that Pader Stanislas could see him clearly as he crossed himself.

"I must be satisfied, then, and I thank you for your vow. You have done a charitable act in telling me," Pader Stanislas declared, giving the dwarf a severe look. "I will accept that the song was free of malign intent, and that it poses no harm to the Konige. There is a severe penalty for false witness, and if I should learn that you dishonor Our Lord . . ." He left the threat hanging and looked from the dwarf to Rakoczy. "And, Comes, see that you sing no more songs to the Konige that are not in Magyar, Bohemian, or Latin." He made the sign of the cross over the dwarf but did not bless Rakoczy; returning to the small table next to the largest brazier, he pointedly ignored the foreigner.

"Thank you, Tahir," said Rakoczy softly in the Antioch dialect.

"I am glad to be of service," said the dwarf, turning away.

"Did you really travel with Chinese jugglers?" Rakoczy asked him before he moved off.

The dwarf laughed aloud. "No. But that kind of sing-song melody with much repetition is in children's songs everywhere."

Overhearing this foreign exchange, Pader Stanislas was rigid with disapproval. "More curses," he exclaimed.

"Not curses, good Pader," said Rakoczy. "That is the tongue of the city of Antioch." He bowed to the juggler. "Tahir does me honor to converse with me in so elegant a language."

Pader Stanislas folded his arms. "I am going to pay close attention to you, Comes. You are too knowing."

"As you wish," said Rakoczy with a fleeting smile.

"Foreigners can be dangerous," Pader Stanislas said.

"So they can, as can those native to this place," Rakoczy said, feeling more isolated than he had felt since he returned from the Land of Snows, more than fifty years ago. As this desolation went through him, some portion of it must have showed in his eyes, for Pader Stanislas leaned toward him.

"How have you been touched by retribution? Is that what makes you so haughty in your ways?"

"Not in the way you suppose." He paused, recalling SGyi Zhel-ri in the distant Yellow Hat Bya-grub Me-long ye-shys lamasery. "In my recent travels I met a most learned youth, a boy who appeared to possess great knowledge and compassion. He had much wisdom."

"A holy child?"

"A monk," said Rakoczy, careful not to fall into the doctrinal trap Pader Stanislas was setting for him.

"Ha." The priest shook his head. "Vanity, it is vanity to suppose that any child but Our Lord could have those attributes."

"I said appeared to possess. I do not know enough of faith to judge these things." He averted his gaze and saw that Konige Kunigunde was weeping. "Your pardon, Pader, but I believe the Konige needs—"

"I will attend to Konige Kunigunde," Pader Stanislas announced. "Such grief requires Christian care, and the consolation of religion." He went to the Konige's couch, his hands clasped in the anticipation of prayer. Everyone in the pavilion watched him silently as he knelt down. "My Konige. Tell me what causes you to weep?"

It took the Konige a little time to gather her thoughts. "Erzebet died. I should have been the one. Why did God take her and leave me to this misery?"

"God does not give us to know all His reasons, just as a father does not tell his children his reasons for his rules; acquiescence is required of us, His children, though His purpose may be beyond our understanding." Pader Stanislas blessed her. "My daughter, my Konige, you must not doubt that God's Will is in all that happens. God has claimed your lady-in-waiting. You have a second daughter, though you sought a son, yet it is essential that you submit to His mission for you. Your daughter will show her purpose in time. For now, resign yourself in true faith to your circumstances, for it is fitting that you are obedient to Him."

Konige Kunigunde continued to cry. "I cannot, Pader; I ask God to restore me to contentment, but He has not answered my prayers."

"This melancholy is a sin, Konige. It shows that your faith is in danger of failing. I exhort you to restore your piety before you endanger your immortal soul." He rose to his feet, although she had not given him leave to do so. "Your obstinacy will bring about your damnation if you cling to your perversity."

Rakoczy watched the two, growing appalled at the eager excitement in the courtiers' faces. So many of them would rejoice if Kunigunde were declared a heretic. He knew that if he interrupted Pader Stanislas' incitation, he would find himself under more intense scrutiny than he had been before. After a moment, he began to play the *Pie Jesu* on his lyre, the sound so quiet that at first it was barely audible.

"Pray!" Pader Stanislas commanded. "Humble yourself before God's Majesty, and be restored to Him again!"

Milica of Olmutz began to sing the *Pie Jesu,* her soft, high voice penetrating the bustle of sounds from outside. Hovarth Pisti knelt and crossed himself; soon after, everyone inside the pavilion, with the exception of Padre Stanislas and Konige Kunigunde, were on their knees, and the melody of the *Pie Jesu* grew stronger. Even the Konige's Hungarian slaves genuflected, although most of them did not understand the Latin words, nor the cause of this sudden demonstration of religiosity.

"Pray, Konige!" The priest raised his hands in supplication.

As the hymn ended, Rakoczy got to his feet and ducked his head to Konige Kunigunde. "What more may I do for you, dear Royal?"

"You can leave me alone. All of you. I want time to myself." She spoke without heat, but there was no doubt that she was sincere in her dismissal.

"I will pray with you," Pader Stanislas said at his most solicitous.

"No, Pader. I must be alone." She made a motion with her hands that sent most of her Court and entertainers scurrying out of the pavilion; only Milica of Olmutz remained at her side.

"Thank you, Comes. Thank you, Pader," Konige Kunigunde said, wiping her eyes with her sleeve. "I will summon you again when the food is ready."

Rakoczy ducked his head and stepped out of the pavilion; a moment later Pader Stanislas followed him, glaring at him.

"This is your doing. I know it is your doing, Comes, and I will be wary of you, as I have pledged to be." To emphasize his point he spat at Rakoczy's feet, then walked away, leaving Rakoczy to stand by himself in the growing chill.

Text of a letter from Zenta Laszlo, Dux of Heves, at Heves in Hungary to his daughter, Imbolya of Heves, lady-in-waiting to

Konige Kunigunde, at Praha in Bohemia, written by Frater Tonku, scribe and Hieronymite monk, carried by private courier and delivered sixteen days after it was written.

To my most estimable daughter, Imbolya of Heves, the greetings of your father, Zenta Laszlo, Dux of Heves, on this, this first day of October in the 1269th year of Grace,

> *My dear child,*

> *In February you will be fifteen, and it will be time for you to be married. Mindful of my duty as your father, I have made inquiries of many Hungarian nobles with sons who would look kindly on an alliance with the House of Heves and the senior House of Zenta, which you embody. I have narrowed the possible husbands for you to four, and in the next months I will be at pains to determine who among them will most advance you in the world.*

> *You may prepare for marriage to take place not more than a year from now, unless the fighting grows more extensive, in which case it may be a year and a half at most until you are a bride. I am determined to see you bearing a child before you are sixteen. I will bring you back to Heves at the end of May so that you may participate in the arrangements for your nuptials. If you would like to spend a month at Santu-Antonia to pray for your happiness and many children, I know the Priora will be willing to have you visit; she has praised you for your learning and humility during the four years you lived there. At the time, I was thinking that you might turn nun, but I see now that God had another plan for you. Certainly there are nobles in Hungary who will see the advantage of a wife who reads and writes.*

> *If only your mother had lived to see this day. Your sisters and brothers have been informed of my intentions and their suggestions for worthy bridegrooms sought. Olya has already recommended her husband's brother as a one to be considered, and I have pledged to pursue the matter, although Konig Bela does not approve of too many alliances among two families, for fear they might take up arms against him. Still, I will present him with a*

reasonable list and I will be guided by his wisdom in whom I choose. Once I have secured the Konig's consent to two of my recommended sons-in-law, I will contact the families and determine what they would want to endorse the union. When we have agreed, I will inform you which man you will marry. You should know by Easter unless the winter is long and so hard that travel is slowed to the point of stopping.

I pray you will conduct yourself honorably at Konige Kunigunde's Court, and that no scandal will attach to your name, for such calumny—as calumny such repute must be—could ruin any hope of a worthy husband. Young though you are, you are as sensible as a woman might be. You are aware of what you owe your family, and what advantage you can bring to our House. That you are a lady-in-waiting to Konige Kunigunde speaks well of you, but I urge you not to taint your duty at Praha. In these war-like times, securing noble husbands is not readily done, and we need to preserve the most laudable reputation for you so that you will have the best opportunity to marry well.

With my most affectionate greetings and my fatherly blessings, I ask you to make ready to leave Praha at the end of winter. I will, myself, inform Konige Kunigunde of these coming changes so that she will not be left without sufficient ladies-in-waiting to support her and her Court. Be grateful that God has favored you in this way, my daughter. May you have many healthy sons to bring honor to our House for generations to come.

> Zenta Laszlo
> Dux of Heves
> (his mark and his seal)

by Frater Tonku, Hieronymite scribe

3

Counselor Smiricti stood in the middle of the main hall of Mansion Belcrady, nodding his approval. "Very fine. Very fine. Comes, you have done very well. All that's lacking is a mirror, like the Konige has. The sprays of pine-boughs over the doors are a good touch; the Episcopus will approve, if he sees them. Any noble in Praha would be proud of such a Nativity display. The Konig will be gratified that you show him such distinction." He straightened the front of his marten-fur-lined huch and rubbed his gloved hands vigorously as he strode to the fireplace, where two large logs were blazing away. His boots were wet, and the front of his soft cap, but the rest of his garments were dry.

"You are most kind to me, Counselor." Rakoczy followed a few steps behind him, elegant in a dark-blue woolen bleihaut over a cream-colored silken chainse. He was curious about the reason for the Counselor's visit, for usually he did not call unannounced, but he knew better than to ask directly; with a little bow he said, "Be welcome, Counselor Smiricti." He clapped his hands, and when Barnon came, he asked, "Is the withdrawing room ready for our guest?"

"Pacar is finishing heating the wine; it will be ready shortly," said Barnon, ducked his head, and withdrew.

Smiricti heard this. "The delay is unimportant; I came unexpected, and so must be satisfied by whatever you give me. Yet I'm pleased to be out of the wet. The first rain of the autumn! What a miserable day; it isn't yet noon!" He made a sound between a laugh and a cough as he began to pull off his gloves. "It's a pity it turned cold so quickly. October is only nine days old and it's as if it were November. I was sure we'd have another month of cooling before this kind of—" He gestured toward the shuttered windows, and the rush of sleet against the wood. "This is likely to slow the Konig's return. The army cannot move far in such rain."

"It does seem that he will be detained because of it," Rakoczy said in his most neutral voice, "assuming the rain has spread through all Bohemia."

"We were going to send a civic escort out to meet the Konig and his men a day's ride from the city, and bring them back with buisines and tabors, but in this weather, it's impossible. The musicians would surely get lost, and the water would ruin their instruments." Smiricti chuckled. "Not even your lyre could brave this storm."

"Have any couriers arrived to tell you when Otakar might be here?" Rakoczy inquired, anticipating the answer.

"Not for six days, and then the weather was fine. At that time the courier said it would be ten days until he reached Praha. But now, who can say it will be four or six or eight days?" He stared at Rakoczy and shoved his gloves into his sleeve. "Have you had any word from your fief? Any news of how things are on the roads?"

"Not for some while," he said, being deliberately vague. "Besides, the Konig is more to the south; my fief is more to the east. Any report I might have would be many days old, and in the wrong quarter of Hungary."

"Surely there is rain in Hungary as well as in Bohemia," said Smiricti.

"Probably, but there is no way to know how severe the storm is away from here. What is a downpour in Praha may be a mizzle in Pressburg," Rakoczy said. "At least there is not likely to be much snow except on the highest peaks. That will allow travel to continue for a time."

"How long do you think it will be until travel stops for the winter?"

"You know as much as I do: what do you think?" Rakoczy replied, again feeling that the Counselor was evading.

"Oh, you know more than I, Comes, being a foreigner with

interests in other lands. You deal with traders and traveling scholars—we all know this of you. You know what they have done, why they have been here, and where they have gone. What have you heard from them?" Smiricti asked. "The farmers at market yesterday said that there are more travelers abroad just now, and they were expecting the weather to hold."

"That was yesterday," said Rakoczy. "This came up last night."

"How could no one have known it was coming?" Smiricti stamped his foot. "Not even the monks expected it, nor my wife's mother, whose hands hurt her before the weather turns."

Rakoczy considered his answer carefully. "This storm must have traveled more rapidly than most do, and so the signs came at almost the same time as the torrent we're having just now. High winds—they pass quickly."

"The wind damaged the roofs of some of the older houses in the old part of the city, and ruined a few of the hovels outside the walls." He scowled toward the windows again as if he could see through the wood to the slanting, biting, icy rain. "May it end soon so that the damage can be repaired before the Konig arrives." He clicked his tongue as if he had a new idea. "You wouldn't know anything about the weather coming up, would you?"

"The last trader I've had business with arrived the day before yesterday, and he said he had encountered rain three days since, to the north of here, which might not be part of this storm. He is staying at the sign of the Golden Ram, if you wish to talk with him." The Polish trader had carried heavy woolen cloth as well as twine and thread in his train of four mules; he had offered to trade for medicaments. "He said the weather had been windy, but made no mention of encountering rain since he left Erdna. I haven't spoken to a traveling scholar in over a month."

"It won't be necessary to ask the trader; he was here when the storm arrived," said Smiricti. "Let's hope it passes rapidly and fair weather returns." He extended his hands to the fire and rubbed them. "Episcopus Fauvinel has asked all Praha to pray for better weather and the safety of Otakar and his men."

"Better weather, and good hunting. The civic feast will need deer and boar as well as sheep and hogs and cattle."

"Amen to that, Comes. At least we had a fine harvest." Smiricti sighed. "Which has only increased the number of rats in the city."

"Where there is grain stored, you will have rats," said Rakoczy, thinking how busy the twenty cats on the Mansion grounds had been of late. He had seen the same in Egypt over the centuries, at the temple on the Irrawaddy where the rats raided rice paddies without fear, in Natha Suryarathas where the rats were treated as sacred, in Tunis where he had slept among them while he was a slave, in the Polish marshes where he had sought refuge . . .

Smiricti cleared his throat. "It would displease the Counselors to have the Konig see rats when he returns to Vaclav Castle."

"I can understand their concerns," he said, thinking that the Counselor had finally arrived at the purpose of his visit, but aware that it would be rude to ask outright.

He shifted uneasily, coughing nervously. "I understand from your staff that you have methods to keep rats away from—" He waved his hand to take in the main hall. "You have the old rushes swept out and new rushes laid once a month. That is trouble and expense, but you do it. Is that one of your ways to keep down the number of rats?"

"It is. The rushes are swept out, the floors washed, oiled with rosemary, and a dozen or so cats are brought in to catch what they can." He would have preferred to have no rushes at all, but that would have given rise to more questions about him, as well as the disapproval of his servants. "The cats have run of the place at night."

"Would you be willing to give your methods to the Council so that we may be free of rats when the Konig comes?" He tugged at his ear, a sure sign of nervousness. "The Council is willing to pay you for—"

"There are several methods I use; you are welcome to them all, at no cost to the Council, but I should warn you that one of them requires the use of a poison." He read the ambivalence in Smiricti's face. "What is wrong about that?"

Smiricti looked even more uncomfortable. "The Episcopus says it is vanity to take such life, and a sin to attack any of God's creatures; he himself does not eat meat except for lamb at Easter. He says that God gave us the task of ruling over all creatures."

"Does that mean that the Episcopus thinks that rats are answerable to God? If they are so dear to God, then surely they would be more prominent in Scripture, and there would be verses to explain their merits." He shook his head. "I have heard the Pope say that rats are a plague of Satan's doing, and that they must be purged or devils will come to work upon men." That the Pope who had said it had been dead for five centuries he kept to himself.

Smiricti considered this. "I will inform the Counselors on this point, and the Episcopus as well. The suit of the Beggars' Guild is still unresolved. None of us wants to act against Episcopus Fauvinel, but surely so many rats as now run in our streets and houses are a danger to the city." He took a long breath. "So you know something of poisons. How much do you know? Or would you rather not say?" He would have asked Rakoczy more, but went silent as Barnon came in with a tray on which stood an earthenware jug and cup as well as a small loaf of bread, sliced into three pieces. "Ah. Most kind; most kind."

"The front withdrawing room, Comes, or the rear?" Barnon asked.

"The front. It is warmer," said Rakoczy. "And when you are done here, will you find Hruther and ask him to come to me?"

"Of course, Comes," said Barnon, going toward the front withdrawing room, his tray held high. "Will you want a meal for the Counselor?"

"Not this time," said Smiricti, speaking directly to Rakoczy, as if the Comes had asked the question. "I am expected home shortly, to dine with my family. On another occasion, it would be my honor."

"We will arrange it," said Rakoczy, leading the way to the withdrawing room

"I will put the tray on the low table," Barnon announced, and set action to his words.

"Thank you, Barnon," said Rakoczy, and noticed that Barnon no longer winced at this unusual courtesy. He nodded to the up-holstered chair. "If you would sit, Counselor?"

"Most gracious," said Smiricti.

"And let me offer you some wine," he went on, taking the earthenware jug and pouring out a good measure of hot, spiced wine into the cup.

"It's a pity you don't drink. Your wines are delicious," said Smiricti as he took the cup and drank. He smiled as the warmth went through him.

"I thank you for your satisfaction," said Rakoczy. He went to poke the log in the fireplace that served both withdrawing rooms; sparks danced in the billowing smoke that rose from the log. "The chimney wants cleaning," he said to himself.

"Better to clean in the summer than the winter," said Smiricti. "There's better weather and the fires aren't needed, so the cleaner can take his time."

"The chimney might not wait so long to catch fire, given how poorly it draws." He thought of the bake-house flue with the rats' nest inside it. It had taken the smallest of the scullions to get the mess cleaned out, and the boy was ill for a week afterward.

"Half the chimneys in Praha smoke like yours," said Smiricti, his words muffled by the section of bread he had popped into his mouth.

"Is there someone you can recommend?" Rakoczy asked, coming back to the table and sitting in the X-shaped chair across from Counselor Smiricti. "I would rather not subject one of my servants to the task."

"Ahil is known to be reliable, for all he's Bulgar; I've had him clean the flues in my house and they smoke much less now. He has two midgets who have worked for him many years; they know what they're doing," said Smiricti, chewing vigorously. "You can find him at the Artisans' Market."

"Thank you," said Rakoczy. He regarded Smiricti for a short while, trying to discern what more the Counselor wanted from him, for clearly he was circling another question. "I will prepare a list of the various ways I deal with rats and have it carried to your house this afternoon. Employ those methods you like." He paused, then took a chance. "Is there anything else I can do for you?"

"The Konige will be pleased that you have contributed so much to the coming festivities. And it is her intention to see that you have citation for your many generous gifts." Smiricti finished the wine in his cup, and made no protest when Rakoczy rose and filled it again. "She has remained melancholy, in spite of all we have done to help her to regain her spirits. Neither musicians nor jongleurs can brighten her heart for very long. The Episcopus himself has exhorted her for her lack of trust in God, yet she remains despondent."

"She was hoping for a son," Rakoczy reminded him.

"But God gave her a daughter. Undoubtedly He has reason for what He has done. The Episcopus and Pader Stanislas have pressed her to embrace Agnethe." He shrugged philosophically. "It would do her a world of good to bow to God's Will. The Episcopus is right about that. She must not continue to languish as she has done. There should be something that will restore her to her former spirits." He took another section of the bread and began to chew it, more slowly than before.

"It is unfortunate, particularly for the Konige," said Rakoczy.

"If there is something—someone—who could alleviate her misery, you would tell me who or what that is, wouldn't you?"

"If I did know, I would." Rakoczy felt more guarded.

"Pader Stanislas has recommended she drink the blood of merry animals—lambs and puppies, or perhaps songbirds. The Episcopus is considering it."

"That could be risky," said Rakoczy, his manner deliberately thoughtful. "Merriment is not the only virtue of those animals, and what the Konige takes could have results that would not please her or the Konig."

Smiricti nodded, then asked, "What kind of poison do you use on rats?"

Realizing that Smiricti would say nothing more about Konige Kunigunde, he answered, "I use wolfsbane and syrup of poppies mixed with grain and formed into cakes, which I put into boxes with holes in them to allow the rats to enter. They die with little pain. Their bodies must be disposed of quickly, to keep the dogs and cats from eating their deadly flesh." He spoke readily enough, though he could see suspicion in Smiricti's eyes. "It is best to put the boxes in places where rats gather—closets and cupboards and granaries. If you put the cakes where dogs or ferrets can find them, the animals may eat the cakes and die."

"Why not just put the cakes inside the rat-holes?" Smiricti's curiosity kept Rakoczy alert. "Why go to the trouble of a box?"

"I use the box for the same reason that I place them prudently—so that no other creature, except perhaps mice, will eat the cakes and die of them, inside the box," Rakoczy told him. "And any creature who might eat a dead rat will not be able to do so, and perish from it."

Unexpectedly, Smiricti grinned. "The Episcopus should approve that, if he approves killing the rats at all." He looked around, his eyes shining with speculation. "Is there such a box in this room?"

"No; most of my boxes are in the kitchen, the pantry, the bake-house, and the stable. I have two on the upper floor." He watched Smiricti finish off his second cup of wine and went to refill the cup, but was stopped as the Counselor held up his hand.

"You are most generous, Comes, but I have a way to go, and cannot linger much longer." He made a moue of regret. "The demands of the Council are with me, day and night, and the rain will not spare me."

"Are you afoot or do you have a carriage—"

"I'm walking. I have two men-at-arms to walk with me: they've gone to the servants' hall. They have my pluvial with them." He patted his huch. "That is why I'm dry." He rose, ducking his head to his host. "I will look forward to your methods for killing rats later today. The rain always brings them out in droves."

Rakoczy accompanied Smiricti to the door of the room and called for Barnon again. "There are two men-at-arms in—"

"—the servants' hall. I will tell them their master wishes to leave. Hruther is in your workroom, busy with the task you assigned him." He left without waiting to be dismissed, offering little more than a nod.

"Insolent fellow," Smiricti remarked.

"He is unaccustomed to my ways, and that makes him brusque. He has not been treated with much respect until now. There is no harm in him." Rakoczy escorted the Counselor into the entry hall, taking care not to rush him, and hoping the Counselor might give some sign of what his underlying purpose for his visit was. "When you learn when the Konig will arrive, will you be good enough to let me know? I want to be sure that Mansion Belcrady is ready for his return, with fir garlands hung from the walls."

"Yes, I will," said Smiricti, his attention on the half-completed mural by the door while he pulled on his gloves. "They say we may have flooding along the river if the rain persists."

"That has happened before," Rakoczy said.

"It is God's Will," Smiricti grumbled, then said more genially, "Well, the Konig will be back shortly. We will pray the rain ends and that no flood comes."

"Are you still planning the civic procession? If the weather remains wet, will you have the procession?" Rakoczy anticipated the answer.

"Of course we will have the procession, but we will wait until the skies clear and Otakar is here; the procession will take place. Even Episcopus Fauvinel has said it is a worthy deed." A loud thump on the door announced the arrival of Smiricti's escort; the Counselor nodded to Rakoczy. "I thank you again for receiving me and for your help." He was startled when Rakoczy opened the door for him. "Too much honor, Comes."

"Hardly an honor," Rakoczy said, taking note of the two bedraggled men-at-arms huddled on the steps. "Why should we all wait for Barnon to return and open the door?"

Smiricti reached for his dark-gray pluvial and tugged it on, raising the hood. "May God guard and save you, Comes."

"May He watch over you, Counselor," he said, and closed the door. He stood in the entry hall for a short while, his thoughts contending within him. With none of his questions resolved, he went back through the main hall to the stairs and climbed up to the floor above. At the door to his workroom he tapped twice before going in.

Hruther was near the athanor, his heavy dull-red cotehardie showing two large stains on the left sleeve. "I would have come, but it is almost cool, my master," he said in Imperial Latin. He nodded toward the beehive-shaped oven at the end of the room.

Rakoczy nodded, and spoke in the same tongue. "Before mid-afternoon we can remove the new jewels; I'll prepare a pouch to present to the Konige tomorrow. I will have more by the end of the month." He went to the fireplace and put two cut branches on the dying fire. "I have to supply the Council my various ways of killing rats. At least that is what Smiricti has requested."

"You think he may have had another purpose," Hruther said quietly; he came down toward the reading-table, a small stand with a tilted top and a lip to hold a book in place. "Do you know what that might be?"

"He seemed inordinately interested in my knowledge of poisons," said Rakoczy, his voice remote.

"Did he say why he was interested?" Hruther asked.

"He wants to kill rats. I pledged to supply him a list of the methods we use," Rakoczy said, making his way to the athanor and testing the heat-plate on the door; he pulled his hand back at once, shaking his fingers. "I may be seeing things in the shadows, but I have the sense that he is seeking something more from me than how to kill rats."

"What did he say that made you think so?" Hruther's austere features revealed nothing of his thoughts.

"There was no one thing, except that he dwelt on the details of how the poison is given, though I did offer him details." Rakoczy began to pace, his dark eyes clouded by worry. "I am fretful. It is as if my soul were itching, or it may be little more than that my mind is growing bored and restive with this place." He turned at the athanor and came back toward Hruther. "My aggravation may be nothing more than a sensation of frustration."

"You do not usually like imprisonment," Hruther observed. "Why should this be any different because the accommodations are amiable?"

"Imprisonment?" Rakoczy stopped moving and stared at him.

"Why yes," said Hruther calmly. "I've been mulling this over for a few months. Praha may be more pleasant than a lightless cell in Kara Khorum, or a barred hut in Tolosa, but you are still confined and constrained: you may not return to Santu-Germaniu without bringing war and rapine to your vassals; you may not leave this city without abandoning your people and your land to the vengeance of Konig Bela. You are bound here as if by chains; half the Konige's Court might as well be your jailers, so closely are you watched. So it is a prison."

Rakoczy considered this, and nodded. "I had not thought of my exile in that light." He folded his arms. "I have let myself become more captive by seeing faces in the shadows."

"Which may well be there," Hruther interjected.

"So they might," Rakoczy agreed. "No doubt there are some of those faces here in this household."

"Only two of the staff can read, and only one can write," Hruther reminded him.

"So if they spy, they spy for Konige Kunigunde, and give their information to other spies," said Rakoczy with a fatalistic nod.

"Unless there is someone from Konig Bela here at Court to whom they report, or a priest who keeps Episcopus Fauvinel clandestinely informed." He clapped his hands in exasperation. "Only one of the Konige's ladies-in-waiting reads—Imbolya of Heves. I was told that Erzebet of Arad could read and write." He looked toward the hearth. "Perhaps she had discovered something in her reading that was secret and that was why she was killed."

"Or one of the women was jealous of her and wanted her out of the way," Hruther suggested.

"That, too, is possible," Rakoczy allowed, his brows lifted to a sardonic angle. He went to the Persian chair that stood near the fireplace and sank into it. "Am I being foolish, do you think, or am I wise to be frightened."

Hruther was startled. "You rarely admit to fright."

"That does not mean I do not feel fear." He tapped his fingers on the arm of his chair. "But I cannot tell if being afraid in this place is sensible or mad."

"It may be both, given the way the Konige's Court functions," said Hruther, "as staying in Lo-Yang for as long as we did was mad and sensible." Their days in the old Chinese capital had been pleasant until the northern part of the Kingdom was threatened by the forces of Jenghiz Khan, when all foreigners had come under suspicion.

"But there, at least, we had been well-regarded for some years; here we have been mistrusted from the start."

"All the more reason for you to feel so discomfited," said Hruther. "If nothing else, you have powerful impositions upon you, restricting the possibilities you can address without hazard." He paused. "I assume you know that Barnon understands Hungarian."

"Oh, yes," said Rakoczy wearily. "I suppose that is why Counselor Smiricti recommended him to me. But I believe he watches me for the Council."

"Very likely," said Hruther, then added, "You've been unusually circumspect since we came here." He saw Rakoczy lift his brows. "You have offered very few medicaments to anyone beyond the treatments to make the wells safe in summer, so you will not draw any more attention to yourself than what Konig Bela requires of you. Your reluctance to provide the Konige and her Court with little more than songs and face-creams is so unlike you that if any of these courtiers knew you better, they would regard you askance for your refusal to treat the injured and ill."

"I would do so, but it would not be safe for me or those I treated: my jewels for the Konige are questionable enough." He slapped the arms of the chair. "They're ensorceled, all of them."

"The people follow their rulers, who are guided by the Church—what can you expect?"

"Precisely what is here," he said, his temper sharpening his words. "If it were possible to travel, even to Austria or Poland, I might be able to do more to help those who are suffering, give them remedies and comfort. But Konig Bela would not approve it, and he would not permit me to come any nearer to Hungary. I miss being able to study. I would like to have my books on medicinal plants with me, but they would be thought dangerous. Counselor Smiricti showed me that when he asked about poisoning rats."

"And they would have to be read and endorsed by the Episcopus," Hruther pointed out.

"True enough, and for what purpose I have studied these things would be called into question; it is awkward to have it known that I have knowledge of poisons. To be seen as someone who treats the sick with methods not approved by the Episcopus, who determines what is acceptable treatment for every malady, is dangerous enough, but since I use poisons as well, what treatment of mine could be trusted? The Episcopus would condemn my sovereign remedy because it is made from moldy bread, since mold is a sign of corruption and therefore cannot heal—which makes it worse if the medicament succeeds, for it compromises the Church in doing so." He shoved himself out of the chair and began once more to pace. "So I must keep from bringing more scrutiny on myself or face the consequences of it."

"You've been careful," said Hruther, alarm brightening his faded-blue eyes. "You have kept to the restrictions placed upon you."

"In most things," Rakoczy said heavily. "But not all. There is Rozsa of Borsod to consider."

"She isn't here any longer," Hruther said, trying to discern the cause for his worry.

"But she has not been completely discreet; think of what Csenge of Somogy said when she accosted me at the Konige's autumn festival; I told you about that. If Rozsa should start to . . . to reveal what she and I have done while at the Bohemian Court, I will be accused of seducing a noblewoman at the least."

"You can't spend all your waking thoughts on what others might do, not when there are more immediate difficulties weighing on you," Hruther warned him. "All of us do as we decide we must, and those decisions are our own, no matter what the Church says. If Rozsa denounces you, then you and I will need to find a way to leave here, and quickly, before we are taken as prisoners. It may be hard for your Santu-Germaniu fief if you do, but once you are accused of diabolism, Konig Bela would have no compunction in breaking his pact with you."

"He may not have such compunction in any case," said Rakoczy sardonically, then lapsed into melancholy again. "So what am I to do to disengage myself from this coil that will not be exacted from the people of Santu-Germaniu?"

Hruther considered the question. "It may not be possible for you to influence that. You are exiled, and Konig Bela is closer to your fief than you are."

"So I am jumping at shadows I have made for myself. No wonder I think I am trapped, in a cage with bars of my own making."

"Probably some of the shadows are yours alone," Hruther agreed. "But that doesn't mean you aren't watched and there are no spies."

The tension went out of Rakoczy's demeanor. "You are right, old friend. We have enemies in plenty." He listened to the moaning of the wind in the chimney, and watched the smoke rise from the fire. "The trouble is determining who they are."

Text of a note from Frater Holeb, scholar to the Konig Otakar, at Vaclav Castle in Praha, to Rakoczy Ferancsi, Comes Santu-Germaniu, at Mansion Belcrady in Praha, written on vellum and carried by Royal messenger.

To the most noble Rakoczy Ferancsi, Comes Santu-Germaniu, the greetings of the scholar to the Court of Przemysl Otakar II, Frater Holeb on this, the 17th day of October in the 1269th Year of Salvation.

Esteemed Comes,

Now that the Konig has brought his officers and his Court once again to Praha, I have been charged by the dear Royal to visit with all foreigners living in the city, to consult them on any knowledge they may have that will aid the Konig in his current campaigns and expand his knowledge of lands beyond his borders. To that end, I ask that you will receive me within the month to impart to me such information as you possess that bears on the present wars and on the places in the world where you have been. It is a service that will do much to advance you at the Konige's Court and in the Konig's good opinion.

I am told by some at the Konige's Court that you are muchtraveled, which interests me not only on the Konig's behalf, but in regard to my own studies. It is not easy to get good information at this time, and most of what is reported is as much fable as it is truth. If you would be good enough to answer questions that do not derive from the Konig's needs but my curiosity, I would be truly appreciative. If this is not possible, then I ask that you will provide me introductions to those who can give me truthful intelligence on the issues I study.

The Konige has given her permission for us to talk, and even the Episcopus has approved the arrangement, subject to his review of my record of our discussion. I have assured both dear Royals and the Episcopus that I will well and truly make note of all you say, and will bear witness to your truthfulness, so I ask you to bear in mind that more than my attention will attend upon your answers, and any mendacity on your part will bear the weight of a lie in Confession.

The civic procession is in two days, and I understand you are assisting the Counselors in their preparations, a most estimable act for a foreigner. I will present myself to you at the conclusion of the procession before the banquet and entertainments. At that time we can determine a time to meet, and the subjects we will address.

With all respect and high regard I sign myself

Frater Holeb, Premonstratensian Monk and Konig's Court Scholar

4

Although the day was clear, the wind was blustery and cold, but that was not enough to keep most of the people of Praha from lining the switch-back route of the civic procession in the hope of seeing the Konig and the city's display to welcome his return. The atmosphere was celebratory, with pie-sellers and musicians working among the spectators, and the inns and taverns keeping their doors open and their tankards full. Reel-dancers wound though the crowds, the bells on their garters jangling, their tabors pounding out a steady rhythm. In the stands set up for the nobility and clergy, courtiers, priests, and monks jockeyed for the best positions.

The stand built for the Konige's Court was in the square at the entrance to Vaclav Castle, where the procession would end. Konige Kunigunde, her Court, and the wives, widows, and daughters of the nobles who had come to Praha for the occasion, all in their most elaborate garments and jewels, took their places there immediately after the triumphal Mass at Sant-Lukas the Evangelist while the Konig and his Court lined up with the rest of the procession at the bottom of the hill in front of the Council Court, preparing to make their way along the main streets and squares up to Vaclav Castle.

"Look, dear Royal," Csenge of Somogy exclaimed, trying to rouse the Konige from her listlessness. "You can watch almost all the procession from here. They say there are fifteen decorated wagons in all."

Milica of Olmutz leaned down toward the Konige, smiling with unctuous satisfaction as she ducked her head to Konige Kunigunde. "Bohemia is the richest kingdom in the world. Gold has brought us more than prosperity, it has made us the envy of all. What other city can match this procession? Not even Constantinople can boast our grandeur, I am certain. And you, dear Royal, are Konige of it all."

Konige Kunigunde, seated with her almost-five-year-old daughter, pointed down the hill. "There, Kinga. Watch for your father. He'll be at the end of the procession, with his knights." She appeared indifferent to the excitement around her.

At the rear of the wagons and companies of Guildsmen and entertainers lining up, Konig Otakar was mounted on a superb bay stallion; he was wearing a golden crown and the new-style armor plated in gold so that he shone like the sun. He was surrounded by his personal guard of twelve German knights, all on spotted horses. They walked slowly in a circle to keep their horses limber and calm. At the head of the procession, the Counselors of Praha fell in behind the beautifully decorated wagon pulled by burnished red horses in which Episcopus Fauvinel rode, surrounded by youths dressed as angels, their wings fluttering in the wind. At the Episcopus' signal, the procession began to move at a dignified walk. After the Counselors came a consort of musicians playing tabors and buisines and shawms. They were followed by a wagon from the Weavers' Guild, in which Otakar's large rampant black lion made of fine mohair cloth glued onto a wooden form received the submission of Austria and Carinthia in the forms of royal heraldic devices laid at the lion's feet; small German horses with golden coats and flaxen manes and tails were led by the Masters of the Weavers' Guild in glorious Damascus silks. A troupe of tumblers came next, Tahir among them, and then the wagon of the Goldsmiths' Guild, adorned with shining spangles of gold leaf and carrying a throne on which sat a woman dressed as the Konige of Sheba, wearing a chaplet of gold and a multitude of rings, bracelets, and necklaces. The wagon was pulled by four chestnut horses led by the Guildmasters, each one wearing a pectoral with the emblem of the Guild. Moorish dancers came next, the slaves of Pan Kolowrat Atenaze, who, rigged out in Antioch silks, rode beside them on a spirited mouse-colored mare. The Saddle-and-Harness-Makers' Guild's wagon followed, bedecked with bridles, saddles, and harnesses in worked leather, and held aloft by their most handsome apprentices; the Guildmasters led a team of three black horses in an ornate Kievan harness. More musicians, these from the choir of Sant-Lukas the Evangelist singing songs of praise to God for the Konig's victories, followed them. The Tapestry-Weavers' Guild came next, four handsome tapestry banners displaying the arms of Bohemia, Austria, Moravia, and Carinthia moving restlessly in the wind and alarming the four gray horses that pulled the wagon. A company of advocates and notaries followed after, solemn in the dark cotehardies and headdresses of their professions. Another wagon came next, this one from the Blacksmiths' Guild, filed with displays of armor, cooking pots, horseshoes, and the tools of smiths: tongs, hammers, and files; the Guildmaster, stripped to the waist and dressed like the god Vulcan, stood over a forge, his hair contained in a wreath of iron laurel leaves. The wagon was pulled by ten apprentices, dressed in what they thought was the fashion in Caesar's Rome.

Watching the procession from a dozen paces beyond the end of the Konige's Court stand, Rakoczy shaded his eyes to keep track of the progress of men and wagons. He could not suppress a smile at the Bohemian notion of Imperial Roman clothing, but kept his amusement to himself. Historical togas and dalmaticas would not have looked Roman to the eyes of the crowd; the semi-Byzantine, semi-Moorish garb satisfied them.

"What do you think, Comes?" asked Imbolya of Heves, approaching him from the Konige's Court stand; her sea-blue silk bleihaut was set off by a collar of silver and pearls, her chainse was white linen embroidered in silver, her gorget was silvery-gray, and her veil that trailed from her elaborate headdress was edged in seed-pearls. She glanced bashfully at him. "I hope you won't mind my company; the Konige's Court stand is a little crowded with all the guests; it's noisy and confused—so much so that the Konige ordered Betrica of Eger to take little Agnethe back to her room: there is too much going on; all the baby could do was cry. Not that things are much better inside."

"The castle must be full to overflowing," he said, knowing it was true.

"And Mansion Czernin"—she motioned to the grand house on the far side of the square—"is also." She giggled, her hand covering her lips in a show of modesty. "We're sleeping four to a bed and even then there aren't accommodations enough. The Konige says that the castle must be enlarged."

"And do you agree?"

"I suppose so, but this occasion is brief, and there would have to be more servants and slaves to care for new rooms, so . . ." She shrugged. "You didn't tell me what you think about the procession, Comes."

"It is a very elaborate display; I hope the Council approves," he said in complete candor, and did not remind her that she had hardly given him a chance to tell her; he attributed her impulsivity to the excitement of the event, an emotion that had not escaped him entirely, much as he had become used to grand occasions over the centuries; he knew that he had to be careful, not appearing too splendid nor too austere, for as an exile, his demeanor during this celebration would be noted and evaluated, and so he had chosen his garments carefully: he wore a black-velvet huch lined in ermine over a chainse of pure-white silk; his braccae were black leather embossed with his eclipse device accented in silver, matching his silver-and-black-sapphire pectoral hung from large silver links. Instead of a hat, he wore a Comes' coronet in brilliant silver, and rather than wearing a sword, he carried a small francisca tucked into the back of his belt.

"Do you think the Konig will be pleased with the honor the city shows him?" She pointed down the hill to the Episcopus riding in his wagon. "Very grand, isn't he?"

"For a man who thinks killing rats is a show of vanity, he surprises me," said Rakoczy, smiling to show he meant nothing against the powerful Churchman.

"This is for the glory of the Church, not his own aggrandizement; anything less would slight the Church," said Imbolya, her voice raised to be heard over the growing excited babble of the crowd gathered in front of the castle gates.

"Indeed," said Rakoczy, wondering why the young lady-in-waiting had sought him out; it was one thing to want to escape the crowding, but he had the impression that she had come to him deliberately.

Down in the Council Court Square the last of the fifteen decorated wagons was moving; the Carpenters' Guild was following the Stonemasons' mule-drawn wagon bearing its perfect cube of marble and display of tools and three stonemasons in the working garb of their trade. Far less austere than the Stonemasons, the Carpenters had a magnificent vehicle with panels of carved wood and a complex throne for three figures: Victory, Honor, and Glory, all of whom wore the heraldic black lion of Otakar's device; the wagon was pulled by six large, black dogs with black manes attached to their harness to add to the allusion of the black lion. Six masked clowns came next, and then the Konig and his escort; cheers and clamor greeted the dear Royal as he and his men started away from the Council Court, beginning the long, zig-zag climb. As if to join in the occasion, the wind gusted more strongly.

Pan Podebrad Athalbrech rode up to the Konige's Court stand on a powerful liver-chestnut; he was resplendent in a cotehardie of cloth of silver, with his heraldic device on his right shoulder, over a deep-green chainse; he ducked his head to Kunigunde. "The Konig, your husband, asks that you join him when he arrives to open the gate of Vaclav Castle. Bring your daughter with you, so that the people may see her."

"If it will please the Konig, we will," said Konige Kunigunde, flicking her fingers in dismissal.

"I will be glad to give you and your daughter escort when the time comes, dear Royal," said Pan Podebrad before moving to the end of the stand nearest the gate, where he swung out of his saddle and stood, waiting.

"He wants a favor from the Konig, that's why he's doing this," said Imbolya to Rakoczy, her disgust with Pan Podebrad more obvious than she knew. "The Konige doesn't need an escort to walk ten paces in front of her own castle—that's nothing more than grandiosity. Who would dare to offer her an insult in this place?"

"There are many men seeking favors from the Konig today," said Rakoczy in a neutral tone.

"Of all kinds," said Imbolya, and glanced up at him, her face flushed, her veil threatening to pull away from her headdress; she seemed pitifully young to him.

Rakoczy considered what she had said. "Doubtless."

"And," she went on with a touch of defiance, "the Konig will not be the only one asked for favors."

"You mean because of the festivities? You assume the Konige will be petitioned as well?" Rakoczy inquired, thinking as he did that Imbolya was very young to be so caught up in Court life.

"Yes, well, that's likely," she said. "But there are many favors to be had." She regarded him with an air of experience that was unusual in her. "You know what sport arises when the people are celebrating."

"That I do," he said, thinking back to the Great Games in the Roman arena, to the bear-baiting at the Court of Karl-lo-Magne, to the Mid-Summer festivals in western France. All manner of excess was excused during those occasions, as, he was certain, there would be through the rest of this day and well into the night.

"There will be riots tonight, unless they're all too drunk," said Imbolya. "Look how worked up they are."

"Then let us hope there is sufficient beer and wine," said Rakoczy.

The Beggars' Guild had managed to create a wagon of their own for the procession: it was a simple cart containing an old statue of Sante Marye Konige of Mercy, pulled by the Guild members themselves. As the wagon began to move people in the crowd threw coins at them, and a dozen of the Guildsmen circled the wagon, picking up the coins and dropping them into the open coffer at the foot of the statue. After a little time a fight broke out among the beggars and the street urchins, who rushed to gather up coins before the beggars could get to them.

"I am to be married, you know," she told him.

"When will that be?" Rakoczy asked, aware that there had been no formal announcement of it in the Konige's Court.

"My father hopes it will be before summer. He is making the arrangements." She bit her lower lip.

"Then nothing is yet settled?"

She shook her head. "At least he has written to me to let me prepare for what is to come. If I could not read, I would know nothing of the agreements until my escort came to take me home."

The eleventh wagon, the one belonging to the Brotherhood of Bakers-and-Brewers, had stopped in Sante-Agnethe's Square in order to pass out cups of beer and throw small loaves of bread into the crowd, an effort that grew in excitement until it seemed that a riot would break out; large numbers of townspeople stormed the wagon, nearly oversetting it; the two stout, black-and-white horses pulling the wagon strove to break free of their leaders, who were doing their best to beat the crowd back. The horses might have bolted had not three of Otakar's knights ridden up and shoved back the populace with the flat of their swords. Once the square was secure, the knights took up positions around the wagon and it moved off again, leaving more than a dozen men injured, and five bag-pipers to make their way through the turbulence, clearing a path for the barge-shaped wagon of the Honorable Company of River Merchants.

"There will be more of that as the day goes on," said Rakoczy.

"Comes," she said in a flash of determination. "Will you show me how to be a wife to my husband?"

Rakoczy gave her a startled look. "How do you mean?"

"You know how I mean." She met his gaze directly.

He said nothing while he considered an answer; finally he spoke. "Why do you ask me?"

"Whom else am I to ask? The Konig's men are at war, and they boast too much, if they would be willing to do as I ask—if they knew what I want from them," she rejoined. "Who would be suitable? The instrument-maker? The tapestry-weaver? The furrier? Or perhaps an apprentice or a servant." She gave him a moment to answer, then hurried on as she turned away so he could not see her face. "Rozsa told me you were a most kind man, who could be relied upon for discretion. I don't know what she needed you to be discreet about, but I know what I need from you."

"What did Rozsa tell you?"

"Nothing more than that you are obliging and discreet," she assured him. "The only other thing she said was that it was a shame you are so carefully watched."

"And you find that sufficient? You make such an offer to me with so little information to guide you? Think what you—" He broke off. "I am much older than you are, Imbolya."

"Yes," she said eagerly. "That's why I thought you'd be safe to ask—that, and you're an exile. You must conduct yourself well. You have regard for women. You must do more than tup." She swung around to face him. "You know it would be folly to refuse me."

"Why is that?"

"Because I can give Konig Bela good report of you, which you need; he will ask if you have done what he has charged you to do. Or I can say things you would rather I did not." She offered him a triumphant smile, like a child anticipating a reward. "I'm one of the Konige's ladies, and for that, I can seek out many things. I've been thinking about this for some time, and I think it would be best if you were willing to comply with my request."

"You are very young, Imbolya, and—"

"All the more reason you should instruct me." The wind whipped her veil across her face; she pulled it back impatiently. "I don't know what man my father will settle upon, but I will do as he wishes. I would like to know how enjoyment may be had." There was a note of desperation in her voice now, a plea that stirred his sympathy for her.

At Sant-Vaclav Dux of Bohemia Square, a third of the way up the hill, the top-heavy wagon of the Upholsters' Guild had to stop when one of its wheels wobbled loose and had to be reattached; the wagon listed dangerously; a dozen men in the crowd helped to prop it up while the wheelwright was brought from the Carriage-Makers'-and-Wheelwrights' Guild's wagon two places behind. The people lining the street surged into the square, pressing close to the wagon and the team of six restive ponies. A company of mummers reached the square and provided a diversion while the wheel was replaced. Soon the mummers had half the spectators in the square dancing and clapping so that they hardly noticed when the wagon moved off again, nor did they pay much attention to the cutpurses who mingled with them as they danced.

"And how would you explain your knowledge?" Rakoczy asked.

"I am one of the Konige's Court—women talk. Everyone knows that." She pulled a pin from her headdress and did her best to secure her veil.

Rakoczy nodded. "Have you not learned enough, then?"

"No." Impulsively she grabbed his hand. "I want to find out everything from you. I want to *know* for myself, not be told."

"That could be a dangerous wish," Rakoczy warned, disengaging his hand without effort; her desire was much too disquieting, he thought. "Your father would not be pleased if it became known that you sought—"

"It will not become known, not unless you reveal it yourself," she said, making this almost an accusation. "Look at me. Am I not comely? Tell me you don't want to share your bed with me."

Rakoczy remained silent for a short while, listening to the distant roars of greeting that moved up the hill with Konig Otakar. He noticed that the Episcopus was almost half-way from the Council Court to the gates of Castle Vaclav, passing through the Artisans' Market to make the turn for Sant-Gabril the Archangel. "I am flattered that you would want to lie with me, but I fear my . . . nature might not be to your liking."

"Let me find out. Oh, please. You *have* to do this for me, Comes, before I am married," Imbolya whispered fiercely. "I will not be bullied the way most wives are. I couldn't bear it. If my husband beats me, I will run away from him; I don't care what the Church teaches about submission to him." She seized his hand again. "I don't care if you don't love me. All you have to do is want me, and show me what I want to learn."

Again he freed his hand. "This is not the place to talk. Too many people can listen." He knew that the Konige had spies in the crowd, as did the Episcopus, and that in spite of the noise, they could be overheard.

"But where else is there? Csenge of Somogy is the Konige's messenger now that Rozsa's gone. How am I to find a way to speak freely with you, if not in this crowd?"

"That may prove difficult. If we were to attempt to have a clandestine meeting it would be more difficult still," he said as gently as he could, adding, "You are watched, Imbolya, and I am watched."

"I don't care," she insisted.

"Possibly not, but I do," he said to her, his voice low.

"Why? What can I say that will persuade you?"

"Nothing right now." He took a step back from her, nettled by how her arousal was working on him; he found her youth too disquieting. "Think about what you are risking."

"I have already."

"Think again," he said without any show of temper. "It would pain me to have you expose yourself to shame and disrepute."

"See?" she persisted. "That's why I want you. You think of me before you think of yourself. How many men in the Konig's Court would do that?" Tossing her head, she slipped back through the crowd to the Konige's Court stand.

Gradually the procession grew nearer, and the welter of sound increased until it was enough to drown out the tolling of the bells of Sante-Radmille that announced the Episcopus' wagon had reached the square. The crowd stamped its feet in growing anticipation. The gathering at the castle gate stopped roving about and settled down away from the gate, leaving room for the wagons and walkers to enter the castle courtyard as soon as the gate was opened. A loud sounding of buisines from the castle walls signaled the opening of the gate; the people started to cry out in exhilaration.

Rakoczy moved back into the shadow of Mansion Czernin's high walls, keeping his attention on the Konige's Court stand, where pages were wriggling through the packed benches, tankards of mead in their hands. He saw Imbolya work her way along the benches into the covered part of the stand where the Konige's Court was seated; she accepted some mead as she sat down. He studied her for a while, reviewing all she had said to him and trying to determine how much he believed her. He could not deny his responsive desire for her, and his cognizance that he yearned for something more than the passionate dreams he provided the widowed innkeeper at the Black Horse, or the Polish dressmaker who lived at her shop at the Virgin's Well Square near the eastern gates of the city.

The buisines sounded again, and the Konige rose in her seat and, taking her daughter by the hand, clambered out of the

Konige's Court stand to make her way to the gate of Vaclav Castle; young Kinga began to bounce in a mixture of anticipation and anxiety. Her mother bent down to speak to her, and the child stood still. Another outcry of buisines heralded the opening of the gate, and caught the attention of all those waiting in the square. The clanking of chains accompanied the buisines, and the gate began to swing inward, revealing the forecourt, where servants and slaves were gathered to assist the members of the procession as they and their wagons arrived at the castle. Konige Kunigunde tugged at her daughter's sleeve, guiding her to the edge of the opening and taking hold of her child's hand to keep her from running off; belatedly Pan Podebrad Athalbrech joined them there, one hand resting on the hilt of his sword, his stance imposingly self-important as he held his horse's reins with the other. The buisines blared once more and now more church-bells joined in.

"Comes Santu-Germaniu?"

The voice came from close behind him; Rakoczy pulled the francisca from where it lay under his belt along his back as he turned, the small throwing axe in his hand as he met the eyes of the speaker. He found himself facing a page in a Royal tabard, who paled at the sight of the weapon Rakoczy held. "Your pardon."

The page shivered from something other than cold; he spoke flatly, no emotion of any kind in his recitation, and he stared at a point somewhere over Rakoczy's left shoulder. "The Konige has asked you to attend her Court within the walls when the procession is over. She and the Konig will hold Court in the Great Hall. She asks that you bring your lyre; there are songs she wants you to sing for her and her Court. I have been charged to bring the lyre to you, if you will tell me what I am to say at Mansion Belcrady to receive it."

"If you will first tell the dear Royal I am honored to be included in her Court on this day." He paused, ordering his thoughts. "At Mansion Belcrady ask for my manservant Hruther, who will bring the lyre to me in your company. Tell him the reason for this summons, and he will reward you with a silver Moravia."

The page ducked his head. "Do you want me to bring him to you?"

"If you would. After you inform the Konige of my answer, use the back-street and you will reach Mansion Belcrady without difficulty. If you try to go down this street, it will take you half a day to get there." Rakoczy slid the francisca back into his belt at the small of his back. He recalled his battle with Saito Masashige at Chui-Cho fortress when the francisca had proved invaluable.

The page signaled his compliance and disappeared amid the flood of people who poured into the square ahead of the procession. A dozen foot-soldiers emerged from the castle and attempted to push back the throng, but without much success. A short while later, Rakoczy saw the page kneel to Konige Kunigunde, then rise and depart again. The soldiers and the crowd continued to jostle as the wind snapped at the banners unfurled along the battlements.

Rakoczy drew back farther into the shadows, making sure his back was against the wall of Mansion Czernin. He was still filled with the sense that he was under observation, and that left him edgy. He could not bring himself to go to the Konige's Court stand although he knew he would be permitted to sit there; the stand was too exposed and so crowded that movement between its benches would hamper any attempt at a quick departure.

There was a sudden burst in excitement around the square; people strained against the foot-soldiers holding them back, and then the Episcopus' burnished sorrels appeared, with the grandly decorated wagon behind it. The Episcopus was standing, his crozier in his hand, surrounded by his shivering angels. The wagon stopped in front of the Konige's Court stand, and the Episcopus made the sign of blessing over the Court, then turned and blessed Konige Kunigunde where she stood in the open gateway before going into the forecourt of Vaclav Castle. The Counselors of Praha, some of them red-faced with exertion, were the next to arrive, and they all bowed to the Konige's Court and then the Konige herself, then followed the Episcopus' wagon. The consort of musicians played a short dance-tune for the Konige's Court, the rendition more forced than spritely, and afterward went through the gate and into the forecourt, their steps faltering. The spectators sent up another cheer of approval for the Weavers' Guild and their wagon with its large black lion.

Two more wagons arrived and were permitted to enter Vaclav Castle, but the dancers and musicians were left to fill the courtyard with their tunes and antics. It was not long before there was an eruption of cacophony as two different groups of musicians began to compete for the crowd's attention. Most of the spectators enjoyed the improvised contest, but some did not; Konige Kunigunde made a point of putting her hands to her ears, her face pale. Next to her, Kinga was bouncing again, grinning at the din. Rakoczy did his best not to flinch at the more strained notes, and hoped that when he played for the Konige he would not have such contention to deal with. As he waited for the next wagon to appear, Rakoczy again found himself thinking about Imbolya of Heves and wondering if she truly wanted his intimacy. He was so preoccupied that he almost reached for his francisca when Hruther laid his hand on his shoulder, saying, "My master, I have your lyre."

Rakoczy took the instrument, holding it carefully to keep it from being damaged by the milling people.

"Perhaps the Konige will allow you to enter the forecourt before the end of the procession?" Hruther suggested. "It's safer."

"So it is," Rakoczy agreed, and started toward the open gate where the Konige stood, greeting all those who were passing through to the next round of entertainment; Hruther followed him, watching the crowd and trying not to hear the worst of the musicians.

Konige Kunigunde accepted the bow Rakoczy and Hruther offered and motioned them on, saying, "I look forward to hearing you, Comes."

"It will be my honor to perform for you, dear Royal," he assured her, and hoped it was true.

Text of a letter from Atta Olivia Clemens in Flanders to Ragoczy Sanct' Germain Franciscus in Praha, written in Imperial Latin on vellum and carried by personal messenger, delivered thirty-eight days after it was written.

To my oldest, most revered friend, the greetings and good wishes of Atta Olivia Clemens on this, the fourth day of November in the Christian year of 1269.

My treasured Sanct' Germain,

Recent trouble here has become truly hazardous, so I have decided that it would be wise for me to leave Flanders for the time being, not for the reasons you might think. This has little to do with my right to own the land or problems of erosion, although both are present, nor it is because I have come under scrutiny that might expose me. I have decided to spend the winter in Sant-Pons and then, when the roads are dry, to go on to Lecco and stay there for a while. My situation has become difficult and I see no advantage in remaining here while all I do is left under a cloud of suspicion from a gaggle of nuns who have nothing else to do but accuse decent widows—I count myself among them—of dealing with the Devil. Already three have been condemned to prison cells for no greater crime than living without the so-called protection of a male relative; as a foreigner and a person of means, I have to prepare to defend myself against the insinuations that I am a tool of Satan, or depart.

How did it happen, that the Church insinuated itself into every aspect of life as it has? A century ago there was a clear line between the laity and the clergy, and each had its recognized province. But since they stopped priests from taking wives—and leaving Church lands to their sons—the Church has been tightening its grip on everything. They find heresy and devils everywhere, and declare no one is safe. The nuns here at Sant-Laizare

are hardly unusual, for there are many convents and monasteries that have seen outbreaks of visionary nonsense that belongs more to fables than to faith, but, of course, we are speaking here of cloistered women who only pray, spin, pray, weave, pray, sing, pray, eat only enough to keep from starving, pray, and pray. On such a regimen, I would have visions, too. Of course, the visions are carnalistic, and that implies, according to the local Episcopus, that there must be an external cause, for no devout ladies ever had so much as a hint of lust or desire for anything but the choirs of Heaven. Thus accusations have fallen on three widows in the area as I have said, and I may well be next.

I was hoping to remain here another five years, but that would be unwise. Niklos has told me that he is convinced this place is unsafe. They've burned heretics in Hainault—six widows, a midwife, four prostitutes, one catamite, and an old woman with a hump—and it may be that they will also burn witches in Brabant and Flanders. If that should occur, it would be better if I were gone from this place. Fire, as you taught me so long ago, kills vampires as well as the living. And if I am burned, my estate will go to the Church, since I would have fallen to the snares of Satan, a consideration that is only an afterthought to the zealous Episcopus. Lecco should be safe enough for a year or two, and by then I will be able to find a place where I would not become the focus of religious disapproval.

It is the Crusades that have done this—this ferocity in the name of Jesus the Savior. They're saying that there will be yet another one. What number is that—seven? eight? Haven't any of the rulers learned that they will not conquer the Holy Land no matter how laudable they claim their cause is? The followers of Mohammed will not give up their faith any more than the Christians will give up theirs. No slaughter will lessen the devotion of either side, but it will create a taste for vengeance and rapine, as we see. That it should spread to those called heretics shouldn't surprise anyone now that the nobles have acquired the rewards of their dogmatism.

I am in the process of helping my so-called half-brother Niklos in deeding my estate over to my "niece" and her "husband," both of whom have written to accept this bequest. I have found a steward to manage the place in my absence and have obtained pledges from the Dux that the deed and its terms will be upheld, which is the most I can hope for, given that there still is no Pope to endorse my claims.

If I lose this estate, then I will lose it, but it is better to go while I still can leave of my own accord. Niklos has already secured a villa for me near Sant-Pons and I will leave in six days. Half of my chests and crates are packed and will soon be loaded onto the best wagons I possess. I am choosing the horses I shall take with me, most of them coldbloods. They're already fuzzy as dandelions, which will help to keep out the cold. I have decided to ride in the saddle most of the way, and will select my riding horses for the journey in a day or two, so they may be given extra feed in preparation for the journey ahead.

In spring I will set out for Lecco and will send you word of my departure, assuming I know where you are. If you are no longer in Praha or Bohemia, I will send messages to Eclipse Trading in Roma and in Venezia, and you may have them sent on to wherever you are. I must tell you that I hope you will stay closer to home for a time. Those years you were in China were most distressing to me, aware you were alive but with no idea where. Spare me that for a decade or two, will you? I know you do not travel on whim, but I ask you to choose a place next time that I might expect a letter to reach you in less than a year.

And with that supplication, I will send you my loyal friendship and my

Undying love,
Olivia

5

Because it was snowing outside, Imbolya had on a wolf-skin mantel with a hood that framed her face in soft gray fur; she stood just inside the door of Rakoczy's workroom, her gloved hands folded in the deep pleats of the mantel. "You are most kind to see me, Comes, unexpected as I might be." She spoke Magyar.

Rakoczy nodded to Barnon. "Hot wine and honey tarts for the Konige's lady-in-waiting," he said in Bohemian, then addressed Imbolya in Magyar, "I understood from you that Csenge of Somogy is the Konige's messenger now." He went to put more cut branches on the fire. "I am pleased to see you, and I apologize for not coming to the Konige's Court, but as you may know, Konig Otakar has ordered me to keep to my house until the Solstice festivities. I am to receive only those persons the Konige or the Council sends to me."

Barnon remained in the room, occupying himself with putting a cloth on the low table next to the fireplace. He did his best to make it appear that he was not listening to them.

"Yes, Csenge is the Konige's messenger now, and ordinarily it would be she who called upon you, but as the Konige wishes to have jewels selected for her daughters for the Nativity: she sent me because of my greater knowledge concerning jewels. I have been charged to examine all the stones you have that might be suitable and to choose for Kinga and Agnethe." She paused. "The ones I approve are to be presented at the Solstice banquet, which the Konig will allow you to attend. I don't know if he will want you to attend Kinga's anniversary "

"If that is the Konige's desire—that I should give her daughters gems—then I am happy to serve her. That is why Konig Bela sent me here."

Imbolya hesitated, then plunged ahead. "The Konig thinks you're a spy for Konig Bela, you know. He thinks your exile is a ruse, and that you have been given a mission to watch Otakar's Court. That's why he has ordered you to remain in your house while he holds Court here in Praha." Color mounted in her face. "I don't think you're a spy."

"Why do you think that?" Rakoczy asked, his curiosity piqued.

"Because you keep to yourself and do not spend your time at Court. If you were a spy, you'd have to find out things, wouldn't you? You can't learn many secrets here, and when you answer the Konige's summons, you take no advantage of it to insinuate yourself into her good graces with flattery and favors." She courtisied to him. "It seems that way to me."

"I do bring her jewels," Rakoczy pointed out.

"As Konig Bela charged you to do," she said. "You do your duty to her, handsomely, but nothing more than that. So if you are spying, you don't do it very well."

"You will want to be comfortable," Rakoczy said, shifting their conversation; he directed her to the upholstered chair facing the hearth. "I will have more candles brought—if you will attend to that as well, Barnon? Two branches, if you would." Low light was no hardship for his eyes, but he knew Imbolya would want brightness in order to examine the jewels. "And see that my guest's carriage is taken to the stable and her horses watered and each given a handful of grain. Her escort are to have cheese, bread, and wine in the servants' room. Make sure the fire is well-stoked."

"Of course, Comes," Barnon said, and backed out of the room, leaving them alone.

"Your bondsman told me where to find you," Imbolya said when they were alone. "He offered to escort me, but your steward—"

"—claimed the honor," said Rakoczy, adjusting the black cotehardie of satin-lined wool he wore over a chainse of deep-red silk. "That is correct for a Bohemian household, is it not?"

"Yes. It is the way of things in Bohemia." Imbolya pulled off her gloves and set them on the arm of the chair. "The fire is very nice."

"That is kind of you," said Rakoczy. "When you are warm enough, I will take your mantel."

"Thank you," she murmured, and fell silent, staring at the flames that were rising in the fireplace. "Carniola has surrendered to Otakar."

"When?" Rakoczy asked. "Is it official?"

"The deputation arrived last night. Otakar has lands all the way to the sea now. He wants the Bohemian Empire to get larger and stronger." She sighed. "The Konig has ordered four of his Captains who were caught stealing supplies to be hanged in chains at the south gates."

"Because of the surrender of Carniola?"

"Because he wants to discourage thieves," said Imbolya. "Now that he is successful he thinks more of his officers will want to share in his accomplishments with . . . allotments of their own choosing."

Rakoczy frowned. "What does the Episcopus say?"

"He says that God has given the Konig power in the world and it is for Otakar to uphold the Will of God, and to root out the Devil and all his works. He says that God gave Otakar Carinthia and Carniola, and Austria, and that Otakar is approved by Heaven or that wouldn't have happened, because God favors the righteous." She looked away from him, feeling the efflorescence in her face and wanting, in some confused way, to conceal it from Rakoczy.

"What does Konig Bela say? Or Rudolph von Hapsburg?" Rakoczy wondered aloud; he was aware of her discomfort and did what he could to allow her to restore herself.

"The Episcopus hasn't spoken about either of them. If there were a Pope in Roma, he might have another view." Absently she crossed herself. "It is hard to see Hungary lose to Bohemia for those of us who have been sent to the Konige from Hungary, and hardest for the Konige, who is torn between her husband and her grandfather. All of us from Hungary feel it, but Kunigunde suffers most."

Rakoczy nodded. "She, too, is trapped."

"I think, no matter what the Konige believes, that it might be just as well that she had a second daughter, for a son could be as torn as she is in where his loyalties might lie." She put her hand to her lips. "You won't tell anyone what I've said, will you? The Konige would be upset to know I think a daughter now is better than a son. She would think me inconstant and might send me away."

"But a girl could be as divided in her loyalties, especially if her marriage is the seal on a treaty, as Kunigunde herself has been; and no, I will not repeat any of what you tell me," said Rakoczy, thinking back to Mnekore, almost two millennia ago. He lowered his eyes to the fire. "It is a pity her father is dead: as Konig of Bulgaria and Grand Dux of Kiev, he might have been able to do something to arrange a peace among Otakar, Bela, and Rudolph."

"The Bulgarian Tsars are too busy murdering and being murdered for any help to come from that quarter. No one trusts the Bulgarian Tsars to uphold their oaths of alliance. Both of the Konige's sisters' husbands were Tsars and they were murdered." For several heartbeats she was still. "Have you thought any more about what I said at the civic procession?" she asked, not looking at him.

"Have I thought about becoming your clandestine lover?" he inquired, to be certain they understood each other.

"Yes. About that."

"I have thought about it," he admitted, leaning against the pillar that flanked the fireplace. "Have you? considered what might happen?"

"Yes," she said with asperity. "I have thought about little else. If you will accept me—"

"It may be more if you will accept me. I am not like most men, and what I can do will not prepare you for marriage," he said; he found it difficult to speak, and he could not keep from thinking of the many conflicts he had: what would Imbolya think of his true nature? What if he disgusted or disappointed her? If she enjoyed him, how would she behave when she was summoned to her wedding? What would happen to them both if they were found out? What if she proved as demanding and capricious as Rozsa?

"Comes?" She spoke a bit more loudly. "Comes, what is it?"

"Nothing," he said, then reconsidered. "I am sure you have questions you want to put to me; I am trying to decide how to answer."

"I haven't asked anything yet," she said almost playfully, "beyond what I've asked you already."

"And that is what concerns me," he told her, his voice mellifluous and soothing as he picked his way through his qualms. "I am deeply obliged to you for . . . for offering me your favor, but I believe you are not fully aware of what you could bring upon yourself . . . You have told me what you seek. You may have . . . expectations of me, or hopes that—"

"So you've warned me. I am not troubled by the strange, or those things the Church dreads, if that is your concern, and you—" she cut in, and would have said more but there was a rap on the door, and the latch lifted.

"Come," said Rakoczy, remaining where he was.

Barnon entered first, a large, brass tray in his hands that held a jug of hot wine, an alabaster cup, and a large plate with an array of fruit-and-honey tarts laid out upon it. He carried this to the low table and set it down; Hruther came after him with two large branches of burning candles in his hands. Both men ducked their heads to Imbolya and then to Rakoczy.

"One on the serving-table, I think," said Rakoczy to Hruther in Bohemian, "and one on the trestle-table where the casket of jewels is kept."

"It's a pity the shutters have to be closed, though of course they must be with the snow and the wind," Imbolya remarked, also in Bohemian, paying little attention to either Barnon or Hruther. "It makes everything so dark."

"I will have paned glass put in place in spring, throughout the manse," said Rakoczy. "Inside the shutters, of course, and with sections that can be opened, so the rooms will not be stifling in summer. I have placed an order with the Glassmakers' Guild and provided the specifications for the windows so that they may assemble the panes and frames before spring, and the installations can begin with the first good weather and be finished by Mid-Summer Eve. The two large windows in the main hall are to have stained glass as well as clear, one showing the eclipse device of Rakoczy, the other showing the Tree of Four Seasons: buds and blossoms, fruit, yellow leaves, and bare branches." It was one of the many things that was supposed to have been done to the manse before he arrived, and it was something he was sorry he had not had done in the summer. "The Master Glazier will supervise the whole project; he has engaged his Guild's most experienced journeymen to do the work. He has pledged to have the windows ready by mid-April; I have promised a bonus if he and his Guild achieve that."

"It sounds very elegant." She looked at him expectantly and motioned Barnon to step back; Rakoczy realized that she expected him to pour the wine.

"How much would you like in your cup, Imbolya?" he asked.

"A good amount, if you would. The day is cold." Her smile flashed but vanished in a frown of uncertainty; she was perturbed by the level of her response to him, as if he were north and she a magnet. Once again she turned her head so that no one could see her burning cheeks or hear the sound of her heart beating.

Rakoczy took the jug and poured out enough to fill the cup almost full. "Tell me if it suits your taste."

Hruther went from the trestle-table to the low one, lighting all the candles, then ducked his head. "Do you need anything more, my master?" He spoke in Imperial Latin.

"Not just at present," he answered, and added in Bohemian,

"Thank you both. You need not linger here. I will escort my guest to her carriage when she is done making her selection. Given the occasions and the youth of the Konige's daughters, it may take us some time to decide which stones are most appropriate."

Barnon bowed his head; Hruther nodded, and without saying anything, they left Rakoczy and Imbolya alone.

"Are you certain your servants are reliable?" she asked in Magyar before she sipped the wine.

"I trust they are, within their lights; they do their work and report to those who require it. But I have complete faith in my bondsman, who has been with me a long time and has shown himself discreet and loyal." That he had found Hruther in the half-built Flavian Circus twelve hundred years before he kept to himself.

"Within their lights," she mused. "Of course they make reports. You have spies among them. Probably more than one."

"It is to be expected."

"Alas," she agreed, and drank more. "This is very good."

"So I understand," he said,

She took one of the tarts and bit into it, holding it so the crust crumbs would not fall on her clothing. "I am to have a new bleihaut of velvet for my Epiphany gift, and Venetian solers."

"From the Konige?" Rakoczy ventured.

"From my father. He will also buy my wedding clothes and give me three sets of clothing for my personal dowry. He has said he will provide for my garments and bedding for five years as part of the settlements. Konige Kunigunde has said she will give me a carriage and horses when I marry."

"And . . ."—he poured her more wine as he tried to frame a question that would not give offense—"is this to your liking?"

"That will depend upon whom I am to marry," she said, and drank again; her cheeks grew more brightly flushed—which she hoped he would attribute to the hot wine—and she shrugged out of her mantel, letting it lie over the back of her chair and revealing a bleihaut of spruce-green wool over a chainse of heavy ivory silk.

She could feel his eyes on her, and with the intention of appearing at ease, she reached up to loosen her hair from the artfully wound loose braid that lay under the silver-fretwork chaplet; the pale-brown cascade spread over her shoulders, with the waves from plaiting pressed into the strands.

"Do you know any of the men your father is considering?" He kept his tone level and his manner unflustered although he was caught up in her tentative abandon.

"He hasn't given me any names, so I don't know. He will inform me in good time so that I may prepare for . . . for my wedding." She took another long sip and set the cup down. "It is a little like a calf being sold at market, isn't it? The calf makes a good trade for the farmer, but who knows if the calf will be bound for the pasture or the kitchen."

"Not a happy state for you," he told her; he realized that her intelligence was too keen for her to be comforted by sophistries, so he said, "I hope your husband is a man who can appreciate you. I hope he is capable of you."

"That's an interesting turn of phrase: *capable of me.*" She thought it over. "Yes, I hope so, too, but it would be folly to expect it."

He could not disagree with her. "Would you like another tart?"

"I would like you to show me the ways of loving," she said, and before he could speak, added, "Don't tell me I am too young, or it doesn't matter, or that it is the Devil's work to rouse a woman's passions." Her eyes shone with tears she would not let fall.

"I would not do any of those things," he said, and bent to add another branch to the fire, troubled by the welling ardor she evoked in him. His own emotions answered hers and he knew he was captivated.

"My father thought at first that I was bound to be a nun, and pictured me like Hroswitha of Gandersheim, with a vast convent and as much power as a lord. He made donations to the Church to found a convent, but Konig Bela would not permit such a convent to be built, for he distrusts the Church, and wants money for war."

She looked up at him, her face emotionless, her eyes forlorn. "So I will disappear into marriage, as women do."

He went to her side and put his hand on her shoulder. "Do not despair, Imbolya."

"Why not? Wouldn't you despair, were you in my situation?" She shook her head. "I know what my duty is, and I will do it. I will marry the man my father chooses for me, and I will bear him children to ensure our House's position, and I will feel so *wasted*. If God has chosen this path for me, why did He instill so many thoughts in my mind? Or did the Devil give them to me?"

"The thoughts, whatever they may be, are yours." He saw her cross herself. "I know that Episcopus Fauvinel would call what I said heresy, but if that is so, then most of the souls on earth are heretics, which is unfortunate for Christians." He paused. "In the lands of the Great Khan there are those who believe that it is the nature of humans to question, and that those who do not question their lives and their behavior are the heretics." He thought back to Kuan Sun-Sze in Lo-Yang, not quite sixty years ago, who had brought him to the university and had sent him away as the forces of Temujin had stepped up their invasion; through Kuan, Rakoczy had studied the work of Kung Fu-Tse and Lao-Tsu, and the Buddha.

"Do they have convents?" Imbolya asked, her attempt at joking an utter failure.

"There are some, I understand, but I know little of their teaching," he answered, remembering the Buddhist nuns he had seen in Tuan-Lien.

"They aren't Christian," she said sadly.

"No, they are not." He could feel her pulse through his fingers and with it, her first trembling excitement; he started to remove his hand, but she laid her own upon it. "Imbolya . . ."

"I am not asking for much, Comes." She touched his sleeve. "Will you refuse me the little I ask?"

"If it is what you truly want, and you understand that it will not last, that I cannot give you more than pleasure." Inwardly he upbraided himself for succumbing to his esurience, but as she rose into his arms, he was captivated by the ardor within her, and her frail hope for a little joy. Their kiss deepened and her ardor became true passion.

"Comes," she whispered triumphantly, and then their lips met again, hers eager, his explorative, and their hands touched as they leaned together; this was more than she had expected and her desire sharpened like lightning in her soul. Since she was almost a head shorter than he, she found the embrace more awkward than he did, and she ended up with her arms around his waist, canted against him, unaware that he was holding her securely, without effort.

When they broke a short way apart, he helped her to the rear of the room, to the low Persian divan that stood to the side of the athanor. "We will be more comfortable here, and the athanor is warm."

"Then you will show me? What I want to learn?" she whispered in her excitement, leaving the wolf-skin mantel on the chair.

"As much as I can without putting you at risk," he said.

She stared at him. "What do you mean?"

"I will not do—I cannot do—the act that might give you a child," he said, for like all the males of his blood, he was impotent, as the females were sterile. Two millennia ago that admission would have discomposed him, but he had long since become accustomed to his state though he knew that many women found this upsetting.

"Can you do that? Really?" She beamed at him. "I *knew* I was right to ask you. I *knew* you wouldn't harm me." An unfamiliar tingle was growing at the base of her spine, and her skin seemed to be more sensitive, as if it had been rubbed with a hair-cloth.

"I hope I would not, whatever I am capable of doing," he said, reaching to loosen the lacing on her bleihaut. "But it is not safe to befriend me, and that may yet be troublesome for you."

She turned so he could work her laces more easily, her pulse thrilling as she touched his arm. "The Konige speaks well of you.

So long as she does, I can do the same." With a hitching of her shoulders, she let her bleihaut drop to the floor. Standing now in her chainse, she smiled tentatively. "Shall I keep this on?"

"If you like," he said.

"What do you prefer?" she asked, trying to hide her nervousness with a coquettish smile.

He picked up her clothes from the floor and laid the garment on the end of the trestle-table. "It is your preferences that matter, Imbolya. If you are pleasured, then I am pleasured. If removing your chainse would add to your pleasure, then remove it. If you would derive more pleasure from having it on, then stay as you are."

"For now, I will leave it on," she decided, then as if she had exhausted all her will, she asked, "What do you want me to do?"

"Sit down and be comfortable," he said; in a remote part of his mind he found this exchange ironically amusing. "Do you want another cup of wine?"

She considered a moment. "Yes. If you don't mind." The flicker of anxiety made the request poignant.

"I will bring it to you, shall I?" He went and filled the alabaster cup, carrying it and the jug back to her. He set the jug next to her bleihaut on the end of the trestle-table, then handed the alabaster cup to her.

"What is in this?" she asked after she sipped.

"Wine, spices, and honey," he said. "Cinnamon, cardamom, crushed nutmegs, and white pepper."

"How luxurious," she approved, and drank a little more before handing the cup back to him. She leaned on the bolster at the end of the divan. "What should I do now?"

"Choose a position that you find relaxing," he said, going on one knee next to the divan; he could feel her anticipation in the tension of her muscles. "I will massage your hands and arms to help you reduce the strain you have."

"All right," she said dutifully, fussing to put herself at ease. "Shall I close my eyes?"

"If it will give you more comfort, then do." He took her hand and began to massage the fingers, gently working them until they released their tightness; he started on her palm, his thumbs pressing the tension away. He moved to her arm, kneading her flesh through the sleeve of her chainse. When he reached her elbow, she lifted her head.

"I want to take this off," she said, plucking at her chainse. "Your hands feel better directly on my skin." She blushed as she said it, then sat up and pulled the garment off over her head, letting it drop to the floor next to Rakoczy; now all she wore was her breechclout.

Gooseflesh rose on Imbolya's arms and torso, more from jittery nerves than chill. Any discomfort she might have felt vanished as he laid his hand on hers. She leaned back against the bolster. "There." She held out her left arm to him. "Do you want to go on?"

"As long as you do," he said, and took her wrist in his hands. He did not hurry his efforts, taking his time to give her the greatest opportunity to surrender her edginess. Finally, as he finished working on her right arm, the quivering tension in her back began to fade, and he changed from kneading her body to caressing it. He made his way from her shoulders to her small, high breasts; he cupped them, teasing her nipples with his fingers, and, when she had finally achieved a welcome transport and her body became responsive to his hands and lips, pliant and apolaustic.

"How do you know to do these things?" she whispered.

"Do you like them?"

She made a giggling sigh. "Oh, *yes*."

"Then I will continue to do them."

"Should I take off my breechclout?" She felt wonderfully brazen just asking the question; she held her breath, waiting for his answer.

"It would be more satisfying if you do." As soon as she unfastened and removed her breechclout, he moved down her body to the hidden cleft at the base of her hips; Imbolya breathed more quickly, a flush spreading over her face and neck and gradually extending onto her chest. When he fingered the soft folds open, Imbolya shivered; her eyes were half-closed. While he teased her little bud into stiffness, she twitched with every flick of his hands and tongue, her body growing taut once more. Slowly he slid a finger into her and felt a preparatory contraction of muscles; he shifted his position so that he was half-lying beside her. The second time he entered her, he used two fingers, and she was caught up in a spasm of elation; he drew her close, his lips on her throat, and shared the waves of rapture that coursed through her.

When she could speak again, she said, "Thank you."

"There's no need to thank me—it is I who should thank you," he said, keeping her in the haven of his arms.

"I could lie here all afternoon, and through the night, and you could tell me tales as captivating as the tales of the troubadours so I could forget what lies ahead," she murmured, and then shook her head regretfully. "But I must choose jewels and return to Vaclav Castle before your servants start gossiping, or my escort." She stretched up and kissed him. "Later, we must find a time to do this again, and do it longer."

"If it is possible," he said, moving back so they could both sit up.

"How do you mean?" She reached for her breechclout and pulled it on, securing the ties at her waist, all bashfulness gone.

"This was an unexpected opportunity, one neither of us can assume will come again." He handed her chainse to her. "What are you going to do with your hair? Do you want a comb?" There was one in the red-lacquer chest that stood against the wall.

"There's no need. I'll tie it in a knot, use the chaplet to hold it in place under my hood." She gave him a clever smile. "No one will think it odd that I take my hair down after being out in blowing snow. They will see that my hair is wet."

"But it is not," he said.

"It will be." She grabbed her chaplet and worked it around the efficient knot she made of her hair. "And with my hood up, who will notice?"

He did not share her confidence, but he kept this to himself, the gratification of their intimacy still heartening him. "Be careful when you do," he recommended.

She smoothed the chainse and got off the divan to take her bleihaut from the end of the trestle-table. "It was wonderful of you to do this for me, Comes. Even if we do nothing more, I will be grateful to you always." Before she got into her bleihaut, she stopped to regard him one more time. "What will become of us? Will we be damned, do you think?"

He took her hands, opened them, and kissed her palms. "It is my profound wish that nothing from this gives you unhappiness." Staring into her hazel eyes, he saw her youth and trust; he tried to banish the misgiving that burgeoned within him.

She pressed her hands together as if to keep the kisses within them. "So do I." Then she resumed dressing, asking questions about the jewels he had ready while she did, striving to regain her composure and the stated purpose of her visit, and all the while her joy was like thistledown within her.

Text of a letter from Episcopus Fauvinel in Praha to Konig Bela of Hungary, written on vellum in his own hand and carried by Church courier; delivered forty days after it was written.

To the most puissant Konig, Bela of Hungary, the greeting of Episcopus Fauvinel of Praha and the Konige's Court, on this, the 29th day of November in the 1269th Year of Grace,

Esteemed Konig,

I have the honor and obligation to tell you that your grand-daughter and her daughters are well and preparing for the joyous time of the Nativity. It is unfortunate that relations between Hungary and Bohemia have not improved and thus you will not be in a position to come to Praha to see these promising girls. Let me tell you that they are modest, pious children, and the Konige sets them a fine example. With the Konig and his Court victorious in

Carniola, the occasion is likely to be a grand one here for all it may cause dissatisfaction to you. The Konige, of course, is less merry, for the losses you have sustained.

The first gifts of the season have been presented, six of them from your nobleman, the Comes Santu-Germaniu, including a golden reliquary studded with amethysts and tourmalines which he presented to me as the representative of the Church for the relics of Sant Iacopus which were brought from the Holy Land a century ago; it is of fine workmanship and the quality of the gems is beyond any I have seen, so fine and so well-polished that they seem to hold the light of the stars within them. For the Konig, the Comes had made a pectoral in the form of a crown augmented with diamonds; for the Konige, he presented a topaz the size of a pigeon's egg hung on a golden chain and a brooch worked in silver of the Virgin surrounded by birds with bodies and wings of rubies, emeralds, peridots, and aquamarines. For the dear Little Royals he gave Kunigunde of Bohemia a chain-collar of gold with white sapphires in the links; for infant Agnethe, he made a bauble of what is called a tiger's-eye and suspended it from a gilded cord. He also presented an anniversary gift for dear Little Royal Kunigunde to be offered to her in January to commemorate her birth.

All of this is said to be in accord with the terms of his exile, and if that is the whole of it, I will say nothing more once I complete this account to you, but for a man in exile, he has wealth beyond all the richest of Bohemians; his is an embarrassment of riches, which inspires envy and avarice in many, surely the result of the Devil at play, as an instigation to covetousness at the least, and less Christian thoughts. My man within his household tells me that the Comes regularly makes more jewels, which smacks of suborning virtue to me, and possible diabolism, although the man in his household thinks not, for he has seen no direct sign of diabolic purpose in these jewels the Comes makes. I admit I am troubled, for, as we know, the Devil and his minions are everywhere seeking to devour the souls of Christians. Yet if you are content that his alchemy is free of any touch of Deviltry, I will defer to your judgment, for you are the one who ordered him here, and decided upon the conditions he would have to uphold. If, however, you have doubts about the Comes, I implore you, for the sake of your soul and the souls of your granddaughter and her children, to impart those doubts to me so that I may take whatever action would protect your family from the threat of damnation that may lurk in his gifts.

It also concerns me that the Comes has, along with his alchemical skills, a professed knowledge of poisons. He provided a substance to the Counselors of Praha to kill rats which has proven most efficacious, and that has caused me much dismay, for surely a man with such skills may well employ them in ways that could be most evil. I have no desire to accuse him of such acts, but I believe there is a danger when any man has the skill to poison another that the man with the skill may not always be governed by charity, nor the righteousness Christians should observe. Yet if you are satisfied that the Comes will do no evil deeds with his poisons, I will declare myself content to bow to your judgment.

May Heaven guide and keep you, Konig Bela, so far as there is no dishonor to Bohemia in those blessings, may your life continue without pain or illness, and may you find Grace in all that you do,

> *In the Name of the Father, the Son, and the Holy Spirit,*
> *Fauvinel, Episcopus at Praha*

PART III

IMBOLYA OF HEVES

*T*ext of a letter from Notay Tibor of Kaposvar at Kaposvar to Przemysl Otakar II at Praha, dictated to Frater Deodor and delivered by him twenty-nine days after it was written.

To the most excellent Konig, Przemysl Otakar II of Bohemia, the most respectful greetings of Notay Tibor of Kaposvar, on the 15th day of January, in the 1270th year of Grace, in accordance with the wishes of the dear Royal.

Most exalted Konig of all Bohemia, Moravia, Austria, Styria, Carinthia, and Carinola,

When you sent me back to my estates last autumn and ordered my wife, Rozsa of Borsod, to return here from your Konige's Court, I was afraid this would mean dismissal from your Court for me and from the Konige's for my wife, given the state of affairs between Hungary and Bohemia. But at that time you assured me that once Rozsa became pregnant and the pregnancy was verified by a capable midwife, my wife might return to the Konige's Court until her delivery is less than two months away, at which time she is to return here for the sake of our child, so that it may be born here at Kaposvar, or so you assured me would be the case. This will provide you what intelligence you may need to put into place the fulfillment of your pledge so that with your approval of these arrangements, I will be permitted to rejoin you on campaign.

As you will recall from our discussion on this point, I believe that Rozsa of Borsod will be far safer in your Konige's Court than here once I am gone from here, at least until her delivery is near, when she will be able to command the company of her cousins and her brother for her guards, and the attention of Sorer Sagitta of Santa-Trava, who will receive Rozsa of Borsod into the convent to await the birth. Too many of my relatives are eager to make a claim on my estates, and if they can control my wife and make a hostage of my child, they will then seek to gain complete hold over Kaposvar and the fiefs within its limits, a development that I fear would bode ill for us all. It is true that Bohemia and Hungary are not truly at peace, but both you and Konig Bela are united against Rudolph von Hapsburg, Comes of Austria, and so I am convinced that Rozsa of Borsod, while she is once again in the Konige's Court, will help ensure that continuing cause to contain von Hapsburg is not allowed to falter, to the benefit of both you and Konig Bela.

Therefore I rejoice to tell you that according to Matra Novea, the midwife for Kaposvar, my wife is two months pregnant and the pregnancy is well-settled. With your permission, I will inform my wife that she may come to Konige Kunigunde's Court from April until Mid-Summer, where she may once again serve the Konige for the honor of Hungary and the protection of our child. She has told me that she is looking forward to seeing the other ladies-in-waiting, and will, if you give your permission, travel with the two new women commanded to serve Konige Kunigunde in Praha. I believe my wife will add to the Konige's comfort and will provide a cushion against intrigue as one who will lessen the degree of mistrust among the ladies-in-waiting as well as give an example of Christian conduct and piety.

To that point I will say that it is a pity about Erzebet of Arad, but her family has always been treacherous, so it may be just as well that she took so deadly a fever and died of it, for then she had no chance to cause harm to the dear Royal or her children, as some of us feared she might. Had she been well for all her days at the Konige's Court, she would have proven to be as disruptive there as she has been in Buda-Pest. I praise God for keeping Er-

zebet from bringing misfortune to the Konige and her children, for the Hungarian and Bohemian Crowns. I myself have instructed my wife to be vigilant against all efforts to compromise the Konige's Court and the honor of Bohemia; you may rely on her good-will implicitly, for as a Hungarian in Bohemia, she knows that she must consider both kingdoms in all she does. May God send more such worthy women to serve the Konige this time.

My scribe, Frater Deodor, has expressed my thoughts for me with true elegance and accuracy, far better than I, myself, would do, if I had the knowledge of letters he does. Through his service to Kaposvar he has earned my trust and my high regard, for he is a man of many God-given gifts, all of which are useful to our shared interests. For his talents as a scribe and his abilities as a recorder, I ask that you permit him to travel with my wife to the Konige's Court so that I may be kept informed of the progress of her pregnancy.

In all fealty and devotion to you as the Konig of Bohemia and the champion of many, many Christians, I submit this petition for your consideration, and I pray that you will grant my pleas to you in every particular. May God show you His Mercy and His Protection, may your kingdom flourish and become the Empire you so ardently seek, may the mantel of the Holy Roman Empire fall upon your shoulders, may the riches with which God has blessed you be the source of prosperity and strength for your House for generations to come, and for all Bohemia; for as long as the Moltava flows may Praha be a beacon of prosperity for all the world.

> With the pledge of my duty and honor,
> Notay Tibor of Kaposvar

by the hand of Frater Deodor, Redemptionist monk

1

During a break in the chain of snowstorms that had belabored Praha for more than a week, the brilliant sun brought people out of doors to revel in the light and to join in efforts to clear away the snow that blocked the streets. Even the Konig participated, ordering his knights and his German Guards into the streets with shovels to open the way from Vaclav Castle to the Council Court Square. As the snow was shoved aside, others came behind them to pack the snow firmly so that it would not simply fall back into the road. At Mansion Belcrady, Rakoczy came out of his gate with an offering of small, double-wheeled hand-carts as his contribution to the endeavor.

"Load them up and push them to the gates," he said to Rytir Guilhelm Leuzay in German. "There will be less to clean up when it all melts."

The German knight looked at the line of four hand-carts. "I've heard about these things," he said, regarding them carefully, distrusting their unfamiliarity. "Can you spare a man for each of them? My servants and slaves are all busy."

"Of course," he said. "They brought them here and they await my summons. Two are from the stable and two are stokers in the back-house and bath-house, all used to hard work, and all use these hand-carts in their work." He signaled to his men, who were standing around a small fire in the middle of the forecourt. "Illes, Megar, Estephe, Kornemon. To your tasks." He stepped aside so that his servants could take hold of the cart-handles and trundle them out onto the newly cleared paving-stones. "When your work is done there will be venison, beer, cheese, and bread waiting for you, and the bath-house will be heated."

Illes spoke for them all. "As you wish, Comes." His Bohemian was a bit clumsy, but everyone understood him.

"If you need more from this household, Rytir Guilhelm, send word and we will do what we can to accommodate you." Rakoczy peered up into the cerulean sky. "It will stay clear so long as the wind is calm, but when it picks up again, the storms will return."

"The Episcopus said that the storms will not return until the Feast of the Departure of the Konigs." Rytir Guilhelm crossed himself with his gloved hand, an act that would have earned him a stern rebuke from any clergyman.

"That will be in eleven days, will it not?" Rakoczy inquired politely, although he knew that in Bohemia, the Feast of the Departure of the Konigs was celebrated on the twenty-third day of January.

"That is what the Episcopus has said," Rytir Guilhelm said. "It would be wrong to doubt him."

Rakoczy did not argue the point. "All the same, keep aware of the wind," he recommended as he prepared to ease the gate closed.

"Where is your warder?" Rytir Guilhelm asked, looking up at the top of the gate-house.

"Minek is in his bed with a hard cough." Rakoczy glanced up. "While it was snowing, I saw no need to keep the gate-house manned, but now that the streets are being cleared, it may be wise to post a guard. My thanks for your timely warning." He swung the gate as the knight moved on, shouting orders to Rakoczy's servants.

Barnon was waiting in the door. "Ambroz has his men clearing the stable courtyard, and they will move to the side-court when the rest is done." He paused, then said, "Those wheeled hand-carts are more useful than I thought they would be. We have restocked all the wood-boxes in the manse and the out-buildings; the hand-carts made it easier than using double-sling hods." He looked about uneasily. "Will the Rytir bring back the ones you've provided, do you think?"

"If he does not, I will order more made."

"Yes," Barnon said, nodding several times. "It's a good thing you brought them."

"They seemed useful to me," said Rakoczy, who had used them often at his fief.

"In the summer they did ease the work of shifting apples and turnips to the root-cellar, but I didn't see the possibilities for winter, for the cart is so new to Praha that it was a novelty that might bring as many problems as those it solved," Barnon burbled on. "It seemed to me that there wouldn't be much use for them once the frosts came. But now I understand how they—"

Rakoczy held up his hand. "I am glad you approve of them. What is it you are trying to avoid telling me?"

"I?" He wriggled his shoulders to make a dismissive shrug. "Nothing, Comes."

Rakoczy fixed his dark eyes on Barnon. "I do not like to accuse you of lying, but I am sure you are avoiding something that troubles you." His expression softened a little. "Why not tell me what it is so I will not have to bother the rest of the household making inquiries."

"It will displease you," Barnon said.

"Then better to do it quickly, and get it behind you. Delay can only make it worse."

Barnon swallowed hard. "Minek wants a priest. For Last Rites."

"Send for one. You do not need my permission for that," said Rakoczy in his calmest voice.

"It's not so simple," Barnon said, fretting. "He wants Pader Tomasek, from the Church of the Apostles. That's well down the hill and it's likely to be hard going to reach the place. If we went to Sante-Radmille, the priest would be here much sooner, but they are Trinitarians."

Rakoczy resisted the impulse to dismiss the matter, for he

realized that many of these various Orders were as competitory in sacraments as companies of armed knights were in combat. "Are there difficulties between the Redemptionists and the Trinitarians?"

"There are difficulties between the Apostles and Sante-Radmille."

"Would it be a problem for Minek to receive Last Rites from a Trinitarian?" Rakoczy stepped into the entry hall.

"He is certain there would be," said Barnon. "I don't know what to tell him."

"Offer him the choice of a Trinitarian before mid-day or a Redemptionist by mid-afternoon," said Rakoczy, wondering if the warder's condition had deteriorated so greatly since the previous night. "Be sure he understands that most of the streets are not clear of snow, and it will be some time before Pader Tomasek can come here."

Barnon scowled. "But how can he be sure of God's Will in this? The cough may have disordered his thoughts. The Devil may be hoping to deny him a good death, so Hell can claim his soul."

"It is possible, I suppose, but the decision about who is to shrive him should lie with Minek. It is his soul, after all." Rakoczy read alarm in Barnon's eyes. "It would not be fitting for you, or for me, to decide for Minek."

"If you are certain . . ." Barnon said dubiously.

"Would you like me to ask him myself?" Rakoczy did his best not to make his question a challenge. He went into the main hall, hearing Barnon's hesitant steps behind him.

"You may be touched by the cough's miasma if you go to him," said Barnon after a short silence.

Rakoczy regarded Barnon thoughtfully. "If there is a miasma, it has touched me already, and if there is not, what have I to fear?"

Barnon considered this. "Put your trust in God and His Mercy."

"As you must do," said Rakoczy, "when you go to him." He saw a flicker in Barnon's eyes. "You do go to him, do you not?"

"I . . . go to the door to the room where he has been taken," Barnon said. After a moment he added, in a tone of ill-usage, "If you had slaves, I would assign one to care for him."

"I see," said Rakoczy quietly. "Then it must be a good thing that I have no slaves." He motioned to Barnon. "Go to the door of his room and find out which Order he prefers for Last Rites. Then dispatch one of the housemen to bring the priest. You may tell him that I will attend to him shortly."

"Yes, Comes," said Barnon, ducking his head and shifting his gaze away from Rakoczy toward the blaze in the central fireplace.

Very gently, Rakoczy said, "Do it now, Barnon."

The steward paled and rushed out of the room.

Left to himself, Rakoczy went along to the kitchen and ordered Pacar to prepare a broth with many crushed herbs in it; he selected the herbs to be used from the hanging bundles of dried herbs. "Use these and no others. Heat the broth slowly with the herbs, then put it in an earthenware bowl and carry it to Minek."

Pacar's hands trembled. "One of the scullions will do it," he said, trying to summon up what authority he could.

Rakoczy pressed his lips together, measuring the fear in his cook. "Have it ready before mid-day and I will fetch it."

"Comes!" Pacar was shocked. "No. You mustn't."

"And prepare a venison stew, bread, cheese, and beer for all those working to clear away the snow." Rakoczy ignored the protests that greeted his instructions. "You need not fear: there is no miasma on them."

Pacar ducked his head as if anticipating a blow for his insolence. "No, Comes," he said as Rakoczy left the kitchen, going toward his workroom.

Half-way up the narrow stairs Rakoczy met Hruther coming down. "Have you seen Minek?" he asked in Imperial Latin.

"Not since last night," said Hruther. "His cough was worse."

"He has asked for a priest, for Last Rites."

Hruther looked surprised. "He didn't seem that far gone to me."

Rakoczy nodded. "How much sovereign remedy do I have left?"

"After treating the innkeeper at the Red Wolf? Ten vials," said Hruther. "I suppose it would be useless to remind you that you're not supposed to treat the sick."

"Yes," said Rakoczy with a swift, ironic smile. "It would be useless."

"I hope you won't regret it," said Hruther, continuing downward.

"I would regret more doing nothing," said Rakoczy, resuming his climb upward, aware that his progress was being watched by Magda.

In his workroom he unlocked and opened the ancient redlacquer chest and removed a vial of opalescent liquid from one of the drawers; he set this aside, closed and locked the chest, then took a little time to build up the fire and to pull a slim volume from the shelves of books. Then he picked up the vial and returned to the kitchen, where he found Pacar bent over a cooking pot of simmering mutton-broth, a bowl waiting on the cutting block at his elbow.

"The broth is almost ready, Comes," said Pacar in as conciliating a manner as he could achieve.

"Very good." Rakoczy turned to the three scullions who were pouring beer into the large cooking cauldron where chopped onions and cabbage lay atop collops of venison. "Make it substantial; the men are working hard in the cold."

The oldest of the scullions summoned up his courage and said, "That we will, Comes. That we will. And have some ourselves, for our labors."

Pacar started to ladle the broth into the waiting bowl; he spilled a little of the liquid, and he swore by the Virgin's tits under his breath, then glanced nervously at Rakoczy. "I will Confess it, Comes."

"As you wish," said Rakoczy, and went to take up the ladle and finish filling the bowl himself. "Do you have a cloth so I can carry it without burning my hands?"

Wordlessly Pacar handed him a long strip of quilted linen.

"Thank you," said Rakoczy, and picked up the bowl. He took the narrow hall to the servants' quarters and made his way to the rear-most room. The odor of sickness and urine struck him as he opened the door, and he realized that no one had removed the chamber-pot or the basin of mucus on the floor next to the narrow bed for at least a full day. The sound of Minek's wheezy breath faltered as the sick warder looked up, his features shadowed; the only light in the room came from the torch in the sconce in the hallway.

"Comes," said Minek, the word ending in a spate of coughing that left him gasping and pale, the fever spots on his cheeks bright. He was clearly very ill, but his eyes were not sunken, nor did he have the smell of death about him.

"I have broth for you, with herbs to help you heal," said Rakoczy, coming to the side of the bed and setting the bowl on the small chest next to the bed. "And there is a . . . a remedy that those of my blood have used to treat illness for a long time." He offered the vial. "Drink it first, and then the broth."

"It's wasted on me," Minek managed to say, then spat into the basin.

"I doubt it," said Rakoczy, and unstoppered the vial. "Drink this. The taste is not pleasant, but it has much virtue."

Reluctantly Minek took the vial, sniffed at it, coughed, then drank it, making a face as he did. "It better have virtue," he muttered.

Rakoczy bent down and without any apparent effort moved Minek into a sitting position. Then he retrieved the bowl of broth and handed it, with the quilted linen cloth, to the warder. "This will take away the taste and should provide you some strength."

"I am dying," said Minek, paying no attention to the bowl.

"Perhaps, and perhaps not," Rakoczy said, unperturbed by Minek's declaration; he put the cloth and the bowl into Minek's hands. "Has Barnon spoken to you about a priest yet?"

"He says"—he broke off, coughing—"that Pader Tomasek is"—he coughed some more—"still snowbound."

"And will be for some while as the Konig's men work their way down the streets," Rakoczy said. "Sante-Radmille is open, but I understand you would rather not ask one of the priests to attend you." He waited for Minek to speak, then went on, "Sant-Norbrech should be cleared of snow in a short while. Do you have any objections to a Servite?"

"I told Barnon Pader Toma—" He coughed so strenuously that some of his broth slopped out of its bowl.

Rakoczy reached to steady Minek's hands. "As soon as the way is open, Pader Tomasek will be sent for. It may be some little time."

"He is my Confessor," said Minek.

"No other will suit you?" Rakoczy asked. "Very well, you shall have him." He bent to pick up the basin and the chamber-pot.

Minek goggled at him. "Comes. No." His coughing was tighter.

"It is unhealthful for these to remain with you. They have contagion in them. I will see they are disposed of." Rakoczy went to the door. "I will leave this open so you will have light. One of the servants will bring you a clean chamber-pot and basin shortly." With that he sought out the rear door and carried the two vessels to the midden to empty them into the steaming heap of garbage, sweepings, and ordure; the severed front hoof of a deer protruded from the pile, which he shoved back into it with the six-tined rake lying beside it.

One of the mansion's nine cats went purposefully past Rakoczy, a mouse feebly twitching in its jaws. Rakoczy watched it go, thinking back to his centuries in Egypt where cats were venerated and worshiped, quite unlike the suspicion they aroused now in most of Europe. His reflections were interrupted by Barnon, who emerged from the herb-garden gate, his steaming breath revealing that he was in a hurry.

"Comes. There you are." He came up to Rakoczy in four long strides. "Counselor Smiricti is here. He desires to speak with you."

"Does he," said Rakoczy, and handed the empty basin and chamber-pot to Barnon. "These were in Minek's room. See they are washed and that he has clean ones."

Barnon ducked his head. "The Episcopus says that it is wrong to wash chamber-pots over-much."

"The Episcopus may say what he likes; in this household, vessels of this sort are to be emptied and washed daily—I thought I made that clear months ago." He swung the herb-garden gate open, going through it ahead of the steward.

"Zenka says she has chilblains from all the chamber-pots you require she wash," Barnon said as if this settled the matter.

"If she washes the chamber-pots in hot water, there will be no chilblains."

"Hot water stimulates lust," said Barnon, dutifully repeating Episcopus Fauvinel's warnings.

"In a laundry?" Rakoczy laughed once at the absurdity of the notion, and again wondered if he should enlarge the washroom, which was a single, small, stone chamber at the rear of the bath-house where Zenka and her niece Bedriska did the linen and clothes-cleaning for Mansion Belcrady.

"The Devil is everywhere," said Barnon, following Rakoczy in the side-door. "Counselor Smiricti is in the rear withdrawing room. Pacar is making a plate of bread and sausages for him. I have already given him a tankard of beer."

"That is good of you," said Rakoczy, and continued on to the main hall, crossing it to the withdrawing room, where he found Counselor Smiricti in a long huch of marten-fur with a hood he had thrown back; his large ears were red with cold; a tankard of beer stood half-empty on the table in front of the fireplace. "Welcome to Mansion Belcrady, Counselor." He gave a polite bow.

"And my thanks to you, Comes," said Smiricti, not bothering to rise. "Your houseman said he would return to build up the fire."

"I will attend to that," Rakoczy offered, going to the bin next to the hearth and taking out an arm-long section of log. "This will catch soon enough, and you will be warm again."

"You wouldn't think a sunny day could be so cold." Smiricti pulled off his gloves and vigorously rubbed his hands together. "The beer he brought me is very good—not cloudy or bitter."

"Thank you," said Rakoczy, studying Smiricti.

"You probably want to know what brings me out on such a day," he began, and not waiting for an answer said, "I'm here to extend you an invitation, but it might not be to your liking." This last he said in a rush.

More curious than circumspect, Rakoczy asked, "An invitation? What is the occasion?" He put the log atop the piled embers of the old fire; sparks flew up like tiny, bright insects.

"The Beggars' Guild is having a burning of rats in Council Court Square as soon as it is clear of snow. Since the Episcopus has decided in their favor in their suit against the rats, and the Council has concurred, the city's beggars have been trapping and killing rats in great quantity." He pursed his lips. "We have been using your poison cakes and trapping boxes in the Council Court, to good effect. We have more than a hundred of the bodies stacked up behind the privy. But doubtless you know that the Episcopus has declared that since the bodies of rats bring fevers and generate wasps and gnats, the bodies must be destroyed or buried a league outside the city walls. The ground is too hard to make a grave-pit, so there will be a fire. The Beggars' Guild is going throughout the city collecting rats to give to the flames."

"Why was I invited?" Rakoczy asked, genuinely puzzled.

"You have helped us to be rid of the rats. The Counselors would like to thank you for your deadly little cakes, and where better than at the burning of poisoned rats? But you may prefer that not half the city know that you are skilled with poisons, being an exile and one of the Konige's Court." He saw Barnon in the door with a tray in his hands. "You're always the gracious host, Comes. Very much to your credit. Some of our Bohemian lords could take a lesson from you." He sat forward in his chair. "Sausages!"

"Of veal with cardamom, boiled in wine," said Barnon, putting the tray on the round table; he glanced once at Rakoczy, then devoted his attention to Smiricti.

"Your master provides well for his guests," said Smiricti, reaching for one of the finger-sized sausages. "Still hot. Good." He popped it into his mouth, chewing energetically.

"Tell me, Counselor," Rakoczy said while Smiricti ate, "why is such a burning of rats afforded so much attention?"

Smiricti looked at him, surprised. "Rats are the bane of the city. Since the Episcopus has granted that killing them is allowed, even on days of the Peace of God, it is just as well to make such an act a grand one, so that all the people can see that they need no longer suffer the creatures to infest their houses, where they do Devil's work."

"We have few rats here," said Barnon. "The Comes sees to it."

"That's good of you to say," Rakoczy told him.

"The Comes keeps an orderly household," Barnon said with more emphasis. "He sees to the welfare of all his vassals."

A number of questions roiled in Rakoczy's mind, but he kept them to himself, not wanting to draw Smiricti into his private business. "Barnon, has Minek been attended to?"

"Yes, Comes. He has." He ducked his head and left the withdrawing room before Rakoczy could ask for more information.

"These sausages are delicious, just delicious," Smiricti enthused as he bit into a second one.

"I am pleased you find them so," Rakoczy said, sitting down across the table from Counselor Smiricti. "Whom else have you invited to this . . . festival?"

"The Konige and her Court, of course, and the Episcopus. The Masters of all the city's Guilds, and all visiting merchants within the walls, since they have often complained of damage done to their goods by rats." He broke off a section of bread from the oblong loaf he had been given. "The Beggars' Guild plan to light their bonfire at sunset. You will want to be in place ahead of that hour."

"So I might," said Rakoczy, "if I come."

"But you must. There are those who will see your absence as a slight." He drank more beer. "You can't want that, can you?"

"No," Rakoczy answered, his attention on his small hands. "But I have had nothing from the Konige informing me that my presence is required." He considered his situation again. "Konig Bela has laid restrictions upon me, as you know, and without an order from Konige Kunigunde, it would violate the terms of my exile to attend so public an event."

"I shall send a messenger to the Konige, then, and have him deliver her decision to you. That should prevent any delays." He bit into the wad of bread he held, and his next words were muffled. "The Beggars' Guild is happy to have this chance to show Praha what use it can be."

"Killing rats is a great service," said Rakoczy with no hint of sarcasm.

"So they say." Smiricti took another sausage.

While the Counselor munched his way through his food, Rakoczy got up from his chair and paced the length of the withdrawing room. The fire was beginning to blaze again, lending its heat to the chamber, and Rakoczy moved away from the flames. He went to the shuttered window, wanting to throw it open, but mindful of the snow beyond, he left the window closed. "How long do you expect the bonfire will last?" he asked Smiricti.

"As long as there are rats to burn. The Episcopus has said that he would allow the gathering to last until Vigil begins."

"So long," said Rakoczy in surprise, for he had not often seen the Episcopus endorse any street celebrations that continued so long after sundown. He had been told that Easter celebrations could go on all night, but for such an occasion as this one the Episcopus most often insisted that strict limitations be imposed, to lessen the chances for public crime and lewdness.

"The Episcopus has rats in his cathedral. He has given the Beggars' Guild the task of killing and collecting them all." Smiricti chuckled and pulled another hunk of bread off the loaf.

"So the bonfire is a reward for the Beggars' Guild," said Rakoczy.

"As much of one as they will ever receive from Episcopus Fauvinel, who has said that the Guild, for being a Guild, has put its members beyond the Church's charity," said Smiricti. "I would count it a favor if you would be willing to attend."

"And the Konige—what of her decision in that regard."

"If she tells you that you mayn't attend, that will be the end of it," Smiricti declared through a mouthful of bread. "She has said that your natal-day gift to her older daughter was the handsomest of any the child received, and for that reason alone she is kindly inclined to you. She may look forward to another display of your generosity."

"What do you recommend I do if she makes no decision at all?" Rakoczy inquired; he wondered whether or not the Konige would want him to be at such a function, where public unruliness would likely be rampant.

"Oh, I doubt she'd do that. She's unlikely to leave her preference in doubt." He picked up the last sausage. "These are really very good, Comes. I thank you for providing them." He began to eat the sausage. "You wouldn't consider providing more of these for the celebration tonight, would you?"

"If I am permitted to attend, I will gladly bring some with me," said Rakoczy.

"Of course," said Smiricti, "if you're permitted to attend."

Text of a letter from Frater Purvanek at the Monastery of the Holy Martyrs three leagues from Praha on the bank of the Moltava, to Episcopus Fauvinel at the Royal Court in Praha, written on vellum and delivered by private Church courier.

To the greatly pious, most reverend Episcopus Fauvinel, this letter from the hand of Frater Purvanek at the Monastery of the Holy Martyrs on this, the 9th day of February in the 1270th year of Grace,

Most excellent Episcopus,

It is my duty to tell you that the Fraters here have done me the honor of electing me to succeed the former Abbott Varengara, who has gone on pilgrimage to Jerusalem. It is the Abbott's hope to die in that most holy city and as his illness is worsening, he has departed so that he will have time enough to reach the Holy Land. To that end, I am taking it upon myself to write to you to inform you of conditions here.

Since it is now my duty to see to the monks and the maintenance of this monastery, I apply to you for what help you can provide us. The storms of the winter have left the cow-barn with a badly damaged roof, and the creamery with water standing on the floor. We will have to be rid of all the cheeses ripening there because the damp has made them unfit to eat, according to Frater Miloslav, who is in charge of the creamery. Without cheese, we will be able to tend to fewer travelers, which will lessen the donations upon which we depend, and without help from you and the city, some of our monks are likely to starve before the damage here is repaired. I beseech you to provide us as much assistance as you can.

Let me ask you to come to the monastery to see for yourself how we are suffering. It would restore the hopes of many of the monks here if they were certain of your attentions in this hard time. God may send us many tribulations but He also sends us you, our Episcopus, to shepherd us through the trials of this world, so that we may join in the celebration of Resurrection on April 13th; for without your help and succor, we will surely by that day be awaiting the Last Trumpet in our graves. We implore you to aid us as if we were your children, for surely your rank puts you in the position of a parent, for we are all vassals of the Church, and we receive Grace from your offices. God has laid His hand upon you, and entrusted many souls to your keeping; ours are among them. With the Devil abroad in the land, we call upon you to help us restore our faith in His Mercy and the protection of the Church.

With my devotion and prayerful submission to our Rule,

> Frater Purvanek
>> Abbott of the Monastery of the Holy Martyrs
>> Benedictine

2

"Where does your cousin think you are? Surely you did not sneak out of Vaclav Castle, did you? Your note said only that you would be coming here clandestinely: how does it come about?" Rakoczy asked Imbolya as they hastily climbed toward the warder's quarters in the gate-house, he leading but facing her, so that he moved backward up the dimly lit spiral staircase. They were making as little noise as possible, for although outside the gate-house freezing rain buzzed on a gusty wind, rattling the slates on the roof and hooting smokily down the chimneys of Mansion Belcrady, they knew someone might well be listening for any unusual sound.

"I am on a mission for the Konige," she said, trying not to giggle; her hair was damp and drops of rain spangled her face in the light from the gateway torch.

"Truly?"

"Yes. As the Konige's messenger, Csenge has sent me to the Sorers at Sante-Zore to secure their agreement to participate in the festival planned when the Konig departs to resume his campaign in the south. Csenge doesn't like going out in the wet, and decided to send me in her stead. The Konige doesn't interfere with Csenge's decisions. Besides, my cousin can't read, so she chose me, because I can. Right now, I'm the *only* one of the Konige's ladies who can." She tossed her head. "It's good to speak Magyar again. I get tired of Bohemian. There's nothing like my native tongue in my mouth." She chuckled at her joke.

"I agree," he said, uncomfortably aware that he was the last surviving speaker of his native language.

"So you give me two pleasures while I attend to my mission, one of the flesh and one of the ear." She was becoming a little breathless as much from anticipation as from their rapid climb. "I yearn for them both."

"I suppose it would not be wise of me to thank Csenge of Somogy for assigning you the task," said Rakoczy sardonically.

"No, it wouldn't," said Imbolya, halting in her upward rush and regarding him worriedly, frowning as she looked at him. Then her countenance lightened and she pushed at his arm in feigned reprimand. "Oh. You're teasing me."

"Not successfully," he said, a trifle chagrined. "What about the festival?" he inquired as they resumed their climb.

Imbolya lifted her skirts to enable her to move more quickly. "Ordinarily the festivities would be held at Easter, but since that won't come until the middle of April, the Konig is determined to be under way by the end of March, so I'm charged with asking the Sorers what they would be willing to do to help send the army on its way with God's blessings and the blessings of His servants before the Resurrection Masses." She saw him nod, and went on, "The Sorers keep stringent Hours; I would have had to wait for some time to speak to Mader Svetla, and that seemed to me to be unnecessary, especially in this weather, and so when I was left at the gate to the convent, I sent my escort to the tavern and I came here—I didn't say where I was going. And you're only two streets away from Sante-Zore; it's not as if I've been wandering about the city unprotected."

"A prudent explanation," he said. "I am glad you decided to come here."

"And I'm glad you got my message in time to admit me yourself; I only realized later that you might not get the note in time."

"The terms of my exile keep me here, inside the walls," he said. "If I am not where the Konige orders me to be, I am here."

She nodded. "I remembered that just before I reached your

gate, thank God and Sant Persemon." She crossed herself. "I might not have sounded the bell if I hadn't recalled that; it would have been awkward explaining my presence to a servant, who would be certain to remember that I came here, and might report me to his Confessor, who would report to the Episcopus, which would be harmful for both of us. Fortunately, nothing bad transpired." She grinned, still a little out of breath, as she burst into the cold room above the gate; it was a spartan chamber, with a bed, a chair, a chest that also served as a table, and a brazier, with pegs on the wall for clothes. A simple wooden crucifix hung on the door. The rushes had been swept out, and so the floor was bare and cold. "When will your warder return to his post? He must still be recovering if he isn't here in his quarters." She wrenched off her gorget and wimple, tossing them on one of the pegs.

"He will be back here in a few more days," said Rakoczy. "He has not put on much flesh since he became ill, and that worries me a little; his tainted lungs have left him depleted and unable to strengthen himself. He needs someone to keep an eye on him, and he needs to stay warm. I have ordered him to remain where he is until he is less gaunt. If his appetite strengthens, it will be no more than five days before he is back here." As he spoke, he went to the brazier in the middle of the room, removed its tarnished copper lid, put a handful of kindling into it, added three branches of rosemary, and used flint-and-steel to strike a spark. "This won't give much heat, but it will be better than nothing."

Imbolya laughed as she unfastened the lacings on her bleihaut. "Then I rely on you to keep me warm." Much of her shyness around him had faded, and she looked at him with sauciness in her eyes. "We haven't much time. You don't have to take time to woo me; I'm yours for the taking." She stepped out of her bleihaut as it dropped to the floor, then sat on the edge of her bed to remove her solers and braccae before skinning out of her chainse and diving under the bear-skin cover on the bed. She wriggled up to the small pillow and poked her head out. "I'm waiting for you."

Rakoczy made sure the fire was truly started, then put a branch on the rising flames. "It may get a little smoky," he warned.

"What fire does not smoke? At least your flues are clear so they draw well." She snuggled the fur around her, shivering in anticipation as well as cold. "Hurry, Comes. I've been dreaming of you and all you do for two weeks."

He unfastened the lacing on his Hungarian bleihaut of Damascus black silk and removed the garment, dropped it over the chair, then pulled off his red-tooled-leather ankle-boots, putting them beside the bleihaut. His chainse hung to his knees and was of dark-red Anatolian wool, so soft that it felt almost like velvet; the braccae beneath were of supple deer-skin leather dyed black. He took off no more clothing. "Make room for me, Imbolya."

She laughed and lifted a corner of the bear-skin. "You'll have to lie close; there isn't much room."

"I think I can manage," he said as he crossed the distance between them in two strides and slid under the bear-skin beside her, gathering her into his arms as he did; the ropes under the thin mattress groaned and the bed swayed while the ropes balanced the load. As they shifted themselves, making room for elbows and knees, he murmured, "It is disappointing to have to be so rushed; I hope you will be fulfilled, but—"

"It's this or nothing, Comes," said Imbolya very seriously. "I would rather have some than none. You have given me so much already." She snuggled to his chest, remarking as she did, "Your body seems . . . chilly. No wonder you keep your chainse on." On impulse she stroked the Hungarian collar of his chainse. "This is wonderful cloth."

"Those of my blood have cool flesh," said Rakoczy, pulling the bear-skin more closely around them. "How long can you stay here?"

"Not as long as I'd like. Until the clock in the German church strikes twice," she said. "You can hear it from here, can't you? even with the rain and wind."

"Yes," said Rakoczy, quickly reckoning their time together. "It is not loud, but we do hear it. Pacar, my cook, depends upon it."

"Then I won't fret about it." She smiled slowly, her eyes alight.

He sensed her eagerness and something more, perilously close to gloating, that private knowledge of a delicious secret she could relish in private. "No word of this must get out, for both our sakes."

"I know," she said with a hint of disappointment. "I would not make a good marriage, and you, most likely, would be gelded or burned at the stake. But Konig Otakar wouldn't dare to hang you in chains—it would be the act of a despot, not a Christian Konig, hanging an exiled nobleman in such a disgraceful way. And Konig Bela wouldn't like it, which would make matters difficult for the Konige. Still, you would be reviled as a seducer, and I would be a fallen woman. The best you could hope for would be a prison cell and torture. I might have to travel to Roma on my knees to make expiation for my lust." She shook her head. "But it *isn't* lust, or not only lust."

"What is it, then?" He moved his arm so she could rest her head on it.

"Something between you and me, Comes. You said so yourself. What we do together is our secret, one that is precious to us both." She touched his close-cropped beard. "I like your face. Your nose is askew and your eyes are a strange color: black with striations of blue, but I like the face. It suits you. I like more than your face."

He kissed her forehead, a little saddened that she had said *like* and not *love,* although he knew she spoke the truth, and answered her truthfully. "And I like you," he told her. "All of you."

She wrapped her arms around his neck. "What would the Episcopus think of us now?" There was a pop and a small shower of sparks as resin within the burning branch exploded, the scent of pine vying with the rosemary to sweeten the air; this gave her an excuse to pull him closer and to hold him more tightly. "We must hurry."

"Are you certain?"

"Yes. Yes."

"That is unfortunate," he said with undisguised sadness in his voice. "You would enjoy this much more if we had a long time to-gether. If we rush, we will have to give up savoring each sensation."

"Then we'll have to gorge and make the most of it." She pulled his head down to kiss him, her body taut as a bowstring. Only her lips were soft, pliant, and welcoming. As they broke apart, she giggled. "Where did you learn . . . so much?"

He did not answer at once. "I doubt you would like my re-sponse."

She rubbed his short beard with the tips of her fingers. "If you think I'll be jealous, I won't be. I know you have had lovers before me, and will have more of them when I am married."

It took him a short while to consider his response. "Whatever I say cannot be unsaid," he cautioned her.

"Tell me," she insisted, a hint of petulance coming into her tone. "If you don't tell me, I'll think worse of you than if you do, no matter how much you may believe I won't be pleased. I do want to know—really."

"Then I will tell you: for the most part I have learned about women in the company of women," he answered, not at all certain this was a wise decision.

"Have there been very many?" Her voice was not quite a whisper, but there was mischief in her oblique glance.

"Yes," he said, his thoughts ranging back more than thirty centuries.

"Did you love them?" As she asked, she pressed her body to his.

"There are as many ways to love as there are people in the world," said Rakoczy, kissing her brow and the bridge of her nose.

"That isn't an answer," she challenged him, arching her back so that her small breasts pushed against him.

"Every woman is different: what each seeks and gives is dis-similar to all the rest. Like you, not all seek love, and like you, not all wish to bestow it." He thought of Melidulci and Olivia, of Tish-try and Gynethe Mehaut, of Padmiri and Thetis.

"I know that: did you love them?"

"Most of them," he said, thinking now of Aloysia in Constantinople, of Csimenae in Hispania, and of Jo-Hsu in western China, then of Rozsa of Borsod: none of them had wanted intimacy from him, only stimulation and release, each in her own way, not unlike the women he visited in their sleep; the dreams he provided them, however sweet, did not include the touching he sought.

She looked at him, her eyes serious, her young face showing the ghost of age. "You said you like me—do you love me?"

This time he had no hesitation in answering candidly. "As much as you love me; what emotion I feel, and how deeply I feel it, is determined by you," he said, thinking his explanation was too simplistic. She tweaked his close-cropped beard then; he kissed her slowly, thoroughly, his hands moving across her back, relearning her contours. He began to caress her, stroking her sides, her arms, her back, seeking out new secrets in her flesh, doing nothing in haste, fitting his attentions to her increasing ardor until she pulled away.

"We shouldn't dawdle," she said, taking his arms and pulling his hands around to her breasts. "You know how to make my desire burn bright."

"It burns brighter if it is not hurried," he said, all the while gently kneading her breasts, small and firm as summer apples, pausing now and then to tease her nipples until they stood, rosy and firm, between his fingers.

"But we haven't much time," she persisted. "Keep doing that, and we'll miss the opportunity for more. The clock will strike and I'll have to leave you and return to the nuns." She strove to kiss him again, her mouth firm, demanding on his, her lips parted. She could begin to feel the first twinge of concupiscence, so she redoubled her efforts, sliding against him and placing one of his hands on her buttock. "Work your way around to the front," she said when she ended their kiss. "It will save time."

"If that will give you fulfillment," he said, and let her guide him. He could sense the urgency she felt, and was surprised at how quickly her passion ignited; it was not her youth alone that inspired her, but the awareness that she would soon be a bride; this was her only chance at the kind of rapture that the troubadours said belonged to legendary lovers and the priests said belonged only to God.

"Hurry. You've got to hurry," she whispered to him, breathing quickly. "My spasm will come quickly once you touch my woman's bud."

"Or it may be too abrupt, and it will take longer to waken your passion," he said, thinking of the many times he had experienced this.

She coughed once and waved her hand. "The smoke," she said by way of explanation. "I want you to be quick and—" She coughed again.

"Do you want me to put the lid on the brazier?" he asked, starting to disentangled his arms from hers.

"I want you to rouse me, to show me the extent of my pleasure," she said emphatically but without raising her voice. "Smoke is everywhere in Praha in winter." She took hold of the hand he had freed, and kissed it. "Time is passing. Give me my rapture."

In answer to her order, he slid his hand between her legs and moved from her knees to the warm, pink petals at the top of her legs. He fingered the soft outer folds while he kissed her mouth with nuances inspired by her educing arousal.

Imbolya felt her insouciance released, as if she floated in warm, perfumed water, her body pliant and tingling. "Comes," she whispered before sinking gloriously into yet another kiss. She wriggled against him, urging herself to greater apolaustic fervor. Her skin felt as sensitive as if it had been scrubbed, but without the pain of scrubbing. She stared into his compelling eyes. "You have so much . . . so much," she murmured, not knowing what she meant. "Comes, sweet Comes." She sank one hand into his hair, pulling him down into another kiss, her body melding to his through his chainse. A delicious spring began to gather in her, its frisson promising a spasm that would exceed the other two she had achieved from him. "Hurry. Hurry." She coughed once, turning her head away as if abashed by it. "Don't stop."

He felt her pulse as he slid two fingers into her and realized that she was not as near her spasm as she thought she was. "Do not chase it, Imbolya," he whispered. "Let it come to you."

"But we haven't *time*," she wailed softly.

He slowed his attentions to her, concentrating on her pulse he felt within her, and how she breathed as her body reacted to his evocation with his mouth and hands. He used his thumb to circle and excite her woman's bud. After a short while, her pulse grew stronger and faster, and he knew her culmination would shortly be upon her; he brushed her lips with his, and felt her quiver as her ecstasy grew more intense, and she reached to draw him nearer.

There was a rap on the door.

The two of them were suddenly still, hardly breathing, listening to the sounds from outside the room. Beyond the wail of the wind and the purr of the icy rain there were shouts and the sound of the kitchen bell.

"My master," Hruther called quietly in Imperial Latin.

"No," Imbolya protested, trying to pull the bear-skin over their heads. "Not yet! Not *yet!*"

Gently Rakoczy disengaged himself from her embrace and slipped out of the bed, getting to his feet. "What is it?"

"There is a fire in the bake-house chimney. If it isn't stopped, it will spread to the manse." He paused. "I can guide your companion to safety. You are needed at the fire."

"A fire, you say—in the chimney?" Rakoczy asked, surprised.

"In the bake-house chimney."

"It was just cleaned," Rakoczy said.

"So it was," Hruther agreed. "Yet it is afire."

Rakoczy nodded, reluctantly shifting his attention away from Imbolya. "I'll be with you in a moment. I will need you to help—"

"—your companion to depart without drawing attention to her," Hruther finished for him. "Yes. I'll see she gets away unnoticed."

On the bed, Imbolya punched the mattress then flung back the bear-skin. "Something's happened, hasn't it?"

"There's a fire," said Rakoczy in Magyar. "I must go. And so must you. It isn't safe here."

She paled, the prospect of a fire gaining her full attention. "Yes. We must. It would not do either of us good if I were discovered here." She got out of the bed, reaching for her clothes. "I don't want to delay you."

He was pulling on his bleihaut. "My personal servant will escort you to Sante-Zore. You may rely on him implicitly, Imbolya: I do." He reached for his belt and secured it around his waist.

"I should thank you for sparing him to me," she said, shivering. "How extensive is the fire?"

"I am going to find out," said Rakoczy, then added quietly, "I apologize for this, Imbolya."

She was tugging her chainse over her head, and as she emerged through the neck of the garment, she shrugged. "I came to you and we knew it would be brief." She took her braccae and began to pull one on. "My solers—"

"Under the bed," he told her, and bent to pick up her bleihaut, holding it for her.

"I see them," she said, pulling on her other bracca.

"As soon as you are ready." He offered her bleihaut to her.

"Just a . . ." She stood up, settling her chainse around her; she caught the cuffs in her hands and held up her arms to help him fit her bleihaut around her. "Don't worry about the lacing. I can tie them well enough."

"If you like."

She blinked against the smoke in the room. "Best put the lid on the brazier."

Rakoczy was already setting the tarnished copper in place. "Your solers." He pointed to them.

"And your boots," she said, bending over to don her footwear.

"Where is Barnon?" Rakoczy asked as he opened the door to Hruther.

"I left him organizing the men to carry buckets from the horse-trough to the fire. He's badly frightened." Hruther held a heavy soccus folded over his arm. "I think your companion would benefit from this."

Rakoczy glanced at the old-fashioned Byzantine cloak. "Yes; thank you, old friend. The weather alone calls for it."

Turning to Imbolya, Hruther said, "You will want to wear the hood up." He ducked his head respectfully.

Imbolya, who was adjusting her gorget and wimple, stopped to look at the engulfing garment. "Oh, yes," she exclaimed. "This is most welcome." She seized the soccus and swung it around her shoulders, permitting it to fall about her before she raised the hood. "I will see it returned to you. It's safer that way."

Rakoczy laid his hand on her shoulder. "Be careful, Imbolya."

"Your man will see to that," she said, and stood in front of him, her face turned up toward him. "Will we have the chance to meet again, do you think? I won't be at the Konige's Court much longer."

"I hope so," he said, kissing her forehead. "If we can meet safely."

"Safely," she echoed disbelievingly, then pushed his chest. "You'd better go. Your servants will need you to command them." With that, she turned away from Rakoczy and addressed Hruther. "I'm ready to follow you."

"Thank you, Hruther," said Rakoczy as he stood aside to permit Imbolya to pass out of the room to the stairs, then descended behind them. At the foot of the stairs, Rakoczy took the larger door and stepped out into the forecourt, one hand raised to keep the blowing rain from getting into his eyes; he did not look to see Hruther open the small warder's door that led to the narrow alley that ran beside the wall to the craftsmen's gate.

"Comes!" shouted Estephe as Rakoczy came around the eastern flank of the manse. "Where have you been?"

"Hruther found me," Rakoczy answered promptly, looking at the billowing smoke that roiled up from the burning chimney, where flames licked at the sooty darkness, spreading heat along with fear. "When did this start? Does anyone know? Who saw it first?"

"The first flames were seen not long ago, but who knows how long they built up? You know how chimney fires can be." He was rushing toward the horse-trough, a large bucket dangling from his rough-gloved hand. "Barnon has ordered us to throw water on the fire. Six of the household men are doing the task."

One of the scullions rushed by, a bucket of water clasped in his hands and held high in front of his body.

"Illes of Kotan—is he helping?" Rakoczy asked, lengthening his stride as he neared the trough.

"He has taken the horses from the stable to the paddock, away from the flames; they were fretting in their stalls—one of the mules was kicking," said Estephe, and crossed himself. "Should I summon him?"

"It is better for him to care for the horses," said Rakoczy.

They were almost at the horse-trough, where Barnon was handing a full bucket to Kornemon while Ambroz lowered his pail into the water. "Make your buckets full and spill as little as you can."

"Very good," said Rakoczy, and reached for one of two wooden buckets standing next to the horse-trough. "Who is commanding the men at the bake-house?"

"Comes." Barnon stared at him. "What are you doing?"

"Helping to put out the fire," he said, filling the bucket. "Who is in charge at the bake-house?"

"Pacar. He says he knows fire from the kitchen."

Rakoczy nodded and hastened away toward the bake-house, his bucket balanced so that he would not lose much of its contents, calling out to Pacar as he came to the edge of the smoke, "Where shall I pour this?"

Pacar stood in the door to the bake-house, his face smirched with ash, his kitchen-smock pock-marked with burns from flying sparks. His voice was hoarse from shouting and breathing in smoke. "Throw it there," he barked without looking at the new arrival, pointing to the maw of the fireplace.

"The fire is in the flue, not on the hearth," said Rakoczy, and swung his bucket so that the water arched toward the chimney, hissing as it struck the bricks. Hot steam rose in pale clouds from the wet patch, getting lost in the black smoke hiding the ceiling. Rakoczy could see that some of the smoke was moving, and he realized that some of the ceiling had smoldered away.

Pacar turned, aghast. "Comes," he gasped, ducking his head twice. "God and His Angels! Why are you here?"

"My property is on fire," said Rakoczy.

"But you . . . you shouldn't be fighting it. That's servants' work." Pacar seemed truly distressed.

"Never mind that," Rakoczy said. "The water must go onto the chimney, not into the hearth. The fire is at least eighteen hands up, inside the chimney." He felt the heat on his hands and face like a desert wind.

"But it may break if the site of the fire is struck with water," Pacar protested.

"It is ruined already, so you might as well get the fire out as quickly as possible; that way, the rebuilding will not require a completely new flue for the ovens and the hearth, the masons can build on the old foundations. Why should cracked bricks trouble you? Pour on all the water you can." Rakoczy backed away from the fire, feeling more than seeing Timoty, the household courier, approaching with a large metal pail held to his chest.

Pacar hesitated as he became aware of Timoty. He sighed heavily and pointed at the chimney. "Throw it there."

Satisfied that the fire would soon be out, Rakoczy went back for another bucketful of water; he could feel the sleet growing thicker as the wind tore at the clouds. He noticed that the men with buckets and pails were moving faster, but whether it was because the storm was worsening or because he was helping to fight the fire, he could not say. He set himself to working steadily, and soon the smoke rising from the bake-house was paler, and the hiss of water on the chimney was fading as the bricks grew cooler and wetter, and the mortar began to crumble. On his ninth return to the bake-house, Rakoczy took time to look up at the ceiling, and noticed the main beams were charred, and in three places the roof had given way, leaving the bake-house open to the sky. "Is the bath-house damaged?" he asked Pacar, for the bake-house and bath-house shared a good portion of the chimney above the three tall ovens.

"No one has looked," Pacar said, his voice barely audible. "The fire doesn't appear to have spread that far."

"Then send someone to examine the bath-house to make sure. I do not want the fire starting up again." Rakoczy met Pacar's gaze directly.

"If that is what you want of us," Pacar said grudgingly. "It is in the Hands of God whether we shall all burn or shall be saved." He crossed himself to make his point.

"Then why did you bother to fight the fire? Why not leave Mansion Belcrady to God?" Rakoczy asked, and spoke before Pacar could frame an answer. "God asks us to use His gifts to help ourselves once we are old enough to fend for ourselves."

Pacar shrugged and bent over to cough. "It will take some days to clear away the damage. No baking can be done until the chimney is made whole again."

"The central hearth cannot be used," Rakoczy said, noticing how close the fireplace was to collapsing; a bundle of sticks lay under the chimney, black where they were not reduced to ash. "The ovens will have to be inspected as well. And the bath can't be heated."

Ambroz came and flung more water on the chimney. "Looks like it's out."

"Probably," said Pacar.

Between the open door and the holes in the roof, the smoke was dissipating quickly; now drops of gelid rain added to the mess on the floor. The household men started to gather up their pails and buckets while Pacar leaned in the door, wheezing. Now that the danger had passed, they all wanted to be away from the bakehouse.

"Comes, come away. Leave it to the bricklayers to fix," said Estephe.

Only Rakoczy remained near the chimney, studying it in the half-light. There was a mass of cracks in the mortar a hand above his head, and the bricks bulged a little. Rakoczy shook his head, then looked down at the fireplace and the mass of twigs and strips of cloth, something like a rats' nest. "But the chimneys have just been cleaned," he muttered to himself as he crouched down to have a better look at the thing.

"Comes, it isn't safe," Pacar warned, shoving himself out of the door.

"Still," said Rakoczy, picking up a blackened length of twine. He lifted it, sniffing it carefully, then rolled it along his fingers, studying the residue it left behind. "Wax," he said in his own language. He picked up one of the remaining twigs. "More wax." He slipped the twine and the stick into his sleeve.

"Comes," Ambroz urged him.

"I am coming," he said in Bohemian, and went to the door, thinking as he went that the fire in the chimney had been set, and the wax proved it.

Text of a letter of introduction from Frater Sandor, scribe to Konig Bela of Hungary, to Konig Przemysl Otakar II of Bohemia and the Counselors of Praha, written in Church Latin on parchment, carried by Royal herald, and delivered sixteen days after it was dispatched.

At the behest of Bela, Konig of Hungary, I send this message to Przemysl Otakar II, Konig of Bohemia, Moravia, Styria, Carinthia, Carinola, and Magna Dux of Austria, and the Counselors of

Praha to present to you the following of Konig Bela's nobles who will be joining the Court of Konig Bela's granddaughter, Kunigunde of Halicz, Konige of Bohemia; this on the 20th day of February in the Lord's Year 1270.

Kustansze of Lugoj, grandniece to Konig Bela and second cousin to Konige Kunigunde, to be one of Konige Kunigunde's waiting-women, housed within the Konige's Court; she is a widow of high repute and the mother of three children currently in Konig Bela's service and care. Past the age of wiles and foolishness, she will provide a pious example to the Konige's Court. She will be escorted by Padnagy Kalman, Dux of Oradea, and four of his officers.

Iliska of Szousa, second daughter of the Comes of Szousa, will take the place of Erzebet of Arad as one of the Konige's Court; she will be escorted by her brother, Antal of Szousa, who will remain with his sister until harvest-time, when he will return to his father at Szousa. Antal of Szousa will have five men-at-arms with him, and bring ten slaves for Konige Kunigunde's use. He will also be in charge of six mares from Konig Bela's stables, a gift to the Court of his granddaughter. He will house himself and his men, so as not to be a charge upon the Konige, and to help to preserve the good names of the waiting-women.

Rozsa of Borsod will return to the Konige's Court until Mid-Summer, when her pregnancy will require her to return to Kaposvar to await the birth of her child at the seat of his father, for surely God will give Notay Tibor a son. Rozsa of Borsod will be escorted by Milan of Gyula, master of Notay Tibor's personal Guard, with six of his men. Rozsa of Borsod will become part of the Konige's Court again, but her escort and his men will take lodgings in the city of Praha and will be responsible for their maintenance and the maintenance of their horses.

In addition, two Passionist monks, Frater Dubede and Frater Isdros, will travel with the company, to minister the Sacraments as they may be needed, and to hear the Confessions of the travelers.

May God yet send you a son, Konig Otakar, and may your wars spare you so that you live to rejoice in him.

*For Konig Bela of Hungary
by the hand of Frater Sandor
Hieronymite and Royal Scribe*

3

"I was sorry to learn of the fire at Mansion Belcrady, Comes," the Konige said as she looked away from the four perfect egg-shaped blue sapphires lying in their ivory box to Rakoczy Ferancsi, who had presented them to her; around them many of her Court were gathered, vying for notice and favor. For this glittering occasion, where all her Court was charged with making a lavish and rich showing, the Konige had donned a long-trained double bleihaut, one of cloth-of-gold, and the other of parti-colored Italian velvet over a chainse of Mosul-cotton. Instead of gorget and wimple, she wore a chaplet of fretted gold and a tall necklace of topazes and pearls with three tear-drop diamonds depending from it in frames of rose-shaped gold. The reception hall of the Konige's Court in Vaclav Castle was very grand, decorated with swags of evergreens, alight with such a vast array of candles that it was deemed brighter than the fading day beyond the shuttered windows. Fresh rushes were strewn on the floor, and odors rising from the kitchens promised a magnificent feast.

"Dear Royal is most gracious," said Rakoczy with a deep French bow. As the occasion demanded, he, too, was elegant in his huch of black-red Damascus silk lined with a herringbone pattern of darkest weasel-pelts, the square, open sleeves lined in red satin and edged in rubies. His chainse was of black Ankara wool, woven to the fineness of Coan linen; his braccae were of supple Persian leather dyed dark-red, and his thick-soled Hungarian estivaux were black, reaching up his leg to just below his knee. The ruby-studded silver-link collar stood out against his clothing, and the pectoral of his eclipse device was magnificent with silver raised wings over a large black sapphire. His silver coronet shone on his brow.

"It is doubly duteous of you to have brought these jewels to me when you have more pressing matters demanding your attention," she said, running her finger over the lid of the box. Her torpid demeanor and downcast eyes were at odds with the splendor of the Court.

"I am here in Praha to serve you, dear Royal."

"You keep to your task quite well," she approved, but in so flat a voice that he would not have been convinced of her sincerity had he not been aware it was her melancholy speaking. "My grandfather did well in sending you to me." This was somewhat more persuasive. Her quirky smile was a bit more animated.

"He wished to see you resplendently adorned, dear Royal, as befits a Konige of such high degree," said Rakoczy, thinking as he did how tedious court-ship could be. "If you and Konig Bela are pleased, what can I be but delighted."

"What gallantry," she remarked. "For someone from so remote a region, you have the conduct of a Prince of the Blood."

Rakoczy could not suppress a faint, ironic smile. "Dear Royal gives me much praise."

She looked away, touching her necklace, her eyes distant. "How is it you do not give me pearls, Comes?"

Rakoczy had answered this question many times over the centuries, and said promptly and truthfully, "Among those of my blood, pearls are said to bring tears, which I would never wish upon you, dear Royal." He assumed she would not pursue the matter; pearls were the one jewel he could not make in his athanor: he relied on Eclipse Trading to keep him supplied.

She considered his answer, her eyes distant, and finally said, "I will inform you when I have chosen the gift I wish to give the Konig through your generosity."

"I await the hour," said Rakoczy.

The Konige acknowledged his bow with a formulaic remark: "For your service you may be sure of my gratitude." She waved him away.

Stepping back with a second bow, Rakoczy found himself next to Csenge of Somogy, whose magnificent bleihaut of peach-colored wool embroidered with colored silks and golden thread to show a vast array of flowers and birds almost concealed her air of deep fatigue. "Good evening," he said to her, lowering his head respectfully.

She returned the greeting in an abrupt fashion. "Comes." She glared at him, as if trying to break his composure; when she did not succeed, she relented enough to ask, "And how do you find the dear Royal this evening? She gave you a goodly amount of her time."

"The Konige seems lethargic," Rakoczy observed. "I had hoped she would be recovered from her delivery by now."

"So has the Konig," Csenge rejoined, looking about sharply to try to discover if she had been overheard. "She likes your gift well enough," Csenge said in a tone that made it impossible to guess whether she meant the remark as a compliment or a recrimination.

"Then I am handsomely rewarded, but that does not lessen my concern for her," said Rakoczy cordially, unperturbed by Csenge's brusque remark.

"Just as well," said Csenge, considering him through narrowed eyes. "My cousin won't be here for this occasion, or not for a while. She is taking care of the Little Royals."

Rakoczy heard this calmly. "If you will be kind enough to remember me to her, I would thank you."

"Certainly." She eyed him suspiciously. "Is it that you're waiting for Rozsa of Borsod to return? Is my cousin less interesting, being little more than a child, than Rozsa is?"

"I had heard that Rozsa was coming back," Rakoczy said smoothly. "The Konige will be glad of her company."

This was not the kind of response Csenge had expected; she shifted the subject. "What do you plan to do for the Konig's departure festivities?"

"I have no notion," he replied genially. "Dear Royal has not told me what she would like me to do for her. I await her instruction."

"And you have nothing to suggest?" Csenge inquired. "No idea that the Konige might settle upon? No inspiration at all?"

Rakoczy took a moment to weigh his answer. "I am charged with pleasing the Konige, so in matters of this sort, it is fitting that I rely upon her to tell me what would please her most. It would please neither of us if I were to provide her with something unsatisfactory. It is one thing to present her and her daughters with jewels, as Konig Bela has charged me to do, but her husband is not the same as her grandfather, and the dear Royal's decision on what Konig Otakar is due must remain with her. She will know best what she wants Otakar to have from her, and it will be my task to make it for her, when she informs me what it is to be; I would not presume to know what she wants." He gave her an urbane smile. "Or do you think I err in that?"

Csenge hardly took more than a moment to consider. "You should recommend something to her; she is disinterested, as you remarked. Surely you can see that she is apathetic, can't you?"

"I can, and that is troubling," Rakoczy said.

"She is in God's Hands, as are we all," Csenge said as piously as possible. "We must all bow to His Will."

"Then I will be content to wait until God moves her to decide." It was an argument that Csenge would never dispute.

"Well, be ready to do her bidding when she finally makes it known." Csenge lifted her head, her jaw at a defiant angle.

"Yes. That is my intention." He lowered his head again. "If you will permit me to—"

"Oh, yes," Csenge said impatiently, having found no nuggets of secrets in anything he said, or his manner. "Go, by all means."

Rakoczy moved away toward Counselor Smiricti and Counselor Hlavka, who stood together near the main fireplace, their

Court garments burnished by the fire's shine. Both men wore several gold rings, but no jewels, and no hats, as the Konig's Law required. Smiricti, in a huch of Damascus silk over a chainse of ecru wool, ducked his head as he noticed Rakoczy. "Comes Santu-Germaniu. A happy encounter. Let me make Counselor Hlavka Innec known to you." He gestured to his companion, who ducked his head.

"Counselor Hlavka," said Rakoczy.

"Comes Santu-Germaniu," said Hlavka with a flourish of his hand, then added, "You're the one at Mansion Belcrady, aren't you? The exile, or so they say." His huch was of heavy, amber-colored Venetian silk and lined in marten-fur; his chainse was of light-blue Anatolian cotton, and his braccae were thickly embroidered with his family trade-mark, a mallet and a pair of farrier's tongs. His color was high and his eyes were shiny, indications that he had drunk all the toasts that had begun the gathering at mid-afternoon, and very likely more than toasts.

"I am he."

"We heard of your fire; a sad misfortune." Hlavka turned to Smiricti once more. "There is a rumor that the fire was deliberately set."

"I have heard the same," said Smiricti.

"A bad business, if it's true." His innuendo was conspicuous; he continued to ignore Rakoczy. "Didn't you tell me that you had recommended Bartech of Tabor for the rebuilding of the damaged furnace and chimney?"

"I did. And Szigmon to make the new roof. Everyone speaks well of his skills." Smiricti smiled, going on effusively, "Masters in their Guilds, both of them, with well-reputed apprentices and reputations of the highest order. Both of them know the Comes is one of the Konige's Court, and will be diligent in their work."

"When will they be able to start that work?" Hlavka asked, still not speaking directly to Rakoczy.

"As soon as the weather improves; to do anything now while the rains continue, that would lead to wasted effort. We are devoting some time to planning what is to be built, and how," said Rakoczy as if he had been included in the discussion. "The damaged parts of the bake-house have already been cleared away. My baker is having to use the kitchen ovens for his loaves while the bake-house cannot be used."

Hlavka nodded, his gaze flicking about the hall as if to make note of everyone in attendance. "It must be inconvenient for you, Comes, not having a bake-house for your mansion. But surely the repairs will begin shortly," he said, sounding a bit distracted.

"It certainly is inconvenient for my cook who wants to have his kitchen back. He and the baker do nothing but wrangle." Rakoczy shook his head. "It's their temperaments; they clash."

"How . . . lax, to have so little authority over your household," said Hlavka with a snide half-smile.

Rakoczy refused to be provoked, shrugging and saying, "You know how it is with exiles. We must depend on the good-will of those around us."

"We would like to thank you for all you've done to help us be rid of the rats," said Smiricti, after an awkward silence, striving to maintain the courtesy required.

"I was gratified that you asked me," Rakoczy said.

"Oh, yes," said Hlavka; his next words were almost an accusation. "Your poisons made short work of many of them."

Smiricti intervened before Hlavka could entirely forget himself and insult Rakoczy beyond all acceptable limits. "Our slaves have been put to work secreting your poison-boxes where rats have been found before. We hope to avoid another such infestation as the one we had last year." He glanced at Hlavka as if to warn him to hold his tongue.

Rakoczy saw that Smiricti was discomfited by Hlavka's behavior, and so he inclined his head. "Perhaps we can speak more privately in a day or two?"

"I will send a messenger; you may assign the time." Smiricti gave him a grateful, chagrined, lopsided smile. "I look forward to it."

Moving away from the two Counselors, Rakoczy saw Hovarth

Pisti standing a little apart from the rest of the company, staring into the dining hall beyond the reception hall, his demeanor both anticipatory and bored; Rakoczy made for the tapestry-weaver, nodding his greeting. "Are your apprentices with you?"

"My apprentices are working on the tapestry for the Konig's departure. We have twenty-two more days, three of them Sabbaths, so we must work on two feast days. Episcopus Fauvinel has granted us a dispensation for those." He gave a harried chuckle. "The Konige didn't decide what the subject should be until four days past, so we will have to labor well into the night to have it ready."

"The work is an honor, of course," Rakoczy said.

"Oh, yes. It is why Konig Bela sent me here. It is a fine distinction he has extended to me and my apprentices. I know that Konig Bela has noted all we have done for Konige Kunigunde. We gain favor from Konig Bela *and* Konig Otakar when we please the Konige." His expression turned smug. "And unlike you, I can expect to be richly recompensed for all I and my apprentices do, by Konig Otakar as well as by Konig Bela."

Rakoczy's deportment did not change; he gave no sign of vexation at Hovarth Pisti's condescension, and no offense at his disparaging remarks. "I do have a reward of sorts," he said. "My fief is safe as long as I fulfill the requirements of Konig Bela and his granddaughter. That reward is more than sufficient for me."

"Not an easy bargain, even for so wealthy a man as you are, Comes." He ducked his head and moved away as three buisines sounded a call from the minstrels' gallery, and a herald stepped to the railing.

"In the most gracious name of Kunigunde of Halicz, Konige of Bohemia," he announced, "you are all welcome to the Konige's Court, summoned for the purpose of arranging the festivities to mark the departure of Przemysl Otakar II, Konig of Bohemia, with his army, to the field of battle, where, with God's Grace, he will enlarge his conquests and be named Holy Roman Emperor. The Konig will leave on the twenty-seventh day of March unless the weather delays

him. The celebration for his departure will begin on the twenty-
fifth day of March and last until the Konig and his army are outside the walls of Praha. May God favor and defend the Konige and
her daughters, and grant victory to our Konig."

A cheer went up, only to be overwhelmed by the braying of
the buisines; as the brazen echoes died, a consort of shawms and
gitterns and a tabor took the place of the buisine-players, beginning their part of the Court's music with the popular song *Praise
to the Virgin.* After that, they played *Hills and Meadow,* an en-
gaging, wistful melody. When they finished, Episcopus Fauvinel
came to the railing and raised his hands; everyone in the reception hall dropped to their knees and crossed themselves.

"In the Name of the Father, of the Son, and the Holy Spirit,
Amen," the Episcopus intoned in Church Latin.

"Amen," the Court echoed, a few of the Konige's Court taking
out their rosaries from under their chainses, and beginning to run
the beads through their fingers, their lips moving in prayer.

Episcopus Fauvinel waited until he was confident of the Konige's attention; when he was sure he had it, he addressed the
Court. "Let us all give thanks to Merciful God in His manifest
Glory. God has given illustrious favor to Bohemia and all its territories, the which you must all show your gratitude, through adher-
ence to God's Law and the offering of Masses. To show your
worthiness for God's Blessing, may you, each and all, serve the
Konige to her honor, the honor of Konig Otakar, and the honor of
Bohemia. May you, each and all, bring esteem to the Konige's
Court and show no contempt for other Courts in doing so. May
you, each and all, seek to ennoble the Royal House of Przemysl
and of Halicz to greater heights. May you, each and all, welcome
the benefices that come to you from your service with humility
and piety. May you, each and all, give praises to God for providing
so excellent an opportunity to demonstrate your fealty, for it is
through Him that you are advanced for your loyalty and devotion,
first to God, then to the Konig and Konige, of which you ought to
be mindful every hour of your lives. Amen."

Another chorus of *Amen* answered him, and a rustle of garments as the assembled Court arose, all silent until the Episcopus stepped back behind the musicians, signaling that the Episcopal audience was at an end. Once again the tabor set the beat; the shawms and gitterns struck up another song—*Love Does Me Great Wrong.*

On the far side of the hall, Rakoczy saw that Imbolya was deep in conversation with Rytir Leutpald Verschluss, one of Konig Otakar's German Guards; her expression was earnest but he was not paying much attention to her words, but was taking in her appearance and the richness of her clothes.

As conversation crescendoed in the vast hall, Rakoczy found a small nook in the wall to the left of the main fireplace and stepped into it; he could watch the Court from here without being readily seen. It was a bit of a risk, for if he were discovered he might be accused of spying, but he was willing to take the chance; there were many questions he sought to have answered, and hoped that this vantage-point would provide him the means to learn by watching.

"Comes," said a voice just outside the alcove.

Rakoczy concealed the twinge of alarm that shot through him. "Yes?"

Tahir moved into the opening, his gaudy clothes showing he would be performing that evening. "Are you well?"

"Yes, Tahir," said Rakoczy. "I am quite well."

"Then you must be hiding," Tahir decided. "Not that I find that unwise, hiding."

"No; I am observing."

"So!" The dwarf tumbler slapped his thigh. "Good fortune to you." He ducked his head and walked away.

Rakoczy remained where he was, watching the Konige's company, taking note of the ebb and flow of the Court until the buisines sounded to summon the Court to supper, when he slipped away from the nook and made his way to the end of the dining hall, looking for one of the Konige's ladies-in-waiting. He finally caught sight of Gyongyi of Tolan, and approached her. "A word with you, Lady," he said, bowing.

Gyongyi blinked. "Comes," she responded, courtisying him. "What do you require?"

"I ask you, if you would, to inform the dear Royal that I will send a messenger to her tomorrow to receive her commission."

"Certainly," said Gyongyi, trying to contain her curiosity.

"You are most graciously acquiescent; you have my thanks," said Rakoczy, and took a step away from her, bowing as he went.

"Comes," she said, halting him. "Aren't you joining the banquet?"

"Alas, no. The customs of my blood forbid it, for we traditionally dine in private, as dear Royal is aware. And in any case, there are those among the courtiers who believe I am a spy for Konig Bela, and are not sanguine when I attend these functions. My presence could prove awkward for the Konige, so it is best if I leave." He bowed one last time before going to the vestibule to claim his mantel.

The under-steward handed him his garment, and asked, "Do you need a horse or a carriage from the Konige's stable to return to your mansion, Comes? Or have you either horse or carriage waiting for you here?"

"Mansion Belcrady is not far from here." He swung the mantel around his shoulders. "I walked up the ridge; I can as easily walk down."

"Then you will need an escort." The under-steward ducked his head.

"For so short a distance? Thank you, but I think not." He passed on into the entry hall, where more servants opened the door for him. He stepped out into the forecourt, and paused to stare at the red, violet, and luminous dark-blue remnants of sunset that flashed under the clouds that stretched over the world like a gigantic tent. He could tell more rain was coming, and that it would be heavier than what they had just had. He went across the forecourt to the main gate and rang the bell to summon the warder.

"Oh. It's you," said the warder when he arrived. "I should have known. No one but you leaves before the banquet." He laughed once before he drew back the massive bolt and tugged the gate open enough for Rakoczy to pass through it. "God give you a good night, Comes."

"And to you, good warder," Rakoczy called back to him, tossing him a golden Vaclav as the warder tugged the gate closed once more. Out in the fading daylight, Rakoczy thought the streets unexpectedly empty; not many people were about, and those who were seemed harried as they rushed along, going down the hill; most of them wore crucifixes conspicuously, and a few had Otakar's lion on simple badges on their shoulders. The reason for this display was soon apparent as a shout went out from the main gates of Praha, and Rakoczy remembered that five deserters were being hanged in chains at sunset, the Konig officiating at the beginning of their slow execution; the first had just been dropped; the other four would suffer the same fate shortly. Frowning, Rakoczy found himself moving more quickly, and as he lengthened his stride, he heard the sound of hasty footsteps behind him. Although he told himself he was being foolish, he swung around, hoping to see who was there, but once again the street was empty.

The distance between Vaclav Castle and Mansion Belcrady was not great, but for Rakoczy it stretched out ahead of him like the vastness of the Silk Road. He considered running at speed— which, for him, was almost as fast as a galloping horse—but quickly rejected the idea, for if he was not being followed, he might draw the kind of attention to himself that he sought most to avoid. Yet he kept moving at a rapid clip, hoping to force his follower to betray himself.

Rakoczy heard the sound of trotting hooves on the cobbles, and a moment later, three of Otakar's German Guard emerged from the side-street, all but dragging two hooded men after them as they turned up the hill toward Vaclav Castle. They paid no attention to the Comes.

At the gate to Mansion Belcrady, Rakoczy slipped in through the warder's door without attracting Minek's attention, or the notice of most of his household. He made his way to the kitchen garden, and entered the manse by the side-door, startling Kornemon, who was carrying a load of wood in a copper tub with wooden handles into the kitchen.

"Comes," he exclaimed. "I didn't know you had returned." He ducked his head respectfully.

"I have, as you see," he told the stoker. "What has happened in my absence?"

The stoker did not answer at once. "The bricklayer and two of his apprentices were here for a time. They left not long ago. They said they would be back in a day or so, if the weather is clear." He looked up at the ceiling, shifting the tub from one hand to another. "Someone from the Council Court came and spoke with Barnon. Illes went to the horse-fair, but you knew that."

"He went on my orders," said Rakoczy, wondering what it was that Kornemon was trying so hard to conceal. "And the rest of the household—what of them?"

"For the most part all is well," said Kornemon.

"For the most part? What is not well?"

"It's not for me to say," Kornemon declared.

"It is, when I ask," Rakoczy said gently but with an authority that demanded an answer.

Kornemon sighed. "Pacar and Tymek fought again."

Rakoczy was silent for a long moment. "Was either of them hurt?"

"Not badly when you consider what they might have done." He shrugged. "Pacar has a lump on his head and Tymek's knuckles are scraped, but Barnon and Ambroz stopped them before anything in the kitchen was damaged, or a knife was found."

"Most commendable. Do you happen to know what the fight was about?"

"I don't know," Kornemon said evasively. He fidgeted, glancing in the direction of the kitchen. "Comes, I ought to—"

"And where was Hruther during all this?" Rakoczy asked; it was most unlike his manservant to allow such a ruction to take place. He could not help but feel anxious; he tried not to show his apprehension.

"I don't know," said Kornemon. "I should get this wood to the kitchen."

Rakoczy nodded and made a sign of dismissal. He waited a short while, in case another servant should happen by, one who would be more forthcoming, who could explain what had become of Hruther. When no one appeared, he went toward the main hall, planning to go to his workroom in the hope that Hruther had left him a message to account for his absence.

Text of a letter from Balint of Santu-Germaniu at Santu-Germaniu to Rakoczy Ferancsi, Comes Santu-Germaniu, in Praha, dictated to Frater Lorand, written on vellum, carried by private courier, never delivered.

To the most esteemed Rakoczy Ferancsi, Comes Santu-Germaniu, presently at Mansion Belcrady in Praha, Bohemia, the most respectful greetings of your steward, Balint of Santu-Germaniu, by the good offices of Frater Lorand, on this, the first day of March in the 1270th Year of Salvation:

My most well-regarded Comes,

This is to inform you that winter is still keeping the Carpathians in its grip, and it appears that spring will arrive later than usual this year. We have had inconsistent weather, all of it bad. There was a week of warm days, when the snows began to melt, which ended in two days of rain, and, as the cold returned, became ice, making your stronghold ice-bound, and giving the appearance of remaining so into April if the local weather-witches are to be believed. This will mean that we will plow and plant later than usual, which may effect the harvest when it comes around, which may mean that we will have to part with more of the harvest than we can spare when Konig Bela's men come for their taxes. I ask you to inform me what you want me to do if we should have such problems as I anticipate. It may be that I am worried for no good reason, but as your steward, you advised me to keep all eventualities in mind.

The commander of the fortress at Santa-Ioanne came here three months ago and claimed ten sheep, ten hogs, and four foals in the name of Konig Bela. Since you instructed me not to deny the Konig's men, I made no objection to their raid, for raid it was, but I am afraid that when the spring comes, they will return with the intention of taking more, which I doubt we can provide without putting your fief at a disadvantage. We have already seen wolves in the forest, and if they start to plunder our livestock, then the Konig's men will leave us in a very poor state. I ask for your permission to send Sylvanu to the horse-and-cattle fair at Cluj in May, to buy a few mares with foals at their sides, and some other livestock as well.

Three shepherds died while driving their flocks into their pens and barns not long after the first snowfall. Rumor has it that they were caught in an avalanche, but others say they were taken by bandits to be sold as slaves to the Byzantines. Some believe that they ran away. This is the fourth time such disappearances have happened in the last year. At first I assumed that it was an avalanche, but almost none of the sheep were lost, as we discovered when we rounded them up, and that leaves raiding parties. Most of the bandits keep to the plains, where they have a greater chance to take captives and plunder, but those seeking slaves are another matter, for they seek to take men, women, and children, and get away with little notice. With you gone, it is likely that these outlaws come here because you are not allowed to keep soldiers to track down those raiders, so they may raid with impunity. I ask you to petition the Konig for the protection of men-at-arms, or allow those of us in your household to keep arms to help drive off the raiders.

There is a record of accounts included with this letter, showing how we have fared since the first snowfall. As you see, the costs for feed has risen. The repair to the cattle barn is complete at the cost of twenty silver coins and eight lambs. We will need to work on the stable next summer, and that may prove as expensive as the barn to repair. As you ordered, the cisterns were cleaned of algae. The dung farmer emptied the latrines and dung channels before the first snowfall. The linen has been washed in saffron-water, and anything in need of darning has been given to the needlewomen. Ten wagon-loads of wood were brought in for the winter, and six of them are still left; the cost was five gold Vaclavs and five silver Emperors. New fences have been built around the chicken coops and rabbit hutches to keep out martens and foxes, and seem to have worked well. We have three barrels of lanthorn-oil left, twenty-two dozen wax candles, and fifty-three barrels of new wine have been laid down. We have turnips, onions, cab-bages, and apples in the root-cellar, and thumb-cabages, onions, peppers, and cucumbers pickling in barrels. We may run short of food by spring, but we will manage.

The weavers are busy this winter, and we will have more cloth than usual to offer at the market fair, unless the Konig's men decide to claim half of it as taxes due. The goat-hair mantels and blankets have turned out particularly well; the woolen bleihauts our needlewomen make should fetch a good price, as well, and if they continue to keep up their present pace of weaving and sew-ing, there will be an extra set of clothes for all the household and still have much to take to market.

May God move the Konig to soon grant you the right to re-turn to your fief. All of your vassals pray for you, and ask God to watch over you in that foreign place.

> Balint of Santu-Germaniu
> Steward of Santu-Germaniu

by the hand of the scribe Frater Lorand

4

The wind was out of the northeast, chilly enough to make the fire in the workroom of Mansion Belcrady welcome to Rakoczy, who rarely felt either heat or cold; he was finishing assembling the elements that would produce amethysts and moonstones—"for the Konige's daughters," he told Hruther—his attention fixed on the vessel that was called the womb of jewels. Behind him, Hruther sorted out the ingredients to make emeralds and rubies, measuring them with care into a similar vessel as the one Rakoczy held. Both of them ignored the whoop of the wind and the answering clatter of shutters, devoting the whole of their assiduity to their tasks.

"There," said Rakoczy, stepping back from the trestle-table; he carried the vessel down the room to the athanor, opened the heavy door of the alchemical oven, set the container into position inside it, closed the oven door, added charcoal to the firebox, and set the bellows working by releasing the spring-driven belt at the rear; this last was an improvement of his own; he had contrived it more than eight centuries before, adapting it from a Roman saw-clock and a Persian mechanical nightingale.

Hruther picked up the large hourglass at the end of the table and turned it over. "One," he announced.

Rakoczy took a deep breath. "We have until sundown. That is three more turns."

"Four turns of the hourglass," Hruther concurred. He looked at the open coffer and its contents of gems. "Will you be able to finish the hilt for the ceremonial sword the Konige will present to the Konig upon his departure?"

"More than enough; the matter is having four of each jewels that match. I should have more than fifty left over when the task is done." Rakoczy regarded the list he had been given. "Two large diamonds for the pommel, ten white sapphires for the hand-grip, four emeralds, four tourmalines, four peridots, four topazes, four rubies, and ten golden tiger's-eyes for the quillons. It ought to impress everyone who sees it."

"That's what the Konige wants, isn't it?" Hruther said. "For the Konig to be impressive."

"So I gather." Rakoczy settled into his Anatolian saddler's chair. "Any more repercussions from your interrogation five days ago?" He spoke in the Cypriot dialect.

"Not yet." He completed loading the vessel and set it in its cradle. "I still don't know what the Episcopus' familiars were trying to get from me, which nettles me."

"I find it interesting that they took you while the Episcopus was speaking at the Konige's Court," Rakoczy observed. "He wants to be protected from what the familiars did, but why?"

"I can only guess." He pursed his lips. "I'm sure they acted on the Episcopus' instructions, no matter where he was while my examination was going on."

"You said they asked many questions at random, or in a succession that seemed disconnected one from another." Rakoczy had undergone just such an interrogation in Constantinople, more than six hundred years ago, and was aware that the random questions were to keep the one being questioned from formulating an effective defense against those questioning him.

"Yes. However, now that I've had time to think about it, most of the questions they repeated had to do with your wealth, directly or indirectly."

"How do you mean?" Rakoczy had until now made only minor inquiries about Hruther's detention, but he was increasingly dismayed that it happened, and wanted to learn as much as possible about the interview itself.

"I've told you that they asked many times about your wealth, and its source, and about the reason for your exile, as well as its terms," Hruther said, as puzzled as he was at the time he was in the familiars' hands.

"Did they do more than threaten you?" Rakoczy kept his voice level.

"They struck me only once, when I refused to tell them what they sought to know, but they kept me on my knees, and that was wearing." He pressed his lips together to stop more words.

"That is typical. That way the Church can claim that no injury was done." Rakoczy looked away in disgust with himself for what Hruther had endured. He leaned forward and slapped the top of the low, round table in front of the fireplace.

"They kept returning to your fortune, but they also wanted to know about your travels and your trading company, and whom among the high lords of Europe you might know. They asked about your studies and your skills. But they put most of their emphasis on your fortune and your fief."

"I gathered that: I would like to know why," Rakoczy muttered, then looked at Hruther. "Yes, old friend, I am aware that you know no more than I do on that point."

"I wish I did. The familiars would not tolerate any questions from me; they required that I answer theirs." He stared at the nearest shuttered window. "They ordered me to pray frequently. I thought at the time it was with the intention to find out if I knew the Psalms, and if I did, how well."

"I trust they were satisfied," said Rakoczy with sardonic amusement.

"I think so." He considered his answer and added, "But I don't know; I can only guess."

"I respect your guesses," said Rakoczy. He leaned back in his chair. "I might as well be bound in chains and confined to a dungeon. I am not safe to know; I am encumbered so that I may not defend my friends or myself."

"Don't tempt the Episcopus with thoughts of dungeons. He would rejoice in seizing your fortune for the Church."

"And Otakar would want it for the Crown, wherein lies my only safety—that those two are locked in stalemate. If they ever decide to make common cause against me . . ." He stared at the flames consuming the two logs in the fireplace. "I wish I could leave here without bringing harm to my fief and my vassals."

"They say Konig Bela will be sending an envoy to the Konige's Court, to assure the Konig that all is well with his granddaughter and her children. Perhaps you could have a private word with him while he's here? If the envoy delivers a good report of you, Bela might reconsider your terms of exile." Hruther brushed away the bits of detritus on the table. "How many more vessels of jewels do you want to make?"

"Two or three, to be sure there are enough to make reasonable matches; the Konige has specified she wants the jewels to match. Additional tiger's-eyes should be part of what I make tomorrow; that will give me a day to polish them before sending them on to the goldsmith for mounting." He stretched and settled back into the chair. "As soon as the current batch is cooling, I will start sorting what I have, and polishing them in the drum."

"And tomorrow?"

"The rubies and emeralds will be tumble-polished while I make the compound for tiger's-eyes. When this is done, I will have to take time to produce more azoth. I am running low on it." A slight frown settled between his brows.

"Celestial mercury can be dangerous to constitute. Think of the Polish marshes." Hruther regarded Rakoczy with worry.

"I do think of them," said Rakoczy. "I will use a triple-vessel to contain the formulation. That should lessen the chance for it to explode."

Hruther nodded. "I'll keep a number of buckets of water on hand, on the chance there is any trouble. One fire in this manse is enough."

Rakoczy smiled. "Such admirable caution."

"Better caution than recklessness when dealing with azoth,"

said Hruther with no sign of upset. "Shall I send the servants out for the day?"

"A clever notion. Yes, of course. Send them to the open market. Provide each of them with two silver Vaclavs, which should allow them to indulge themselves. Tell them they may have the day until Vespers, when I expect them to return."

"And if any of them should ask why you extend yourself so generously? what do I tell them?" Hruther inquired.

"Say it is the custom of those of my blood to give their households a sign of appreciation of service after the Christ Mass and before Lent begins." He managed a twisted smile. "In case any of the Episcopus' familiars should ask."

Hruther nodded once. "The scullions as well as the rest?"

"All of them. The swineherd and the shepherd, too." He paused thoughtfully. "Tell them I would join them, but I must finish the commission from the Konige."

"Joining them is another tradition of your blood?" He kept most of his incredulity out of his voice.

"Let them think so," said Rakoczy.

"Good enough." Hruther thrust his hands into the large, closed sleeve of his bleihaut, drawing out a twice-folded note. "This was handed to me this morning. I was told not to give it to you until after mid-day."

Rakoczy took the note, studied it, but did not open it at once. "Where did you get this? Who gave it to you?"

"One of the Konige's Court pages handed it to me as he accompanied the heralds. They were going to deliver more plans to the Counselors, for the Konig's departure."

"And the page just happened to encounter you?" Rakoczy made no excuse for his skepticism.

"He said it saved him stopping here on their way back," Hruther told him. "I took the note; I thought I would draw attention to it if I refused to accept it, with the escort to make a report in any case."

"That is probably true," said Rakoczy.

"You have received many notes from the Konige."

"So I have, but always my title was on the outside, with her sigil. There is nothing on this." He held up the folded note. "Quite blank. It may be a trap of some kind," Rakoczy mused aloud. "If a page carried it, any number of the Konige's courtiers might have written it."

"That's possible, and it would be like the Episcopus to try something of the sort," Hruther agreed. "So it might be a device on the part of the Episcopus to snare you."

"That, too, is possible," Rakoczy said, then unfolded the note; he recognized the neat hand at once: it was Imbolya's.

My most dear Comte,

It has befallen that I will be at the Sant-Mattiza Chapel this evening for Mass, at the conclusion of which I am charged with coming to you for the purpose of choosing the jewels for the hilt of the Konig's ceremonial sword. I will be accompanied by two men-at-arms and two pages, whom I ask you to receive with your usual hospitality.

The Konige is aware that such careful sorting of jewels as the sword requires may take a good portion of the night, and so has excused me from attending bed-time prayers in her private apartments while I meet with you to make the best selection possible. The castle guards have been ordered to admit me and my escort upon my return at any hour without question or hindrance, so I need have no reason to be hurried in choosing the stones needed.

Dear Royal is distressed at the thought that the sword will not be ready in time for Konig Otakar's departure; this has caused her much distraint, and to lessen her anxiety, she seeks to be informed on the progress of all involved in its making: my cousin Csenge of Somogy will be attending to the goldsmith, and Gyongyi of Tolan will be dispatched to the smith fashioning the blade. All of us will

be suitably escorted, so that no disrepute may bring dis-
honor to the sword.

The Konige has been kind enough to let me write this
note to you rather than have her heralds announce my ar-
rival formally. She sees my writing as a kind of modesty,
although the Episcopus does not. I trust you will not be of-
fended by this means of informing you of my coming visit.

In the name of Kunigunde of Halicz, Konige of
Bohemia,

Imbolya of Heves

"Trap or not, we should prepare for a visit," said Rakoczy
when he had read the letter twice. "If it is a ruse, it is a bold one.
The Konige would disapprove of mischief done in her name."

"So she would," said Hruther, his voice completely neutral.

Making up his mind, Rakoczy said briskly, "Have Pacar prepare a supper for the men-at-arms and pages. Ask Illes to invite
the men-at-arms to dice with him and the grooms. Make the servants' hall available to the pages, in case they should grow tired."

"You are planning to receive her?"

"Since it appears that the Konige requires it, I must."

Hruther gave a little sigh. "Shall I inform the household that
the Konige wishes the jewels to go unseen by all but her ladies-in-
waiting and the craftsmen working on the sword until the weapon
is presented to him at his departure?"

"Adroit as ever," Rakoczy approved. "Thank you. Yes, indeed,
spread warnings throughout the household, and make it plain that
to attempt to see the jewels will be against the will of the Konige."
He got up from his chair and went to put another log on the fire.
"Pacar will want to prepare a tray for the Konige's lady. If you will
carry it up to this room, I will be most grateful."

"Certainly," said Hruther, a glint in his faded-blue eyes. He
looked around the workroom. "Do you want the room swept?"

"That would attract too much speculation. At least I have carpets on the floor instead of rushes, which are more suitable than rushes to receive the Konige's envoy. And most of the rats are gone." Rakoczy gazed at the hourglass. "The current jewels should be out of the athanor by the time Imbolya arrives. I will attend to them if you will arrange a proper reception with Barnon."

"I'll start the household in motion now, if you will excuse me." Hruther ducked his head as he went to the door. "My master? Do you need anything more from me just now?"

"I doubt it." He paused. "When Vespers begins, meet me in my quarters to help me change clothes. The Konige's lady, who is Kunigunde's deputy, must not be welcomed in an old cope and stained braccae."

"Of course. At Vespers." He pressed down the latch and let himself out.

For the rest of the afternoon, Rakoczy kept to his workroom, turning the hourglass as it was required, taking out a blanket fashioned out of bear- and wolf-skins and spreading it over his Anatolian saddler's chair, lighting two braziers and adding incense to the cut branches in them. He put his trestle-table in order and set up a velvet-covered stand where the jewels could be examined. By the time he took the vessel from the athanor and put it on the cooling-rack, he was ready to change clothes, and went along to his own rooms to meet Hruther.

While he donned black, sculpted-Antioch-velvet braccae and a chainse of dark-red silk, Hruther summed up all the preparations under way in Mansion Belcrady. "I've suggested that bread and beer be taken to the stable for the men-at-arms and grooms."

"Will their supper be served there?" Rakoczy asked as he chose his huch of black Damascus silk shot with silver thread.

"If they request it," Hruther said. "Which is likely."

"Well done," Rakoczy approved, and continued his dressing. As he set his silver collar in place around his neck, his eclipse pectoral hanging at the middle of his chest, he remarked, "My appearance shows my respect for the Konige, as everyone in the household will be aware, including the spies."

"If we only knew beyond doubt who they are," said Hruther, running a comb through Rakoczy's hair. He nodded his satisfaction and went to open the door. "The envoy should be here shortly."

"Is Pacar ready?" Rakoczy asked as he locked the door.

"Probably. He was setting out trays and plates when I left him."

"Very good," Rakoczy approved.

The main hall was brightly lit, as was the entry hall. Barnon stood near the door in his most impressive garb, trying to appear at ease. He ducked his head to Rakoczy. "The Konige's envoy will bring honor to Mansion Belcrady."

"As the Konige herself has done," Rakoczy agreed.

"To be able to add to the Konig's departing gifts, and you no Bohemian." Barnon clasped his hands. "It is a fine thing for you."

"It is."

A cry went up from the warder's tower, Minek announcing the arrival of the Konige's lady-in-waiting and her escort. A few moments later the main gate swung open, and an enclosed carriage painted iris-blue and drawn by a pair of brown-and-white spotted horses came through, accompanied by two men-at-arms and two pages, all in bag-sleeved cotehardies with Otakar's lion blazoned on the chest of all four. Two grooms hurried from the stable to take the horses' heads.

Rakoczy opened the door and welcomed them all to Mansion Belcrady. He said to the escort, "My steward, Barnon, will take you and the wagon to where you will be given hospitality." With that, he pulled back the carriage door to assist Imbolya, offering her a French bow. "For the Konige's sake, you are welcome as her envoy." For the sake of his staff, he spoke in Bohemian.

Imbolya, in a bleihaut of turquoise wool over a high-necked chainse and wimple of rose-colored cotton, stepped down and courtisied him. "In the name of the Konige I thank you, Comes." She spoke in Magyar, then repeated herself in Bohemian, adding, "The Konige is grateful to you for your efforts on her behalf."

Rakoczy stood aside to allow her to enter the manse, where the household servants were gathered to make their greeting. Barnon went on his knee on behalf of the entire staff, then rose and clapped his hands to send the servants back to their work, and only Hruther remained in the entry hall. "May your stay here be pleasant." This time he spoke in Magyar.

"I'll tell the dear Royal how well I have been received." Imbolya looked at him with a suggestion of hope in her face.

"The servants would appreciate that."

"And you?" The playfulness she might feel was lost in the tentative note in her voice.

"Tell me when you leave how pleased you are, and I will take my satisfaction from that." He bowed to her. "If you will come with me to my workroom, we can begin to sort the jewels."

She looked a bit crestfallen. "Will it take long, do you think?"

His smile was gone almost as soon as it was begun, but there was no mistaking the anticipation in it. "That will depend entirely upon you."

Imbolya's demeanor lightened. "In that case, let us set to work at once, Comes."

Rakoczy signaled to Hruther. "If you will bring the tray of food and drink up to us as soon as it is prepared?"

"Of course, my master." He inclined his head, and was about to leave the entry hall, but paused. "Will our noble guest want hot wine?"

"I would," said Imbolya.

"Then, good lady, you shall have it," Hruther assured her with a bow as he left the room.

"If you will come with me, Royal envoy?" He said it loudly enough for anyone listening to hear. "I have a good selection from which you may choose; if they are not sufficient, there will be more tomorrow."

She followed his example. "I look forward to seeing what you have."

They went through the main hall and up the stairs beside the fireplace to the gallery, saying nothing so that they would not be overheard. Only when they were in the corridor leading to his workroom on the left and his private apartments on the right did she dare to speak. "I want to be sure we have the best matches possible. It may take some time."

"Whatever you wish," he said as he unlocked the workroom door and led her inside, where the fire was burning brightly and the room was pleasantly warm. He indicated the saddler's chair with the fur blanket thrown over it. "I think you will be comfortable there."

"I have good memories of that chair." She looked warily around the room. "We are alone?"

"We are. And when he has brought the tray for you, Hruther will keep guard." He smiled as he went to the trestle-table and took a small case of ivory and brought it to her. "For your inspection, while we wait."

She opened the lid of the box and gasped. "They're lovely," she said at last. "Is the count complete?"

"Very nearly. You may review them for yourself."

She turned the contents of the case into her lap and began studying the gems, putting them back in the ivory box as she reviewed each of them. "Four emeralds, all the size of a fingernail, all polished. Three peridots, the same. The Konige will be delighted. Four topazes, the color of butter. Four rubies. Four tourmalines. Two diamonds." She held them up in turn to the shine from the fire. "Excellent. And as large as pigeon's eggs. The Konige will be delighted." Picking up the white sapphires, she counted under her breath, ". . . eight, nine, ten. There's an eleventh!"

"In case there is any trouble setting one of them into the hand-grip," Rakoczy explained.

"Is there an eleventh tiger's-eye as well?" she asked, not bothering to count the stones.

"There will be, and for the same reason." He took the ivory case from her as soon as she had put the last of the tiger's-eyes in, closed it, and returned it to the trestle-table; he paused to open the casket of gems that stood at the other end of the table near the athanor. "I will leave this open, so that any servant who sees it will know that we have passed all our time together sorting jewels."

She laughed, drawing her knees up to her chest and wrapping her arms around her legs. "You are a very clever man, Comes."

He went and knelt next to the chair, pushing the jointed frame so that its back half-reclined. "I am glad we will have this time together."

"It will probably be our last. The new ladies-in-waiting will arrive shortly, and when their escort departs for Buda, I will have to go with them. I will be married soon, I believe. Married." It seemed that she was on the verge of weeping, but she made her face pleasant and managed not to cry. "So this will have to be enough to suffice for all my lifetime."

"Are you sure you will not come to love your husband?" He took her hand in his and kissed the palm; he was suddenly aware of how very young she was.

"I hope not, for he isn't apt to love me. My father is seeking alliances, not a lover for me, as Konig Bela did for the Konige. My duty is to have children, preferably sons, and to oversee my husband's estate when he is away from it. And to be virtuous, or appear so." She pulled her hand away from him and stared into the flames lapping at the logs in the fireplace; he saw the youth had gone from her eyes. "If I am fortunate, I will love my children."

Her desolation transfixed him, and he took her into his arms, encompassing her knees as well as her torso. "Imbolya, I am sad that you are so constrained."

"You're constrained, too," she said, and slipped out of his embrace as a tap sounded on the door.

"I have the tray," Hruther said. "If you will allow me to bring it in to you?"

Rakoczy got to his feet. "Yes; bring it in." He brought the low table nearer to the saddler's chair, where Imbolya was now sitting upright.

Hruther brought in the tray and set it on the low table. "For your delectation, Lady," he said, ducking his head and withdrawing.

"The wine is hot: would you like some?" Rakoczy inquired with great court-ship.

"I would," she said, looking at the large earthenware pitcher with its wispy crown of spice-scented steam. She reached for the green glass cup as soon as he filled it, her eyes bright. "You have wonderful wines."

"It may burn your lip," he warned her.

She put the cup down and shook her hand. "Yes."

He took a linen polishing towel from the end of the trestle-table and handed it to her. "Use this. It will keep you from being hurt."

"Thank you." She wrapped the linen around her glass, lifted it, and blew on the dark wine before attempting a little sip. "There's bread and cheese, too," she observed, needing to say something. She took a second sip, looking up at him as she did. "I wish you'd stop acting as if we were in the Konige's Court."

He came to her side again, laying his hand tranquilly on her arm. "When you are ready, we will seek your pleasure."

"I'm ready now," she said, putting the cup of wine down. "The food can wait, but I cannot."

"Then let me move the table away," he said, and went to pull the table back a full stride; the legs of the table made no sound on the magnificent carpet.

"Where are we going to lie?" She bent over and touched the carpet. "Here?"

"Not unless it would gratify you," said Rakoczy, coming back to her. "The chair will let you lie back, and I will kneel beside you."

She considered this. "That might work," she allowed. "But I suppose you know it will already."

"Yes," he said, and pressed on the side of the chair so that it rocked back. "You will be comfortable."

"And warm, too, when I get out of my clothes," she said, sitting up and turning away from him so he could loosen her laces. She unpinned her veil and removed her gorget, handing them to him. "Don't wrinkle them."

"I will not," he promised, and rose to hang the veil and gorget on pegs near the door. "If you will give me your bleihaut . . ."

She struggled out of the garment, muttering, "My hair must be a mess."

"With a little luck, you will have the chance to repair the damage before you go." He took her bleihaut and hung it on the largest peg, then waited for the chainse and her braccae.

"Are you sure your man can be trusted?" Her voice was low and a bit unsteady.

"With my . . . life," he said, and took her chainse.

"Then I suppose I must rely upon him for my honor," she said, suddenly sounding very old and world-weary. She tossed her braccae to him.

As he caught them, he regarded her with concern. "What troubles you, Imbolya?"

It took her a little time to frame her answer. "I have realized that no other living man, not even the greatest hero, will ever please me as you have—and that you are something not entirely natural, not if you gain your pleasure as you do, through mine; you are like the heroes in songs. Perhaps you are an earthbound spirit, or perhaps an incubus, such as the troubadours sing."

He remained very still. "What makes you say that?" He hung up her braccae and came back to her side.

"You have taken my blood and nothing else, and only a little blood. You do not take my body with your flesh as most men would do, but you still have desire, and your desire fulfills mine. You seem to have no reflection: I saw you in front of the Konige's mirror in her Court and there was no sign of you in the glass that I could see. You have no fear of holy things, but you take no Communion. When you speak of your travels, it's hard to think you have gone so far in your life, if you look your age." She laughed sadly and held out her arms. "The stories of embodied pagan spirits are like the stories of the Saints, but opposite, violent, and goatish, yet you're kind beyond what is asked of any courtier. You may say that it's alchemy that gives you these qualities, but no other alchemist has ever been like you. You tell me about those of your blood, so you must be an elemental force in flesh or an earth-bound spirit. If that is what I have in you, then I am satisfied. What is better for me than a lover who is not of this world?"

He returned to her side, his emotions in tumult, but his face revealing little of his consternation. "Would you like me to tell you if you're right?"

"No," she said. "Because then I would have to Confess it, and that would be dreadful for us both. Besides, if you tell me, then I will have to give up my imaginings, dangerous though they may be." She took his hands and pulled him close to her. "If I'm wrong, don't tell me. I prefer my illusion to whatever might be real, even though both are damnable. Take what you want of me, and let me have the ecstasy of your passion." Rising up in the chair, she kissed him with an intensity she had never shown before. Their kiss deepened and his hands moved over her slender body, inviting response and apolaustic joy; she clung to him, moving only to give him access to all of her body and to increase her passion. His esurience was made keen by her desire, and, when she achieved her ecstatic culmination, as his lips touched her throat, he succumbed to her fulfillment with rapture fully equal to hers.

Text of a report from Bartech of Tabor, Master Bricklayer in Praha, to Rakoczy Ferancsi, Comes Santu-Germaniu, written in Church Latin by Frater Jedric, scribe at the Two Fishes Inn, and delivered by Guild messenger the day after it was written.

To the noble foreigner, Comes Santu-Germaniu at Mansion Bel-crady, on this, the ninth day of March in the 1270th Year of Grace,
   Most esteemed Comes,
   We have in hand the plans for your new double-chimney for

your bake- and bath-house. I agree that rats' nests will not so easily be made in flues of your proposed design. I also believe that the rats' nest where the fire began was not accidentally set alight. The bricks we have taken show that the rats' nest was touched with oil, or wax, and rats rarely take either of those things for their nests.

We will begin work as soon as the sum we agreed upon is in our hands, and we will work all days but Holy Days and during the Konig's departure celebration. I will bring eight men with me, and if the weather does not interfere, your chimneys should be finished within a month. If the weather works against us, we may need another ten days to finish the task.

Our work is guaranteed to last through storm, through snow, through rain, although we do not guarantee it will last if it is struck by lightning, or other manifestations of the Will of God.

It is the honor of the Bricklayers' Guild to serve you.

Bartech of Tabor
Master Bricklayer
(his mark)

by the hand of Frater Jedric, scribe

5

Although the morning was cool, Konige Kunigunde had ordered the windows in her reception hall thrown open, not only to give the room more light, but to provide the new arrivals with an opportunity to view Praha, spread out below Vaclav Castle, a reminder of the power of the Court. There were sprays of blossom-covered branches over the windows, and fresh rushes on the floor. An air of strained expectancy hung over the Court, the delay in the presentation of the new ladies creating restiveness everywhere, for there was to be a parade of the Konig's army later that afternoon, a grand occasion no one wanted to miss, least of all for the presentation of three Hungarian ladies.

At the far end of the reception hall, Konige Kunigunde sat on her throne that glowed with gold-leaf; she glistened with jewels in her profusion of necklaces. Her crown, too, was studded with pearls and polished gems. Her posture was stiff as the golden cloth of her huchine encouraged her to be, and her face was expressionless; her gaze was fixed on the far wall where a new tapestry depicted the life of Sant Vaclav, Dux of Bohemia, featuring a central scene of the Dux and his page trudging through the snow; Hovarth Pisti and two of his apprentices stood next to the wall where the tapestry hung, all three of them glorious in new Court finery.

The Konige's current ladies-in-waiting stood around the throne, each in her newest formal Court garments, displaying the wealth and beauty of Bohemia and the grandeur of its Court. All the women wore cloth-of-gold huchines over their bleihauts, the long, open-sleeved garments the most opulent sign of luxury in all the sumptuous display. Only Milica of Olmutz was absent so that she could take care of the Konige's daughters.

In the broad corridor beyond the reception hall, the new arrivals waited with their escorts. Two of the women, new to the Court, fretted, fidgeted, and tried to hide it; they both were still weary from their long journey and as yet unsettled in their own quarters. The third woman, Rozsa of Borsod, affected a kind of boredom to remind all those around her that she was accustomed to the rituals and trials of Court life. Her displeasure was the ache in her back from standing too long; her pregnancy was beginning to show, her breasts had become larger, and she was hungrier than she wanted to admit.

As the younger of the two new ladies-in-waiting, Iliska of Szousa was the most restive; she made mincing steps around her brother, who was escorting her, shaking her hands as if to rid herself of her edginess.

"Stop it," her brother hissed in Magyar.

"I'm nervous," Iliska answered in an undervoice. She stroked the elaborate belt of braided silver that hung low on her waist; her bleihaut was of Hungarian cut, with deep sleeves edged in more silver thread, setting off her blue-silk chainse.

The escorts of the other two women ignored Iliska's complaints, their attention on the reception room and the magnificent Konige's Court.

"Why do we have to go through all this elaborate ceremony?" Iliska bounced on her toes. "Why can't we just join the Konige at table? We could be more easily introduced there, couldn't we?"

"You know the answer, sister mine: that would do no honor to Bohemia and its territories and it would insult Hungary, into the bargain." He reached out his hand. "Be still and comport yourself with dignity. You are a Konige's woman now. You are observed."

"Why must I do that? Doesn't the Court ever get excited?" She rounded on Rozsa. "You have been here before. Do we always have to behave as if we were watching the Pope celebrate Mass?"

"When there are strangers present, yes we do," said Rozsa, her mouth turned down in disapproval. "If the occasion is made a Court function, then we are more than ourselves, and we must never forget that." Her ruby-colored silken bleihaut was lavishly embroidered with patterns of birds flying worked in thread that ranged from wine to purple to black, and her chainse was golden Persian silk. She tried to smile at the newcomers, but only achieved a rictus.

"Are you glad to be back at Court?" Iliska persisted.

"Under the circumstances, yes, I am."

"Iliska, be quiet," her brother ordered her.

She paid no attention. "Under what circumstances?" When she received no answer she bounced closer to Rozsa. "Tell me; what circumstances?"

"Why ask me? I would have thought that you'd worm it out of my escorts while we came here," said Rozsa, her patience strained.

"I didn't realize you might have more than the honor of serving the Konige to bring you back to the Court," said Iliska, offering a brazen grin. "Traveling in your condition shows dedication."

"It shows prudence, you child; Bela is ailing and my husband is away," Rozsa said sharply, hoping to quell Iliska's questions. "I am here at the behest of my husband, and the pleasure of the Konige."

"You have a task to perform," Iliska decided aloud.

"As have you, as have we all," said Rozsa, growing more weary of their game.

"Then you will know if we will be presented to Golden Otakar before he and his army departs, or whether this will be our presentation for both Konige and Konig." There was a hard light in her honey-colored eyes.

"Do be quiet," said Antal, glaring at his sister. "This isn't the time."

"We're waiting. Why can't we talk while we wait?" She glared at him. "If we must remain still, can't we talk?"

"We wait at the pleasure of the Konige," said Antal. "Be grateful you are here and ask God to give you contentment for it."

"But must we all keep silent?" Iliska flung up her hands in frustration.

Kustansze of Lugoj gave Iliska a hard look. "We are waiting upon Episcopus Fauvinel, who has been delayed with the Konig's men. He has blessed the criminals being hanged from the walls and now he is saying the farewell Mass for the Konig's army, since it departs tomorrow at dawn, and the men wish to be shriven before they go."

Iliska pursed her lips in annoyance. "Doesn't he know it's ill-mannered to keep the Konige's Court dependent on him to begin, but unable to on his account because he can't be bothered to arrive when everyone else does? Can't another religious open the Court if the Episcopus is attending to the Konig? It's allowed in Hungary."

"Bohemia isn't Hungary," Kustansze reminded Iliska as if she were talking to a child of eight.

"We are in a foreign land, for the sake of the Konige Kuni-gunde and Konig Bela." Rozsa stared directly at Iliska. "And don't forget that the Episcopus has as many spies in the Konige's household as anyone. Nothing you say, and nothing you do, will go unnoticed. Nothing." Something self-satisfied flickered in her face, but vanished before Iliska was sure it was there.

"All right—I'll be quiet," Iliska said, sulking.

Kustansze managed a near-smile. "Cultivate patience, Iliska. You'll need it at Court."

Iliska gave a heavy sigh. "We shouldn't have to stand here like this."

"Yes, we should," said Kustansze, reaching up to push a holding pin into the elaborate braid that encircled her head. "It is required of us for the Konige's sake."

"Will you both be quiet," Rozsa exclaimed. "We are being overheard. Keep that in your thoughts at all times."

"Spies." Iliska sighed. "Everyone knows spies can be bought."

"Iliska, hold your tongue," Antal told her more forcefully as he raised his hand. "You wouldn't want to make your courtisy with a mark on your face."

Iliska glowered at him, then turned away, her lower lip quivering in fear and chagrin. She muttered something about unfairness and the ill-conduct of brothers. The others pointedly looked away from her, for which she was grateful, but she suspected it was because they wanted to divorce themselves from her jejune behavior. A short while later, she sighed again and said, "At least the windows are open."

"On the Konige's order," Kustansze reminded her.

"Of course," said Iliska; she had taken the end of her long white veil in her hands and was pressing minute pleats into the cloth.

A sudden squeal of buisines announced the arrival of the Episcopus, and a second ostentation informed all of Vaclav Castle that the Konig was accompanying the Episcopus. Servants rushed to man the doors of the reception hall, almost shoving the women and their escorts aside in their haste.

"Move to the wall," Rozsa recommended. "The Konig is going to pass."

Iliska glanced at her brother, giving him a wicked grin. "And you said he wouldn't have time for the Konige's Court."

"He may not linger. Don't assume he'll notice you," Antal said blightingly.

"Of course," Iliska said, slipping next to the window so that the light would fall on her face.

"Courtisy him, but do not speak unless he addresses you," Rozsa reminded the other two women. "And the Episcopus as well."

The doors at the end of the broad corridor banged open, and the Konig's German Guards strode toward the reception room, their armor shining, their weapons jangling as they walked. At their rear came Otakar himself, crowned and in full armor but for his helmet. His breastplate and the chain mail of his coif were gilded, and his new ceremonial sword with its gem-encrusted hilt hung in a jeweled scabbard. He barely glanced at the women and their escorts, the women courtisying, the men kneeling, but went directly into the reception hall of the Konige's Court, her herald crying out his name as he came into the hall.

"Remain as you are," Rozsa warned Iliska, who was starting to rise. "The Episcopus is coming."

Iliska clicked her tongue but remained in the half-crouch position of the courtisy. "Where is he, then?" she whispered.

As if responding to her remark, a company of Trinitarian and Assumptionist monks entered the corridor in double-file, two of them bearing a large golden monstrance between them. At their rear came Episcopus Fauvinel, his vestments and miter glistening with gold and silver thread and studded with pearls and diamonds. He carried a tall crozier that thumped with every second step he took. He paused long enough to make the sign of the cross over the three women and their escorts, then passed on into the reception hall to the greeting of the herald's stentorian voice.

"Can I straighten up now?" Iliska asked impatiently.

"Yes." Rozsa rubbed at the small of her back. "It is many, many days until September," she remarked to Kustansze.

"And you will feel the days more keenly than we will," said the Konige's second cousin. "Especially after June. I know how it was with my children."

"You are to return home in June, do I have that right?" Iliska inquired with apparent solicitousness.

"You know you do," Rozsa told her. "You've asked me about it often enough coming here."

Iliska said something under her breath and looked away from Rozsa. "The Konig is bowing to the Konige."

"He is in her Court. Of course he bows," said Rozsa. "Didn't your father tell you *anything* about Court?"

"He told me what I had to do for Szousa, and what I ought not to do," said Iliska, trying to show more confidence than she felt.

From the reception hall came a rustle of clothes as the Court knelt, followed by the Episcopus' voice droning out his blessing on the Konige's Court and the dear Royals themselves, and admonishing all attending to strive to be worthy of the gracious friendship the dear Royals extended to all, and explaining that failure to be upstanding in the name of the Konige would also mean that the courtier had failed God, Whose Will it was that Konig Otakar and Konige Kunigunde should rule here. Last he called upon all the Konige's Court to welcome the new-comers and to show them courtesy for the sake of Konige Kunigunde. At the sign from the Episcopus the Court rose, and the Konig went to kneel to his wife and charge her with the safety of Praha in his absence.

"May God guide me in all ways to serve you, dear Royal, and the Kingdom of Bohemia," the Konige said to her husband.

The herald bawled out the names of the women to be presented and their escorts, giving their titles and their estates; in the reception hall, the Konig, his personal guard, and the Episcopus stood aside, leaving an aisle for the women to approach the Konige's dais.

"Kustansze of Lugoj, daughter of Kazmir of Lugoj, kinswoman

of Konige Kunigunde, escorted by Padnagy Kalman, Dux of Oradea."

Kustansze stepped forward and courtisied the Konige. "May God show you all favor, dear Royal," she said in awkward Bohemian.

"Be welcome in Bohemia, good cousin," said the Konige, and nodded to her so that she would step aside.

"Iliska of Szousa, daughter of the Comes of Szousa," announced the herald, "escorted by her brother, Antal of Szousa."

Iliska felt a warning jab in her side from Antal's thumb as she stepped away from him to courrtisy the Konige. "The blessings of God and man be with you, dear Royal."

"Prettily said," Konige Kunigunde approved, and waved her away.

"Rozsa of Borsod, wife of Notay Tibor of Kaposvar," the herald declared.

Rozsa's courtisy was not as deep as Court usually required, but the Konige made allowances for Rozsa's pregnancy. "I am greatly honored to return to your resplendent Court, dear Royal," she said, using Milan of Gyula's arm to steady herself.

"I am happy to have you here again, Rozsa of Borsod. Kinga has missed you." For the first time there was animation in Kunigunde's face. "You will find your friends are glad of your return." She held up her hand to indicate her ladies-in-waiting. "And I will be happy to have news of my grandfather and my brother."

"Dear Royal is all kindness; it will be my most pressing duty to speak with you of all that has been happening at Konig Bela's Court," said Rozsa, stepping back and taking a surreptitious glance around the room caught sight of Rakoczy Ferancsi standing with Tirz Agoston of Mures; Rakoczy held a new lyre in his hands, softly testing the strings and listening to Agoston's instructions as he did. Rozsa kept herself from smiling, but she felt encouraged to find him still at Court; she had plans to see him again.

Konig Otakar stepped up onto the dais, the Konige's women moving back from her so that they would not offend the ruler. "I have members of your Court to thank, dear Royal, before I leave for battle, and it is fitting that I do it here."

"You are welcome, my Konig," said Kunigunde, rising to honor him.

"If you will call forth those who have done service for you to my benefit?" He raised his new ceremonial sword. "I will bestow my thanks upon them."

The herald called out, "Hovarth Pisti of Buda."

The tapestry-weaver came through the assembled Court, not quite strutting, his face flushed with pride. "Dear Royal," he said as he went on his knee in front of the dais.

"For the magnificent tapestry that now adorns this hall, and the two others that hang in the Konige's private apartments, I show you my thanks and bestow upon you this ring"—he took a gold band from his sleeve—"and ask you to wear it in testament to your service to the Konige and the glory of Bohemia. A stipend of ten golden Vaclavs will be paid to you annually for a period of ten years as a sign of our gratitude, and one golden Vaclav annually for a decade to each of your apprentices."

Hovarth Pisti put the ring on his middle finger—the only one on which it would not be loose—and lowered his head. "I and mine will thank your generosity for all generations to come."

"Most worthy," murmured the Konige as she signaled the Master Tapestry-Weaver to rise.

"Tirz Agoston of Mures," bellowed the herald, and the instrument-maker ducked his head to Rakoczy and went to the dais to kneel.

Konig Otakar whispered a few words to Rytir Steffal von Passau, the German Guard nearest to him, then turned his attention to Tirz Agoston while Rytir Steffal departed on an errand. "Good musician and maker of instruments," the Konig said, "you and your instruments have brought many hours of pleasure to the Konige, and have soothed her in times of sadness, for which we are deeply grateful. In recognition of your excellent service, I present you with a badge of your service, set in gold, and dependent from a gold chain, so that all may witness our esteem and thanks. We also bestow upon you a grant of fifty golden Vaclavs to encourage you to help to bring your craft to greater perfection. In addition, we pledge to match that amount for a period of five years to enable your work to continue without hesitation or let." He took the chain with its pendant badge from his capacious sleeve and dropped it around Tirz Agoston's neck.

"I . . . am overwhelmed by your k-kindness, dear Royal," Tirz Agoston stammered, touching the links as if he couldn't believe he wore them, his eyes dazed. "May God reward your goodness."

"Most courteous," said the Konige, motioning him away from the dais.

"Pader Klothor," the herald summoned; a buzz of conversation rushed through the hall, for it was unusual to summon the Konige's treasurer to such events as these.

A thin, elderly man in Redemptionist priest's habit came from the corridor leading into the private parts of the Konige's Court; he carried a ledger as if it were made of solid Bohemian gold. He stopped before Episcopus Fauvinel before he went to the Konig. "Dear Royal," he said in a dusty voice as he went onto his knee.

"Pader Klothor," said the Konig, raising his ceremonial sword, "tell the Court the accounting on this splendid symbol of Bohemia's power that my Konige has presented to me."

Obediently the little priest opened the ledger and began to read, "For gold, a measure equal to twenty-eight roundels of lead was used in the hilt, which is ornamented with two diamonds in the pommel, ten white sapphires in the grip, four emeralds, four tourmalines, four peridots, four topazes, four rubies, and ten tiger's-eyes in the quillons. The blade is of Luccan steel, weighing equal to fifteen roundels of lead. The scabbard is of silver the equivalent of twenty-one roundels of lead ornamented with ten amethysts and eight rose zircons. The gold is the work and the gift of Hrodperht von Ratisbon; the jewels are the gift of Rakoczy Ferancsi, Comes Santu-Germaniu."

"A princely treasure, provided by men who are not Bohemians, which is an excellent omen, for it says that the reach of this
sword extends beyond this kingdom. It is a pledge of greater
things to come beyond our present borders, one I will display
to all the world when I am Holy Roman Emperor," the Konig
proclaimed, hefting the sword above his head, smiling at the
general acclaim. When he lowered the sword, the clamor qui-
eted. "In recognition of this imperial treasure—" He signaled
the herald.

"Hrodperht von Ratisbon," the herald called.

The goldsmith made his way to the Konig, kneeling down
with a great show of deference. He lowered his head and waited
for Otakar to speak.

"Your workmanship and your gift have distinguished you
among the Master Goldsmiths of Praha, and to demonstrate my
appreciation, you will henceforth be known as Goldsmith to the
Konig. As part of that advancement, you will be awarded a pen-
sion of twenty golden Vaclavs a year for life, and for ten years beyond for your heirs."

Hrodperht was overcome with emotion; tears welled in his
eyes and rolled down his face. He flung himself forward to seize
Otakar's steel-booted foot and kiss it, exclaiming through his sobs,
"Most, most dear Royal, nothing can say how greatly your munificence has honored me."

The Konig grinned. "May I be so beloved by all my vassals,"
he said, and watched as the men in the reception hall went down
on their knees to him, and the women courtisied. "Rise, rise, all of
you," he ordered a long moment later, using his sword to motion
them upward. "And you, my goldsmith, you have set a most admirable example. My choice of you is an excellent one."

Nearly stumbling, Hrodperht got to his feet; he was still weeping, and his hands were clasped in devotion. "Dear Royal is—"

"Yes, yes," said Otakar. "I have no doubt that you will show
yourself fit for my favor."

"Your gift and work are beyond price," said the Konige as Hrodperht staggered away.

At the Konig's sign, the herald yelled, "Rakoczy Ferancsi, Comes Santu-Germaniu."

This was the moment Rakoczy had been dreading, but there was no avoiding it without giving unpardonable offense to Bohemia. He moved through the Court with no sign of his dismay at this recognition; he paused to bow to the Episcopus, and then knelt to the Konig, his demeanor calm and self-contained, elegant in his black-and-silver velvet huch over a chainse of darkest-red silk against which his eclipse pectoral shone with the luster of the night sky.

"Comes, your jewels have made my sword and scabbard an object of beauty and a symbol of wealth and power. Were you a vassal of mine, I would be hard-pressed to reward you, for you have more riches than most of Bohemia together. I will not insult you with paltry riches when you are so clearly monied past all want." His chuckle was dutifully echoed by the Court. "But as you are an exile, and your movements are restricted to Mansion Belcrady, the Konige's Court, the Council Hall, and the public streets of Praha, on the order of Konig Bela, I can at least reduce your restrictions and grant you free movements within five leagues of Praha, and all the buildings within the city's walls, your safety and protection assured through this, my grant to you."

"Dear Royal is most gracious," said Rakoczy, thinking of how irate Konig Bela would be when he learned of Otakar's modification of his exile. Nothing about him betrayed his anxiety as he lowered his head in another sign of respect.

"You have more than earned it," Otakar declared. "You have enriched the Konige's Court, you have eased the Konige's sorrows, you have aided the Counselors, you have conducted yourself with probity, and you have cost the treasury nothing. I would be a fool not to give you what little I can in return." Before the Konig could launch into more fulsome praise, the Konige spoke up.

"You have my gratitude, and that of my daughters," she said, and dismissed Rakoczy with a turn of her hand. "And I thank

Pader Klothor for his careful accounts." A nod of her head sent the priest away.

More relieved than he dared reveal, Rakoczy got to his feet and returned to the far end of the reception hall, his thoughts roiling: how was he to behave now? If he did not travel outside the city, Konig Otakar would be insulted, but if he did travel outside the city, Konig Bela would send his soldiers to pillage and ransack Santu-Germaniu. He was still deep in thought when he felt a hand on his sleeve; he turned and saw Rozsa of Borsod smiling conspiratorially at him. "Dear lady," he said with an automatic bow.

"Oh, very prettily done," she said, staring directly at him. "I didn't know you would still be here. I thought Konig Bela might have relented and summoned you home."

"That has not happened," said Rakoczy.

"More fool Konig Bela, then, for surely you could enrich his treasury as you have done for Konig Otakar." She studied him silently for a short while, then said, "At least you haven't forgot me."

"No, I have not," he agreed, trying to discern her intentions.

"I'm glad you haven't."

He bowed to her again, curious to learn what she wanted. "Your husband must be pleased that you will give him a child."

She laughed angrily. "He may be, but his cousins are not. I'm here so that they won't be able to cause me to miscarry. They have been Tibor's heirs and want to remain so. At home, with Tibor gone, they might do anything to remain his heirs."

"Ah," he said.

"The Counselors of Praha," the herald announced as the crowd parted once more to admit ten of the Counselors.

"My husband has gone to join Konig Otakar in his on-going war with Rudolph von Hapsburg; the Comes of Austria is determined to reclaim his fief from Bohemia. Tibor knew he would have to protect our child, and he couldn't do it sending me to Konig Bela's Court, for his cousins are there as well as at Kaposvar, and my position wouldn't protect me there." She touched him again. "So he sent me back here—isn't that fortunate."

"If it spares your child, it certainly is," said Rakoczy, wishing he had reason to excuse himself from the Court.

"Yes, but there may be other reasons as well," she said, her eyes provoking him.

"For your child's sake, I think not," said Rakoczy drily.

"You can do me no disgrace now, no matter what you do to me," she persisted, relishing the risk she was taking in speaking so directly to him. "I am pregnant, and no other seed shall quicken in my womb until this child I carry now is delivered. I have to protect my husband's heir."

Rakoczy held up his hand. "Say nothing more if you wish to keep your reputation."

She laughed in her practiced way, her head tilted to beguile him. "Are you afraid of what might happen to me? Then you aren't indifferent to my fate, are you?"

"I have tasted your blood, Rozsa," he said in a hurried whisper. "I cannot be indifferent to you."

"How that must vex you," she said, moving away from him to greet Gyongyi of Tolan, who had just stepped down from the dais on an errand for the Konige.

Rakoczy stood by himself while the Konig spoke confidently of the victory that he knew would be his by the end of summer. Each assertion he made was greeted by the Court's acclaim, though the Konige's eyes were distant and troubled.

"They've gone to get the two daughters," said a voice beside him; Rakoczy glanced around, then down, to discover Tahir standing next to him. "Otakar is already planning brilliant marriages for them both."

"It is what all Konigs do with their daughters," said Rakoczy, feeling a pang for the two girls.

"Too long has Bohemia been denied its place in the world. God now shows us the way to the highest place in the Holy Roman Empire. What can I, and all of you, be but grateful for His gift to Golden Otakar?"

"Would you repeat what you said?" Rakoczy asked the dwarf.

"I told you to be careful of spies. With so much favor from the Konig, your enemies will multiply as maggots in a corpse." He ducked his head and went away through the crowd, while Rakoczy resisted the impulse to look about in the hope of discovering whom Tahir had had in mind when he gave his warning.

Text of a report on the damage done by the Moltava's flooding, presented by Pader Baltzsar of Budejovice to Episcopus Fauvinel and the Counselors of Praha six days after the flood-waters receded.

To the most reverend Episcopus Fauvinel and the most esteemed Counselors of Praha, the dutiful greetings of Pader Baltzsar of Budejovice, with his report of the flooding of the Moltava on the 23rd, 24th, 25th, and 26th days of March in the 1270th Year of Grace. May God guide me to report aright. Amen.

Pursuant to the Episcopus' instructions issued in his capacity as deputy to Przemysl Otakar II in his absence, I have now completed my initial inspection of the countryside for ten leagues upriver and ten leagues downriver and herewith offer my observations for your considerations.

The tillers of the fields tell me that at least one third of all they have planted is lost. Some may be planted again, but they will not have a full harvest even if they plow and plant again. No assessments of orchards and vineyards has yet been made. The current loss of livestock for the region I have covered stands at 162 drowned cattle, 248 drowned goats, 429 drowned sheep, 754 drowned chickens, 127 drowned geese, 81 drowned horses, 96 drowned asses, 722 drowned swine, 358 drowned dogs. Of the peasants themselves, 16 men have drowned, 24 women, and 53 children; there may be more, but these are all that have been reported to the priests and monasteries, most of whose losses are accounted in these figures, with the sole exception of the monks of the Monastery of the Holy Martyrs, where all but six of the monks there have perished. Not all the bodies have been found, but they will receive the blessing of the Church and burial in sacred ground when they are.

Uncounted numbers of peasants are without food or shelter, and only two monasteries are in good enough repair to take them in: Sant-Phedor and Sant-Weilant, and they are strained to the limit. Food is needed in both establishments if the peasants who survived the flood are not to starve instead. I beseech both you, Episcopus, and you, Counselors, to gather together as much foodstuffs as you can spare and dispatch wagon-loads of bread, cheese, sausages, and wine to help relieve the monks who have extended their charity to these unfortunates.

Eleven roads are in great need of repair, three bridges have been washed away entirely, leaving only their foundations behind, and another five are badly damaged, including two which will be used by the Konig and his men for their triumphal return, and therefore must be brought into good repair as soon as may be. Masons and woodmen will be needed to begin the rebuilding as soon as they may be dispatched so that they may begin their work.

I will revisit all the places I have seen in another week and prepare an amended report to this one for your perusal.

Gloria in excelsis Deo, et pacem in terris,

Baltzsar of Budejovice
Trinitarian Pader

PART IV

ILISKA OF SZOUSA

*T*ext of a decree issued by the Counselors of Praha; published throughout the city and read in every church on the 6th day of April, 1270.

Be it known to all the people of Praha:

1)   At the order of the Episcopus Fauvinel and the Counselors of Praha, the Beggars' Guild is given continuance on their order to hunt and kill any and all rats found in the city, and to be paid one silver Apostle for every ten rat bodies presented at the Council Court.

2)   Every resident of Praha has the permission of the Episcopus and the Counselors of Praha to kill rats; they may also claim the same bounty as the one provided for the Beggars' Guild.

3)   Those owning property within the walls of the city are charged with the duty to kill any and all rats that may be found on said property, regardless of the use made of said property; they may also claim the bounty levied against the rats.

4)   The bounty on cats is herewith rescinded; no cat, with or without a household to claim it, may be killed so long as it is able to catch and kill rats and mice, and no charges of witchcraft may be made against any cat or household with cats within the city walls; those who are uncertain regarding any cats may take them to any priest in the city to be blessed.

5) *All warehouses within the city walls henceforth are required to keep cats to control the rats that are known to infest warehouses, where they proliferate in great numbers.*

6) *Those failing to observe the orders of this decree will be subject to fines up to four golden Vaclavs for failure to comply with the terms herein. Repeated offenses will cause the assessed fines to be doubled at every lapse.*

God bless the City of Praha, the Konig, the Konige, the Episcopus, and the Counselors of Praha.

1

"Do you plan to venture outside the city?" Hruther asked Rakoczy in the language of Persia as they sat together in Rakoczy's workroom while the athanor produced another load of jewels; it was late afternoon and Holy Week was beginning, announced by the ringing of bells throughout all Praha.

"Not yet, and if I do, it will be limited to Otakar's park, as I have done before at the Konige's order. I think it would be best to wait to see what Konig Bela has to say about Konig Otakar's benevolence before testing the limits of what I may actually do." Rakoczy leaned back in his saddle-chair, his dark eyes enigmatic as he stared up at the ceiling. "No matter what I do, one of the Konigs is going to take umbrage."

"Which one can do you the most harm?" Hruther inquired; he had his own opinion, but he wanted to discover Rakoczy's thoughts on the matter.

"It is not a question of harming *me,* it is my fief that stands in the greatest danger, and Bela knows it." He rubbed his close-trimmed beard. "What I need to ascertain is some means of leaving Praha in such a way that neither Bela nor Otakar can hold it against—"

"The people of Santu-Germaniu," Hruther finished for him. He got up from the upholstered bench. "Do you think Konig Bela would relent and permit you to return to Santu-Germaniu? You have enriched the Konige with so many jewels, might not Konig Bela want some of the same bounty?"

"Probably not," said Rakoczy. "My . . . heir will have to wait until Konig Bela dies to return to Santu-Germaniu." He had long since made a habit of leaving property and businesses and fortunes to himself in the form of a nephew or a cousin; in this instance the device was crucial, not simply convenient, and he had gone to great pains to make the succession secure. "My cousin will claim the fief when next I go there."

"Otakar holds you in high esteem just now, and for all he is away on campaign, his orders protect you. Konig Bela is the one who is in a position to do you harm," Hruther said, reflecting Rakoczy's understanding. "He, and the French Episcopus."

"So the city walls are still my prison, because Konig Bela would exact a higher price for my venturing beyond the city than Otakar would," said Rakoczy as if confirming something he already knew.

Hruther studied Rakoczy, his long years of serving him giving him insight into Rakoczy's behavior. "My master, you have done as much as any man in Bohemia to support the Konige and her Court, as her grandfather ordered you to do. You have shown no favor to the Konig Bela's heir, for all that he rules in Transylvania, nor have you allied yourself with the Hapsburg interests. You have not looked beyond the Carpathians for alliances to the east. You have not taken part in any rebellion against Konig Bela. Your service to Konige Kunigunde is beyond any question. If you were to take a day to go into the countryside to evaluate the extent of the flood damage, how could Konig Bela possibly object, since it would be in service to the Konige as well as to Otakar? You are doing what you would do for your own fief if such misfortune befell it. If you took one of the Hungarians from the Konige's Court, Bela would never regard that as a breach of your exile."

"If it suited his purposes, he would," Rakoczy said, unmoving.

"You won't make the attempt?"

"Not yet," said Rakoczy. "It is too much risk."

"Do not despair," Hruther said bracingly, his ascetical features lighting with sympathy. "You will find the means to leave here."

"And go where?" Rakoczy shook his head. "I could not return to Santu-Germaniu without bringing Konig Bela's or his heir's wrath upon my fief. I would have to get away unnoticed and find a place where I could remain untouched and unknown for as long as Konig Bela lives, and hope that Bela's suspicions are not shared by his son." For a short while he said nothing more. "If Konig Bela offered sufficient reward, I might have to go back to China to be safe." He chuckled sadly to show he knew that was not possible with the descendants of Jenghiz Khan spreading from China to Baghdad.

"Where *would* you go?—if you could leave here without hazard?" Hruther inquired, hoping to turn Rakoczy's mind to more energetic cogitation. "Constantinople? Alexandria?"

Rakoczy considered his answer for a moment, then said lowly, "The Pays d'Oc would be a possibility. Perhaps Lisboa. Grodno might be a safe place for a few years. So might Bruges, or Uppsala, or Novgorod, as long as we are beyond the reach of Hungary and the Holy Roman Empire, and so long as my vassals are not held to account on my behalf."

"Then you think Otakar will become Emperor," said Hruther.

"He may, but if he does, it will be hard-won. He has done much to expand Bohemian territories, but that has created spite in many of those rulers around him who have lost ground to him. They will not be likely to support him, and that could end his chances." Rakoczy sighed. "Where would you like to go, old friend, assuming we find some means to leave here safely?"

"I?" Hruther looked startled. "Roskilde, or if that is too near the Holy Roman Empire, then Opslo or Aberffraw, or perhaps London, at least for ten years or until Konig Bela is no longer a threat. His heir has little reason to continue to hold your fief and vassals hostage."

"He may decide he does," said Rakoczy.

Hruther shrugged. "He would do better reclaiming Hungarian territory from Otakar if he wishes to strengthen Hungary."

"I worry for Balint. It would be poor return for good service to have him taken prisoner by Konig Bela as a means of forcing my hand." He paused, sinking into thought. "If I knew what Konige Kunigunde has told her grandfather in my regard, I would be more able to decide."

"Would she be likely to tell you what she has said in her reports?" Hruther asked, anticipating the answer. "No, I suppose not."

"No," Rakoczy agreed.

"This is an impasse for you," Hruther said, concern showing in his faded-blue eyes.

"True enough, but there should be a way to work through it, given enough time." He sat up, his face shadowed. "I wish I knew how matters stand at Santu-Germaniu. It would ease my mind."

"Assuming Konig Bela has upheld his pledge."

"It remains my hope that he is too caught up in war to turn all his attention to a place like my fief." Getting to his feet, Rakoczy began to pace, his black huch and red chainse swinging with the energy of his movements.

"Bela is still at war with Otakar."

"And Bela is no longer a young man. He is not in a position to squander his army or his own resources," Rakoczy said. He stopped. "I am summoned to the Konige at sunset. I should choose a suitable gift."

"Gems for Easter." Hruther recognized that Rakoczy would not discuss the predicament any further for the present. He nodded. "I'll lay out something for you."

"Thank you." Rakoczy went to his coffer, opening the bands and tipping back the lid.

"Do you want to bathe?"

"Yes, but I had better not. Barnon has already commented on my bathing, and I do not know whose spy he is, or what he makes of my preoccupation with cleanliness." Rakoczy stood still. "I loathe this sense of bitterness I feel, and there is little to alleviate it." He shook his head, but went on, "It is as blighting as frost on blossoms, and it takes away from so much that could be affirmative, or revivifying, like the return of spring. But it lingers, like a slow poison."

"My master," said Hruther with stern sympathy.

"We will have to leave here, I know, before it numbs me to all joy." That had happened in the past, and the memories still rankled within him.

"If it does, you will thaw: you have before," Hruther reminded him.

"Oh, yes," he said quietly. "In time."

Hurther closed the door and went to set out Court clothing for Rakoczy. He had seen the Comes in morose moods before, but he had not been aware in the past of the degree of revulsion he sensed now, and it troubled him. The trials they had endured in India were still sharp in his memory, and he thought that Rakoczy had not yet put them entirely behind him. Perhaps he felt echoes of Tamasrajasi in some of the women he encountered, and had failed to find the intimacy that was so necessary to him. As he took the black-velvet huch and the pearl-white silk chainse from the garderobe, he considered what he might do to make Rakoczy's escape possible. He was choosing between black Damascus silk and fine, black Florentine woolen braccae when the door opened and Rakoczy stepped in.

"I am glad you are still here," he said to Hruther. "I want to ask your pardon for my fit of saturnine self-indulgence." His smile faded as soon as it appeared.

"You have nothing to apologize for, my master."

"Not for someone who has the luxury of time that I do," said Rakoczy bluntly. "I ought not to forget that everything passes. As much as I may rail against my circumstances, they will not last."

"As you remind me, there is no certainty that you will survive." He sat down on the straight-backed chair.

"But I have three millennia behind me. My patience should be greater," said Rakoczy levelly. "So I ask your pardon, and I hope you will not be appalled by my outburst."

Hruther did not smile but there was a change in his austere

features, an easing that showed around his eyes and mouth. "You are more bound to life than I am; it doesn't surprise me when there is a price for that bond." He stopped any more conversation by asking, "Would you like me to help you to dress?"

"I will manage, thank you, old friend."

"Then I will tell Illes to saddle which horse for you?"

"Asza. As I recall, she is not in season just yet; the Konige would not be pleased that I would bring to her stable if Asza is."

"It would keep the grooms busy," said Hruther with a suggestion of a grin. "She will be ready, or Phanos, if Illes thinks it best."

"A fine choice," said Rakoczy as Hruther left him to his preparations.

Phanos was saddled and bridled and ready, waiting near the horse-trough, his reins in Illes' hands. Rakoczy patted the gray gelding on his neck, tested the girth, and swung up into the high-backed saddle. "Thank you," he said, tossing a silver coin to him. "He will have earned a good brushing when I come back. What of Asza?"

"Asza is turned out in the paddock for the day. She was kicking at her stall."

"I wish we could settle on a stallion for her," Rakoczy said as he gathered up the reins. "Maiden mares feel their blood more keenly than those who have had foals." With a nudge from Rakoczy's heels, Phanos started for the gate.

The streets were busy but not so crowded that making his way through them was impossible. At Mansion Czernin a group of noble pilgrims had just arrived, and the confusion at the gate slowed Rakoczy's progress through the gates of Castle Vaclav. Leaving his horse with stable grooms, he went toward the Konige's part of the huge stone building. Pages escorted him to the Konige's Court, and her herald announced him.

He approached the tall, gold-plated chair where Konige Kunigunde sat, resplendent as a sunrise in a bleihaut of red silk embroidered with gold and silver thread. For Holy Week, she wore a gem-studded gold crucifix larger than her hand on a heavy chain around her neck; beside her, the Episcopus glittered with rubies and garnets on his white-silk vestments. Rakoczy knelt and held up a pouch of figured velvet. "May God grant you and your children His Mercy at this sacred time, dear Royal."

One of the Konige's pages took the pouch and carried it to her, kneeling as he did.

Konige Kunigunde opened the pouch and poured a scintillating cascade into her lap, the look of disinterest fading as the jewels streamed through her fingers. "Gracious, Comes," she exclaimed. "How many!" She picked up an emerald the size of the end of her thumb, holding it up to the light from a tree of candles set up behind her. Putting the emerald down, she chose an opal to inspect. "This is lavish, even for you."

Rakoczy studied her. "With the Konig gone, I had hoped to provide you and your daughters with a pleasant distraction."

"*Most* generous," she exclaimed with a faltering smile, motioning him to rise.

"If this brings you joy, dear Royal, I am more than rewarded." He took a step back and gave a deep French bow to her.

As if it were an afterthought, she added, "If you have had word from your fief's steward, I would be glad to hear what has been said." She sounded only mildly interested but there was a need in her eyes that held his attention.

"When you like, dear Royal. I will be here until the meal is served." He moved aside, puzzled by the intensity he had felt from the Konige. What had she heard that she was so overstrung?

"How do you contrive to keep giving her such fine gems?" Rakoczy swung around to see Rozsa of Borsod coming up to him, her feline smile widening. "I would be jealous if she were not the Konige."

"Jewels are expected of me; presenting them is my duty," said Rakoczy, inclining his head respectfully; he looked to see if Imbolya was in the room, but he caught no sight of her.

"A half-dozen perhaps," Rozsa said. "But you bring them by the peck." She smoothed the front of her burnt-umber bleihaut, subtly emphasizing her pregnancy. "Have you kept yourself amused during my absence? Or need I ask?"

Rakoczy did not answer her question; his manner remained affable. "You look well, Rozsa. I trust your child thrives."

"He grows," said Rozsa, a flash of anger in her eyes. "You appear much the same as you were."

"Did you suppose it would be otherwise?" He made sure there was an arm's-length of distance between them, certain they were being watched.

"I had hoped you might have languished without me." She looked away to hide the spite in her face. "But men do not languish, do they? no matter what the troubadours sing."

Rakoczy would not be dragged into the wrangle Rozsa so clearly wanted. "Troubadours tell what their listeners want to hear."

"So you believe that I—"

He held up his hand. "The Konige would not approve our talking together in this way. It draws undue interest to our conversation."

"She isn't paying any attention, not to us or anyone else," Rozsa snapped, but she turned away from him, saying softly as she did, "Would you like to meet again, as we have done in days past? I haven't forgotten the hours we spent together."

"Not while you are with child," he said in an undervoice, watching the men and women milling around them.

"My pregnancy repels you?" Her question was a furious whisper.

"This is not a prudent discussion for this place."

"Spies. I know. We will talk later," she said, her brows angling into a frown. Abruptly she walked away from him, going toward Pan Kolowrat Atenaze, who was entertaining Betrica of Eger with a display of amateurish juggling.

The Angelus bell began to toll, first from the bell-tower of Castle Vaclav, because the Episcopus was attending Court, then from the churches of Praha. Episcopus Fauvinel rose and pronounced the blessing for Holy Week while the Court knelt. This was followed almost at once by Sant-Boleslav's carillon ringing the anthem *Vinea Mea Electa,* the mournful notes darkening with the day; while the bells rang, conversation in the Konige's Court was subdued, and only after the last peal had echoed away did the reception hall begin to seethe with words and the courtiers to circulate through the hall.

When the Episcopus had moved from his place beside Kunigunde, Rakoczy was summoned to the Konige once again; she had left her throne and was standing in the largest of the window embrasures, her unguarded expression filled with aching, a look that vanished as soon as she realized she was no longer unobserved.

"Dear Royal." Rakoczy was about to drop to his knee, but she motioned to him to remain standing.

"Comes," she said without inflection of any kind.

"How may I serve you, dear Royal?" He saw that she was still troubled.

"What have you heard from your steward in the last month? What has he to say of my brother?"

"I have heard nothing from Balint, which has caused me some worry. I hope it may only mean that the courier was delayed by the floods."

"Yes," the Konige murmured. "The floods. I, too, have had only scant news of my grandfather."

"Do you have a particular fear, dear Royal?" He knew it would be folly to press her, but he shared her anxiety.

"Only a rumor. As such, it means very little, as rumors so often do. I should probably pay it no notice." She forced a smile. "No doubt both of our concerns will prove baseless by the time May comes and our reports reach us at last." For a long moment, she remained quiet, then said forlornly, "It's just that my grandfather is old and my brother hates him so."

It took Rakoczy an instant to form a response. "That has been the case for several years, dear Royal, and the rumors that filled the Court of coming war or open confrontation meant nothing.

Your brother has not raised an army in spite of his threats, nor is he likely to."

"Thus far," said Kunigunde. "If my husband did not war with my grandfather, I would not be troubled by my brother's malice, but as it is—" She stopped herself from saying more.

"It is a hard circumstance for you, dear Royal," Rakoczy said with genuine sympathy.

She did not seem to hear him. "I was supposed to prevent the war. That's why the marriage was arranged, so that Hungary and Bohemia would not go to war, and so that the Hapsburgs in Austria could be contained between them. I was the assurance of peace! How could they have gone to war? Why did God turn against me?"

Rakoczy regarded her solemnly. "Their war is no fault of yours, dear Royal. You do yourself a disservice to think so."

"The Episcopus tells me that if I had had sons and not daughters the war would not have happened." She crossed herself; her eyes shone with tears. "God has not heard me."

"Why would anyone assume sons would have brought peace, when your own brother is prepared to take as much of an army as he can raise against your grandfather? Are not daughters more useful than sons?" Rakoczy saw a flicker of something in her face that suggested the Konige was distressed for her children. "They will surely find worthy husbands, and do so without war."

The Konige sighed. "May they succeed where I have failed," she said with more emotion than she usually revealed. She put her hands to her temples, her eyes closing. "My head hurts."

Rakoczy signaled to one of the pages. "Would you fetch one of the Konige's ladies?"

The boy ducked his head and hurried into the crowd to find the nearest lady-in-waiting. He reappeared with Iliska of Szousa trailing after him.

Iliska gave Rakoczy a speculative smile as she courtisied the Konige. "Command me, dear Royal."

Konige Kunigunde blinked. "I need to be alone for a short

while," she collected herself enough to say. "Take me to my apartments. I will be better soon."

"Of course, dear Royal," said Iliska, looking at Rakoczy as she spoke, measuring him with her eyes. "I will find you to tell you the Konige is . . . is improved. I will stay with her until she is." She offered her arm for the Konige to lean on, patting her hand gently. "You'll be more yourself in a little while, dear Royal."

The Court parted to permit the Konige and Iliska to pass, the departure marked by a susurrus of inquisitive whispers. At the door, the Konige turned and said, "I will join you when you go to eat. Until then, you may amuse yourselves as you think best."

Feeling uncomfortable from the notice he was attracting, Rakoczy soon found an excuse to depart. He reclaimed Phanos at the stable, mounted, and left the central courtyard by the main gate, letting the gelding pick his pace down the hill to Mansion Belcrady. A luminous light in the west was fading as night closed in, and the town was shut up for the night, households devoting the evening to simple food and prayer.

"You are returned early," Minek remarked as he opened the gate for Rakoczy.

"That I am," Rakoczy agreed, dismounting and looking about for Illes; the wavering torchlight emphasized the darkness and turned Illes' approach into a flickering apparition. Although Rakoczy's night-seeing eyes were not deceived, the impression was a disquieting one.

"I have warm mash for him, Comes," he said as he took the reins to lead the gelding away.

"Good. And some olive oil with the mash; he is shedding, and the oil will help him to be rid of the hair."

"As you wish, Comes," Illes promised, clucking at Phanos.

Barnon admitted Rakoczy to the entry hall. "It is good to have you home, Comes."

"Thank you, Barnon." He noticed that Barnon was trembling. "Are you well?"

"Yes. But I am cold," he said.

Relief went through Rakoczy like a gust of wind. "Then have Kornemon stoke the fireplaces and set the fires. There is no reason for you to be so chilled." He went into the main hall, pointing to the hearth. "The Episcopus has not banned heat for Holy Week. You need not hesitate to light the fire."

"Yes, Comes. Thank you for that." Barnon ducked his head more respectfully than he usually did. "The household will be glad."

"There's no point for you to have to huddle around the spits in the kitchen to keep from succumbing to cold." Rakoczy went toward the staircase. "Is Hruther in my workroom?"

"I don't know," Barnon answered.

"Um," said Rakoczy, to make it plain that he had understood, as he continued upward, his thoughts in a tangle and his worries multiplying with every step.

Text of a letter from Antal of Szousa in Praha to his uncle, Szygosmund, Comes of Czongrad, at Konig Bela's Court in Buda, Hungary, dictated to Pader Bedo, Premonstratensian scribe and Court clerk, carried by private courier and delivered twenty-three days after it was written.

To the most respected and esteemed leader of our family, Szygosmund, Comes of Czongrad, the duteous greetings from your nephew, Antal of Szousa, at the Court of Konige Kunigunde in Praha:

My venerable uncle,

I have, at your request, been at pains since arriving here to be vigilant in the care of my sister, Iliska, serving Konige Kunigunde as a waiting-woman, and to seek out likely husbands for her, a task that has been made more difficult than either of us anticipated with the Konig away at war with most of his Court accompanying him. There are men at Court, but not many of them offer the kind of alliance that would improve our family and increase its holdings.

*One of the men at the Konige's Court is a Transylvanian
Comes, Comes Santu-Germaniu, who is formidably wealthy, but
who is here under terms of exile. Apparently he is unmarried,
about forty, judging by his appearance. There are those who say
that he is actually a spy for Konig Bela, and others who say that
he is an ally of Konig Bela's heir. In either case, he would be a
poor bargain for us to make. Unfortunately, my sister has become
fascinated with him, either because of his elegance or his fortune,
but neither of those things will serve to advance our family, so I
am doing what I can to discourage Iliska from setting her hopes
upon him. She may be a willful girl, but she knows what she owes
to the House and to her blood. I am confident that she will turn
her thoughts to more appropriate noblemen than this discredited
Comes.*

*Now that Easter is over by a day, the Court is preparing for
the Konige's May Festival. There will be jousting and feasting and
as many kinds of competition as can be possible in a Court so
lacking in suitable men. I've granted Iliska the right to wear the
gold necklaces you have entrusted to me for her adornment, and
I will let her wear the pearl earrings. She has appropriate bleihauts for all Court functions, of course, but I am mindful of your
recommendation that she not be encouraged to make too great a
display, not only to keep her from the envy of the Konige's other
ladies, but to depress the greed of potential suitors.*

*The Konige herself is well, if a bit downcast by the absence of
the Konig. She and her daughters are surrounded by all manner
of entertainments, and although Agnethe of Bohemia is still a babe-
in-arms, she is not a difficult child, and she has taken a liking to
Iliska, so Iliska has been much assigned the task of looking after
her, which should benefit her while she remains at Court.*

*We have heard rumors here that Konig Bela is unwell. Two
cloth merchants from Bologna have arrived here bringing news
that he is not in the field yet, although Konig Otakar's armies
have been on the move for three weeks and more. One of the men
said that he had heard that Bela's heir had hired an assassin to*

poison him, but the other said that was a baseless tale. Whatever the case may be, I ask you to let us know as soon as you receive this, what the condition of Konig Bela's health may be. For the sake of Konige Kunigunde as well as Bela's courtiers here in Praha, such information may prove crucial in days to come.

Never doubt that I have the welfare of our House always foremost in my thoughts, and with God's help, I will serve the family honorably. You may be confident that I will continue, as long as God grants me life, to protect and promote the good of our House and the heritage we will bequeath to those who come after us.

Antal of Szousa
(his mark)

By the hand of Pader Bedo, Premonstratensian clerk and scribe to the Court of Konige Kunigunde of Bohemia at Praha the 20th day of April in the 1270th Year of Man's Salvation.

2

"I am so glad that Easter is over and we can wear bright colors again," said Iliska, stretching luxuriously in her new chainse, a glowing leaf-green that added brightness to her eyes and brought out the color in her cheeks.

"Better for you not to make too much of a show," Csenge of Somogy warned her. "The Episcopus doesn't like ostentation. He says it leads to envy and pride."

The two of them were alone in the ladies' hall, waiting for their turn in the bath-house. The day was balmy, so their second-story windows stood open, letting in the air and sunshine in equal measure. Below in the stable courtyard there was a bustle of activity as three new German knights made ready to depart for Austria to take their place among the Konig's German Guard.

Iliska rounded on her. "Then why does he wear a jeweled robe and carry a golden crozier? Or does he think no one could envy an Episcopus such treasures?" She ignored the snort of disapproval that remark earned her, and instead went twirling across the ladies' hall, laughing and flicking her hands over her head.

"The Episcopus' vestments and crozier show the way our faith magnifies God in His Majesty." Csenge shook her head.

"And no one ever begrudged the Episcopus his grandeur? Not even for a moment?" Iliska laughed. "What monk would not like vestments of silk instead of stuff?" She gave a little hop and spun more quickly.

"You're a hoyden, Iliska of Szousa," said Csenge with a scowl of disapproval.

"As God made me," said Iliska with the assumption of piety.

Csenge did not laugh. "Be careful that your mischief is not your undoing."

"Why should it be?—since it is God's Will," she challenged, whirling more rapidly still, and growing dizzy, laughing loudly.

"Light behavior means a light character, and the Konige will not have such women around her." This time the severity of her expression left little doubt as to her meaning. "You can be sent away if you bring disrepute to the Konige's Court, and then no honorable man will have you to wife."

"That's ridiculous," Iliska declared; nevertheless, she stopped turning and faced Csenge, blinking to steady her vision. "Why do you insist on dampening everything?"

"I don't dampen, as you call it. I devote myself to the Konige, as should you. I have as many expectations as you do, but I know better than to show them, or to display myself, or to undertake something so unwise as your roguery." Csenge kicked at the rushes, dislodging the small carcase of a mouse as she did. "The house-slaves are being lax again."

"Then arrange for the stewards to beat them. That should make them keep to their duty." Iliska moved toward the window. "The breeze is chilly today, for all the sun is warm."

"If the sun is warm, then the bath-house will hold its heat. Today and tomorrow it will be used, and not again after that for a month." Csenge stretched slowly. "Be sure your gorget is clean for Mass tomorrow. If it isn't, you will cast disapprobation on the Konige in your remissness."

"And my veil must also be clean," said Iliska, not succeeding in keeping the resentment out of her voice. "My brother has already issued instructions. I have to abide by them."

"You would be wise to obey him; he is here to defend you." Csenge made her way to the single chair in the room and sat down. "Remember not to linger in the bath—you do not want to indulge your flesh."

Iliska grinned. "Why shouldn't I indulge my flesh? God gave it to me, didn't He?"

Csenge stiffened in her chair. "That is blasphemy. If you say such things again, you will bring the Church upon you, and no one—not your brother, not your House, not the Konige, or the Episcopus himself—will be able to save you from the consequences. The Konige and all her Court will suffer the opprobrium of your behavior."

"It isn't blasphemy," said Iliska, but her voice shook as she spoke.

"I wouldn't put it to the test if I were you; women are known to be more inclined to sin than men are, and we must be diligent in keeping to the ways of the Godly," said Csenge, and glanced toward the door as Sorer Zuza knocked upon it. "Your levity may yet bring you down," she added just above a whisper.

"Your drying sheets are ready for you," the nun called out. "The bath awaits."

"Come, Sorer," Iliska said, opening the door to the nun. "We thank you for bringing us our sheets."

"It is my task so to do," Sorer Zuza said, holding out the engulfing sheets. "See you keep your modesty even bathing, for God sees all."

Iliska bit back a retort as she took the sheets. "May God reward your service."

"Amen." Sorer Zuza stepped back, crossed herself, and closed the door.

Getting up, Csenge took her drying sheet from Iliska. "Do you remember how to get into the bath so that no one can see you?"

"Yes," Iliska said, sounding ill-used. "Fasten the sheet to the hooks in the wall and stay behind it once it is in place."

"And when you get out, stand behind it and wrap it around you meekly so that your body is not exposed in any unbecoming way."

"I then give my garments to the laundresses and they will hand me clean garments from my own garderobe. That is the ritual, is it not?" Iliska's lower lip protruded.

"Yes. You have it. Then we should go down. Imbolya and Betrica should be gone by now; Sorer Zuza will alert Gyongyi and Milica to make ready and then to wait here." Csenge thought carefully about what she should say to Iliska next. "Do keep your place in mind, and be a credit to it. If you please God, you will please the Episcopus."

"So I have been told," Iliska said, and swung the door open for Csenge to lead the way to the bath-house. "One bath at the end of every month and one before the Mass of the Nativity and one before the Mass of the Resurrection. So we will have twice bathed in April. Does that make the Episcopus more wary for our souls?" She pursed her lips as if trying to decide if it would be wise to say anything more, then fell silent as she caught sight of the Greek eunuch who guarded the corridor to the Konige's Garden and the bath-house beyond, her bare feet making her wince as she trod the rough gravel of the path, thinking as she did that this must be mortification of the flesh for going without solers.

On their way across the Konige's Garden Iliska and Csenge

passed Rozsa of Borsod, who was rebraiding her wet hair; Rozsa was freshly dressed in a bleihaut of blue-green patterned Damascus silk over a chainse of embroidered white cotton. She courtisied the two women and went on with her task.

"Is it true that her relatives want to kill her child?" Iliska asked just after they entered the bath-house.

"There are rumors," said Csenge, not wanting to discuss such matters.

"No wonder she's so brusque," said Iliska, and hung her drying sheet so that it concealed her as she removed her chainse and her breechclout, which she hung on a broad peg before stepping into the large oblong wooden tub of warm water. She sighed as the water rose around her, and she began to unfasten her hair. The room smelled of damp and of rosemary, which was strewn about the floor to keep the fleas down.

"The soap is on the tray near the head of the tub," Csenge told Iliska as she took hold of the gray lump sitting next to her tub.

"I know," said Iliska. "It's rough on my skin."

"They say the lye does the damage. All the more reason to use it only once a month, and then sparingly," Csenge said, beginning to rub the soap over her arms, watching the bubbles form.

Iliska started with her feet, deliberately splattering as she worked the soap over her toes; she enjoyed having the opportunity to move her body in the warm water, with or without the soap. "They say the Comes Santu-Germaniu bathes as often as twice a week. His skin doesn't look as if he does." She worked the lather up her legs, her flesh stinging from the washing, for the soap was coarse and rough. "They say the followers of Mohammed wash often."

"The Comes is no apostate—he's an alchemist, among the best of them," Csenge told Iliska. "He has told the Episcopus and the Konige that in order to make jewels, he must have newly clean skin, or there is a chance he will produce clods of earth instead of gems. The baths are part of his ritual to create jewels."

"Then he would have to spend hours—perhaps days—in the

bath, since the Konige has increased her demands for jewels. I should think that the Episcopus would reprimand him for such excesses." She could feel small insects on her body, trying to escape the soapy water as she sank more deeply into the tub.

"The Episcopus is glad of jewels to adorn the saints and the crucifixes of his cathedral, and he knows that Konig Bela has charged the Comes with the task of ornamenting the Konige and her daughters with the finest jewels to be had throughout the Holy Roman Empire. There is no vanity in what the Comes does, only duty." Csenge unfastened her elaborate braids and let her hair float around her. This was one of her favorite parts of bathing, the loosening of her hair; it made her feel unfettered and unconstrained for all of the limitations that confronted her daily, and which she was compelled to uphold. She closed her eyes and let the water hold her.

"Why does Konig Bela want to give such splendor to Bohemia? Isn't the war between them enough for him to summon the Comes back to Hungary?"

Csenge did not answer at once; she was luxuriating in the pleasure of her bath, and reminding herself to Confess it to Pater Lupu before Mass tomorrow, for it was most certainly sinful to enjoy washing her body so much, as were the thoughts that awakened in her when she did it. Finally, as she heard Iliska splashing more energetically, she said, "Konig Bela wants his granddaughter's magnificence to come from Hungary. Let Otakar laden her with gold and silver, but let her jewels come from Hungary, so that her beauty will outshine her wealth." She held her nose and slipped under the water to allow the soap to drift free of her, then, reluctantly, she stood up, shivering a little as the heat of the water fled her, then she took the small pail beside the bath and twice filled it and poured it over her. Now rinsed, she climbed out of the tub and pulled her drying sheet around her.

"I wouldn't send such a man as Comes Santu-Germaniu to my enemy's Court. Not with his riches."

"Konig Bela didn't send the Comes to an enemy, he sent him

to his granddaughter," Csenge said; she put down the pail and secured the drying sheet more securely. "This is not a matter for us to speak of."

"When is your cousin leaving?" Iliska asked a bit later. "She was supposed to leave yesterday, wasn't she?"

"Imbolya? The Konige has requested that she remain through the May Festival, and her escort agrees that it is fitting, since the bridges they will cross are still being rebuilt and will delay their arrival in any case. A little postponement now will mean a swifter return, for more of the bridges will be usable." Csenge found herself shivering in spite of the warmth of the room. "She'll be departing soon enough." She started toward the side-door.

It took Iliska a little longer to emerge from her tub than it had taken Csenge, and she rinsed herself three times, sighing as she did. "Where is the laundress?"

"Through the door in the north wall; you have to slide the door, not open it," Csenge said as she went to collect her clean garments; a short time later, Iliska did the same.

A small dressing room with three clerestory windows provided the two women a place to finish drying all but their hair and to dress, each being assisted with lacings by the other. Large ivory combs were set out; they both took one and stepped out into the Konige's Garden to tend to their hair.

"Where's Rozsa?" Iliska asked, a bit surprised at finding her gone.

"She must have returned to her room," said Csenge, who was relieved that Rozsa had left the walled garden.

"No doubt to think of some new way to draw attention to herself," muttered Iliska. "For a woman with child, she has not learned humility, has she? She makes a show of everything."

Csenge made no response, afraid of being overheard, but continued on into the private door that would lead them back to their rooms. As she walked, she hummed a hymn to discourage any more conversation with Iliska.

Rozsa had wandered into the reception hall, where Konige

Kunigunde was with the Episcopus, discussing the plans for the Konige's May Festival; she courtisied the Konige and lowered her head to the Episcopus, then lingered near the door, her attention fixed on the Konige.

"—and with the Konig away at war, your display should reflect a gravity as well as celebration," Episcopus Fauvinel was saying.

"It should also be festive enough to express the certainty of his prevailing," said the Konige, unaware that she and the Episcopus were overheard. "As Konig Bela's granddaughter, I must not be seen to favor Hungary over Bohemia."

Episcopus Fauvinel sighed. "Dear Royal is correct. I will not protest the hanging of garlands. But I believe it would be wrong to encourage jongleurs and acrobats to perform. Perhaps musicians and singers, but dancing . . ." He pulled at his beard. "I will meditate on how much jollity you may properly show." Looking about, he caught sight of Rozsa standing behind them. He scowled at her, but he took the time to acknowledge her presence with a lackadaisical blessing. "I will speak with you tomorrow, dear Royal, and pray for you and the Konig's triumph." He rose from his upholstered bench, bowed in the French manner to the Konige, and stalked out of the room, the sharp report of his crozier striking the floor marking his progress.

The Konige studied Rozsa as she courtisied her. "Have you come on some urgent errand?" she asked.

"I have come to ask what I might do to help you in arranging the May Festival. You have much to arrange, and I am at your disposal to assist you in any way that dear Royal commands." She smiled, a bit more carefully than she usually did.

"Your offer is much appreciated." The Konige stared into space for a long moment. "If you will ask Tirz Agoston what new instruments he has made, ones that will be ready by the May Festival, then I will send one of my courtiers to search out musicians to play them. New songs and new instruments for a new spring." She folded her hands in her lap. "It is fitting that we have songs of heroes sung."

"When would you like this done?"

The Konige pondered her answer. "After Vespers would be appropriate, I think."

"Of course," said Rozsa, then added, as if the notion had just occurred to her, "Have you decided which of your courtiers should make this search?"

"Not yet. Perhaps Thokogy Lecz. He has some knowledge of music, and he is old enough not to be distracted by beauty. No one would accuse him of taking advantage." She pressed her lips together, cutting off whatever else she had wanted to say.

Rozsa made one more offer. "Would you like me to ask the Comes Santu-Germaniu if he might sing to you? You have liked his songs in the past, and he must be willing to prepare new ones for you."

"That would be very welcome," said the Konige, her eyes still a bit dazed. "Yes, tell him I want him to sing for me, something I have never heard before. And, of course, he will bring more jewels. Tell him that I would prefer diamonds this time."

Rozsa courtisied the Konige. "At once, dear Royal," she said, concealing her satisfaction as best she could as she slipped out of the reception room and called for a page and an escort. This was going to be much less difficult than she had feared. She could call upon Rakoczy with the approval of Konige Kunigunde, so no one could speak against her.

Albrech answered her summons, straightening his sleeves and pushing back his hair; at eleven, he was looking forward to the next year, when he would become a squire to one of Konig Otakar's knights, and in anticipation of that, he made a point of practicing his manners. "Lady, command me," he said, not quite bowing.

"Go fetch an escort for me, and an enclosed wagon drawn by four ponies or two horses, and meet me in the forecourt as soon as possible with the escort and the wagon," Rozsa said, her orders crisp, her green eyes alight. "Make haste, boy. I have a duty to perform for the Konige that cannot be delayed."

The young page nodded and sprinted off, eager to do something that might gain him the Konige's notice; Rozsa watched him go, her thoughts rapid and acutely clear.

By the time she reached the forecourt, she had changed from the blue-green bleihaut she had been wearing to one of wine-red sculptured velvet that made the white of her chainse seem brighter. For a gorget she had more white cotton, and her veil was of iris-colored lawn. She stepped into the wagon and pulled the door closed. "Mansion Belcrady, to speak with the Comes Santu-Germaniu," she said, smugness making this sound like a declaration of victory. "At the Konige's pleasure." She gained admission to Mansion Belcrady without any hesitation from the staff, and was escorted by Barnon to the larger reception room off the main hall, and promised a tray of bread, cheese, and wine, along with the assurance that the Comes would soon be with her, that he was just now busy in his workroom. She nodded her approval, and sat in the largest chair to wait.

"Rozsa of Borsod," said Rakoczy some short while later. "I am honored to have you in my manse."

She looked around, shocked that she had not heard his approach. "Yes," she said, trying to conceal her discomfiture; she spoke in Bohemian. "I am come at the order of the Konige in regard to her May Festival. I won't require much of your time; other duties await me." She neither rose nor courtisied him as she held out her hand. "I have been looking forward to this."

Rakoczy did not ask for an explanation, certain that one was coming. Instead he gave a little bow in recognition of the wishes of the Konige but did not approach her. "And what would the dear Royal like me to do for her?" He came into the room, his blehaut slightly stained from his labors in the workroom above, his hair slightly disordered. Taking Rozsa's hand, he bowed over it. "I am honored to serve the Konige in all things."

"As well you should be," said Rozsa sternly. "Konige Kunigunde would like some new songs for her May Festival."

"It would be my honor to provide them," he said, looking up as Barnon brought in a tray with wine, bread, cheese, and a small saucer of salt set out on it; at Rakoczy's signal he set it down on the table in front of Rozsa.

She waited until Barnon left the room, then reached to pour herself some wine, and said to him in Magyar, "She's requesting diamonds from you for the occasion. She didn't mention how many she wanted, but don't offer too few. You don't want anyone saying that your fabled fortune is becoming exhausted. That could lead to trouble for you."

"I will keep your recommendation in mind," Rakoczy said, and waited for her to speak again.

"It is always wise to keep high in the Konige's regard." Rozsa took a long sip of the wine. "There could be demands on your purse beyond those the Konige makes."

"The Episcopus, you mean? I have given him a goblet filled with rubies." He said it without any sign of rancor, but Rozsa sat forward.

"No, I don't mean the Episcopus," she said, her eyes daring him to protest. "I am going to make you a . . . proposition." Although he said nothing, Rakoczy felt as if the whole manse had shifted around him. His disquiet increased as she went on, "I have dreamed of you often, you know. All those months with my husband, I dreamed of you." He offered Rozsa an ironic bow; she paid no attention to him. "I would like you to resume our arrangement."

"Not while you are with child," he said, his memories casting back to Csimenae and her son.

"I know, I know; sad as it is, it must be. So while I am here for now, I have other uses for you," she said impatiently as she tore a handful of bread from the loaf. "My husband's blood must not be compromised, not with his cousins waiting for me to make any show of infidelity. They would like nothing better than to see me discredited, so that they may continue as his heirs." She began to eat, swallowing more wine to help the bread go down. "My husband wants a son. He certainly beat me enough to produce a boy. But with him away at war, I must be vigilant for the child's sake. I will have the child at my husband's estate, of course, but I will not remain there; it wouldn't be safe." She turned toward him, her smile wholly without mirth. "When I return in a year or so, we will make new arrangements."

Rakoczy studied her. "And for now? What are your plans."

She relished telling him. "Since I will be deprived of your skills in passion, I will have the fruits of your skills in alchemy. You, who scatter gems like grain for chickens, I want jewels from you—many, many jewels. I want jewels enough so that if my reputation should be ruined, I will be able to keep myself from destitution or harlotry. I will do as the old Konige did, when Otakar changed her for Kunigunde, and endow a convent where I can live in comfort, where my husband's relatives cannot reach me."

Rakoczy let no emotion show on his features. "When you say many, many jewels, what did you have in mind."

She cocked her head and studied him. "I will send you a coffer to fill by the May Festival. Surely you can accommodate me to that extent. Later I will send you another, and a third, before I leave to return to Kaposvar. That should make a good beginning."

"And if I do not comply: what then." He spoke cordially, but there was a blue light in the depths of his dark eyes like the heart of a flame.

"Oh, then, I fear I must Confess what indecent intimacies you have forced upon me, and the ungodly rites you used to subdue me to your will," she said with exaggerated lamentation. She pulled off more bread. "Not even the Konige could save you from the Episcopus then." With a flourish she downed the last of her wine and poured more into her cup.

"I see," said Rakoczy quietly.

"I hope you do," Rozsa told him, and ran her tongue over her lower lip. "It will be better for you if you agree to my demands without dissembling. You have to uphold the terms of your exile, and what I report to Konig Bela can praise or defame you; do not forget that." Her green eyes were shiny. "And it needn't be unpleasant, accommodating me, in jewels or in ecstasy." She rose and walked up to him. "I can be most devoted in my way, so long as I have no rivals."

Rakoczy studied her face. "An odd requirement for a married woman."

"Think of Erzebet of Arad." She flicked the corner of his mouth with the tip of her finger. "It could happen to others of the Konige's ladies." She offered him an elaborate courtisy, then left the withdrawing room, calling for Barnon to have her wagon brought to the main door, leaving Rakoczy to ponder her threat; as the main door opened, an unexpectedly cold wind rushed through the manse.

Text of a letter from Imbolya of Heves to Rakoczy Ferancsi, written in Church Latin and carried by a scullion with the permission of Pater Lupu.

To the most worthy Comes Santu-Germaniu, on this, the first day of May in the 1270th Year of Salvation,

Esteemed Comes,

The unexpected snow that fell yesterday has delayed not only the Konige's May Festival but, yet again, my departure, which will now be in ten days—days that will be filled with my last obligations within the Konige's Court. I am taking this unexpected time to write to you not only to say farewell to you, but to ask your pardon for my fancies that led me to say such inappropriate things to you the last time we conversed, for surely no such monster as I said you reminded me of could have been able to be one of the Konige's Court, not with the Episcopus and so many faithful Churchmen about to protect us from the Devil's minions. I fear it may have been on account of the songs of the troubadours and the tales foolish women tell one another late at night, and that some Confess in the morning. It may also have sprung from the jealousy of some of the courtiers, who openly envy your riches, and hint that you do not come by your jewels through al-

chemy alone, but by the favors of the Devil, for the corruption of good Christians. Whichever weakness accounts for my imaginings must be attributed to my womanly weakness: my Confessor has exhorted me on my failings, and I humbly ask your forgiveness for the things I said, and beg you will not regard me with the contempt I deserve.

Recently I realized that I have found in you the nearness I should only find with God, that the troubadours have lied to us and offered us the fruits of damnation; daughter of Eve that I am, I allowed myself to turn away from Heaven for the sake of your love. Let me beseech you to abandon the lures of the flesh and turn your sight on God.

I have had word from my father that I will be married in July, and that the terms are beneficial both to Heves and to Szarvas, for which I am most thankful; I will seek to prove a virtuous wife so that I will bring esteem to my House and honor to my husband. I will thank you now for the handsome jewels you presented to me as a nuptial gift, which I shall treasure for all my days, and which is so typical of your many kindnesses to me. The Konige has also given me two chests filled with fine cloth, and four linen sheets for my marriage, once again showing her generosity. I have pledged to remember her in my prayers every morning and every night, and to pray also for her children. Since I am returning to Hungary, she will not put me in the difficult position of having to pray for Konig Otakar while he and Konig Bela remain at war. That, at least, is something for which I am grateful.

May God guard and protect you, may He be gracious to you and your House, may He bestow His Mercy upon you.

> With high regard, and by my own hand,
> Imbolya of Heves

3

All of the uncanny snowfall was gone; blossoms showed edges of brown and rust as token of the late freeze, and the roads beyond the city walls were stiff with mud, but otherwise spring resumed as if there had hardly been any interruption at all; throughout Praha the markets were busy and the streets were full. As if to join in the city's activities, Vaclav Castle thrummed with excitement in anticipation of the May Festival. Six large wagons were laboring out the south gate toward the Konige's Field for the celebration that would be held the following day, all of them manned by servants and slaves whose task it was to set up the pavilions, fire-pits, lists, and stands for the grand occasion; the Konige watched their progress from the solarium at the top of her wing of the castle.

"Dear Royal," said Teca of Veszbrem from the solarium door.

"What is it, Teca?" the Konige asked without turning away from the open windows.

"Episcopus Fauvinel is waiting in your withdrawing room." She sounded so apologetic that Kunigunde blinked.

"Episcopus Fauvinel? Was I to expect him?"

"No, dear Royal. He said he was moved by the fervor of his office to seek you out to discuss what remedies your ladies might aspire to through penance to remove the peril of damnation that now hangs over us. The danger is real." Teca crossed herself, fear hidden in her eyes. "Csenge is still claiming that she has seen ghosts and fiends about her."

"Csenge herself may be possessed, and her accusations made

at the instigation of the Devil," said the Konige, sounding tired; since Csenge had made her Confession, Kunigunde had been filled with anxiety for all her Court. That Csenge was Hungarian only made it worse, for there were those in Otakar's Court who would use Csenge's accusations as proof of the danger that having Hungarians in Praha created. "We must pray that God will restore her wits and bring her to His care again."

Teca shook her head as she crossed herself. "The Episcopus wants to examine all your ladies-in-waiting to be sure that none are—"

"I trust it will not have to come to that." The Konige closed her eyes for a long moment. "But I should settle the matter of how we are to proceed before the May Festival begins; otherwise the Episcopus may require that we not have it at all. There are those who think the late snowfall was a sign that God wants no merriment in time of war." She glanced at Teca and saw the distress in her eyes. "Have I put you in an awkward position?" she asked, and turned so that she could no longer gaze on the beautiful day.

Teca did not answer directly. "The Episcopus' welcome-tray is being brought, but he is . . ." She floundered for the right word, and shook her head.

"I know; ever since Csenge made her Confession about the Devil and demons and fallen angels and hobgoblins and imps and enchanters and incubuses, and witches and vampires and night hags, and whatever else—" She made herself stop her outburst. "I am sure the Episcopus is concerned for the safety of our souls."

Crossing herself once more, Teca whispered, "Amen."

The Konige came to Teca's side. "Well, I suppose it is best to deal with him now. I want the May Festival to go splendidly." She smoothed the front of her dark-gold bleihaut and adjusted the hang on the gold pectoral crucifix that hung on a jewel-studded chain around her neck. "The May Festival will be over in three days, and the Episcopus may resume his hunt for all that is unholy."

Teca coughed gently. "Do you think he will insist that we burn anyone?"

"I'm sure he will tell me," said Konige Kunigunde, falling silent as she went behind Teca down the two narrow flights of stairs to the broad corridor that led to the three withdrawing rooms set behind the reception hall. "Who is attending to my daughters this morning?"

"Betrica and Gyongyi; Milica and Kustansze will replace them at mid-day. Iliska is Court messenger until mid-afternoon; she's in the ladies' withdrawing room."

"Very good," said the Konige automatically. She noticed a rat in the shadow of the main door. "It is time to order something done about the vermin again. They're everywhere and bolder than before."

"I will inform Cyrek that you have given the order," said Teca, frowning a little as she spoke the Bohemian under-steward's name, for it was well-known that he was one of the Konig's spies in the Konige's household.

"If you would," said the Konige, her voice remote. "I don't know how long I'll be with the Episcopus."

"No," Teca agreed.

"So you will supervise the nursery meal," said the Konige as she waited for Teca to open the door into the largest withdrawing room for her.

"Of course, dear Royal," said Teca as she courtisied the Konige, then opened the door for her.

Episcopus Fauvinel rose and blessed the Konige as she knelt to him. "May God smile upon you and upon the Kingdom of Bohemia," he intoned before he held out his hand to assist her to rise; on the table beside his chair the welcome-tray with its wine, bread, pickles, and cheese sat untouched. "I thank you for seeing me although I am unexpected."

"It is the least the Konige can do for the Church, Episcopus," said Kunigunde, feeling dispirited, anticipating the worst from this zealous man. She took her place in her chair, and nodded to the Episcopus to be seated. "I understand you want to discuss the

Confession of Csenge of Somogy and what it may mean to the May Festival."

"That I do," said the Episcopus, and launched into the explication of his purpose in coming without an announcement of his arrival. "Csenge of Somogy's Confessions have continued much the way they began—she herself has not yet been attacked, or so she claims, but she fears that several of your ladies-in-waiting have become the abject servants of the forces of the Devil, and through them the whole of the Court is in danger. If her Confession is an honest one, your Court is at grave risk, dear Royal."

"So you have said," the Konige responded calmly. "Do you tell me that Csenge has added to her Confessions?"

"A great deal more," the Episcopus said with a nod. "She has recalled a night when she sat with Erzebet of Arad before she died, when Erzebet declared there were witches and devils gnawing her entrails, and that Csenge saw specters hovering over Erzebet, all of them with knives and spears in their hands, attacking the vitals of Erzebet. She fears now that Erzebet died from a malign spell." He paused to cross himself. "With all that she has claimed already, and the dangers she has revealed, I feel that it would be prudent to examine your women to see who among them is bound to the infernal beings that are the enemies of all that is good and holy."

"Have you any reason—beyond what Csenge has said—to think that my ladies-in-waiting have been corrupted by hellish—"

Episcopus Fauvinel held up his hand to silence the Konige. "We have yet to be certain that this has happened. It may be that the Devil has visited Csenge and filled her mind with visions of damnation and the denizens of Hell, so that the Devil might triumph over God in your Court, dear Royal, through the offices of a single woman who is possessed rather than the corruption of all of your ladies. You can see why I would like to investigate your ladies further than their Confessors have done." He pointed his hand at the Konige. "With Konig Otakar at war, it is apparent that we must be circumspect in all we do so as not to endanger anything that the Konig is undertaking in the field."

"I am agreed," said the Konige, keeping her manner accommodating, "but I would rather that we be allowed to have our May Festival before we subject my Court to your inquiries." She felt a sensation in her vitals, as if a serpent had coiled there and was starting to squeeze the breath from her body.

"Then we should be able to set the seal upon our agreement shortly." The Episcopus gave a smile of satisfaction. "You must know that I am concerned for the welfare of your Court, and the preservation of the souls of your daughters."

"They are very young for such worries," said Konige Kunigunde. "Agnethe is hardly more than half a year old, and Kinga is very much a child."

"All the more reason to take precautions," said the Episcopus. "They do not yet have the judgment that would keep them from becoming the servant of Satan. You know that children and women are especially susceptible to the workings of the Devil, and so must be diligent in preserving their souls from peril."

"There are monks and priests at Court. Their presence must count for something," said the Konige, trying not to bristle.

"Professions of faith do not keep the soul from falling into evil. Think of how readily the monks of Sante-Wisie succumbed to the temptations of the flesh so that not even imprisonment was sufficient to drive the Devil from their monastery, and they had to be burned to eradicate their iniquity."

The Konige paled. "That was twenty years ago, Episcopus. Since then the Church has been more vigilant in matters of monks, and errors such as the ones the Trinitarians committed at Sante-Wisie are now guarded against by authorities, such as yourself. Surely, with so many holy men to watch over them, you don't think that young children would become possessed by lust as the monks were? What child feels lust?"

"It is not what I may think, dear Royal," said the Episcopus smoothly, "it is what the Devil seeks to do to bring about the destruction of the world." He cleared his throat. "It would be well to encourage your courtiers to show their devotion to God and His Church with donations and public displays of penance, some of which could begin during your May Festival."

So that was the bargain the Episcopus was seeking, the Konige thought. "What kind of donations and public penance did you have in mind?"

"Those who are burdened in their souls could carry a cross around the Konige's Field, reciting such prayers as are determined to be appropriate to their sin; it would make all the Court aware of the demonic enticements that surround all men, and point them the way to a virtuous life." He held up his hand as he considered the matter, his eyes rolled upward as if he expected to see a revelation in the air above him. "I would think that four times around the Konige's Field, in homage to the four Evangelists, would provide a fine example, and one that would do much to expiate the sins in question. And those courtiers who want to improve their standing with the Church could make an offering of gold and silver—and jewels, of course. There is much virtue in giving donations to the Church." He looked around the withdrawing room, pointedly noticing its luxurious appointments. "The Court is a magnificent place, as befits the Kingdom of Bohemia and its wealth, but surely God, Who has given the wealth to Bohemia, deserves equal splendor."

Konige Kunigunde bit back a sharp retort, reminding herself that this man had it in his power to end the celebrations of spring and to impose severe self-abasement on all her courtiers. She took a deep breath. "It may be that there are some in my Court who would benefit from the penance you describe. And there may be some who may be moved to make donations to the Church in thanks to God for His smiling upon us."

The Episcopus nodded benignly. "Your ladies-in-waiting will have to be examined, but I will postpone that inquiry until the May Festival has ended. Unless I see there is too much licentious behavior among those attending."

"The penitents circling the Konige's Field should dampen the urge to debauchery," said the Konige more sharply than she had intended; the penitents would have a chilling effect on any revelry that might occur. With an effort she went on more humbly. "Your fears for my Court may be founded in the Confession of delusion, as you have already allowed, and it seems to me that had such excesses as Csenge has Confessed been occurring here, I must have known of it, yet I did not. I dislike having my ladies' honor impugned, and as Konige it falls to me to see any aspersions cast upon them are not allowed to stand unchallenged."

"That is your duty, yes," said the Episcopus, his geniality fading. "As it is mine to guard against all the depravity of Hell."

"You are most diligent in your task, Episcopus," said the Konige in a tone that might be construed as praise.

The Episcopus offered Kunigunde a faint smile of approval. "Then we are agreed—members of your Court who wish to make an act of penance tomorrow will be allowed to carry a cross around the limits of the Konige's Field for the purpose of acknowledging their sins and making an example for others to follow. I will attend the festival to monitor the penitents and to accept the donations of those courtiers who wish to contribute to the magnification of the Church in Bohemia. When the two days of the May Festival have concluded, you will arrange for your ladies-in-waiting to be questioned by me and four of my priests to determine whether or not the Confesssion of Csenge of Somogy is as she has described it." He stared at the Konige. "You are wise to comply, dear Royal, for it persuades me that whatever Deviltry may be going on among you ladies, you, yourself, have no part in it."

"For which I am grateful," said the Konige. "And I will be thankful to Heaven when my ladies all stand exonerated of all wickedness."

"May your faith in them be requited," said the Episcopus, standing and motioning to the Konige to kneel. "May God bless and keep you safe; may He smile upon you and your children, may you ever serve His Will, and may the Devil never ravage Bohemia."

"Amen," said the Konige, crossing herself.

The Episcopus nodded again. "I will leave you to make the necessary arrangements for tomorrow." He started toward the door, his crozier tapping on the rush-strewn floor. At the door he turned and regarded her fixedly. "God will surely look kindly on many penitents and on generous donations."

"I thought He might," said the Konige, her eyes downcast to conceal the flare of anger in them. The Episcopus would never make such demands if Otakar were still in Praha, she told herself, and schooled her temper so as not to give him cause to add further restrictions to her courtiers beyond what he had already imposed. As soon as the Episcopus was gone, she rose to her feet and raised her voice, summoning her page Albrech. "I must ask you to fetch Iliska of Szousa to me at once. I have a task for her."

"Yes, dear Royal; at once," the youth said, and ran off.

Alone, Konige Kunigunde paced her withdrawing room, trying to calm herself. She ran through her concerns in her thoughts: how am I to protect my ladies-in-waiting from the inspection by the Episcopus? What is it he wants of me? How am I to convince any of my courtiers to make public penance tomorrow? she asked herself. I would need at least a week to accomplish the task, and well the Episcopus knows it. She clapped her hands and called for another page: Bertik answered her summons. "I have a charge for you."

"Dear Royal," said the youngster. "Command me."

"Listen to what I say to Iliska of Szousa and then go to the stable and to the barracks."

"I will," said Bertik.

"May I come in, dear Royal?" Iliska asked from the door, Albrech at her side; she courtisied the Konige. "You have a task for me?" She glanced at Bertik, then gave her full attention to the Konige.

"I do," said the Konige. She motioned Iliska to approach her. "You are to call upon all of my Court who do not live within the walls of Vaclav Castle. You are to tell them that the Episcopus has set aside a part of the Konige's Field for a penitential procession. Any courtier who wishes to show the Episcopus the depth of his faith should present himself to the Episcopus after morning Mass. Any of my Court who can do so are asked to make a donation of gold or jewels for the churches of Praha, or to the Church itself. You are to ask a pledge from all of them, and, if all goes well, half of the courtiers will promise to do their part for the Episcopus." She felt her body clench as she gave this order. "The pages will know where all the Court outside the castle live, and the escort will protect your name and the reputation of the Court. Go and put on a grander bleihaut and be ready to enter your wagon by mid-day."

Iliska courtisied the Konige again. "I am ready to serve you in all things, dear Royal. You honor me with your trust."

"Then be about your duty, and my thanks for your service," said the Konige.

As she backed out of the withdrawing room, Iliska tried not to grin; she was being allowed to go beyond the castle walls, and to call upon courtiers in their homes, a prospect that delighted her; long days in the Konige's Court had left her yearning to be outside, if only for a few hours. To be received by all the Konige's courtiers would add to her satisfaction, for she would enjoy hospitality at some of the finest mansions in Praha, and that would include calling on Rakoczy. Her step was bouncy as she went down the narrow hall toward the room she shared with Milica of Olmutz.

"What's the cause of your light step, sister-mine?" Antal asked, stepping out of the shadows near the door to the Konige's Garden. He had been gaming with some of the Konige's Guards when the Episcopus made his visit, and had decided to seek out Iliska to learn more of what had transpired.

"I'm to be sent to give a message to all the courtiers outside the castle walls. *All* of them." She laughed.

"That makes you merry?" He shot a questioning glance in her direction, not trusting her to observe the dignity of the Konige's Court in such a frame of mind.

Her reply confirmed his worst suspicions. "That means I am to call at Mansion Belcrady."

"Does the Konige require that you go there, or can you send a page to him?"

Iliska spun toward her brother, all laughter gone from her demeanor. "No, I cannot send a page. My task is explicit. I must deliver the Konige's request in her stead, as her deputy, to all of her Court outside the castle." She glowered at him. "You will not tell me that I am to defy the Konige's commission, will you?"

"No," he admitted.

"Then I will go to Mansion Belcrady to deliver the Konige's requests, as I will go to all the others."

Antal sighed. "That's unfortunate."

"No, it's not," she declared. "It is the Konige's wishes. I know I shall do well in speaking with the Comes."

"You will say no more than the Konige demands, and you will not spend any time alone with him. You will have an escort, won't you?"

"Of course," she answered, lifting her chin and glaring at him.

"Then make sure one of the escort is with you at all times. I won't have you claiming he's compromised you or made you an offer in order to force a marriage upon him."

Her face paled. "I wouldn't stoop to such devices."

"You're lying, sister-mine."

"I am not," she insisted but with enough hesitation to give him cause to doubt her; she stamped her foot, her eyes snapping with annoyance. "Besides," she said more calmly, "his House is much older than ours and he has wealth enough to let us broaden our holdings. It would be a worthy gift to Szousa for him to add to our lands." She met his eyes boldly. "Who in our family would not want to extend our lands?"

Antal's face darkened and he took a step toward her, his fists clenched. "I've told you that you are not to fix your thoughts on him. He has a grand manner, no doubt, yet he's a poor connection for our House, for all his riches: he is an alchemist, and were he not under royal protection, he might well be in the hands of the Church. More to the point, however, his fief is controlled by Konig Bela to prevent the Comes from taking up the heir's cause, and that alone makes him ineligible as a husband for you. You will have to choose another, or have one chosen for you."

"I won't," she told him. "Of all the men I have met, he pleases me the most. I will not marry if I cannot marry him."

"But you will," Antal said, his voice suddenly smooth. "You will abandon all hope of him, or I will send you home."

"You can't," said Iliska, her defiance tinged with dread.

"I can. I have excellent cause if I decide to remove you. With Csenge of Somogy Confessing to dealing with the Devil, no one would fault me for taking you away from such dire influences as the Episcopus believes may be active in the Konige's Court. Do not think that anyone in our House would take your part, for no one will." He bowed to her. "So go about your mission, Iliska, but bear in mind that what becomes of you is wholly in your hands."

She would not deign to look at her brother. "So you tell me."

"You would be wise to listen," he said.

"Because you tell me so? Because you have already chosen a husband for me, but won't tell me who it is? Or are you still waiting for better offers?" She flung her accusations at him without apology.

"No—so that you may keep your reputation." He lifted his brows in surprise. "Of course I tell you. Our father doesn't wish to endow a nunnery for you, so marriage it will be, and not to some minor lord with small holdings and no influence."

"I know that," she said, carefully emphasizing each word.

"Our father will not let you throw yourself away on—"

"A nobody, I know. All the more reason to encourage me to fix Rakoczy's interest," she persisted.

"Not so long as he is an exile. His fief means nothing if Konig Bela will not allow him to live on it, and keeps him confined in Praha. If you continue to pursue him, he will have to be removed."

"Konig Bela has sent him here to the Konige's Court. You

can't remove him," said Iliska, enjoying the satisfaction she got from besting her brother.

Antal shook his head. "Women are fools about men, and will be swayed, like Eve was, by honied words. See you do not bring about the fall of our House through your self-indulgence."

She wanted to scream at him, but she knew what that implacable note in his voice meant, so she ducked her head and turned away. "I must change. I can't do the Konige's business looking like a frump."

"It is only a matter of time before you will be betrothed. Keep that in mind, sister-mine."

She flounced down the corridor, not looking back; she was seething. How dare he! she thought. "He will not command me in this way," she said under her breath as she entered her room and found it empty. She opened the door again. "I need a 'tire-maid," she called out, and went to get out of her bleihaut.

Rusalka, one of four 'tire-maids assigned to the Konige's ladies-in-waiting, answered Iliska's summons, coming into the bedchamber just as Iliska dropped her bleihaut on the floor. "Lady? What am I to do for you?"

"Help me to dress, of course," Iliska snapped. "The Konige is sending me to deliver a message to all her courtiers living outside the castle walls, and I must present an appropriate appearance." She pointed to the bleihauts hung in the main garderobe; the odor from the vials of camphor-oil hung with the clothes was very strong in the room. "I will need some perfume, as well," she added, wrinkling her nose.

"Yes. But shall you choose your bleihaut first, and do you want to select another chainse?" Rusalka pointed the clothespress. "You have a pretty one in pale-blue silk."

"So I do," Iliska said. "Yes, all right. I'll change my chainse, too. And I think the white sculptured velvet bleihaut will do, with the blue veil and gorget." She began to smile, aware of how pale colors set off the golden-peach color of her skin.

"Then let me help you out of your chainse," said Rusalka. "I will help you to get into it in a moment." She went to the clothes-press and lifted its lid. "Oh! There are mice in the press," she cried.

"There are mice in the pillows, if it comes to that," said Iliska. "And the Devil has sent a miasma of flies to the castle well, to plague us." She crossed herself.

"God between us and harm," said Rusalka, and made the sign of the cross for the whole chamber. "Pray that no harm comes from them."

"Let the Episcopus entreat God—it's what he does." Iliska was about to laugh but stifled the impulse as she saw the appalled expression on Rusalka's face. "Well, it *is* what he does."

"With all that Csenge of Somogy has Confessed, you would do well to be less light-hearted."

"And since you are a servant it would be well for you to be less impertinent." Iliska pulled her chainse over her head and handed it to Rusalka. "Give me the pale-blue one."

Rusalka ducked her head. "Yes, Lady."

"And find me those pearl-topped pins for the gorget." She glanced at the small mirror that hung on the garderobe. "At least the weather is improving. That's a relief."

"As you say, Lady," Rusalka murmured as she held out the chainse to Iliska, averting her eyes.

Iliska pulled the garment over her head and shifted it on her shoulders. "This should do," she approved. "The bleihaut."

Rusalka handed it to her. "I have the gorget and veil here as well."

"Lace me up," Iliska ordered.

"Yes, Lady," Rusalka muttered, and said nothing more.

"Tight enough to make my breasts swell," Iliska added, cupping her hands around them to move them into the preferred position. "Like this."

When Iliska was finished dressing, she turned to Rusalka. "While I'm gone put out my clothes for the May Festival. You know which things I want. And make sure you include perfume with my garments."

Rusalka nodded, but held her tongue.

"Pray for me," Iliska said to the 'tire-maid. "If I do the Konige's desire correctly, I will come out of it with a pledged husband." With this as a final announcement, she bounced off toward the door, humming in anticipation.

Text of a report to Rudolph von Hapsburg, Comes of Austria, from his most highly placed spy at the Konige's Court in Praha, written in code and delivered by private courier seventeen days after it was written.

To the most worthy Comes of Austria, Rudolph von Hapsburg, the faithful greetings of your servant at the Court of Kunigunde of Halicz, Konige of Bohemia, on this, the fifth day of May in the 1270th Year of Man's Salvation, by my own hand.

Most noble Comes,

As she has done in years past, the Konige celebrated the coming of spring with a May Festival, one that had to be postponed from the first or second day of May to the fourth and fifth days. I have just returned from the Konige's Field and before I retire to bed, I am taking my pen in hand to tell you of how the festival was kept this year. You may decide what significance the events may have.

As I informed you two weeks since, the Konige's lady-in-waiting, Csenge of Somogy, has Confessed that she has witnessed Devil's Rites practiced by the Konige's ladies, and that for her knowledge she has been tormented by imps and devils and other creatures of Hell. Because of these accusations, Episcopus Fauvinel has declared that he will examine the ladies-in-waiting to determine if Csenge's claims are those of virtue or those of possession, and to set the tone for what is to come, the Episcopus required that many courtiers make public penance by carrying a cross in much the same way that Our Lord did to His crucifixion, while reciting penitential Psalms. In all, twelve members of the Konige's Court made the four circuits the Episcopus had ordered. Their presence certainly reduced the gaiety of the festival. Not even the troubadours who were singing for the Konige's entertainment were able to infuse the usual delights into the courtiers, although it is fitting to say that only one of them made any serious effort.

The lists—usually filled with jousting—were used only little, and those knights who decided to show their skills were ordered to pledge whatever prizes they might be awarded to the Church. The few knights who did joust were displeased by this condition laid upon them, but none of them were so outraged that they refused to give their winnings to the Episcopus. It is said that a number of the men have sworn not to compete again next year unless they are allowed to keep their winnings, but the Konige has not been able—or perhaps has not been willing—to offer such an assurance. Some of the knights said they feared that Konig Otakar was trying to buy the favor of the Pope in his bid for becoming Holy Roman Emperor. While that may be true, I doubt it is the way the Episcopus views his requirements, for he made no mention of the Konig, only of the Konige. It may be that he is playing a subtle game, laying traps for Otakar's supporters, but he has never seemed so crafty to me; he is more a zealot than a schemer from all I have seen of him. But it may be that I am underestimating the depths of his contrivances.

Tomorrow the Episcopus begins his examination of the Konige's ladies-in-waiting, to determine how many of them the Devil has claimed for his own. The one lady excused from this process is Imbolya of Heves, who departs in two days to return to Hungary to prepare for her wedding. Her Confessor has said that she at no time exhibited the kinds of depravity that Csenge has claimed occurred, and while Imbolya admits to taking delights in the tales of the troubadours and the stories of marvels that are

told in the marketplaces, she is cognizant that these are the inven-
tions of clever men, not creations of God. So she will be gone and
the Konige will once again lack a lady for her service. It will be up
to Konig Bela to decide who among his noblewomen is to come to
Praha to serve the Konige.

When there is more to impart, rest assured, revered Comes, I
will again take up my pen so that you may be apprized of all that
goes on in the Konige's Court in Vaclav Castle. If there is any way
in which I might serve your interests further, I ask that you in-
form me in the same code with which this is written, in case that
this or any other dispatch falls into unfriendly hands. Know that I
pray for your victory morning and night, and that my dedication
remains fixed on you and God.

Your secret servant

4

"Estephe is not in the household today," said Hruther in Visigothic
Spanish as he entered Rakoczy's workroom on a warm afternoon
three days after the Konige's May Festival. "Barnon says he left last
evening and hasn't returned."

"Where was he bound when he left—do we know?" Rakoczy
asked, looking up from a large, leather-bound volume with *Res
Naturae* stamped in gold on its cover and its spine; he was wearing
a black-silk gambeson of Hungarian cut over braccae of black
leather, much simpler than anything he would be seen in outside
the gates of Mansion Belcrady.

"Barnon says that Estephe told him he was going to church;
he didn't mention which one." There was a note of doubt in his
voice. He glanced toward the open windows. "The glaziers are
busy in the main hall."

"I can hear them; they have promised to be finished in another four days," said Rakoczy, and closed the book. "Is Barnon worried?"

Hruther nodded. "When he told me of it, he was troubled. He says that he fears the Church has detained Estephe, if he truly went to church, that, or he has gone to inform upon you, but whether to the Council or the Church he didn't venture to say." He noticed the disassembled Roman saw-clock spread out on the trestle-table, and recognized it as the sign of frustration it was. "I don't think it would be prudent to make a close inquiry for him."

"No doubt: it would be seen as an upset or a concession, and either way, there may be trouble. I trust we can deal with it, old friend." Rakoczy sighed.

"Then you *do* share Barnon's vexations," said Hruther.

"I believe that Estephe's absence could mean . . . difficulties," Rakoczy admitted, a rueful smile tweaking the corners of his mouth and then fading. "If he has not returned by nightfall, I suppose I will have to make an inquiry through the Konige's steward, since it would be considered suspect for me—or anyone else in the household—to seek him out directly."

"Is there something you'd like me to do in the meantime? Do you have anyone you could tell to look for him without exposing yourself to risks? Are there preparations we should make?" Hruther asked, adding, when Rakoczy volunteered nothing, "I could send one of the household to ask for him at the Hive and Bees. It would be a start, and one that no one would think strange."

Rakoczy considered this. "Not yet, I think," he answered slowly. "If there is no trouble beyond his being out for the night, then . . . We do not want to create misgivings where none exist."

"This might have nothing to do with you. He might have run away from the household. He might have been set upon by street toughs. He may have accepted other employment, to avoid being in a foreigner's household," said Hruther.

"If he has been set upon, we will hear of it soon enough," said Rakoczy, his manner remote—another sign that Hruther recognized for the anxiety it was. "If he has run away, that may be less easily found out."

"But you can do so, can't you?" said Hruther. "Without increasing your exposure to the malice of others."

"If no one forces my hand, it should be possible," Rakoczy conceded.

"When are you next bidden to the Konige's Court?"

"Tomorrow after Mass; that gives a little time to decide upon a way to discover what has happened to Estephe and what it can mean for us. If I must rely upon the Konige to address the matter, then there are apt to be more questions than any of us would like," said Rakoczy. "Still, the Konige does feel some little obligation to me, and I have another two pouches of jewels to present to the Konige and her children tomorrow."

"Does that strike you as excessive? The Konige has increased her requests again, hasn't she?" Hruther watched him while he answered.

"Not from her view of the matter; she is adding to the riches of her daughters, which will give them fortunes of their own. I know she fears she and they may be in danger," said Rakoczy. "She's fretting about the lack of news from Konig Otakar, and adding to her display gives the Court the appearance of confidence of victory."

Hruther nodded. "And how convenient that the display costs the Konige nothing."

"I wonder," said Rakoczy. He started ruminatively at the athanor at the far end of the room. "She is far from . . . content."

"The wealthiest Konige in Europe is discontented." Hruther took a long moment to mull over Rakoczy's remark. "It is most unfortunate for her if she is. There are rumors that the Konig was not her first choice for a husband."

"There are always such rumors about Koniges, for most of their alliances are for political ends," Rakoczy said, then added, "But that does not mean that they might not be true of her. She has the air of loss about her."

"She is far from her home and her husband is at war with her grandfather." Hruther hitched up his shoulders. "Not an easy course for any woman."

Rakoczy raised his fine brows. "Did you see what the Episcopus made of her May Festival?"

Because he was worried, Hruther exclaimed, "That one!"

"He enjoys having power over the Konige," said Rakoczy.

"That he does. He enjoys having power over everyone." Hruther turned to Rakoczy, wanting to shift the subject. "Some of the servants are complaining about the taste of the well-water again."

"Let them complain—at least they will not spend the spring infested with the animacules that bring flux and fever," said Rakoczy, recalling the time, long ago in Egypt, when he learned to treat well-water to prevent flux in spring.

"They might be more inclined to accept what you add to the water if they thought it held off demons and suppressed miasmas." Hruther waited a long moment before he asked, "Have you decided how we are to leave, my master?"

"Not yet," Rakoczy admitted. "Since nothing has changed, I am still powerless to act without endangering my fief. I cannot put Santu-Germaniu at risk. Konig Bela has not yet relented toward me in any way; he has not looked kindly on anything I do here. That is what causes me to hesitate."

"Is it possible that Konig Bela might have already ordered his troops into your fief? You haven't had a report from Balint in some time, and Bela's heir might be troublesome again." He saw Rakoczy nod. "Do you think that Istvan could have done something that made Konig Bela to forget his pledge to you when he sent you into exile here?"

"It would be unlike Konig Bela to act against his promise—one made in writing and witnessed by his Confessor," said Rakoczy but with an expression in his eyes that ran counter to his words.

"Konig Bela has had to fight Otakar to the west. Who knows what his heir has done to the east? Mightn't that give Bela the excuse he seeks to claim Santu-Germaniu, to hold Istvan in check?

Is there any way you can discover what has transpired at your estates?"

"Not that is beyond suborning," said Rakoczy.

Hruther coughed. "One day you will have to deal with him, I suppose—Istvan."

"Perhaps," said Rakoczy.

Hruther brought his thoughts under control and gave Rakoczy his full attention. "What is it? What makes you so indefinite?"

Rakoczy shook his head. "I do not have all the information I need, and so long as Konig Bela reigns, there is little I can do that will not bring misfortune to me and my vassals. Istvan has a hormetic character, and will not readily abandon his ambitions, not with his father growing old." He began to pace.

"Do you think you could enlist the enemies of Hungary to help you?" Hruther asked. "There are other fiefholders who are in a similar position to yours—"

Rakoczy shook his head. "No; that game is too mercurial for me; too many allies could become foes in an instant, leaving me and Santu-Germaniu to carry the burden of treason."

"Have you no other means of preserving Santu-Germaniu beyond this . . . this exile?" He permitted his frustration to show and offered no apology for it.

"If we could provide an acceptable reason for leaving, then I would use it, and go far from Hungary and Bohemia, but Konig Bela wants me here, and the Konige is pleased with my service to her, so if we leave, we will be doubly hunted."

"That's happened before," said Hruther. "Think what we've discussed before and consider if it might be worth addressing Konig Bela directly."

"Not with Santu-Germaniu in the balance," said Rakoczy. "That is what troubles me more than—" He broke off as there was a knock on the door. "Yes?" he called in Bohemian.

"It is Barnon, Comes. Counselor Smiricti is below, wanting to talk with you. He tells me it is urgent."

There was a hesitance in his voice that Rakoczy found puzzling, but which he attributed to his own sense of oppression. "Ask him to wait for me in the larger withdrawing room. I will be with him directly." He turned to Hruther. "I will do what I can to find out if he has information about Estephe. Then we can decide how to go on."

"Yes, my master," said Hruther, his faded-blue eyes clouded with dubiety.

Rakoczy nodded, then went toward the door. "Do you think I should change, or will this do to receive him?"

"Tell him you are making more jewels and he wouldn't mind if you wore sacking," said Hruther drily.

"Very likely," said Rakoczy, and let himself out of the workroom. He went down the corridor to the stairs, doing his utmost to calm his thoughts; if Counselor Smiricti had come unannounced, the reason, he told himself, need not be minatory; there were many reasons the Counselor might call at Mansion Belcrady. He descended to the main hall, where the glaziers were busy putting the stained-glass windows into place and adding inner sills to help hold them. He nodded to the men as he crossed the room to where Counselor Smiricti waited.

It being now officially spring, the Counselor was wearing a tan huch of linen twill lined in samite, over a chainse of pale linen; his braccae were of a wool-and-linen blend the color of iris, and his hat was like a soft mushroom in shape and hue. He caught sight of Rakoczy approaching and got to his feet. "Comes. I thank you for seeing me."

"It is I who should thank you, I suspect," said Rakoczy, his manner somber and cordial at once. "I trust Barnon has sent for a welcome-tray for you."

"It doesn't matter," said Smiricti, dismissing this courtesy with a wave of his hand.

"But it should," said Rakoczy, and was about to summon Barnon to ask why the welcome-tray had not been presented when Smiricti went on.

"The City Guards found your man Estephe this morning. He was unconscious so they took him to the monks at Sante-Natike, where he regained consciousness a short while ago. When the monks learned whose servant he is, they sent word to the Council Court, and I have come to you to tell you of his . . . misfortune." He clasped his hands together nervously, not meeting Rakoczy's steady gaze. "He is badly bruised and the monks say his shoulder is broken, and that he has a damaged head."

Rakoczy heard him out in silence, and when Smiricti stopped talking, he inquired, "Did he say who had hurt him, or why?"

"He said only that he remembers meeting some men near Mansion Belcrady who invited him to come with them to the Hive and Bees for dicing and drink. He decided to go with them because they seemed like pleasant fellows. Beyond that he knows nothing. He has become confused." Smiricti sat down as if having imparted this news had left him enervated.

"Did you speak to Estephe?" Rakoczy asked.

"No; the monks did and two of them came to inform me of what they had learned. They are praying for him, that he may recover his wits." He paused. "If Estephe had any money with him when he left here, it's gone now."

"Hardly surprising," said Rakoczy with a fatalistic nod. "Is Estephe still at Sante-Natike?"

"As far as I know. They said nothing about allowing him to depart in his present condition." He coughed; it was a nervous sound. "The monks said he was in no condition to walk, being unable to keep his balance when he is on his feet." Then he cocked his chin toward the main hall. "Your windows are finally being installed, I see. Very grand."

"Yes. I will have clear glass put in upstairs." Rakoczy made a puzzled frown. "Where did the City Guards find Estephe: do you know?"

"Near the Sante-Agnethe fountain, or so the monks told me." Smiricti tugged at the lobe of his large ear. "I haven't spoken with the Guards who came upon him, but I will, if it would gratify you."

"I would like to speak to Estephe myself," said Rakoczy, his face unreadable.

"I will ask if the monks will permit it," said Smiricti.

"Why would they not?" Rakoczy concealed the rush of dismay that he felt.

"You are a foreigner, and . . . and the Episcopus might not be in favor of it." He looked around uneasily. "The Episcopus is demanding that he be given the right to keep watch on your household. He believes that what has happened to Estephe is proof that you have sinned against Bohemia."

"Sinned against Bohemia," Rakoczy echoed, more bemused than wary. "In what way have I done that: do you know?"

"The Episcopus hasn't been more precise in his observations—it is sufficient that he knows you have enemies, and he is using that knowledge to his advantage. He has declared that as an exile, you must be watched closely." He cleared his throat and spat. "He has wanted to place his men in your household since your arrival was announced in the Konige's Court, but hasn't been permitted to, officially." He lowered his head, and stared at the floor. "Against our agreement, he has placed a spy—or perhaps more than one— among your servants."

Rakoczy felt a kind of apprehension come over him. "What were the terms of your agreement with the Episcopus, Counselor, that you and the Episcopus negotiated?"

"It was not the Council that decided the matter: the Konige had said that it would be the Council who would keep watch on you, not the Church. You are not here as a suspected heretic, but— as you say—an exile, which places you under the Konige's Court's purview. Therefore, she has appointed the Counselors to observe you. In the discharge of her orders, we were allowed to place two spies in your household- -"

Rakoczy nodded grimly; the only thing that surprised him about this was that the Counselor admitted it. "Will you tell me which two?"

Smiricti went on as if he had not heard the question. "The

Episcopus was not supposed to have any, but he is the Episcopus, and two days ago he boasted that his spy in your household has told him more than my two have told me, and he is sure that what his spy has said proves that he is right to suspect you of nefarious intent, for his spies always report what he wishes to hear. He claims that, if she knew what he has discovered about you, the Konige would not refuse him the right to be the one to observe you, and so he has acted on his own authority, to spare her the necessity. He claims this shows his devotion to Bohemia's interests." He finally looked directly at Rakoczy. "It were better for you, Comes, to have the Council watch you than the Episcopus."

"Probably so," Rakoczy conceded, wondering who among his household was listening.

Smiricti cleared his throat and straightened up. "My spies have defended you often, spoken well of you, and sworn that you are no follower of the Devil, nor are you an ally of the Konig's enemies. You have earned their good opinion in spite of being a foreigner. They have been ready to take your part in our investigation; they continue to counter the suspicions of the Episcopus." His voice dropped to a near-whisper, as if he feared he was over-heard. "The spies said you have been true to the terms of your exile; even your manservant has been estimable in this regard. They say he does not work against your vow in any way."

Rakoczy smiled wryly, briefly. "He is an excellent—"

"That is what we all hope of our servants, and what we often believe to our folly," Smiricti said, waving his hand in dismissal. "Yet we often see that they are suborned, that they betray us for their own gain, that they are ready to place their advancement in the hands of others. If your man has never done these things, you have a most rare man in him."

"So I think," said Rakoczy, again wondering why the welcome-tray had still not been offered to his guest. He went to the door and looked out into the main hall, where the glaziers stood on ladders, fitting in the fourth window and putting shutter-levers into place; neither Barnon nor Pacar was anywhere in the large room.

"You needn't trouble yourself, Comes," said Smiricti.

"You are a guest in my manse, Counselor," Rakoczy reminded him, offering him a slight nod.

"Still, I came unannounced," said Smiricti as if making excuses for his servants. "You have no need to—"

"You say your men in my household speak well of me—then let me requite their good opinion of me."

Smiricti allowed himself to be persuaded. "I will accept your hospitality with gratitude."

Rakoczy clapped his hands loudly. "Barnon!" he called out. "Barnon! Where are you?"

"He isn't in the manse," said Smiricti, sounding defeated. "He has left Mansion Belcrady."

"Why is that?" Rakoczy asked.

"Because I sent him away, as soon as he informed you of my arrival. The Episcopus ordered me to do so." A little color rose in his face. "He is my man, you see, and the Episcopus wants him out of here, so that others of his own choosing may take his place."

"Then Barnon is one of the two?" Rakoczy shook his head, wondering why he had not seen Barnon's divided loyalty.

"Yes. I had hoped to keep that from you for a little longer." He offered a jittery smile. "You will have to assign another to his duties."

"Someone who may or may not be your man, as well? Or shall I assume that anyone I hire is in the pay of others?" Rakoczy made a gesture of apology and stepped out into the main hall. "Hruther! Have a welcome-tray prepared for the Counselor!" Then he returned to the withdrawing room, certain that Hruther would attend to this courtesy.

Now Smiricti was truly chagrined. "Comes, it isn't necessary."

Rakoczy held up his small hand. "This is not just for you; I will not have my servants say I neglected a guest."

"Even one who has abused you as I have done?" Smiricti looked truly shocked.

Rakoczy sighed, a short, hard sound. "You forget that exiles cannot afford to ignore the customs of their hosts. Servants talk, whether by assignment or by inclination, and what they say, I need hardly remind you, is often noted by others. You are a man of position and authority in Praha and you deserve to be received well, as all the household knows: you will be, for my sake as well as yours." He had a brief, uncomfortable recollection of his time in Tunis, before he was seized and made a slave to the Emir's son.

"You are too severe," Smiricti said, a suggestion of relief in his voice. "I don't expect any display of welcome from you, not today."

"I should hope you will not mind accepting my hospitality. I will be diligent, for the sake of the Episcopus' man and my reputation." Rakoczy came across the room and drew up the small upholstered bench to the table, straddling it as he sat. "Since you are being forthright with me, let me press you on a few points."

"I suppose I owe you that much," said Smiricti, suddenly cautious.

"Then, if you can explain it to me, why has the Episcopus taken this opportunity to claim jurisdiction over me and my household?"

Smiricti slowly shook his head. "I don't know. I believe he is exceeding his authority, but my opinion has little weight with the Konige; with the Konig away she depends heavily on the Episcopus, who is the Konig's deputy in Praha during his absence." He got up and went to the newly glazed window. "If it were left to me, I would only keep one spy in your household, Comes. The Episcopus has taken that possibility out of my hands." For a short while he remained silent. "And I am alleviated from bearing a burden because of it."

Rakoczy heard him out, outwardly unfazed by Smiricti's admission. "Then the Council is no longer . . . concerned with me and my affairs?"

"By order of the Episcopus, we are not," said Smiricti. "Keep in mind that the Konige must have consented to this."

"Of course," Rakoczy said, swinging around on his seat to motion

Hruther into the room, a welcome-tray in his hands. "Place it on the table if you would, Hruther."

As he did, Hruther said, "I am told Barnon is no longer in the manse. I have taken the liberty of telling Pacar and Kornemon that he has gone to find Estephe."

"Thank you," Rakoczy said, glancing at Smiricti. "That should satisfy them for a while—would you agree?"

Smiricti came back from the window and sat down. "You have a clever manservant."

"Yes, I do," said Rakoczy, pouring a cup of wine for his guest and indicating the bread, cheese, butter, and sausages set out for him on the welcome-tray. "If you would select what pleases you."

"It would please me to take my leave of you," said Smiricti, coming back to the table and looking over the bounty set out for him. "But I will have some wine and bread so that no one can say that I disdained your cordiality." With that, he took the cup of wine and drank half the contents in a single gulp. "You have excellent wine."

"Thank you," Rakoczy responded ironically.

As he sat down again, Smiricti held out the cup for more. "I should probably ask if you are aware of your enemies at Court, as a gesture of respect."

"I suppose I have them," said Rakoczy carefully.

"You may be certain of it," said Smiricti; he drank avidly again. "And not just the Episcopus. There are others."

"Ah?" Rakoczy turned the whole strength of his dark eyes on Smiricti, and waited for him to speak.

Smiricti took a sausage in his fingers and began to chew. "You have . . . angered some of the Konige's . . . waiting-ladies . . . and their families." He licked away the grease from where it had run down his palm.

"How have I angered them?" Rakoczy was puzzled, thinking again that his position at the Konige's Court had become untenable.

"You have disappointed some. You know what women are:

they set their sights on what they want and become outraged if they cannot attain it."

What had Rozsa done now? he wondered. "It has never been my intent to offend anyone in the Konige's Court."

"Then marry, Comes, and put an end to foolish jealousies. So long as you have no wife, the Konige's ladies will vie for you, for your fortune, for your title." He laughed and took another sausage. "Even without the title, you are too rich not to have women eager to wed you. No doubt you can have your pick of the Konige's Court."

"It is not advisable for me to marry," Rakoczy said.

"Certainly that is a prudent answer, but it won't keep the ladies from trying to win you. They woo as heartily as anyone." He laughed again and drank the rest of his wine, then waited for the Comes to pour him another cup. "More than half the Konige's ladies are Hungarian. You are Hungarian. They have lands. You have lands. Those things would be sufficient for them to be interested, but you have wealth, and that"—he quaffed most of the contents of his cup in sarcastic salute—"ensures their attention."

"Without a fortune, I would be a poor match, in spite of my lands and tittle," said Rakoczy, once more refilling the Counselor's cup.

"True enough, but since you are a very rich man . . ." He shrugged to finish his thought.

"In what way does this lead to enemies? It may bring envy, but enemies?" Rakoczy gave himself a little time to consider who among the Konige's Court would have reason to call him an enemy.

"Envy is reason enough," said Smiricti, pulling a handful of bread from the oblong loaf on the tray. "So is ambition."

"Whom do you believe could be so envious or so ambitious as to become my enemy?" Rakoczy asked, watching Smiricti sway in his chair, and realized that the man was well and truly drunk.

"Best not to know," Smiricti said, wagging an admonitory finger at his host as he raised his cup and drained it.

Text of a letter from Frater Sandor at Sant-Gidius in western Hungary near Pressburg, to Kunigunde of Halicz, Konige of Bavaria, at Praha, carried by Royal courier and delivered eighteen days after it was written.

To the most excellent Kunigunde of Halicz, Konige of Bohemia, the greetings of the Hieronymite monk and scribe to Konig Bela of Hungary, on this, the seventh day of May in the 1270th Year of Grace,

 Dear Royal,

 It is with a grieving heart that I write to you to inform you of the death of your grandfather, Konig Bela of Hungary, yesterday. He had been stricken with a fever five days since, and was brought here to be cared for by the monks. I accompanied him so that he might continue to exercise the obligations of his rule. From the time he arrived here, it was his intention to return to the field of battle as soon as his body was healed.

 God has willed otherwise. Two days ago Konig Bela worsened, his fever increased, and he became disordered in his thoughts. The monks urged him to make Confession and accept Extreme Unction, but he refused, declaring that God would minister to him and restore him. Late in the afternoon he sank into a dreamy swoon, and by sundown, his last breath had left him.

 A company of six knights have been dispatched to Transylvania to inform Konig Bela's son and heir, Istvan of Transylvania, that his father is dead and now he reigns in all Hungary. The knights will escort him to Pressburg to receive the Crown of Sant-Istvan and the allegiance of the army. There are those who see a good omen in Konig Istvan and Sant-Istvan's Crown, but my sorrow is too great to consider such matters.

 Since Konig Istvan will want another scribe near him, I will remain at this monastery, although the monks are Benedictines, until the Superior of the Hieronymites sends me otherwhere. This will be the last time I address you, Konige Kunigunde, and so, in

our hour of mourning together, I send you my blessing and the
assurance that God will console us, as He will welcome Konig
Bela to the Glory of Heaven and a place at His Right Hand.

Gloria in excelsis Deo, Amen,
Sandor, Hieronymite Frater and scribe

by my own hand

5

"Rozsa of Borsod has been claiming that you have been impor-
tuning her, suggesting that she take you for her lover, but I know
that's not true," said Iliska of Szousa as she laid her hand on Rakoczy's heavily embroidered sleeve, a desperate smile transfixing
her countenance. "I don't believe what she's saying. You aren't like
that. You wouldn't deny me for her." Her face darkened. "My
brother does believe her. He says that you are not a man of honor."

The reception hall of the Konige's Court was filled with courtiers and a number of entertainers who juggled, tumbled, or made
music, according to their talents, while the Konige and the Episcopus watched from the dais. The windows had been thrown
open and the full light of mid-May streamed into the reception
hall, limpid and glowing. A squad of servants passed among the
Konige's Court bearing tankards of wine and plates of bread-and-
cheese.

"It would appear that Rozsa seeks to discredit me: I do not
know why." It was the truth as far as it went, but not an explanation. He ducked his head politely, and tried to step away from
Iliska, his black-silk gambeson whispering with his movement.

"It is a dangerous stance for a married woman to take." Iliska's eyes shone with rascality. "That's why my brother believes her. He says no woman would say so much if her husband might hear of it."

"He is trying to look after you," said Rakoczy.

Iliska shook her head emphatically. "He's trying to bend me to his will." Her voice lowered. "She says she has been troubled in her sleep, all on your account."

"That is unfortunate for her," Rakoczy said, and saw that Antal of Szousa had seen Iliska at his side. He took a determined step back. "Your brother would not like us to talk."

"I suppose not," she said, pouting coquettishly. "But what is he to do about it? He would have to create a disruption in front of the Konige, and that could get him sent back to Hungary."

"He can take you back to Szousa with him," said Rakoczy. "That would mean leaving the Konige's Court with a blot on your reputation, and your brother would not be pleased, for it would discredit him to have you return to your family unmarried and unpledged."

"Do you think that he would dare to take me home? Wouldn't it disgrace him more than me? Wouldn't it mean that he neglected his duty?" Iliska demanded; the long, open sleeve of her bleihaut was polished, pale-blue linen lined with flame-colored silk, and as she flung up her arms in frustration, she flickered and shone like a candle.

"I think that he is entrusted with your protection; he would do anything to keep you safe." He made a gesture of withdrawal, which she did not acknowledge.

"Then let him settle matters with you. You are rich enough to make him accept your offer with satisfaction if not gratitude," said Iliska.

"I have made you no offer," Rakoczy reminded her as politely as he could.

"All because you have allowed Antal to refuse to consider you as a suitor for me." She shook her head. "You are too modest, Comes. He is supposed to find me an acceptable husband." She licked her lips.

"I am not acceptable," said Rakoczy, holding up his hands to placate her.

"Rich men are *always* acceptable, if they are rich enough," she said, staring at him. "The Konige will agree, and if she does, how can Antal refuse?"

"Your family might not want you to marry an exile," said Rakoczy. "I understand their position and I esteem them for it."

"Why?" Her smile broadened. "Think how you could use my position and restore yourself to Hungary. You will have your fief again, and I will have a rich husband. Then we will all have what we want." She stepped a little closer to him. "I know you want me; you don't have to tell me. I am the way for you to restore yourself in Hungary."

Rakoczy gave a single, ironic chuckle. "Konig Bela is the way for me to be restored in Hungary, Iliska of Szousa. There is no other for so long as Bela reigns in Hungary."

"My family would see to it. They are well-placed in Bela's favor," she told him, annoyance sharpening her tone. "They are in good graces with Konig Bela—that's why I've been sent here, as a sign of Szousa's high standing."

"What would your family gain from me?" He shook his head slowly. "No, your brother is right. I am no bargain for you or your House."

"Riches. They will gain riches, which they need," she said as if it were obvious. "Give them half the quantity of jewels that you have offered the Konige, and even my Uncle Szygosmund will be satisfied, and he is the most greedy of them all." She was about to continue when Antal strode up to them, his features set in severe disapproval.

"I told you not to associate with this man," he said to Iliska, his fists balled; he deliberately ignored Rakoczy. "He isn't worthy of your notice."

"Antal!" Iliska exclaimed as he slapped her, then swung around to face Rakoczy.

"Leave her alone, Comes. I will not have her defamed by you."

"As you wish, but do not revile her." He ducked his head in a show of respect he did not feel.

"He's right, Antal. You are—" Iliska protested, stopping abruptly when Antal raised his hand again.

Satisfied that she would not continue to make a spectacle of herself, he went on in a tension-quieted voice, "If you behave like a willful child, you will be treated as one." Antal took her by the arm and all but dragged her away, saying loudly so that Rakoczy would hear him, "You are not to speak to the exile again. Do you understand me?"

Iliska shrieked and strove to break free of his hold upon her. "You *won't* reprimand me this way! Not here!"

"I will, and the Konige will support me," Antal said, his voice hard; the gathered courtiers made a path for Antal through their midst to the corridor to the chambers of the ladies-in-waiting. All conversation was halted, so that Antal's castigations were heard by everyone. "Be silent. It's bad enough that you comport yourself so like a strumpet. Have the good sense to control your character, or it will be the nunnery, not the marriage-bed for you."

"Antal!" Iliska shrieked, trying to twist out of his grasp; he struck her again, this time with more force.

"If you will permit, dear Royal," Antal said, addressing Konige Kunigunde from near the door, "I find I must spend time with my sister to explain our family's wishes once again."

"Go, then," said the Konige, her wince slight enough to go almost unnoticed; she signaled to Rakoczy to approach her dais. "And you, Comes: I would be grateful if you would depart for now. You must see the wisdom of it. I will summon you again in a few days. The sooner this contention is forgotten, the better it will be for all of you."

Rakoczy offered a French bow, recollections of Pentacoste and Odile flickering through his mind. "Dear Royal, I hear and obey." He went toward the door opposite the one Antal had propelled Iliska through, and found himself facing Rozsa of Borsod, resplendent in a silken, rose-colored bleihaut with broad Hungarian sleeves over a sheer linen chainse and a veil of Mosul-cotton pinned to her golden chaplet.

"She won't have you, you know," Rozsa said, her words silky, her green eyes lambent. "I won't allow it."

This promise struck him emphatically, and although he maintained his composure, he felt an inward trepidation that chilled him. "You need not fret. She will not have me in any case; *I* will not allow it to happen," said Rakoczy, adding with a self-deprecating gesture, "She knows nothing of my true nature or what I would need from her, she knows only what she has heard in the troubadours' songs. I cannot fulfill her dreams." For an instant, Imbolya's plea that he turn away from the flesh in favor of God disquieted him; he shut the memory away.

"She won't know that until she has you, which she will never do. Even if I would countenance it, her family wouldn't." She flicked her tongue over her lips. "That brother of hers listens to me, and is willing to accept what I say as the truth."

"You are telling him that I am attempting to seduce you, to bring shame upon you." He nodded. "If you are persuasive enough, you may succeed in having me banished from Praha and beyond your reach." He turned his enigmatic gaze on her. "Is that what you want, Rozsa? to drive me away?"

"Better that than abandon you to that ambitious child." She beckoned him to come nearer with the summons of one finger. "Erzebet of Arad isn't the only one of the Konige's waiting-women who could die in her service."

Rakoczy's eyes remained unflinching. "If there is another suspicious death, and so soon, there will be many more questions to answer, and the Konige will not be able to protect any of you, even if she wanted to." He gave her a little time to consider this. "The Episcopus will not hesitate to—"

"They will not know that I had anything to do with it. I will see to it that if there is any blame, it lights upon you."

"Think what your are doing, Rozsa," he admonished her, his face revealing nothing of his alarm. "If you drive everyone away from me by raising misgivings that would engage the attention of the Episcopus, you will not be allowed to approach me. Neither the Episcopus nor the Konige would permit any of the Court to seek me out, not even for jewels. I will be exiled more completely than I am now, especially if you continue to say that I have compelled you through ungodly forces to seek me out for sinful delights. What will happen to your plans then?"

Rozsa's smile became a rictus grin. "Oh, well said, very well said. But I know you better than you think, and I know you would accept a headstrong girl and fill a tun with jewels to regain your place at Santu-Germaniu." She reached out and touched his chin with one finger. "But do not invest your faith in Szousa, Comes. There is nothing for you there." With that, she courtisied him and went back into the reception hall.

Rakoczy watched her go, wondering what she would do next, and trying to discern what she intended, for he was certain she would use Iliska's misfortune to her advantage. With a sigh, he turned and continued down the broad corridor and out of the Konige's Court, through the main gate and down the hill. He paid little heed to the beauty of the day, the warmth of the air, or the activity in the streets as he made his way to Mansion Belcrady, where he found Hruther in the main hall supervising three servants washing the floor with stiff brooms and soapy water.

"My master," he said in surprise as Rakoczy came through the door.

"I know I have returned early; I have no wish to interrupt your work," Rakoczy said, pausing only briefly, preparing to climb the stairs. "If you will have the bath-house heated and the bath made ready?"

"Certainly," said Hruther, barely able to conceal his curiosity; Rakoczy did not often come from Court before he was expected, and his arrival did not bode well. He pointed to Jurg, the newest servant in the household. "You heard the Comes—find Kornemon and have the bath-house made ready for the Comes' use."

Jurg, a loose-limbed fellow with a broken nose, hesitated. "There is work to do here."

"It will wait for you to return," said Hruther, waving Jurg away; the other three servants tried not to notice. As an afterthought, Hruther called after him, "It will take the bath-house some time to heat, even on so pleasant a day as this one. Tell Kornemon to make the fire long-burning."

Jurg ducked his head and ambled out of the main hall of the manse.

"He's lazy," said Hruther, shaking his head.

"Because he knows he will not be beaten for it," said Rakoczy, his manner mildly distracted.

"Did anything happen at the Konige's Court?" Hruther inquired.

"Later," said Rakoczy in Imperial Latin, continuing on to the stairs. "I will explain it all to you. After my bath."

Hruther watched him go, thinking that he would have to get to the heart of the matter as soon as possible; after his twelve hundred years with Rakoczy, he could tell when the Comes was vexed. He saw that two of the men had stopped scrubbing their brushes on the floor and gave them his attention. "It must be clean before any new rushes are laid down," he reminded the servants and clapped his hands for emphasis.

"Jurg isn't here," the younger of the two said to Hruther.

"True enough," said Hruther. "He is doing his duty."

The other servant laughed, but resumed his work; a moment later the younger man did the same.

Vaguely aware of the confrontation behind him, Rakoczy paused in his upward climb, then went on as he heard the scrape of the brooms; the ruction was over. What was it about this day, that there should be so many disputes in it? he wondered. Perhaps some balefulness in the heavens, or a rising of bellicose humors brought on by the rapid change in the weather, had caused tempers and passions to flare. He reposed no assurance in any explanation, and

continued to mull the events as he went along the corridor to his
private apartments, unlocking the door discreetly and putting the
bolt in place once he was inside. He stood for a while, staring at
the closed window, an expression of superb blankness in his face.
"I cannot continue to do this," he whispered in his native tongue.
"One way or another, I will have to leave." He unfastened his
gambeson and took it off, hanging it on one of the pegs on the side
of his garderobe, revealing his chainse of deep-red silk. He found
a braided-leather belt and secured it around his waist, then kicked
off his solers and chose instead a pair of thick-soled Roman peri,
sighing a little as the anodyne presence of his native earth spread
through him. All his soles were lined with his native earth, but the
peri were thicker-soled and more restorative than the solers.

A book lay open on his clothes chest, a knotted silken cord
keeping the pages from shifting. He removed the cord and picked
up the leather-bound volume. It took him less than a moment to
find his place on the page; he resumed reading the *Tsou Ping Tao*,
finding comfort in its elegant observations on the well-regulated
life for educated men, comparing the sentiments of Djien Hsu
with the demands made by the customs of the Konige's Court and
Episcopus Fauvinel; he preferred the thoughtful Mandarin to the
hectic Court, and the concept of good conduct to righteousness.
Not that China was free from troubles, he reminded himself as he
sank onto his upholstered bench. When he had been in China, sixty
years ago, the impositions made upon foreigners were almost as
stringent as those made upon exiles in Praha, and that was before
the arrival of Jenghiz Khan and his Mongols. Rakoczy's departure
from Lo-Yang for Mao-T'ou fortress had come as the Mongol incur-
sions increased in ferocity. Still, before the invasion, Rakoczy had
been allowed to teach at the university and to appear in society, so
long as he wore Western clothing on public occasions; he had not
felt as trapped in Lo-Yang as he did in Praha. He continued to read.

Some while later, Hruther knocked on his door. "My master?
The bath-house is almost ready. You will want to gather your things."

Rakoczy closed the book, marking his place with a scrap of

black silk. "Thank you," he said loudly enough to be heard through the door.

"Do you need anything from me?" Hruther inquired, a host of unasked questions hidden in this single probe.

"Not just at present, thank you," said Rakoczy, getting to his feet. "When I return to my rooms, you and I will talk. If you will, bring your basin and razors; my beard is getting a bit unkempt."

"That I will," Hruther promised, and left.

Rakoczy opened the garderobe and removed a Persian caftan made of soft-woven cotton, the color of dark wine. He folded this over his arm, then took a vial of oil-soap from the small coffer at the side of the clothes chest. Moving smoothly and rapidly, he unbarred his door, took the key from its hook, stepped into the hall, closed and locked his door, then strode off to the stairs, descending quickly to the main hall, and passing to the kitchen corridor and out the side-door, and into the long, deep-blue shadows of afternoon.

The bath-house was in good repair at last, and the smoke rising from the chimney promised the interior would be warm. Rakoczy opened the door and stepped into the damp warmth, his eyes adjusting to the half-light provided by a single, small window set high in the wall beside the chimney. He noticed that the steamy, smoky air smelled slightly of rosemary—Kornemon had tossed a handful of branches of the herb in with the logs when he laid the fire.

Rakoczy undressed quickly, putting his clothes into the small closet near the door where they would stay dry. Naked, he walked to the deep wooden vat that sat atop a base of Rakoczy's native earth, climbed up the small steps, and sank into the wonderfully warm water that rose to his shoulders. Opening the vial of oil-soap, he began to rub the fragrant lotion over his chest, moving to the upper ring inside the vat that allowed him to wash his arms and the striated scars that covered his abdomen, the last token of his execution more than thirty-two centuries ago. He extended first one leg and then the other for washing, working the oil-soap down his thighs and calves to his feet, taking time to inspect his toenails, deciding that it was time to trim them again. Throughout his long, long life, he had always taken pleasure in bathing when protected by his native earth, and today was no different than any others; he welcomed the lassitude that the warm water offered.

Finally he stood up in the vat and poured the last of the contents of the vial into his hair and then worked the lather over his face and neck. Satisfied that he had done his best to get clean, he settled back in the water and slipped under the surface to rinse the oil-soap from his hair. Then he shook his head to keep his hair from dripping, stretched, and leaned back against the edge of the vat; he hooked his arms over the edge of it and let himself doze, willing the tension to leave him, and his thoughts to find more pleasant subjects to explore than the perfidy of the Konige's Court and his own perilous situation within it. Gradually his eyes closed and he drowsed as the sunlight faded from the window and the activities of the manse became centered in the kitchen as the household servants gathered for their evening meal.

The fire that heated the bath and the room was dying and it was quite dark when the door to the bath-house opened with hardly a sound and a small figure came silently inside; he paused to take stock of the place and to confirm that Rakoczy was still in his bath. He swung around, making a summoning gesture; a moment later three larger figures came after him. The door was closed softly as the figures gathered together before starting toward the vat.

Although Rakoczy's eyes remained closed, he was now alert to the presence of unknown men in his bath-room. He wished now that he had brought a dagger or a francisca with him. He listened attentively for every step the men took, marking their progress in the gloom.

Somewhere outside two cats shrieked at each other and prepared to launch into battle. One of the men swore under his breath and was hissed to silence by another.

Taking advantage of this, Rakoczy sat up and drew his arms

into the vat. "Hruther?" He looked about, his dark-seeing eyes taking stock of the four men. The smallest moved forward.

"Not your manservant, Comes, a juggler," said Tahir, climbing up the steps at the side of the vat. He carried a double-bladed misericordia in one hand and a had a spiked glove on the other.

"On what errand, Tahir?" He saw the other three men moving toward him.

"On a mission from Antal of Szousa. I am to deliver a message," said Tahir with such satisfaction that Rakoczy knew the men had been sent to kill him.

"Why did he choose you?" Rakoczy asked, thinking rapidly.

"Your warder knows me; he let me in. My comrades dispatched him before he could raise the alarm." He grinned at the cleverness of the plan.

"You wanted to kill him," Rakoczy said, certain of it.

The tallest of the three men muttered a warning, hefting his battle-hammer.

"Szousa disapproves of your interest in his sister," Tahir said, making his voice menacing as he took a testing swipe with his spiked glove.

"I have no interest in his sister: she has interest in me." Rakoczy did not flinch; he knew it was useless to tell the men that he had grown tired of Iliska's relentless pursuit, and of Antal's determination to punish him for Iliska's infatuation, just as he realized that any show of fear on his part might well set Tahir on the attack.

Tahir laughed, his voice harsh. "So you say."

Rakoczy kept his eyes fixed on Tahir, who was now leaning over the lip of the vat, a fierce shine in his eyes. "Why are you doing this?"

"Why do you think?" Tahir countered. "Because he has paid me handsomely, and vowed to place me in his household."

"Are you certain he will keep his Word?" Rakoczy asked, knowing that so long as Tahir was talking, he would not attack.

"He pledged on the Cross," said Tahir, adding, "You won't turn me from my purpose. If you must waste breath, pray; God might hear you."

Rakoczy ignored the juggler's mockery. "What did Antal offer the other three: do you know?"

"They are here to help me carry out our mission," said Tahir, preening. "He gave me the privilege of killing you."

Rakoczy saw a flickering look pass among the other three men; he wondered if he should warn Tahir of treachery when he felt a blow on his shoulder next to his throat and saw the two prongs of the misericordia pulled out of his flesh. The pain struck him as water sloshed over the pair of wounds. "You are . . ." The words trailed off to a groan. He took a breath and added in a soft hiss. "Be wary. Those three will kill you."

Tahir uttered an incoherent cry of rage and pushed Rakoczy's head down beneath the water, yelling curses as he did. "You are the Devil's spawn! Die and go to him!"

Rakoczy coughed as he stopped breathing and sank down in the vat below where Tahir could reach. The remnants of oil-soap stung his eyes but not enough to force him to close them; the pain from the two stab wounds was intense but not spreading, and he was able to resist the urge to place his hand over the punctures. He knew long submersion would leave him weak and disoriented, but he preferred that to having to fight Tahir and his three fellow-assassins, which might result in serious injury, or perhaps the True Death. He made a last, feeble flailing with his arms, then let himself hang in the vat, moved only by the motion of the water.

Tahir remained at the rim of the vat, his spiked glove lifted, ready to strike if Rakoczy should make another movement. He repeated the *De Profundis Clamavit,* as much to be certain that the Comes had been under the water long enough to drown as to implore God to hear him. While he prayed, he thought about what he was saying, his voice faltered, knowing that God might well condemn him for killing Rakoczy, though he did it at the behest of Antal of Szousa. At last he straightened up, noticing for the first time that the front of his clothing was soaked and that there was blood on the sleeve of his chainse. He turned to his three companions. "There—you see? You can tell Szousa that I didn't need your help."

One of the three glanced at the other two, gave a nod, and launched himself at Tahir, grabbing him and pulling him from his place on the steps.

Startled, Tahir whispered a protest. "I can get down by mysel—"

The man who held him turned so that the tallest of the three of them could help subdue Tahir with a sharp blow to the abdomen with his battle-hammer.

"What?" Tahir gasped, trying to bend over and get air back into his body, but the leader of the three held him upright.

"Hurry," said the oldest of the three in the Bulgarian tongue. "There's been too much noise. Someone will come."

"The Comes is dead. Szousa told us to leave the juggler's body with the Comes'," the tallest whispered.

"Then have done with him," said the leader, and clapped his hand over Tahir's mouth as the dwarf began to scream. "He's strong for a poppet."

Tahir wrenched and twisted, bucked, kicked, and bit, but aside from getting out a single yelp, he was held securely enough for the third man to drive a falchion two times into Tahir's broad chest. Blood erupted from the second wound, covering the man who held him with the gory flow. Tahir jerked and managed to free one arm, but when he attempted to batter at his captor with his fist, there was no strength left in him; his blood still pumped out of him, but the amount was diminishing.

"Drop him," the oldest man snapped. "We must leave. We've done our work."

"And we can claim the rest of our fee," said the tallest man.

"Ten gold Angels each," their leader gloated as he released Tahir, letting him fall as he might.

Tahir was distantly aware that he had been betrayed, but it hardly seemed to matter now. He could feel the stone floor beneath him, but it was unimportant. He was vaguely aware that there was something unfinished, that there was a wrong that was unredressed, but it was no longer worth the effort to recall it; he let it go as he let all the world go.

"He's gone," said the oldest, going toward the door and pulling it open carefully. "I hear noises."

"The household at supper," said their leader, picking up his falchion and slipping it into the scabbard in the small of his back.

"No; listen," said the oldest, holding up his hand. "Someone is coming."

"What's another body?' the tallest asked, swinging his battle-hammer.

"It's trouble, and there's no money in it," said the oldest. "Come on. Now!"

The other two went to flank the door; the leader stepped over Tahir's body and slipped out into the darkness.

Lying in the cooling water, Rakoczy had a fleeting, ironic thought that he now had the means to leave Praha.

Text of an edict issued by Konige Kunigunde, Episcopus Fauvinel, and the Counselors of Praha, distributed to all churches throughout the city.

To the people of the city from Konige Kunigunde, with the blessings of Episcopus Fauvinel, and the approval and duty of the Counselors of Praha on this, the 27th day of May in the 1270th year of Grace:

On the occasion of the reception of the notification to the Konige Kunigunde that her royal grandfather Konig Bela has been called to Heaven and the presence of God, for which the Konige's Court and the people are now to mourn until the season of the Nativity, when the Konige's Court will celebrate the ascendency of her maternal uncle, Istvan of Transylvania, to the throne of Hungary, there will be one hundred Masses said for the repose of Konig Bela's soul, and one hundred more for the long and glorious reign of Istvan of Hungary. All residents of Praha will show mourning by placing a black crucifix on their doors and in distributing alms to the poor in the name of Konige Kunigunde. All officials of the Council and the Konige's Court are to dress in red or black through the period of mourning; any lapse in such demonstrations of respect will require a fine be paid to the Counselors and the Episcopus of three golden Vaclavs for each offense.

No weddings are to occur until thirty days of deep mourning have passed. No music but the chants of monks will be allowed within the city for sixty days. No entertainments such as bear-baiting and cock-fighting will be allowed inside Praha's walls for sixty days. No dancing or other wanton games are to be permitted for sixty days. All failures to abide by these dictates will be met with fines, and, if repeated, public whipping.

There will be, in honor of the Konige Kunigunde's grief, a cessation of all executions for a month; all those condemned to be hanged in chains will be kept in prison until the thirty days have passed, at which time their sentences shall be carried out. The sole exceptions to this degree are the three Bulgarians captured by Antal of Szousa and condemned for the murder of Rakoczy Ferancsi, Comes Santu-Germaniu, and the Konige's juggler, Tahir. These vile assassins have claimed that they were employed by Antal of Szousa, but admitted, under the boot, that they lied when they accused Szousa, which Confession will grant them absolution of their sins and the glories of Paradise.

The Mid-Summer Festival will not be held, nor will any tournaments, until the principal six months of mourning have passed, at which time there will be a civic procession to mark the end of the Konige's grieving. The end of mourning will also be recognized

*with dignified demonstrations of thanksgiving and renewed fealty
to Konig Otakar, his Konige, and their daughters.
Witnessed and signed in the presence of Episcopus Fauvinel*

*for Konige Kunigunde
and
the Counselors of Praha*

6

Cases and chests stood in the entry hall of Mansion Belcrady, ready to be loaded into wagons for the authorized departure the following day of Rakoczy's Hungarian household for Santu-Germaniu. Despite the warm afternoon, the sky was glary with high, thin clouds that made the light inside the manse more muted than was usual on a June day. Activity in the household was on-going but muffled, a reminder that they were mourning not only the death of the Comes but the coming end of the servants' employment; each of the household members had been given generous service payment and the pledge that the Counselors would see that they found new work, but unease hung over them all. As if to punctuate that restiveness, there was an occasional clash of pots and pans as Pacar loaded up the kitchen supplies; the scrape of rakes marked where the rushes were being taken up.

Hruther was occupied among the packed chests with checking off the items on his inventory that were to go to Santu-Germaniu; a second, smaller list was for the things he would need himself. He was dressed in a dark-gray huch of linen over a chainse of black-cotton, with black-velvet bands on his cuffs indicating his mourning state.

"How many more horses do you want me to purchase?" Illes

of Kotan asked as he came in through the door; he, too, was in dark clothes with black bands on his cuffs. "I am off to the market shortly; I plan to return before sundown."

"How much money do you have?" Hruther asked. "How many horses do you plan to buy?"

"I have twenty-five gold Angels and twenty silver Apostles, and a few copper Agnethes," he answered, fingering the pouch that hung from his belt. "I had planned to buy four or five horses and perhaps a pair of mules, since you are taking three of them. They should be sufficient for our journey home. I might be able to buy another two horses without needing any more money than I have now." He gave Hruther a speculative look.

"If you see a pair of good riding horses, you may purchase them. I would like to have a pair of remounts at the least." Hruther made a mark on his inventory, then regarded Illes directly. "How much grain will you need for the journey to Santu-Germaniu? Is there enough in the stable for your journey and mine, or will you need to buy more?"

"I will know when I know how many horses we will have," said Illes, his tone level. He looked up at the new windows. "Seems a shame to go, with the manse finally finished."

"Yes. But the Comes' heir needs to be provided with his bona fides, and to do that, I'll have to find him first. Until the heir is found, no one can live here; it is protected by the Konige and the Counsel."

"Do you know where he is?" Illes asked. "I know it isn't my place to ask," he added hastily.

"I know where to begin my search." Hruther looked away from Illes, his demeanor reserved. "I will find him, and in time he will come to claim this fief; I will see to it. Tell Balint that when you arrive in Santu-Germaniu. I will send word to inform Konig Istvan when I have located the heir, and I will notify Santu-Germaniu, of course."

"Of course," Illes echoed. He filled in the awkwardness of the sudden silence by making a show of examining the nine chests set out nearest the door. "These are the ones that will go with you? loaded on the mules?"

"Yes." Hruther glanced up from his inventory. "Those chests and four sacks of grain."

"Three mules and four horses . . ." Illes studied the chests. "This big one—you'll have to use the strongest mule to carry it."

"Very likely," said Hruther. "That is my plan."

"And this old chest, with the legs off? It will need to be wrapped well in canvas if the lacquer isn't to be damaged."

"We brought it here in a canvas shroud: it will leave the same way," said Hruther.

Illes studied the chests. "You aren't taking an escort?"

"No. If I need one, I will hire men along the way."

"Not so much of a chance of spies," said Illes with a knowing nod.

Hruther nodded a little, then consulted his inventory once more. "There are eleven more crates to be packed and bound for your return to the Comes' fief. You'll need to put most of them in the wagons that will be in your charge. Only a few will go on pack-animals." His thoughts drifted for a long moment, back to the bath-house ten days ago where he had found Tahir dead on the floor and Rakoczy, in stupor, floating in the vat, a wound in his shoulder, his breathing stopped. After bolting the door, Hruther had pulled Rakoczy from the vat, assured himself that Rakoczy was only in a stupor before laying him out next to Tahir, then unbolted the door and summoned Pacar and Kornemon to witness the deaths and to report the murders to the Konige's Court and the Episcopus— He heard Illes repeat his question.

"Can they be loaded tonight, or will they have to wait until tomorrow morning?"

"All can be loaded tonight." Recovering himself, he patted the nearest chest, a banded one of medium size. "Only my cases need to wait. There's no point in loading up a pack-saddle before it's on the mule."

"Um," said Illes. He looked toward the door. "Then I'm off to the horse-market in Sante-Radmille Square. If you want to inspect what I buy?"

"I'll want to see the two riding horses you buy for me, but otherwise you're capable of choosing animals that will best suit your travels." Hruther's expression lost a little of its asceticism. "The Comes accounted you a fine horseman, and a dependable groom. You know what you will require."

Illes flushed, turned on his heel, and left the manse. He returned at dusk, leading a string of horses and mules; he put them in the stable, fed and watered them, then returned to the manse for a light supper and the last meal he would share with the household. By the time the trenchers were gone and the beer and wine drunk in honor of the Comes' memory, Illes was weary; he found Hruther in the Comes' workroom with a final crate of books.

Hruther greeted him in Hungarian in a desultory manner, then asked, "Is everything ready?"

Iles shrugged. "As much as it can be tonight. Tomorrow we'll get the rest done. I bought two horses for your remounts," said Illes.

"Excellent. Tell me more." Hruther sighed as he closed the lid on the crate of books. "You'll need to make sure this stays out of the rain."

"I'll put it in the lead wagon and remind the driver to be careful."

"Very good." He paused. "Which stalls are the remounts in?"

"The eighth and ninth, across from the dun gelding." He waited to see if there was anything more that Hruther required.

"Rest well—you have a long way to go," said Hruther.

"At least I know where I am bound," said Illes, and went off to his room in the stable and his bed.

Clouds thickened during the night, and Praha woke to a sullen, lowering, canvas-like sky and the heavy, still air that promised rain by the end of the day. Sapped of energy, most of Praha moved slowly, but at Mansion Belcrady, industrious loading and packing began before first light; the lanthorns were kept burning well after the east showed the arillate nimbus of sunrise. As the morning advanced, the pace increased, approaching the frenetic as the loading of wagons progessed; now that the end had come, the household was eager to be shut of the place.

Hruther met Illes in the stable shortly after dawn; he inspected the two riding horses Illes had bought and nodded his approval. "I'll saddle the calmest one for me to ride; with the mules and all their burdens, I don't want to have to contain any frisks from my mount." He picked up his saddle with its pad atop it, and carried it to the stand, and then fetched the bridle.

"The dun gelding is the most steady of the horses, but he is not a plodder; he can walk out all day long. He should suit your purposes." He cocked his head as if listening to the horses. "You'll want to keep him on a slack rein; I had him from a merchant who goes between Carinthia and Lorringaria. He sold his horses because he is ill and is going to enter Sant-Toluc so the monks may treat him."

"The dun gelding it shall be," said Hruther. "Do you have a spare set of reins and a pair of extra lead-ropes?"

"Yes." Illes retrieved them from the back of the wagon that stood in the stable door and handed them to Hruther.

"I have the Comes' saddle and bridle with me, and his saddle pads to present to his heir," Hruther said calmly. "You have his bones to carry back to his native earth, so that he may lie with his fathers."

"Yes," said Illes a second time. "As the great knights were brought back from the Holy Land." He crossed himself.

"Yes. Like that." For a short while Hruther thought back to the night that Tahir had done his utmost to drown Rakoczy, and all that he had done in haste and secret to ensure Rakoczy's protection as well as his escape from exile: the speed at which Hruther had arranged for disposal of the bodies, the search he had made alone through the night for a body that could be used to supply

bones to be carried to Santu-Germaniu; it had been well toward
the end of night when he had found a monk with four deep wounds
in his side, newly perished. He had brought the dead monk back
to Mansion Belcrady and to the large cauldron behind the storage
sheds that Rakoczy had filled with water, where the monk's carcase would be boiled in his stead. For the following nine days,
Rakoczy had remained in the shed, enervated but recovering,
until Hruther had conspicuously packed the bare bones in a casket like a reliquary and entrusted it to Illes, and then, one day ago,
he had surreptitiously brought an iron-banded chest lined in his
native earth to Rakoczy and locked him in it before ordering
three of the servants to carry it to the entry hall, where it now
waited to be loaded onto one of the mules' pack saddles.

"Hruther?" Illes inquired.

Aware that he had been distracted too long, Hruther shook
himself. "I have much to do; I don't want to forget any task. How
many wagons are packed?"

"Four are filled; the rest will be ready before mid-day."

Hruther glanced down at one of the mansion's cats. "We
should provide food for them so that they won't wander off, but
will hunt here. The Comes' heir will not want to live in a place
filled with rats."

"I suppose that's a good plan," said Illes. "I'll get the pack-
saddles." He started for the tackroom, but paused. "Will I ever see
you again after today?"

"If God wills, I trust so," said Hruther.

"If God wills," Illes repeated, crossing himself, then brought
out the first of the pack-saddles and its pad. "Which of the mules
shall I—"

"That one," Hruther said, pointing to the one with the broadest back. He picked up the nearest brush and went to work on the
coat of the dun gelding he would be riding. "Do you think I can
be away by mid-morning?"

"If the rain holds off, yes," said Illes, brushing down the broad-
backed mule. "Rain will slow loading the pack-saddles."

"Do you suppose it will? so soon after dawn?" Hruther asked as two of the household servants brought another large wooden crate to put in the wagon in front of the stable door.

"It's likely. There's no thunder yet, and the rain won't start until the thunder awakens the clouds." He picked up the harness for the wagon and gave it to one of his assistants. "The piebald mule and the liver one." He pointed them out to the under-grooms.

"Do you have the Konige's safe-conduct with you?" Hruther inquired.

Illes touched the wallet that hung from his belt. "I will keep it with me until we reach Santu-Germaniu, as you told me."

"Very good," said Hruther, and went on grooming the gelding, taking time to pick out his hooves and to comb the tangles from his mane and tail. As he secured the saddle-girth, he said, "Will you bring the mules and the remounts around to the front of the manse so they can be loaded? I'll lead this horse." He patted the gelding's neck.

"I'll be there shortly." Illes put his brushes away. "As soon as this team is harnessed."

"I'll have the chests and crates in position for you."

"As you like," said Illes, ducking his head respectfully as he stood aside to let Hruther lead his gelding down the aisle between the stalls, past the wagon awaiting loading, and out into the dim sunlight.

Illes was as good as his word: by mid-morning the mules were loaded, the remounts were tethered to their lead-line, and a few of the household staff had gathered to wish Hruther farewell and safe travels. Pacar was the only one of the household who appeared to be sad about the coming separation.

"I thank you all for your good service, and for your care of my master and Mansion Belcrady," Hruther said, gathering up the reins and the leads. "May God send you good fortune, good employment, many children, and good health. And may God guide and guard Konig Otakar, Konige Kunigunde, and Episcopus Fauvinel."

Since Minek had been killed the same night as the Comes was drowned, Kornemon served as warder, opening the gate and waiting until the mules and remounts were through to close and bar it again. No one paused in their activities to wave or offer any other farewell; there was still much work to do before Illes and the wagons left and the keys to Mansion Belcrady were given into the care of the Counselors of Praha to hold in trust for Rakoczy's heir.

Passing through the south gate, Hruther could see the bodies of the three Bulgarians hanging in chains beside a forger, a pair of tergiversistic monks, and a blasphemer; the weather intensified the stench from the decaying flesh; crows flapped around the corpses, and high overhead kites shrieked.

Hruther took the river road, carefully avoiding the places where the bank had sunk. He maintained his horse, the remounts, and the mules at a steady, fast walk over the level ground, slowing only slightly as the land began to rise, so that by the time, late in the afternoon, that the first thunder grumbled overhead, he was almost six leagues from Praha, the city long lost to sight behind him. Half a league farther on, lightning ripped the clouds, thunder thudding after it. "Time to find shelter," Hruther told his gelding, and began to watch for tracks leading away from the river; he chose a path that was narrow and old, leading off toward a spinny of larch and oak, and what appeared to be ancient, tumbled walls with an abandoned almshouse beside it.

He dismounted and led the horses and mules into the long, narrow almshouse, taking care to be sure it had not become a den for foxes or bears before stepping inside. The place was musty but not too dilapidated; it would do for the first night. Hruther unsaddled his dun gelding, securing his reins to a half-fallen beam. He found two more substantial beams where he could tie the mules and the remounts, all at the same end of the almshouse; then he unloaded the pack-saddle on the largest mule, setting the single large chest down away from the door and the tethered animals, leaving space for the other chests and crates and easy reloading. Taking great care, he next unloaded the iron-banded chest, putting it next to the large one. He unlocked the banded chest and held out his hand. "My master," he said in Imperial Latin.

From his cramped, folded position within the chest, Rakoczy looked up at him, an expression of relief in his dark eyes. "Old friend." Slowly he straightened up, stretching carefully, his back and shoulders stiff from almost two days in the chest. "Where are we?"

"South of Praha; I reckon it about six leagues, or perhaps a little more." He helped Rakoczy to rise, brushing away the small clods of earth that clung to his gambeson and high boots. "A fair distance."

"Good. We're beyond prying eyes," Rakoczy approved, stretching carefully, favoring his left shoulder where the wounds of the misericordia were concealed by a thick bandage; then he brushed the grime from his face.

"I hope you haven't had too difficult a time in the chest," said Hruther, still steadying Rakoczy so that he could move without falling.

"I've spent years in an oubliette; two days in a box was nothing." He hitched his right shoulder. "Well, not nothing, but far from trying."

"You must have been bored," said Hruther, suiting his tone to Rakoczy's. "There was so little to do."

"No, I was not; I used the time to think—I needed to think." He inhaled gradually and let the breath out slowly. "And Illes? where is he?"

"As far as I know, he left some time after we did. He is bound for Santu-Germaniu with six wagons, a pony cart of food, and an escort of ten men-at-arms. He carries a safe-conduct from the Konige."

"Will he stop at Pressburg to report to Istvan, do you think?" Rakoczy was becoming more alert as he spoke.

"He plans to." He took another case—a small one of leather and iron—from the third mule's pack-saddle. "Jewels and gold."

"All of it?" Rakoczy asked.

"All that wasn't paid to the Counselors and the household," said Hruther. "We may yet have to bribe our way out of Bohemia."

"It is not impossible," said Rakoczy, and looked at the largest chest. "What have you there?"

Hruther opened the chest. "Your bed, and your native earth."

"Thank you," said Rakoczy. "You anticipate everything."

"After so long, I would think so," Hruther said with a touch of amusement in his faded-blue eyes.

"It is good to be away from Praha," Rakoczy said as he took a turn around the almshouse.

"You couldn't remain there, could you?—not after what happened," Hruther remarked, taking the lanthorn from the pack-saddle of the second mule. He used flint-and-steel to strike a spark, and put the lanthorn down on the large chest.

"No," Rakoczy said, accompanied by another mutter of thunder.

"No doubt you are pleased to be free."

Rakoczy considered his response. "I could not remain there as I was."

"And that is no answer," Hruther said.

"No, it is not," Rakoczy conceded. "We are still in Bohemia, so I am not yet free."

Hruther nodded. "But your bones are being carried back to Santu-Germaniu. That should keep anyone from pursuing you."

"They have no reason to assume I have got away, unless Rozsa convinces them that has happened." There was a note of dismay in his voice.

"Who will believe her, even if she should decide that you aren't dead."

"But I am dead," Rakoczy said gently.

"You are undead," Hruther corrected him. "As you have often reminded me, you haven't died the True Death yet."

Lightning filled the almshouse with cold, jagged light and

vanished; the horses sidled and pulled, and the mules laid back their ears.

"I believe this is the first time that anyone has tried to drown me deliberately," said Rakoczy; there had been another time, but it was centuries before that day in the Year of the Four Caesars when he had come upon the exhausted and beaten Rogerian in the shadows of the half-built Flavian Circus and restored him to life.

"Not easily done, in your case," said Hruther with the hint of a smile. "Do you want me to build a fire?"

"Unless you would like one, there's no need. I am not cold."

"No," Hruther agreed, thunder silencing him for a long moment. "Smoke would make our presence known, if anyone should be searching for isolated travelers. I won't bother with a fire." He unloaded the largest sack of grain and put down generous measures for the three mules and three horses. "I have your tack, for the morning."

"I never doubted it," said Rakoczy, swinging his arms to loosen them.

Hruther resumed untacking the mules; after a few more stretches, Rakoczy took over stacking the remaining crates and chests with the others, then, while Hruther wiped down the pack-saddles and shook out the saddle-pads, he brushed down the mules and horses, taking his time while the animals ate.

More lightning flashed overhead, cracking and spitting.

"I'll lead them out for water. There must be a stream nearby," said Hruther as Rakoczy finished with the hoof-pick.

"Or a well inside the old walls," said Rakoczy.

The thunder was louder now, more ominous; one of the mules brayed his disapproval.

"Perhaps I'd better bring a pail for them to drink from," Hruther said as the mule continued to protest the storm.

"A good notion," said Rakoczy. "The rain will come very soon now."

"And you won't want to be out in the water, not after—"

"Being drowned," Rakoczy finished for him. "Thank you for that consideration, old friend."

Hruther picked up a large bucket from the assortment of un-crated supplies and let himself out through the leaning door. He found an old well inside the broken stone walls, where Rakoczy had surmised one would be, filled it with water, and hauled it back to the almshouse, shoving his way through the door, then setting the bucket down where the mules and horses could get at it. "I'll take them outside in a bit."

"No need," Rakoczy said from the earth-filled mattress that lay atop the long, narrow chest of his native earth. "We will not be here longer than the night, and both of us have slept in worse places than stalls."

"True enough," said Hruther, his expression sedate; he could see that Rakoczy was finally out of the stupefaction his drowning had imposed upon him. "What is it about drowning that is so ter-rible? You can't die from it."

"That is what is terrible; water enervates me, leaves me in a state of stupefaction so that all I can do in water is drift and wait to be pulled out or be devoured by one of the many hunters that live in water."

"But the vat stood on your native earth—that should have preserved you: it has in the past," said Hruther, finally giving voice to what had been troubling him.

"Ah, but I had been stabbed and Tahir aimed to reach my heart." He touched his left shoulder. "It left me as incapacitated as the open sea would do."

Hruther considered this, then said, "It must have been un-speakable." He saw Rakoczy nod once; he deliberately changed the subject. "I have a haunch of lamb that I can eat from. The lamb was killed late last night and the meat is fresh enough. It should serve for another day as well." He opened one of the supply boxes and pulled out a joint of meat wrapped in a sheet of vellum. "Will you take sustenance from one of the horses?"

"Not tonight. Tomorrow I may," said Rakoczy, and leaned

back on his sustaining bed, only a slight furrow between his brows revealing the discomfort he still felt from his stabbing and drowning.

"It has been many days," Hurther remarked as he took out a skinning knife and sliced a section of lamb, then cut it up into edible strips.

"It has," said Rakoczy. "But one more night will not harm me."

The first rattle of rain sounded on the roof, accompanied by another shudder of thunder.

"Did you manage to visit one of the women you sought out while they slept in the days after your attack?"

"Not after the drowning, but the night before I did." He paused for a long time. "I am grateful for them, for the women at Court . . ."

"But there were only two ladies, weren't there?" Hruther asked, startled by the enigmatic tone of Rakoczy's voice.

Lightning blanched, cracked, and vanished.

"Rozsa, because she insisted, Imbolya, because she is too young to marry," Rakoczy paused. "Rozsa sought no intimacy from me, nor, I suspect, from anyone. She wanted no touching beyond skins. Imbolya is an intelligent girl, and that is enough for her to want her aspirations fulfilled, though most of them are based upon the songs of troubadours. Both of them believe what the Church tells them: that the gratification from union is possible only with God, that all other satisfaction is carnalistic and therefore debauched." He stared up into the rafters. "They have forgotten that profane is not depravity, it is only outside of the Church. So Rozsa demanded the full pleasure of her senses but would not extend any of herself to me. Imbolya was more willing to risk a kind of touching, but she would not abandon herself to what she so deeply desired."

"And the third? The one whose brother sent your killers?"

"Iliska? She is a child: Imbolya is painfully young, but she is no longer a child. Iliska is like the Konige's daughters, who see a bauble and demand to have it. Iliska is of the same nature. She has no sense of what she is playing at." He went silent again, thinking back on his time in the Konige's Court. "It is . . . so sad."

"For them, or for you?" Hruther asked, taking another strip of lamb and chewing it vigorously.

"For all of us," said Rakoczy slowly, the rest of his observation overwhelmed by the peal of thunder that brought a deluge from the clouds, one that thrashed the almshouse unrelentingly for half the night, stilling their conversation and lulling them into rest with the steadiness of the downpour. As the thunder rumbled into the distance, the horses and mules drowsed and the lanthorn burned down, leaving the almshouse in darkness.

Morning brought watery sunlight and soggy ground. Rakoczy and Hruther fed the mules and horses, groomed them, saddled and bridled them, then loaded up the pack-saddles. They went back to the main road and turned south. When they had gone another league, Hruther asked, "Have you decided where we are going yet?"

"Out of Bohemia and Hungary," said Rakoczy.

"Have you decided anything more than that?"

"West," said Rakoczy tersely.

Hruther nodded. "West it is."

Text of a report from the Counselors of Praha to the Episcopus Fauvinel and Konige Kunigunde, dictated by Counselor Smiricti to his scribe, Frater Ulric, and delivered by Council messenger.

To the most puissant Episcopus Fauvinel and the most honored Konige, Kunigunde of Halicz, the report from Smiricti Dedrich, Counselor of Praha, concerning the death of Rakoczy Ferancsi, Comes Santu-Germaniu, submitted on this, Mid-Summer Day in the 1270th Year of Salvation:

Most exalted Episcopus and most Royal Konige:

Having been charged with the determination of responsibility in the murder of the Comes, we of the Council have made a thorough inquiry into the events, and we have found that the jug-gler Tahir was paid by some unknown enemy of the Comes to kill him. He was accompanied by three Bulgarians, whose bodies are now little more than bones, for the purpose of ensuring that the Comes would not escape them. Since the Bulgarians were taken before they could be questioned, and their execution carried out promptly, who may have paid them could not be learned from them.

Therefore, the Council instigated a Process to try to discover who had spoken out against the Comes, and who among those people could be said to be willing to order his death.

We have dismissed the various accusations of Rozsa of Bor-sod, for a pregnant woman is prey to all manner of visions and delusions that are part of her condition. Between the news of the death of her husband, Notay Tibor of Kaposvar, the day after the murder of Santu-Germaniu, and her impending departure, hers are unreliable opinions. She will be returning to Kaposvar in three days, in any case, and will not have her remarks included in the records of the case.

Three household servants have told the Council that they knew of no revealed enemies of the Comes here in Praha, and of-fer no explanations for the murder. They did remind us that the warder at Mansion Belcrady was killed after admitting the mur-derers, so it may be that he was part of the scheme and was be-trayed by his fellows.

Among the Hungarians of the Konige's Court, no one has any revealed enmity toward Santu-Germaniu, and therefore it is our conclusion that the murderers were in the employ of an unknown person who has probably fled Praha and was probably neither Hungarian nor Bohemian, but perhaps in the pay of Rudolph von Hapsburg, who is known to be envious of Bohemia and a foe of Hungary. Arranging for such a killing as this one is a way to strike at both kingdoms and to sow dissension in the city and the Ko-nige's Court.

May God bear witness to the truth of this, and protect the Episcopus and the Konige's Court from all malice and treason.

Given by duty in all fealty,
Smiricti Dedrich (his mark)
Counselor of Praha

by the hand of the Hieronymite monk and scribe to the Council, Frater Ulric

EPILOGUE

*T*ext of a letter from Atta Olivia Clemens at Lecco to Rakoczy Sanct' Germain Franciscus in Alexandria, written in Imperial Latin, carried by Eclipse Trading Company courier and the ship *Golden Moon*, delivered two months after it was written.

To my most dear, most vexing, most enduring friend, the nettled greetings of Atta Olivia Clemens on this, the 29th day of March in the 1272nd Christian Year,

I am too perplexed to rebuke you, although I am sorely tempted. I have your letter of last November in hand at last. So you tell me in this most recent letter that you plan to leave Alexandria in a year or so and go to Constantinople. Why not come here instead, to Lecco, and spend a few months with me? It has been a long time since we have seen one another, and it would do us both good, I think, to have time to talk face to face, and not have to rely on the delays and vagaries of sending letters that may take months to arrive, if they arrive at all. I had hoped that when you left Praha you might have stopped here at Lago Comu for a few days at least, but instead, you went off to Narabonnis and sailed from there to Egypt. Why did you go so far out of the way to take ship? Neither Otakar nor Istvan had reason to pursue you, even if they had been aware that you had survived.

Doubtless you have heard that Otakar has not done well recently in his fight to make an empire out of Bohemia, and he has probably lost all chance to be Holy Roman Emperor when Richard of Cornwall finally dies. Frederich of Hohenzollern has been promoting his brother-in-law for the position; I'm sure that Rudolph von Hapsburg, Comes of Austria, would do the work as well as any of those eastern European barbarians could, and with unsteadiness to the south of Hungary, no one would take a chance on Istvan, who is rumored to be going to war with Bulgaria. I'm told that Urosh of Serbia may not honor his treaties to Constantinople and could enter the side of Bulgaria.

Never mind. I am being inconsequential; the fate of Kings is not yours to bear, nor mine. You had your reasons for going to Alexandria, and they are not for me to oppose. But still, I would like to see you for at least a little while, before you continue on to Constantinople. Like you, I become lonely from time to time, and I miss speaking the language of my youth with someone who comprehends it as you do. Niklos is very reliable and he indulges me from time to time with Imperial Latin, but he did not know me in my breathing days, as you did. As I write this, I am made aware of how much more you are alone than I am, and how the loneliness must ache in you more than the yearning for touching the living. Or perhaps it is that loneliness that fuels the hunger those of your blood have, more than the need for the only sustenance that can support us. I, too, have found that those I have sought out are less willing, or perhaps less capable, of embracing us and our nature as others have been in the past, preferring to indulge the flesh but to withhold the soul, for fear of slighting the Christian God, or his minions on earth.

It is unfortunate that the Church has claimed so much of the understanding of the people, and has become the clerk for the nobility. I think back to the Priest of the City in the Roma of my youth, a position that was a political one achieved by election, a time when the Vestal Virgins could over-rule the Senate and even the Emperor for a century or two. The people worshiped by choosing the god or goddess who best supported their cause, and respected them as they respected the civic virtues they represented—at least enough of them did to provide an even keel for the Empire. You remember this time, and although Niklos has heard about it, he came after the Roman state was (if you will pardon my putting it this way) in eclipse, and riddled with corruption, as so many European Courts are now. You have told me the corruption was always there, and that may be true, but not so blatant as it became, and not so devoid of consequences.

Such morose maunderings! You will think me lost in melancholy, and I am not. I will admit to being disappointed in the world around me, but that is far from despondency and the lethargy that comes with it. I know that I must not give way to despair, nor will I, but I am certain that I should put my efforts toward finding those partners who are willing to find exultation in more than the Mass. Is that why you went to Alexandria? Are the women there more willing to extend themselves to you? I have assumed most of them live cloistered lives, away from men, but there may be some who will be happy to have a lover as devoted to their fulfillment as his own. I admit this causes me misgivings I have not felt before, and that leads to restlessness that erodes my serenity. But it will pass, in time. You have assured me many times that all things do.

You will say I continue to quetch, which I will agree I do. You continue to wander, searching for what? solace? rapture? acceptance? endurance? Whatever it is, I hope you will find it, and that it will be all you have yearned for. Until that time, be certain that my love is yours

Eternally,
Olivia